The Key Thief

Christina Van Starkenburg

The Key Thief

Cover designed by GetCovers.

www.christinavanstarkenburg.com

ISBN: 9781070176062

For Joshua and Evelyn,
who believed in me
even when I forgot to
believe in myself.

CONTENTS

— CHAPTER ONE —

Keeping Shop

Ethelwynne hugged herself close and tried to remember the feeling of her mother's arms around her. She forced her body to relax. They were only going to be gone for one month, and they hadn't even left yet. If Ethelwynne burst into tears now, her mother would never leave. She drew in a shaky breath and pasted on a smile as she followed her parents out of the family fabric shop.

Meredith was adjusting her skirt on the wagon bench. "Maybe we can ask the Mayers to send Danny over as we pass their place. Surely they'll be willing to spare him."

"Mother, it's the harvest. They need him."

"At the very least, he could check in from time to time."

William climbed into the wagon and squeezed his wife's knee. "We can mention it to them, but I'm sure Danny intends to come and check on his sister whenever he has the chance." He waved to Ethelwynne and flicked the reins. The wagon rattled down the road.

Ethelwynne waved to her parents as they headed away from Sweet Briar towards the Greisgebied Mountains and the Elven Kingdom of Grahamadon. They rounded the corner. Tears filled Ethelwynne's eyes. *I can do this. Everything is*

going to be fine. She listened to the clatter of the wagon
wheels and the clop of the horse's hooves as they moved
farther down the lane. One month. She sniffed and rubbed
her eyes.

The hoofbeats were barely audible now. Ethelwynne
took a few deep breaths, but the tears spilled over and ran
down her cheeks faster than she could blink them away. She
wiped both of her eyes and looked down the blurry road her
parents had gone on. "Goodbye," she whispered to the trees.

*   *   *

The month passed quickly. There was only one hiccup
when a traveling merchant tried to mark up his prices in light
of her perceived inexperience, but it was nothing she couldn't
handle. *Mother and father are going to be so proud.*
Ethelwynne beamed as she wandered around the store and
adjusted the different bolts of fabric. Everything was going to
be perfect.

Mrs. Tarleton walked through the door. "I need some
material for my boy. His old work clothes are absolutely
tattered," she said. Her arms flailed about in her usual
dramatic way.

If she hadn't been in charge of the store, Ethelwynne
would have rolled her eyes at all of the arm waving and
urgency of the woman before her. As it was, Ethelwynne
nodded and headed to the undyed wools which would be the
most likely options for a blacksmith. "This way, Mrs.
Tarleton."

"Hmm. I'm not sure how I feel about this." Mrs.
Tarleton huffed and held up a corner of the beige cloth
dejectedly. "What do you think, my dear? Do you think my
lovely Eric would look good in something this... shade?"

Ethelwynne blinked a few times. She bit her lower lip to
resist the urge to laugh and looked around her parents' store.

8

Most of the material was some version of brown, beige, or white, especially the fabric they recommended to use for work clothes. Once she regained her composure, she answered Mrs. Tarleton's question: "This material is sturdy enough to withstand the heat Eric will encounter in the forge. We wouldn't want him to burn."

"Yes, but do you think it will look becoming on him? If your parents were here, I'm sure they would be able to find me sturdy fabric that also emphasizes my child's stature."

This time Ethelwynne did roll her eyes. Nicer clothing would not stop Eric from being a self-absorbed dolt. "While beige might not be the best color for some individuals, until the next shipment of fabric comes in, it's the best I can do."

Mrs. Tarleton wandered around the store to look at the options available. "What about that one?" She pointed to a lone bolt of pine green silk on the back wall. "Eric absolutely loves the color green."

"Silk isn't a suitable material for work clothes. But I could take it down and cut you some fabric for a dress shirt if you would like."

"Silk? Do you ever hold it up to yourself and pretend you're wearing a fancy evening gown like the ladies do?" Mrs. Tarleton said as she spun around in an imagined gown. "You should ask your mother to make you a dress from it when she gets back." She smiled wistfully, "You'd look so becoming next to my beloved child. But no, the Festival of the First Frost is still a little ways off. Today Eric requires work clothes, not a dress shirt. Is there anything else?"

Ethelwynne shook her head in response to the question and the idea of her attending the festival with Eric. Not even the gift of a silk gown would compel her to dance with that boy. "Perhaps my parents will have something more suitable for your son when they return later today." Although she highly doubted it; blacksmiths weren't among those who wore green or blue fabric.

Mrs. Tarleton frowned. "I shall come back tomorrow then."

"If I see anything that suits your needs, I'll set it aside," Ethelwynne promised as Mrs. Tarleton left the store.

Ethelwynne shook her head and wandered back to the wool to rehang the material. The bell rang and Mrs. Cohen stepped inside.

"Good afternoon, Mrs. Cohen," said Ethelwynne as she adjusted the bolt. "Are you here for another dress for Sarah?"

"Yes," Mrs. Cohen smiled. "I'm hoping to find her something nice to wear to the festival in a few weeks." She glanced at the door that joined the family home to the store. "Is your mother here yet?"

"Not yet. Shall I show you some options for fabric while we wait?"

"Lead the way, my dear," Mrs. Cohen said as she started walking to the finer fabrics near the back of the shop. "I'm looking for something that will flow nicely, but that will still keep her warm if she's not right beside the fire."

Ethelwynne joined the older woman and pointed out a few selections. Mrs. Cohen hemmed and hawed over fabrics for a while. Every so often, she glanced out the door behind her. After she rejected the fifth option, she sighed.

Ethelwynne looked over at her from behind the sixth bolt.

"It's not that I don't trust you, dear," said Mrs. Cohen, "it's just, your mother has always made our clothes, and she has such lovely ideas. It doesn't seem right to make these decisions when she's not here yet." She walked over to Ethelwynne and patted her on the shoulder.

"It's alright, Mrs. Cohen. My mother has taught me well, but it always does seem a little magical when she makes dresses," said Ethelwynne smiling to suppress a frown. She wondered if anyone in her home town would ever think of her as capable. "If you come back in two days, she will definitely be working."

"Thanks, dear." Mrs. Cohen patted Ethelwynne once more as she left.

Ethelwynne paused in the doorway and looked down the empty road. Shadows were beginning to stretch across it as the sun sank lower in the sky. *Where are they?* Ethelwynne bit her lip and walked back inside. Maybe they left later than they intended, or stopped for a picnic along the way and lost track of time. She leaned against the closed door and shut her eyes. There were many reasons they might not be home yet.

Ethelwynne walked to the window and flipped the closed sign. After one final peek down the road, she shut the curtains. The clopping sound of horse hooves echoed up the road and stopped in front of the shop. Ethelwynne's brows furrowed. She hadn't heard the clatter of the wagon wheels. *Who's here?* She stepped outside and locked the door behind her before she walked around the corner to the hitching post.

Danny was busy tying his horse up. "Hey Eth, I don't see a wagon by the stables. Are they not home yet?"

She shook her head.

Danny frowned and pulled a bag off of his horse. "I brought over some ingredients for soup from the farm. So, I might as well make supper while we wait."

Ethelwynne opened the backdoor, and together they walked up the stairs and into the house. Danny dumped the contents of the bag on the kitchen table. "Chop these, will you?"

The corners of Ethelwynne's mouth lifted as she started chopping the carrots. "Yes, I can see how you are preparing a wonderful meal."

He gave her one of his biggest fakest grins. "Quit your whining and get back to work. I'll get the water."

Ethelwynne laughed and continued chopping up the vegetables. Once she was done, she dumped them into the pot Danny had filled and wandered over to the cupboard to grab four bowls and spoons. "Just in case they're late," she muttered. She glanced at the window. She couldn't make out individual trees anymore. Ethelwynne tried to ignore the queasiness in her stomach as she set out their places. She didn't want Danny to know how worried she was feeling.

"Mrs. Tarleton stopped by the farm today," Danny started to say from his position stirring the soup. "Apparently, you're very concerned about the well-being of her most beloved son."

Ethelwynne wrinkled her nose. "How's Annie?"

Danny put the spoon down and leaned against the wall by the stove. A smile spread across his face. Hopefully, he would simply talk about her and leave off with his questions about Eric; she'd had enough of him for one day.

"Good." The smile vanished as he studied her. "Please tell me you're not interested."

"I'm not interested." Her whole body shook with revulsion as she went to grab the cups from the cupboard. "Better? How could you honestly think I would be?"

He turned back to the stove and resumed stirring the soup.

She shook her head at him as she put the cups beside the bowls. "Eric?" She shuddered at the thought.

Danny sipped some soup off of the spoon. "Perfect. Pass me the bowls." He ladled out the food then replaced the soup pot with a second, water-filled pot so it could be ready for dishes by the time they were finished eating.

Neither sibling reached for their spoons as they looked at the still-closed door. Finally, Danny began to eat. "They won't mind if we don't wait for them," he whispered. Ethelwynne nodded and pulled her own bowl closer. Silence filled the room as the two of them ate their lukewarm food and stared at the door.

After he put his bowl in the wash bucket, Danny sat

down and drummed his fingers on the table. "I'm going to ask Annie to marry me."

"I know that. Everyone knows that."

"Yeah, but I'm going to do it. Once the harvest is over, we'll have time to relax and plan for a spring wedding."

Ethelwynne nodded and glanced at the window again, absentmindedly braiding her hair.

"We're going to build a house across the road from her parents so we can help out on the farm. I'm thinking about getting some sheep of my own. Or maybe goats. Do you think mom and dad would be interested in the wool? It'll just be a small flock. Nothing too fancy..."

Ethelwynne got up and lit the lantern. "They're alright, right?"

Danny walked around the table and hugged her tightly. "Yes. Of course. I'm sure they'll be here tomorrow."

Ethelwynne nodded into his chest and willed it to be the next day already. Since she couldn't make that happen, she pulled away and started on the dishes. Danny fell in beside her.

When they were finished, Danny grabbed his coat and headed back to the Mayers' farm. Ethelwynne desperately wanted to ask him to stay. The house seemed even emptier now than it did the night before. At least then she had anticipated being alone, but this time she had been expecting to hear the sounds of other people. But she knew the Mayers would need his help with the morning chores. Cows did not like to be kept waiting at milking time.

The next morning, she stumbled down the stairs to get the store ready to go. She promised her parents she could handle things here without them, and that had to include unexpected setbacks like her parents' late arrival. However, she was grateful when Mrs. Tarleton did not return.

Danny came back in time for supper once more. This time he showed up with some food that Annie and her mother Bethany had prepared for them. The two ate in silence.

"What if their wagon crashed?" Ethelwynne asked as she put her parents' unused plates back in the cupboard for the second night in a row.

Danny exhaled loudly and shook his head.

An uneasy stillness settled around them as they worked together. Danny paused with the drying rag on a cup. "Nathaniel, Zachary, and I were thinking about taking the horses down the road a bit if they didn't show up today. On my way home tonight, I'll swing by their place and let them know mom and dad aren't here. We'll head out after chores."

Tears streamed down Ethelwynne's cheeks as she nodded. It didn't surprise her the Tanner brothers were the first to offer to help look for her parents. She studied their cupboard to find a place for her cup. As much as she wanted Danny to head out and look for their parents, she was terrified by what answer he might bring back. "What if they're not alright?" she whispered.

She heard the soft clunk of the cup and cloth being placed on the table before her brother's arms wrapped around her. "They're fine."

She nodded once more, but his words couldn't reach her heart—the 'what ifs' drowned out any hope she wanted to feel. "Let's get these dishes done," she said, stepping away from him.

When they were finished, Danny left. Unwilling to sit in the silent kitchen alone, she blew out the candle and went to bed.

Eight days later, Danny and the Tanner brothers returned from their ride. Danny shook his head. His eyes were bright with tears. "We rode to the mountain pass, but we didn't see them."

Ethelwynne felt like she would break. She squeezed the hitching post until her fingers hurt. "Maybe they missed the gate's opening," she said weakly. She didn't even want to entertain the possibility that the wagon had an accident on the pass. With all of the sheer drops, she knew they would never find them if that were the case. They had to be alright. What would she do without them?

*   *   *

As days turned into weeks, Ethelwynne's life settled into a new routine. Every morning, she'd get up and tend to the store like nothing was the matter. Each evening, Danny would stop by for supper. Sometimes Annie was with him. Sometimes she wasn't. He told her these visits were to check and see if their parents were home yet, but Ethelwynne suspected they were mostly to make sure she was alright.

Mrs. Tarleton returned for her fabric. While she was there, and every time she saw Ethelwynne around the town, Mrs. Tarleton suggested more and more forcefully that her son would be an excellent companion to help keep the lonely nights at bay. When she came back to the store for more clothes for her son, Ethelwynne staunchly informed her she was not interested.

"Well, then," huffed Mrs. Tarleton dropping the buttons back on the counter. They bounced off the smooth surface and hit the floor scattering under the table and the nearby displays. "Perhaps I will just have to take my business elsewhere if my dear boy is so distasteful to you." She spun and marched to the door. Pausing in the threshold she whirled around and faced Ethelwynne, "Your mother would never have tolerated this foolishness from you. She knew how to treat her customers. You should be ashamed of yourself." She sniffed and slammed the door behind her.

The bell was still ringing when Danny opened it. He pointed in the direction Mrs. Tarleton had gone.

Ethelwynne glared at him and slammed one of the

buttons back on the counter. "Don't ask. Just go do something useful."

He knelt beside her to gather the remaining buttons.

"Not this," Ethelwynne huffed.

Danny threw his hands up in the air and disappeared through the adjoining door leaving her alone once more.

"I am doing the best I can," she hollered to the closed front door. "And you're wrong, Mrs. Tarleton. My mother would have agreed with me." Ethelwynne slammed another button onto the table. "She wouldn't have tolerated your behavior, especially after I had made it perfectly clear I'm not interested in that stupid son of yours."

When the last button had been found and shoved back in the button box, Ethelwynne stormed to the shop's door and locked it. Then she followed her brother through the back door and into the house.

Danny was sitting at the kitchen table with his forehead cradled in his hands, ignoring the screams from the kettle.

"How's the harvest coming?" Ethelwynne snapped. She took the steaming kettle off the stove and poured both of them a cup of tea. She couldn't believe the nerve of that woman. Her parents were missing, they might even be dead, and there was that despicable human being trying to force Ethelwynne to marry her horrid spawn.

The hot water sloshed out of the kettle and burned her hand. Ethelwynne yelped and sucked on the burn. Of course she would burn her hand today. It fit with everything else that was going on.

Danny shrugged. "It's coming."

Ethelwynne sat down beside him and stirred some sugar into her cup. Her anger subsided as she stared into her tea. Nothing was going the way she planned anymore. It was supposed to be one month. Simple. Easy. Expected. Everything had gone so well until her parents didn't come home. Tears blurred her vision. She wiped them away and took a sip.

Looking up from her cup, she noticed Danny hadn't touched his drink. He had been there for her so many times when they were growing up, but right now, he needed her to be the strong one, if only for the evening. Ethelwynne took a deep breath as she cradled the now-tepid liquid. "Why haven't you proposed to Annie yet? You were so excited about it a couple of weeks ago."

Danny looked at her with a mix of disbelief and disgust. "You honestly expect me to propose right now? What's the matter with you? What about mom and dad? Aren't you worried something happened to them?" He slapped the table.

Ethelwynne jumped at the sound.

"They could be dead, and you want me to think about marriage?" The chair clattered to the floor behind him as he stood quickly. Danny stalked to the coat rack.

Ethelwynne wrestled up more confidence than she felt, and followed her brother to the door. "Danny, they're fine. They're probably late because some elf wanted to buy fabric and forgot how much material they needed or they wanted to barter over prices for much longer than necessary. You know how invested our father gets when he's bartering over things. They probably just missed the opening of the gates."

Danny paused with his hand on his jacket.

"It's happened before," Ethelwynne continued. "I bet you and Mom didn't freak out this much when Dad and I missed an opening. They're fine. But Annie's hurting." Ethelwynne gave Danny a quick hug. "She's trying not to say anything because she knows you're worried, but Annie isn't very good at hiding what she's feeling. When she came over a few nights ago, I asked her what was wrong, and she told me she's worried that you might have changed your mind about marrying her."

Danny sank to the floor by the coat rack. His jacket slumped across his lap. "It's hard. I don't want to propose to

Annie when I'm not focusing on her or us—it wouldn't be fair to her." He wiped his face on his sleeve.

Ethelwynne sat on the floor beside him. "I know Mom and Dad aren't here, but they would be upset if you paused your whole life for them." She felt him turn to face her as she leaned her head on his shoulder. "You know mom would never leave again if it turns out nothing is wrong, and she found out you didn't propose because they're late."

Danny nodded. Tears spilled down his cheeks as he hugged her. "You're probably right," he mumbled. He stood up and put on his jacket. "I'll think about it."

Ethelwynne followed him down the stairs. She watched him walk away and leaned against the door frame. "You really need to come home now," she whispered to the road. "We miss you." She locked the door and plodded into the house to pour out Danny's untouched tea. "Maybe tomorrow," she told herself, but the words were no longer hopeful, just habit.

Danny didn't stop by the next day.

Ethelwynne stared at his empty spot dejectedly. After trying to be happy and confident in front of all of the customers all day long she really wanted to just be with someone who understood how she was feeling.

More than that, she didn't want to be alone. The first night her parents were gone the house had picked up more than one new and unusual sound. Ethelwynne thought she had gotten used to those eerie creaks and whistles, but now that there was a chance they might never return the noises multiplied.

She wiped away the tears pooling in her eyes. Maybe she shouldn't have judged Eric so harshly. Perhaps, once you tuned out his incessant chatter about himself, he was a decent person. Ethelwynne laughed mirthlessly and cleared the food off the table, uneaten.

Briefly, she considered heading to bed early in hopes of

rushing into the next day, but she knew despondency waited for her in the morning as well. Instead, Ethelwynne grabbed her cloak and a lantern and headed for Meghan's house. If she was so alone that she was considering crawling back to Mrs. Tarleton and apologizing for insulting her child, she needed to get out more.

*   *   *

The night out at The Sturdy Stag with Meghan refreshed Ethelwynne's spirit. While she didn't feel joyful, she still found it much easier to act happy around her customers throughout the morning, an act made even easier by the promise of another night out with friends after work today.

It was almost noon when the bell above the door rang. Ethelwynne looked up from her sweeping as Mrs. Cohen entered the store. "Hello, Mrs. Cohen." Ethelwynne swept the dust to the side and leaned the broom against the wall. "How can I help you today?"

Mrs. Cohen sighed. "The festival is nearly upon us. I cannot wait any longer for your mother to return."

Ethelwynne stood a little straighter. Mrs. Cohen was going to ask her to make a dress for Sarah. Judging by the heavy snow clouds in the sky, the festival might only be a week away now, but Ethelwynne was sure she would have time to finish the gown.

"I was wondering if I could look at some buttons," Mrs. Cohen continued. "I decided to let out the hem on the dress Sarah wore last year, but I noticed that the gown is missing a few buttons."

Ethelwynne felt her shoulders slump a bit—Mrs. Cohen still did not trust her—but she managed to keep the smile on her face and a light-hearted bounce in her voice as she headed towards the counter and the button bins. "Of course. If I recall correctly, that dress was blue with some white flowers embroidered into it?"

Mrs. Cohen beamed. "Yes, that's the one. It's so lovely. I'm glad your mother had the foresight to add some extra fabric to the bottom so Sarah could wear it again."

Ethelwynne nodded—that was something her mother would do. "I think I have just the thing." She pulled out a few buttons covered in a light blue fabric and held them out to Mrs. Cohen. "Do these work?"

Annie burst into the shop. She threw her arms around Ethelwynne and nearly knocked her over. The buttons Ethelwynne had been holding scattered across the floor. "We're going to be sisters!" Annie squealed.

Mrs. Cohen's eyebrows arched as a small smile slipped across her face.

Ethelwynne hugged Annie. "He finally asked!"

"Yep." Annie bounced on the spot.

Mrs. Cohen offered her congratulations and told Ethelwynne she'd be back to finish discussing the dress later. "I'll leave you two to celebrate," she winked, "but I did like those buttons. Perhaps you should pick them up so we can find them again tomorrow."

Annie's cheeks flushed. Ethelwynne giggled and grabbed the broom to sweep up the buttons.

Annie bounced around the shop as she told Ethelwynne how Danny proposed. "I'd given up hope of it happening while your parents were gone, but then, out of nowhere, he just asked! We were walking home after bringing some eggs to the Tanners." Her face shone as she wrapped her arms around herself. "It was perfect."

Annie laughed and spun back to where Ethelwynne was standing. She squealed as she gave Ethelwynne another hug and almost caused Ethelwynne to drop the buttons all over again.

Ethelwynne laughed. "I'm meeting up with Clarissa, Moira, and Meghan at The Stag this evening. Do you want to come?"

Annie shook her head. "That's very sweet and all, but I mostly came by to tell you thanks for convincing your brother to stop dragging his feet. He told me about your conversation." She paused for a moment. "Afterwards. Not before he asked. It was more romantic than that. Anyway, we're going over to my Nana's for dinner. We want to let her know." With that, she waved and danced out of the store.

No one else came into the store for the rest of the afternoon. The weight of the emptiness pressed in around her and the calm she felt in the morning faded away. Ethelwynne rubbed her eyes and closed up the shop a bit early and got ready to walk down to The Sturdy Stag. Maybe she could forget her parents were missing and likely dead, for just one night.

"After all," she said out loud to break up the silence, "it is possible they missed the gates to the realms being opened the first time, and they're just waiting for them to open again." As she pointed out to Danny, it had happened before. The gates were only open for a few days each month because the key's magic was tied to the lunar cycles. So, while the gatekeepers did their best to warn people when it was coming time for the gates to close, if a deal took longer than normal, or if the Keeper of the Keys was in a hurry, humans and elves alike could miss it and have to wait until the next opening. There was no reason to panic.

She grabbed her cloak and a lantern to help her get back in the dark and headed to the tavern. As she got closer to the inn, she recognized Michael's caravan. Ethelwynne bit her lip as a grin crept across her face. She hadn't known they had come into town.

Their families were good trade partners. When her parents came home from Grahamadon they would often set aside some of their purchases specifically for Michael's family. In return, Michael's father would let them have first pick of the fabrics they purchased from the other side of the country. Michael was a few years older than her, but over the past few years, the two of them had grown pretty close. She wondered if he was with them, or if it was just his father or brothers. Her heart lifted at the thought of seeing him and her steps quickened as she bounced towards the inn.

— CHAPTER TWO —

Tavern Talk

Music and laughter wafted out of the inn along with the smells of supper. Ethelwynne sighed and opened the door; it smelled like stew again. As much as she loved stew, she was getting a little tired of it, and winter hadn't even officially begun yet.

She scanned the room to see if Michael was around. He wasn't in the crowded tavern, but that didn't mean he wasn't in town. As she was looking for him, she saw her friends sitting at the table in the far corner. She waved to them and walked over.

"Hi everyone," Ethelwynne said, as soon as she was close enough to be heard over the hubbub. "How's it going?"

Clarissa shrugged and answered for the group. "We're good. What about you? I saw that Michael's in town."

Ethelwynne slipped into the empty spot beside Meghan. "So it's actually him? I just saw the wagons."

"Mmhmm. Think you'll try to convince him to stick around?"

Moira giggled. "You two are so good together, and it'll be so perfect. You can run your shop here, and he already has all of the experience needed to buy and sell fabrics in different places. With your family's elven merchant license, people will come from the capital to look at all the unique materials you have."

"We haven't actually talked about it." Ethelwynne blushed. "We hardly talk at all, just, you know, when trading fabrics and strings and stuff. My father is usually there for that, so, it's not really ideal for conversations."

"Well, I've seen the way he looks at you. He looks about ready to eat you up. Surely he'll make a move soon, especially now that your parents are, well . . ." Clarissa sighed, and looked at the other two women, "and then it'll just be us three looking for a match. I think I know who I want." She bit her lip and waved demurely to someone behind Ethelwynne.

Ethelwynne sneaked a peak as the barmaid handed her a drink. "Eric? You're interested in Eric?"

"Why not? He's strong and handsome, and he has a good job."

"He also talks about himself so much that he probably does it in his sleep," Ethelwynne replied.

"No wonder his mother has to try and sell him so hard," Meghan laughed. She nudged Ethelwynne, "She has to marry him off before everyone realizes there's no brain in there."

"Guys," chided Moira.

"You two just don't understand him," Clarissa huffed.

Meghan smiled. "Yes. That's what it must be." Her expression changed into one of concern and she rested her hand on Ethelwynne's knee. "So, Ethelwynne, while Clarissa is ogling over the guy who's going to ignore her like he ignores everyone else, how are you really doing today?"

"I—"

"Meghan, she doesn't want to talk about it," Clarissa interjected.

"I want to know. We're her friends. What kind of friends would we be if we didn't ask?"

24

"We did. When she got here, I asked how she was doing, and she didn't answer."

"Guys," Ethelwynne tried to interrupt.

"You didn't give her a chance to answer," Meghan continued.

"Yes, I did. Meghan, we talked about this before she got here. If she didn't want to talk about it, we weren't going to force her. And she obviously doesn't want to talk about it. Now, come on."

"No, you obviously don't want to talk about it. Just because it doesn't fit into your perfect rosy world, doesn't mean we shouldn't talk about the fact that our friend's parents never came back after their last trip to the elven realm. It's kind of a big deal."

"Guys!" Ethelwynne raised her voice to talk over top of the two women. "I'm okay. Really. I'm sure they probably just missed the gate's opening and have to wait for the next one, or the one in the spring when the mountain path is safe to travel again. It's happened before where we've missed the gate. Not at this time of the year, but, you know, it's happened."

Someone at the table behind her coughed. "Sorry to tell you this missy, but you might be waiting a real long while— longer than springtime—if your parents missed the gate." Ethelwynne turned to face the man. Even before she saw the worn patch on his sleeve depicting the Brown's family store symbol of a bear in a jacket, she recognized him as the driver of Michael's caravan, Charles.

"What do you mean?"

"Well, it's just that..." He looked around as if to see if there was anyone else who might want to jump into the conversation and spare him from having to continue. Those who were close enough to notice the exchange looked away or resumed talking to the people closest to them with some urgency. Since no help was forthcoming, he turned to face

Ethelwynne again. "Uh, well, you see, there's been talk that, well, that the gates might be closed, you..."

"Well, of course, the gates are closed right now. Everybody knows they're only open for a few days a month, and even then, it's only if the elves open them," Ethelwynne responded.

"Well, normally, that's the case, yes, but there's, uh," he blew out a series of short breaths that made his mustache bounce, "well, there's been rumors, mostly they say that, that they, uh, that the key to the gates has been lost." He tried to take a swig from his drink, but it was empty. Charles stared into it forlornly for a moment. He coughed and swung his cup out towards her and pointed to it as a way to excuse himself from the conversation before walking to the counter to get more ale.

The four girls sat in stunned silence as they digested the news. "How could the key be lost?" Ethelwynne swallowed and blinked back tears as she looked up at her friends. "The Keeper of the Gates has the key with him at all times. He wears it on a necklace. I've seen it."

"Maybe he had to leave the gates for a bit and something came up, you know, like a family emergency or something, so maybe he just hasn't gone back yet to unlock the gates?" said Meghan as she rubbed Ethelwynne's arm.

Moira nodded. "Yeah, that makes sense. If he always has it on him, then it's not like it could be lost. The driver has to be wrong."

Ethelwynne turned back to the caravan driver and watched him walk up to the counter and down his drink, immediately ask for more, and guzzle it a second time. After his mug was filled a third time, he sloshed over to a different table and sat down. She took a deep breath and rubbed her arms, chilled despite her proximity to the tavern's fireplace and the warmth of the room that was filled with bodies.

Meghan hugged her.

26

"He's wrong, Eth. He has to be," said Clarissa.

Meghan and Moira both nodded and stammered about how Clarissa was right; there was no possible way for the key to be lost. That just couldn't happen. Ethelwynne only half heard them. She was still staring at Charles. Charles was now downing his fifth mug. Judging by the amount he was drinking, he believed it. Ethelwynne pulled her gaze from him and looked around.

"There are other caravans in town. Perhaps they've heard other rumors." She stood up and turned to her friends. "I'm going to go and ask around for more information from the other tables. If the gates are closed forever, guaranteed more than one person has heard about it."

This week would likely be the last time merchants came through their town until spring. Some merchants thought traveling through the winter months was worth the extra money they could make. Most didn't want to risk their own necks and wagons on passages that might not be passable. The snow could become very deep this close to the base of the mountains. And roads that were very apparent when the ground was clear could be lost to the monotonous shroud of snow-covered trees.

If things got desperate and spring refused to come like it did a few winters back, word could be sent south to Helmsville and, if a snowstorm wasn't likely, a skyship could fly over the forest and deliver supplies. However, supplies weren't what she needed from these men at this time. She needed more information and the other drivers and guards would likely have heard something about the key when they were passing through all the different villages and cities on their travels.

"Oh Eth, don't be ridiculous," said Clarissa. "The gates are fine. You're right, your parents probably just missed the last opening and are simply waiting for the next one and a safe passage home." She looked to the other two young women for support.

"It's true. She's absolutely right," said Moira.

Meghan looked at the other two then stood up and faced Ethelwynne. "Do you want some help asking around? If you start working your way around the room that way, I'll go the other way, and we can meet up back here in front of the fireplace and talk about what we've learned."

Ethelwynne's gaze settled on the ground as her shoulders drooped. "Thanks, Meghan."

"No problem," Meghan said, squeezing her arm. The direction Meghan chose for herself would take her past Charles's table. She squeezed Ethelwynne's arm again and gave her a sympathetic smile as she strode to the first table.

Ethelwynne turned to face her two remaining seated friends. "No," said Clarissa, "I'm not feeding your paranoia. Your family is fine. Come on, Moira, let's go." She stood and pulled a sheepish-looking Moira out the door behind her.

"Thanks for your help," muttered Ethelwynne to their retreating backs. The pain of their departure stung almost as keenly as the pain Charles inflicted when he first mentioned the rumor. With one last wounded look in their direction, Ethelwynne turned towards her side of the room. Meghan was already at her second table when Ethelwynne approached her first.

When the two women met up to compare stories by the fireplace, the theories they had gathered from the tavern's patrons were vast and varied. Some said there was a war in the elven realm, others that all the humans who went there were taken as slaves, and still others claimed the key was stolen from the elves. While Ethelwynne tried to take comfort in the fact that no one knew exactly what was going on, what was very clear was that something was definitely wrong with the gates. If her parents hadn't gotten out in time, they were trapped.

Meghan walked her home using her own lantern to light

the way. Ethelwynne's unlit lantern bounced and rattled against her thigh. The weight of it felt like it was going to pull her to the ground. Tears blurred her vision and her shoulders shook.

By the time they made it back to her place, Ethelwynne was an outright wreck. She could hardly breathe; she was sobbing so hard. They shuffled inside away from the cold wind which threatened to freeze Ethelwynne's tears to her cheeks. Ethelwynne crumpled on the bottom step and leaned forward on her knees, hugging them closely.

Meghan sat down beside her in the narrow stairwell. She hugged Ethelwynne deeply and rubbed her back as she waited for the tears to pass.

"Let's get you upstairs," she said tenderly, once Ethelwynne's tears subsided.

Ethelwynne's breathing hitched as she tried to respond. In the end, she gave up trying to speak and nodded as she turned to climb up. Meghan followed her. After Ethelwynne opened the door to the kitchen, she succumbed to the weight of the news once more. She sank to the floor and leaned against the wall. All she wanted to do was curl up forever and cry; she was never going to see her parents again.

After a while, Ethelwynne had no more tears left in her. "What am I going to do?" She leaned over into Meghan's shoulder and looked up at her with glassy eyes.

"I don't know," Meghan whispered and hugged her tight. "I don't know."

They sat there in the soft glow of Meghan's lantern and watched it burn down. "You should get some rest," Meghan said in a low voice and pulled Ethelwynne to her feet. "We can't fix anything right now, but there is always tomorrow, and maybe another caravan will come in with news that the key has been found."

Ethelwynne leaned on her friend's strength as she let Meghan pull her towards her black bedroom. While stray beams of moonlight trickled in through the kitchen windows, her bedroom's curtains were closed tight.

Blindly, she navigated the two of them towards her bed and sat down. The heavy quilts she had worked so hard on didn't bring the usual sense of pride and satisfaction. She ran her fingers along the stitches as she sat there in the dark. Some of the seams on the top blanket were done by her mother; Ethelwynne wondered if the line she was tracing was one of them.

"We shouldn't have let the light go out," she murmured, as somewhere in the part of her mind that was still connected to the present she realized that Meghan would have to find her way out in the dark. Unlike her, Meghan didn't have any experience navigating this room in the middle of the night.

"It's fine. You have spare blankets in the hope chest, right?"

Ethelwynne sniffed and rubbed her eyes. "Why?"

"You need me. I'm not going to leave you alone after all that."

Fresh tears began to fall. "Thank you," she squeaked.

"No problem." Ethelwynne could hear the small smile in Meghan's voice even though she couldn't see it on her face. Meghan slowly made her way to the foot of the bed and yelped softly when she kicked the back leg and again when she hit the side of the hope chest.

"Would you like help?" Ethelwynne leaned across her bed and opened the curtain to let some of the scarce moonlight in.

The hope chest's hinges creaked as Meghan lifted up the lid. "Nope," said Meghan. "I've got it now." She shuffled around some more without bumping into anything else and made herself a place to sleep. Ethelwynne listened to Meghan's breathing slow and deepen. Soon she drifted off into sleep as well.

*   *   *

The next morning, even though every motion felt nearly impossible, Ethelwynne opened up the store.

"Ethelwynne," Meghan consoled, as she shook out some linen and rehung it, "you don't have to do this. Everyone would understand if the store was closed today."

"I know." Ethelwynne adjusted the material Meghan just hung so that it draped nicely. She stepped back and scanned the store. "The cotton needs to be touched up, I also need to grab the buttons for Mrs. Cohen, and then I can flip the sign."

"Ethelwynne." Ethelwynne looked up at Meghan who smiled at her, but the concern in her eyes and voice took any joy from the attempted levity of her mouth.

"I can't just sit around and do nothing," Ethelwynne remarked, as she pulled out the buttons for Mrs. Cohen. "I promised my parents the store would be here when they got back, and I intend to keep that promise." *Even if it ends up only being open so I can buy food for myself,* thought Ethelwynne sadly.

"Okay," mumbled Meghan, as she headed towards the cotton to shake off any dust that may have settled on the material.

Once Ethelwynne readjusted the bolts she opened the curtains to flip the sign and show everyone that they were open. Thick clusters of snowflakes fell from the sky and blended into the white tegument on the ground. She sighed heavily. Last year, the fluffy white flakes would have excited her because it meant the Festival of First Frosts would happen on the weekend, but now the snow forced her to admit the pass through the Greisgebied Mountains would be too dangerous for her parents to travel through. Even if the gates opened, they wouldn't be able to return until spring.

Day by day, Ethelwynne continued to go through the motions of opening the store. As deep banks of snow shut

Sweet Briar off from the rest of the country, Ethelwynne prayed fervently to the goddess Satia for spring to come early to the mountains. Maybe, once the mountain paths were passable, the problem with the key would be solved and her parents could come home.

*   *   *

When the days grew longer and the water dripped off the tips of the icicles, hope swelled in Ethelwynne's heart again. Soon the first caravans would begin to arrive and with them would come news from the rest of the country. Maybe her parents would be among them; she didn't admit it to anyone other than herself, but she didn't really believe they would roll up with the spring melt.

Ethelwynne was up early, as was her norm this past winter. She rarely slept soundly or for long. The creaks and echoes that reverberated through the house often woke her. Depending on whether or not she was in the middle of a rare good dream or, more commonly, a bad dream, she would either think her parents had come home while she was sleeping or that someone was breaking into the store or her house.

Danny, Annie, and Meghan stopped by at least twice a week to check in on her and see how she was holding up on her own. While she was mostly truthful when she told them how she was feeling, she never told them about the sounds or her nightmares. Their frequent visits told her how worried they were about her well-being, and she had no desire to fuel their anxiety.

Ethelwynne sighed as she swept the new dusting of snow off of the store's front step. The sun was just starting to crest the trees and the warmth of the rays would melt it. Ethelwynne did not want the snow to be there long enough to create a mud puddle in front of the door. "I'll have to deal with enough mud as it is," she muttered, as she envisioned everyone tramping through her store with their mud-covered boots. It would take forever to clean the store before she could go and make supper at the end of the day. But, with any luck, no one would knock any fabric off of the racks and step on the bolts as they tried to get away from their mishap unnoticed.

She shook her head as she remembered the time Eric did that when his mother dragged him to her store to try one last time to get the two of them together. Mrs. Tarleton was livid when Ethelwynne informed her she'd have to pay for the torn top layer because it wouldn't be salvageable even if Ethelwynne washed it.

Mrs. Tarleton had stormed out of the shop without paying, leaving her blushing son behind. Eric apologized brusquely and dumped some coins on the table before he followed his mother out. The amount was far more than the cloth was worth. As a gesture of good will, Ethelwynne had painstakingly cut around the torn and stained area and made Eric a shirt.

When she brought it and the remaining change to Eric, she mentioned that Clarissa loved this style of shirts. Shortly after that, he and Clarissa started seeing each other more frequently and Ethelwynne started seeing her friend—and Mrs. Tarleton—less. The loss of Clarissa's company stung a bit, but Ethelwynne was more than ready to see Mrs. Tarleton leave her shop and never return.

A robin landed in the tree across from her and started to sing, drawing Ethelwynne from her reverie. Spring was here. Ethelwynne leaned the broom handle against the wall and massaged her arms and hands as she surveyed her handiwork. She always seemed to hurt. "Why does spring have to be so muddy?" she asked the bird. "Couldn't the snow just melt into rivers or forests or anywhere else that isn't here?"

The robin twittered something Ethelwynne took for

agreement before it flew off. With a sigh, she went inside to set up the shop for the day.

Ethelwynne paused after she opened the curtains to bask in the warmth of the early morning glow. She hugged herself tightly and tried to remember when her mother hugged her. The familiar feel of tears filled her eyes as she looked out the window and stared at the curve her parents vanished behind. "What am I going to do if you don't come back?"

Drying her eyes, she moved to flip the sign around to let the other villagers know the shop was open. The first caravan of the season sloshed past. The crew looked miserable. The wagon's sides, the horses' bellies, and the men's entire bodies were covered in mud. Ethelwynne cringed.

She dropped the sign and the closed symbol thumped gently against the window. She doubted anyone would come. After winter, when there was nothing exciting to gossip about except what ones' neighbors were doing, Ethelwynne suspected that most villagers would be in the square with her, eagerly waiting for information from the outside world. *Besides,* she reasoned, as she slipped into the back hall to grab her cloak, *if anyone does decide they need to buy fabric right now, they'll probably see me beside the caravan. Or, at the very least, they'll hear the crowd gathering and assume I'm there.*

As Ethelwynne was coming back down the stairs, the bells by the front door jingled, followed by the sloshy sounds of swishing skirts and shuffling muddy feet. "I was just heading out to see the caravan," Ethelwynne called and tried to ignore the annoyance that threatened to bubble up. She had just swept and the sign said she was closed. Ethelwynne ran down the last few steps, slowing only to walk back into the shop.

Annie slumped her way to the counter. Her face was splotched from crying, and her chin trembled as though she might burst into tears at any moment. "Ethelwynne?" She flopped onto the stool and lay her head down into her arms. "Danny..." Her voice hitched and she broke down.

Ethelwynne darted to her side. Her heart pounded and her lungs forgot how to breathe. She dropped her cloak carelessly on the counter. It slid off and fell to the floor. "Is he alright?" Danny had to be alright. Ethelwynne couldn't do this on her own. She needed to know her older brother was there if she ever needed him. She couldn't lose her parents and her brother in the span of one horrid winter.

Annie lifted her head a bit to look at Ethelwynne. "Yes." She sobbed and shook her head. "No." She took a few shaky breaths. "I don't know."

Ethelwynne exhaled slowly as she leaned on the table beside Annie. Blinking back her own panic, she put her hands on Annie's. As calmly as she could muster, Ethelwynne asked, "What's wrong?"

Annie sniffed. She pulled out a handkerchief and wiped her face. "He wants to go looking for your parents. But he's just going to get himself killed." She shuddered and burst into fresh tears.

Ethelwynne hugged her until the tears stilled enough for Annie to continue. "I mean, you saw the wagons pulling in."

Ethelwynne looked out the window at the road with its muddy tracks. In the forest, the ruts from wagons going over the soft earth would be even deeper. If he headed north towards the Greisgebied Mountains, there would still be deep banks of snow barring his way and hiding any branches that had fallen during the winter's storms or the rocks that were there all along. If he went, she likely would lose him. She suppressed a shudder and squeezed Annie's shoulders more tightly. "I'll talk to him. I promise."

Annie sniffled and nodded. "Do you... do you need any help here? Danny has been doing all the chores at my parents' farm so there's nothing for me to do, and I could use a chance to just be busy."

"Uh..." Ethelwynne glanced out the window in the direction of the town square. Annie was not a salesperson, but there was a good chance no one would come to the shop, so she wouldn't be able to ruin any sales. "I haven't had a chance to mop the floor yet." Ethelwynne decided against mentioning that she hadn't intended to mop it either, but since the new muddy tracks on the wooden boards begged for water and soap, it was as good a task for Annie as any. "And, um, if any shoppers happen by, you could let them know I'll be right back."

Annie gave her a small smile. "I can do that."

"Okay. There's some water in the washbasin and a clean cloth is on the shelf, if you wanted to freshen up first. The wagons aren't going anywhere. I can wait."

Annie sniffed and headed out through the door to the stairs. Ethelwynne heard her trudging up to the kitchen. Once Annie was back in the store, Ethelwynne put on her cloak and boots for her trek through the mud. She didn't bother to flip the sign. Ethelwynne decided she could deal with the repercussions if Annie noticed that the sign said closed, but for now she would give the woman some privacy to cry.

Even though she held up her skirt, the mud and moisture were still up to her knees by the time she made it down the road to the square.

The wagons were easy to spot. They set up beside the village green and a large crowd was already gathering around them. The people were unusually silent as they listened to the merchant addressing them from where he stood on one of the wagons. It took Ethelwynne a few moments to figure out who he was underneath all of the mud, but as she approached, she realised it was Ronald Perera. With all of his arm-waving and shouting, he could give any showman a run for his money.

Ethelwynne spotted Meghan in the crowd and went to stand beside her. Mrs. Tarleton, Zachary, and a few others

36

gave her angry glares as she squeezed passed them. Ethelwynne opted to ignore them.

"Did I miss anything?" she whispered to her friend.

CHRISTINA VAN STARKENBURG

— CHAPTER THREE —

Finding the Truth

Meghan hugged her, "Apparently the gates are closed because the elf king and his brother aren't speaking to each other."

"What does that have to do with the gates being closed?" Ethelwynne huffed. "Can't the two of them go through the passage, let the people out, and have their royal spat in their own realm?"

Several of the villagers standing in front of the pair turned around and shot the women angry looks, and more than one person hissed at them from behind and demanded their silence.

Meghan chuckled softly, but Ethelwynne's cheeks prickled as the two women turned to face the wagon where Ronald was continuing with his tale.

"King Orrin had Prince Damien sent away to..." Ronald snapped his fingers as he ran through some names, "Hammond? Hambell? Heatherbell? You know, King Kellan's hunting lodge—Heatherfield." He threw up his hands triumphantly. "That's the place."

"What does this have to do with the gates?" Ethelwynne called out.

While the merchant didn't hear her, the people standing around her did. "If you don't want to be quiet, leave. I want to hear," Zachary whispered, as he tried to pull her out of the crowd.

Ethelwynne shook her arm out of Zachary's grasp as the merchant started speculating about what the elves' disagreement was about. She could not care less about whether or not the king killed the boar the prince was hunting, or if the prince insulted the king's choice of weapon, or whatever other petty argument it might be. She just wanted to know what happened to her parents.

"Excuse me," she yelled, louder this time so Ronald could hear her over the sound of his own voice as he continued to make up potential disagreements that the two royal elves might be having.

His jaw dropped open. He opened and shut his mouth a few times before he stammered, "I was on a roll." He surveyed the crowd with his palms outstretched. They nodded their agreement and glared at Ethelwynne. "What do you want? You can wait to buy something. Your people want news."

Considering the disgusted expression on his face, Ethelwynne knew she shouldn't buy from him this trip if she wanted a fair price. She gripped her skirt—the cloth would have to wait. She wasn't ready to give up on getting answers just yet. "If the brothers aren't speaking to one another, why does that mean one can't just go back through the gates and open them again?"

He pointed his finger at her. "Now, that there is a good question." He tapped the side of his finger against his lip a few times before answering with a slight shake to his head, "I don't know. There are lots of rumors 'bout that too. Some think the elves lost the key. Others say it was stolen. And there are those who believe the king has the key, but that he still has business in the human realm so he won't let his brother go back to Grahamadon without him—even though the two can't stand each other—because he doesn't want him to bully the queen. I suppose that makes sense, if their argument is about the queen, and honestly, what better thing to have an argument about than a lady?" He smiled, and several men in the crowd chuckled. "But," he paused dramatically and looked over the crowd, "whatever happened, people do agree the king was the one who was supposed to have the key."

Ethelwynne and Meghan listened for a bit longer. However, after the merchant's tale veered away from the elves to more mundane things, like how much mud he and his men had braved to bring the good people of Sweet Briar their very first news and spices of the season, they decided they had heard enough.

The people around them willingly parted to let them pass when they realized that the two women wanted out. "About time," muttered one particularly surly villager whose name Ethelwynne couldn't recall, as he stepped out of the way and on to Sarah Cohen's foot. Sarah yipped in pain, but quickly clapped a hand over her mouth to stifle the sound.

"Come on," Meghan said, once they broke away from the crowd. "Let's go to my place and have some tea." Around them, other villagers were beginning to disperse. Evidently, they had just come for the news, as well.

Ethelwynne shook her head. "I left Annie in charge of the shop while I was gone. Now that the crowd's dispersing, I should probably head back. I might actually get a customer."

Meghan grinned. "Not if the angry looks Zachary and the others were shooting at us say anything. Did you see the look Barry Cohen was giving you? It'll be weeks before Deborah is able to convince him that your store is the best place to buy gowns for his granddaughter."

"Nonsense. Just give them a few days. Once the caravan

is gone, they'll be back. They'll need fabric and clothes eventually." Ethelwynne smiled as they walked down the road together.

Meghan laughed. "Fine, but first let me get some tea leaves from my place. Your supply was pretty pathetic the last time I was over." She veered off the main road towards her house. Ethelwynne knew it was the fifth house on the street, but she always double-checked that she was in the right place by looking for the herbs drying in the window. No matter what time of year it was, Meghan's mother always had some in her window in case she needed to quickly grab a few sprigs of some herb or other as she was leaving the house to help someone with labor pains or bring down a fever.

"I have tea."

"Right. Just like you have customers." Meghan disappeared into her house and reappeared with a small bag that contained her opinion of a suitable amount of tea leaves and a larger bag hiding a change of clothes she could slip into once they arrived at Ethelwynne's place.

Before long, they made it back to the store. Annie had finished mopping and was contentedly shaking out the fabric and rehanging the bolts on their stands. Ethelwynne suppressed a groan and forced a smile on her face that she prayed looked natural as she looked around. The different materials were no longer in their correct places. Instead of matching the fibers, it looked like Annie had matched shades and colors.

"Oh good, you're back," Annie called, as she shook out a bolt of white linen. "After I finished mopping, I thought I'd shake some dust off of the different fabrics so they have a fresh look when your customers come in." She smiled as she hung the cloth up beside a bolt of white cotton.

"I'm glad the work has helped you feel better," Ethelwynne managed. Her voice sounded a little tense, but neither Annie nor Meghan seemed to notice.

"It looks great in here, Annie," Meghan said.

Annie beamed. "Thanks. I hope you don't mind I rearranged things a bit. I just love it when the different colors match like this. It's a shame you don't have more colors. It would be so cheery in here."

Ethelwynne nodded instead of responding. She wouldn't be able to open the store today. She wouldn't know where anything was. *It's a good thing everyone in town is currently mad at me,* she thought wryly, *at least I'll have time to sort this out.*

"I'll just finish up these last few sheets, and then I'll get out of your hair."

"We can help," offered Meghan.

Ethelwynne shook her head and frantically thought of an excuse to get out of the room. "We need to wash our hands first. You," she looked at Meghan, "you've been touching herbs. One of them could have properties that could dye my fabric. So let's go, and then we'll come back." *Hopefully,* thought Ethelwynne, as she opened the adjoining door to head to the kitchen, *Annie will be done with the last three bolts before we come back down.* Ethelwynne really did not want to help her destroy the normal order.

While Ethelwynne was drying off her hands, she looked down at the floor beneath her feet forlornly. She couldn't face the downstairs disaster yet. If she did, she might cry in front of Annie and then Annie would be a miserable wreck once more. "Why don't you go help Annie finish up, while I start boiling water," she suggested. She pulled the key out of her skirt pocket and handed it to Meghan. "Here's the key so you can lock up after her. The sign should still say 'closed,' but it might be a good idea to check anyway."

Meghan studied her. "Is everything alright?"

"Mmhmm," Ethelwynne murmured.

"Alright," Meghan said, but her facial expression clearly stated that she didn't believe Ethelwynne was fine for one moment. She turned to head back down the stairs.

"I can't face the room right now," Ethelwynne blurted. "Annie messed everything up—it could take me days to rehang all of the fabrics in the right spots. I sort them based on the type of material it is, and while some are obviously not the same materials—I mean, I can easily tell the wool from the fur—other fabrics look the same so I'll probably have to touch each and every bolt to make sure I'm putting it back properly. But I don't want her to know that, because I don't want her to get upset all over again."

"So you'll wait a few days until she comes over and sees that you've put everything back to address this?"

"Yes." Ethelwynne wrung her hands in front of her waist.

Meghan threw her hands in the air and stepped out of the kitchen and onto the top steps. "I will go lock up your store for you so you don't have to face your sister-in-law yet," she said, low enough that her voice wouldn't carry to the room below.

Ethelwynne quickly changed and put a pot of water on to boil. As she waited for the water, she resolved not to think about the store. Instead, she mulled over what she had learned from Ronald. Ethelwynne grabbed the teapot from its place on the shelf and put the tea leaves Meghan had brought over inside it. The water steamed and roiled. Ethelwynne picked up the pot and carefully poured the liquid into the kettle.

"You know," Ethelwynne said, when Meghan re-entered the kitchen, "Heatherfield isn't that far from here."

"It is in this mud," Meghan answered. She put the key on the table and slipped into Ethelwynne's room to switch her undergarments. "Annie is on her way home," she called through the open door.

Ethelwynne nodded and returned the key to her pocket.

"You're not going to do something foolish, are you?"

said Meghan, as she adjusted her skirt and rejoined Ethelwynne in the kitchen.

Ethelwynne shook her head and poured the tea, "It's too muddy. Besides, I promised Annie I would convince Danny not to do something like that, and I have the shop."

Meghan nodded slowly.

Ethelwynne fidgeted under her studious gaze and changed the topic as they moved downstairs. But, as she sipped her tea, she couldn't help glance out the window and wonder how long it would take for her to get to Heatherfield Manor to find out the truth.

*   *   *

A week later, Ethelwynne sat behind the counter as she refolded one of seven remaining bolts of misplaced fabric. She'd begun reorganizing the store right after Meghan left but it was taking longer than she anticipated because she had chosen not to close the shop while she fixed it. And, like she had predicted to Meghan, people hadn't stopped coming to the store because she'd interrupted the merchant's tale. Every day several villagers came in and prevented her from reorganizing the shop. In the beginning, it had taken her at least twice as long to help them find what they were looking for. More than one person had huffed in annoyance and remarked, "Perhaps you should simply put things back the way they were when your mother was managing the store. It never took her this long to find something."

Ethelwynne had bitten her tongue more than she could count to stop herself from replying that she hadn't been the one to rearrange everything. Annie had been highly apologetic when she learned what her decision had done and she offered to help reorganize, but it was clear she couldn't distinguish the different materials, so Ethelwynne had politely turned her down.

She sighed and supposed she should be grateful this happened before she had purchased a new order of materials. As it was, there was space on the different racks for her to hang extra bolts as she moved them back to their rightful places. Her store should finally be back to normal this afternoon.

Being very careful not to mess up her hard work, Ethelwynne carried what she thought might be the last bolt of linen to the rack in the front of the store. While she adjusted the way the fabric draped on the rod, she thought about the conversation she had with Danny the night before. He looked like he was getting even less sleep than she was and his hair was standing on its ends from him raking his fingers through it all the time. He was adamant he was going to walk to Heatherfield and demand the elf prince tell him when the gates were going to be opened.

Ethelwynne wasn't sure she convinced him to stay home. She had begged, pleaded, and reasoned with him to stay. She brought up how she might need help around the store, Annie's family would need help to prepare the fields for this year's crop, and how he needed to build a house for himself and Annie. "Unless," she had pointed out, "you want to sleep in her parents' place or with the hired hands after your wedding."

"Fine," he snapped as he stormed to the door to leave, "I'll stay until the crops are in the ground. But then, I'm going. Someone has to find out the truth." The door slammed shut behind him as he rode back to the Mayers' place.

"Ouch!" Ethelwynne yelped as she kicked one of the racks on her way back to the table. She hoisted herself onto the wooden counter and rubbed her bruised toes. The house had been so quiet last night after Danny had left—too quiet. He was right. Someone did need to find out what happened with the gate. Ethelwynne wiped away a tear. She doubted demanding information from the prince would be the best way to get it. He was probably too busy with other demands on his time to take questions from lowly peasants such as herself.

Ethelwynne picked up another bolt and rubbed the material between her fingers. One good thing about this whole debacle was she was getting very good at recognizing the different materials and the different quality of the bolts she had in her store. Although, in this case she wasn't entirely sure why she bothered, she knew this bolt was made from cotton.

She hopped down off the table and picked up the bolt to bring it to its correct place, but she didn't make it more than two steps before a merchant wagon rumbled past her door. Ethelwynne put the fabric back on the counter and debated going after the wagon to see if there was any new news. Every time a caravan passed through the town, people gathered around it to hear more news of the quarreling elves. The details never changed: the visiting king was angry at his brother for some unknown reason and, because of that, the gates were still closed.

She didn't want to go and hear the same message over again, but the shop was starting to look a little bare. She needed her parents to come back with their latest purchases from the elven realms. Since that wasn't going to happen, it was up to her to barter for materials to sell. Sighing, she headed into town to see if this wagon had any good items for her to purchase. As she walked to the town square, Michael's caravan rumbled past her. Ethelwynne smiled and veered towards his wagon instead.

While Michael's crew set up, Ethelwynne chatted with him and took the first look at all of the fabric. She put aside the ones she wanted to purchase once Michael was ready.

Michael glanced at the stack she created and laughed. "Gents, we might not need to go any further. I think the Tregown's intend to buy up all our stock."

Ethelwynne blushed, "Well since my parents aren't back yet, our store is looking pretty barren."

He squeezed her arm and went back to setting up the shop in the back of the wagon.

"Where are you heading afterward?" Ethelwynne asked, biting her lip.

"Helmsville." Michael waved his hand over her pile, "And not just 'cause you're buying everything. It's time for us to go home. But," he said hopping off the wagon and picking up Ethelwynne's hands, "before I go, we should have lunch and talk business. There's always lots to talk about with new shopkeepers."

Ethelwynne's hands went limp as she stared at him. "Yeah, okay," she smiled sadly. "Shall I pay for this now, and then we can meet up after I bring it to the shop?"

"Charles won't let anyone touch it. Come on, let's go and get something to eat now." Michael folded her arm in his and walked to The Sturdy Stag.

*　　　*　　　*

A few days after her lunch with Michael, Ethelwynne leaned against the wall in Meghan's home and sipped some peppermint tea. "I'm going to Heatherfield, Meg."

"What?" Meghan looked up from the herbs she was grinding into powder for her mother.

"Can you watch the store for me? I'd ask Danny, but..." She took another sip to avoid finishing that sentence.

Meghan put the pestle on the table before putting her hands on her hips. "But you don't want him to know you're going. What about not doing anything rash?"

Ethelwynne cocked her head to the side and lowered the teacup. "It's not rash, I've been thinking about it since I learned the prince was there. Can you watch the store?"

Meghan threw her hands up in the air. "What about your

48

brother? Can't he go?"

"He's supposed to be getting married and building a house."

Meghan scoffed and crossed her arms. "This is ridiculous. You're going to get yourself killed or something."

Ethelwynne put the teacup on the table and clasped her hands together pleadingly. "It won't be dangerous, I promise. Michael is taking me, so I won't be traveling alone. And it's not like I haven't been on the road before. Please?"

Meghan sighed. "Fine. I'll watch your store, but," she poked Ethelwynne in the chest, "if you die, I'm going to kill you."

Ethelwynne smiled and hugged her. "Thanks. Michael's caravan leaves this afternoon. I have to let him know I'm coming, finish packing—oh, and there's Sarah's dress. I still need to finish that." Ethelwynne put the cup down. "Before I go," she grabbed a piece of paper off the table and jotted down a few reassuring words. "Here's a note for Danny."

Meghan rolled her eyes as she snatched the paper from Ethelwynne's hand. "He's going to kill you when he finds out."

Ethelwynne studied her feet "Don't let him come after me. Annie needs him here." She looked up at Meghan. "I'll be fine."

Meghan crossed her arms and shook her head.

"What? He's busy helping his fiancé's family plant their crops, and he has to start building his house. I can't take him away from that. I'll only be gone for two weeks."

Meghan arched her eyebrows.

"Two weeks," Ethelwynne held up two fingers. "Come on Meghan, help me out. Please."

Meghan raised her face up to the ceiling and closed her eyes as she let out a long deep breath. Then she looked back at Ethelwynne and waved her hand with the note in it at the door. "Go, before I change my mind and try to stop you. I won't tell your brother until tomorrow, so your caravan has a chance of getting away before he can saddle a horse and catch up to you."

"Thanks." Ethelwynne hugged her and smiled in what she hoped was a reassuring manner. "I'll leave the key in the pot by the back door." She left Meghan's place and headed for Michael's caravan in the village green.

Michael wasn't with his caravan. Before returning his attention to the work at hand Charles told her he'd be back shortly. Ethelwynne nodded and turned down the dirt path to her family store to pack and finish the dress.

Michael was leaning against the store's door. Her stomach fluttered when she saw him. He was here. He was going to help her figure out what happened to her family. He was going to keep her safe. Her cheeks tingled.

His face lit up in a smile when he saw her. "Figured I'd help you carry your stuff over to the wagons."

Ethelwynne returned his smile and opened the door to the shop. "Thanks."

"So, is Meghan going to watch the shop for you?"

Ethelwynne nodded and picked up the dress and thread that she'd left lying on the counter. "I just need to finish sewing on this ribbon, grab a few clothes and I'll be good to go."

He watched her silently as she finished sewing. There was about a hand's breadth of ribbon left to sew. It didn't take long for Ethelwynne to finish. Then, she headed upstairs to grab the plain canvas pull-top bag she had sewn together from the ends of a few rolls. She had already filled it with a change of clothes for everyday wear, some soap, a brush, and a few other personal care items. Michael promised she could share his food and drink and he assured her he had a spare tent so she didn't worry about finding space for those items.

Michael followed her up. "Nice place," he remarked, as he looked around.

Ethelwynne flushed; she had forgotten this was his first time here. She glanced around as she headed to the dress hanging on her bedroom door. She hoped to save it for her meeting with the elves and wanted to keep as many wrinkles out of it as possible by packing it last. As she carefully folded the dress and wrapped it with paper, she hoped he didn't notice the fine layer of dust starting to settle on everything.

Ethelwynne delicately placed the dress in the bag and pulled it closed. Michael shouldered the bag and together they walked back to town. By the time they got there, his caravan was almost packed up and ready to go. "Do you need to hide while I smuggle you out of town? Or does your brother know you're going?" Michael asked as he dumped her bag in with his own supplies.

Ethelwynne scoffed. "I don't need to hide. I can leave if I want to."

Michael arched his eyebrows and nodded indulgently.

"It's true," Ethelwynne playfully swatted him, "but we probably shouldn't wait too long before we leave, just in case Danny comes into town."

Michael laughed and helped her onto the wagon. Before he climbed on beside her, he walked back to the other wagon to speak with Charles and the guards to make sure everything was ready before they set out. A moment later he hopped up beside her. "There's a blanket behind the seat in case you feel the need to hide," he teased and flicked the reins to get the horses moving.

Ethelwynne gave him a perfunctory glare. But, once they drove past the Mayer's farm without seeing Danny, Ethelwynne let go of the breath she'd been holding.

Michael chuckled beside her. "All clear now," he purred.

Ethelwynne scowled.

Michael just laughed more.

Shaking her head Ethelwynne settled back onto the wagon's bench.

As the caravan rumbled down the road, Ethelwynne watched the familiar scenery roll past. Every year, for as long as she could remember, she'd come this way with her father as they headed towards the Greisgebied Mountains and the elven kingdom beyond. When they'd approach the next fork in the road, they would turn their wagon right and pass Riderless Ridge. All the trees there had an unusual bend in them like someone had been sitting on them for a hundred years and the trunk had to grow around them before turning to the sky again. As a child she'd always thought they looked a little like horses, and, even though their journey had barely begun, her father would stop here and let her "ride" them. Ethelwynne stared down the right fork to see if she could catch a glimpse of the trees from here. She knew she wouldn't be able to—they were around a few more bends, but still, she tried.

The wagons rumbled over the ground as they veered down the left path and began heading south towards Heatherfield. Ethelwynne shivered as she blinked back tears and tried not to dwell on the thought that she might never turn right at that bend again. She rubbed her arms, but it didn't warm her up at all. Ethelwynne peered behind them. She just wanted her parents to come home. Her shoulders slumped as she grabbed the afghan Michael had teased her about and wrapped it around herself.

Michael raised his eyebrows when he noticed. "If you are cold now, you might as well keep the blanket, because you'll be freezing tonight."

Ethelwynne didn't hear him. Even though Michael was sitting close enough that his arms bumped hers every time he adjusted the reins she felt so alone. *What if the elves won't speak with me? What if the key is gone?* When she could no longer see the fork, she turned to face forwards and studied her hands, as they clutched the blanket close. *What if the key wasn't missing?* She tried to wiggle even further into the blanket. *What if it's just my parents who are gone?*

Crack! Ethelwynne jumped and looked up as a tall birch tree fell across the road and smashed into a young oak on the other side.

CHRISTINA VAN STARKENBURG

— CHAPTER FOUR —

Heatherfield Manor

The front guards kicked their horses forward to avoid being hit by it. Branches crackled and leaves fluttered as the fallen tree scraped down the side of the trunk. The two mounted men calmed their animals as they scanned the surrounding area for any signs of danger.

The wagons rolled to a stop. Ethelwynne held her breath as she looked around. The previously quiet forest seemed alive with noises now. Birds cawed in the shadows. Leaves rustled in the wind. Branches snapped in the undergrowth. Ethelwynne craned her neck to see what caused the noises. She saw nothing.

Her stomach muscles tightened. She squeezed her elbows into her sides to try to make herself as small as possible as she huddled in the blanket.

One of the lead guards handed his reins to the other. The mounted guard continued to scan the forest while his companion walked along the trunk to inspect the stump. Ethelwynne watched his route with wide eyes. He drew his sword as he stepped off the road and disappeared behind a tree. Her heart pounded in her ears, and she bit her lip as seconds passed.

Michael turned around to grab his bow and quiver from behind the bench. He grunted as he jumped off the wagon. He swore when he twisted his ankle. "Stay here." He nocked an arrow and limped after his men towards the fallen tree.

Ethelwynne looked around anxiously. Michael's men wandered around in pairs. Every one of them was armed. She shifted uncomfortably on the bench and watched Michael's back. He disappeared behind the same tree as his guard. Ethelwynne held her breath and waited for him to reappear.

Michael walked out from behind the tree. He no longer had an arrow nocked and was putting it back into the quiver.

Ethelwynne breathed a small sigh of relief as he came back to the wagon.

"The tree was rotten," he called to his men. "We need to get it moved. Jordan, grab the rope from the back wagon. We'll tie it to the horses, and they can pull it off the road."

One of the guards who stood beside the horses ran to the rear wagon to grab the rope.

Ethelwynne hopped off the wagon and wandered to where the men were gathering to see if there was anything she could do to help.

Several of the men noticed her approach and nodded their heads in her direction. Michael turned around. "I told you to wait in the wagon."

"I wanted to see if I could help."

Michael scoffed. "Yes, you can," he grabbed her arm and pulled her back to the wagon and lifted her onto the bench, "by staying here."

"I might not be able to move the log, but I can gather some branches so the horses don't pick up any slivers and get hurt."

"You'd be in the way," he snapped and stalked back to his men.

Ethelwynne crossed her arms as she spluttered indignantly. "I'm not useless." But Michael was already too far to hear her soft retort.

"Get moving," Michael called to his crew. "That tree won't move itself."

His men nodded and ran up to the tree to try to figure out how to tie the rope to it.

Ethelwynne glared at Michael's back as he joined his men by the tree. She flexed her fingers before balling them into fists. "Unbelievable." She hopped down and walked up beside the horse on her side of the wagon. She rubbed its nose. "Maybe I would be in the way," she whispered to it. "Maybe they plan for these types of things. But," she glowered at Michael, "he had no right to pick me up like that. I am not a child." She took a deep breath and continued to rub the horses as she tried to calm down.

"I told you to wait in the wagon," snapped Michael.

Ethelwynne jumped and spun to face him. She hadn't heard him coming back. His arms were crossed over his chest, and his expression looked tightened. "How's it go—"

"Get in the wagon." He pushed past her to unhitch the horses from the lead wagon.

"No. I'm not a child and I'm not in the way."

His face turned red and his lips thinned as he glared at her.

Ethelwynne stepped back into the horse's flank.

He visibly vibrated as he relaxed his fists and took a few breaths. "Ethelwynne, please," he said in a strained voice, "you're making me look bad in front of my men."

Ethelwynne flinched as he grabbed her arms.

"Just get in the wagon like I asked and stay there. If you don't respect me, they won't either. We'll lose the business my parents worked so hard for and I won't be able to support you if that happens."

Out of the corner of her eye, she noticed several of his men were watching them. "Fine." She hopped back in the wagon and watched him stomp back to the tree with the horses.

When his men stopped staring at her, she shuddered and rubbed her arms. Small bruises had already begun to form where his fingers had been. Even though she was no longer cold, she picked up the blanket and pulled it over her shoulders and arms to hide the marks. He'd never acted like this around her before. He was always so cheery and kind to her, to her parents, to anyone she saw him interact with. *Maybe he's worried about letting his parents down. I know I am. I just want them to come home and be amazed by how well the store is running.* She briefly glanced back the way they came. She'd only be gone for two weeks; Meghan could handle it for that short amount of time. Ethelwynne rubbed her arms again. Everything was going to be fine.

Ethelwynne watched as his men finally got the rope tied to the tree. The animals strained as they pulled it to the side of the road. There was a lot of swearing and yelling when the log caught on another tree, but, soon enough, the horses dragged it off to the side.

Michael didn't say anything as he hitched the horses back up to the wagon.

Ethelwynne flinched when he hopped up beside her. She shuffled over as far as she could on the bench so his arm wouldn't constantly brush hers. *Please don't let him notice,* she thought as she bit her bottom lip. She wouldn't want him to think she was making him look bad in front of his men by continuing to be obstinate, but if she could she would rather be riding back with Charles right now.

"It's going to take us an extra day to make it to Bewdley," Michael said gruffly as he flicked the reins and the horses started pulling the wagon down the road again.

Ethelwynne refused to look at Michael as they rumbled down the road. Instead, she focused her gaze on the ground rolling along beside them and tried to guess what color the flowers would be on the buds that were beginning to appear.

She'd never been very good at identifying plants but she thought the ones bunched under the tree were daffodils. She guessed they were yellow—since daffodils were really only yellow, white or some combination of the two, her chances of being correct were pretty high. That is, if the plant was, in fact, a daffodil. If she remembered she could always check on the way back.

After a while, Michael broke the silence. "Ethelwynne?"

She continued to stare into the foliage on her side of the wagon.

He grunted. "I'm sorry."

She turned her head slightly and looked at him from the corner of her eye.

"Most of the time this is a very safe passage between the two towns. But when the tree fell, I was worried something would happen to you. Especially when you wouldn't listen. I don't know how to keep you safe if you don't listen." He rested one hand on her knee. "I need you to promise me that the next time something goes wrong you will listen to me."

Ethelwynne looked at him and dipped her head in acquiescence. "It's okay," she breathed, even though it wasn't. She was grateful that it was still early enough in the spring for her continued cocooning in the afghan not to be glaringly obvious and that he had apparently not noticed her cringe when he lay his hand on her knee. "I'm sorry, too." She turned her gaze back to the earth beside the wagon. Underneath the protective shelter of the blanket, she traced the small marks on her arms with her thumbs. Ethelwynne winced at their tenderness. "I'll listen."

Michael squeezed her knee before withdrawing his hand. Then he raised his voice to let the others in their company hear him. "We'll make camp in the clearing up ahead."

The rest of the members of the caravan murmured in agreement, and soon the tents were pitched and supper was served.

After supper, Ethelwynne retired to her tent, but even though the night was quiet except for the occasional owl and the wind whispering through the trees, Ethelwynne found it difficult to fall asleep. Every time she closed her eyes, she saw Michael's angry face. She shivered and pulled her cloak overtop of the spare blanket she grabbed from the wagon. "He didn't mean it," she whispered into the night.

The next morning, Michael was his usual bright and cheery self. He teased Ethelwynne about her long sleeves as he helped her take down her tent. "How did you ever make it through the mountains if this early spring air is too much for you?"

She laughed apathetically. *If I got too cold I could always sit closer to my father*, she thought as she double-checked to make sure the sleeves covered the marks on her arms. *I didn't have to worry about whether or not I was making him look bad in front of the men.* Not that her family traveled with guards; only a fool would pick a fight on the mountain ledges. Michael continued on with his jovial remarks while Ethelwynne finished packing her bags and putting them on the wagon.

After a quick breakfast, the caravan rolled out. Michael chattered happily as they rolled down the road, oblivious to the silence of his traveling companion.

Ethelwynne tried to smile, but she was too lost in her own thoughts to even see the white daffodils that had opened up this morning as they rumbled past them. *He was just worried about me and my safety. He didn't mean to hurt me. I don't even think he realized he did. He'd probably be devastated if he knew he left bruises on my arm.* She considered showing him, but worried that the guards might be too close and see the marks. *If my getting off of the wagon made him look bad, having proof that he hurt me would be much worse.*

They pulled into Bewdley around noon and stopped at

the Busy Boar Inn. "We'll spend the night here," Michael remarked. "It'll be easier for us to find a place to park the wagons tomorrow night if we don't have to hunt for new clearings."

It was smaller than The Stag, which surprised Ethelwynne. She knew Bewdley was smaller than Sweet Briar, but it was in a more central location, so she assumed more traffic would come through here. The Busy Boar was empty; although, Ethelwynne reasoned that could be because of the hour. Perhaps more customers would trickle in as the dusk approached.

Michael shook his head at her ignorance when she mentioned it to him. "We're only staying in the inn because sleeping outside has been so difficult for you. Normally, caravans pitch their tents in the surrounding fields, which is where Charles and the others are right now." He turned and spoke to the owner before turning his attention back to Ethelwynne. "I'm going to go and check on the men. Stay here."

Ethelwynne nodded to his retreating back. Where would she go? It's not like she knew anyone in Bewdley to visit, and since Michael was taking her to Heatherfield Manor tomorrow there was no point in heading out now. She sighed and grabbed one of the books the inn kept in stock and curled up by the fire where she pretended to read while she tried to decide what to say to the prince's attendants.

*   *   *

The next morning, Ethelwynne got up and wandered over to her room's vanity to splash some water on her face. The bruises on her arms had faded to a sickly yellow color. Sighing, she pulled on her long-sleeved dress again, braided her hair, and headed down to the dining room for breakfast.

The room was still empty. Besides her, there was an old

man sitting with a young town guardsman eating breakfast in silence.

She ordered her food and sat in a booth while she waited for everyone else to show up. By the time the serving woman brought her a cup of tea and a bowl of porridge with rhubarb, Ethelwynne began to wonder what was keeping Michael. "Maybe he got up early to prep the wagons," she muttered. Her fingers tapped on the table as she glanced at her breakfast. "It can keep a few more minutes."

The barmaid came out to refill the men's drinks.

"Excuse me?" Ethelwynne called to her.

"Hmm? What can I do for you, miss?" she asked as she swished over to Ethelwynne's table.

Ethelwynne played with the edges of her sleeves. "Have you seen the gentleman who came here in the caravan with me?"

"The caravan left already. But he did leave you a note." She pointed to the piece of paper peeking out from under the porridge bowl. The woman tilted her head. "You didn't forget something with them, did you?"

"No. I just... I..." Ethelwynne stumbled over her words. *He left me? He promised he would take me safely there and back.* She could feel her anxiety levels rising, but she didn't want the serving woman to know how distraught she actually was about his desertion. Before the fear could show on her face, she swallowed her panic. "Never mind. It's fine. I just didn't thank them for bringing me this far, that's all."

The young woman smiled. "Well, as long as you paid them, I'm sure they figured you thanked them well enough. Shall I top up your tea before I head back to the kitchen?"

Ethelwynne shook her head.

"Alright then. Well if you think of anything, feel free to holler and I'll come help you. The name's Lanie."

As Lanie moseyed backed to the kitchen, Ethelwynne reached for the note. All Michael's note said was he had to continue on their normal route to make up the time they'd lost with the tree, but she was to wait there for him. She crumpled the note and shoved it into her pocket. She didn't have time to wait. Danny would be worried, and Meghan had other things to do besides babysit her family's shop.

She sipped the tea and blew out a slow breath. The drink was sweeter than she usually liked it, but after taking a few bites of the porridge, she figured it was a nice way to offset the tartness of the rhubarb. *I can't believe he left me here without saying something.*

Ethelwynne dropped her spoon irritably into her empty bowl and headed back to her room to change and gather up her things. "Thank goodness everything was in one bag," she muttered as she pulled out the dress she intended to wear when she spoke with the elves and unwrapped the paper covering, "otherwise he would have taken it all with him and then what would I do?"

She had hoped that she would be able to sit in a wagon all the way to the gate so there would be no chance of her skirt getting muddy or dusty, but that wasn't an option anymore. Hopefully she'd be able to keep her feet beneath her as she walked to the manor. Like the dress she'd worn to breakfast, the sleeves on this one also covered her arms so there would be no questions about the bruises from either Lanie or the elves.

Even though she hadn't unpacked anything beyond a change of clothes and brush, after she shoved her gown back in the bag, Ethelwynne thoroughly searched the room to make sure she wasn't forgetting anything. Her eyes watered; her mother had always told her to do this whenever she went with her father to the elven realm as a child. Her father was rather notorious for leaving things behind accidentally and more than once the two of them would have to return to an inn or picnic site to retrieve something that had been left behind.

Ethelwynne wiped the tears away, fastened her cloak, shouldered her belongings and headed down the stairs. Before the day ended, she would arrive at Heatherfield Manor, speak to the elves, and learn when she would see her mother and father again. It wouldn't be long now.

As she paid for her bagged lunch, Ethelwynne said goodbye to the innkeeper and Lanie. "I'll see you tomorrow," she called over her shoulder as she stepped outside.

She set a brisk pace as she walked down the street towards the road that would lead her to the manor. If Michael was in such a hurry to return home to continue his sales trip that he left her behind, surely, he would appreciate only having to bring her home instead of also heading to see the elves.

As the houses gave way to trees and budding flowers, Ethelwynne forced herself to slow down. She wouldn't be able to keep up this pace the entire time, and she knew as long as she wasn't delayed for any reason, she would reach Heatherfield Manor by the end of the day. Rushing wasn't going to make it happen much faster.

Grey clouds hung overhead, and, by the time Bewdley was hidden behind the hills, a light drizzle began falling. Ethelwynne groaned and pulled her hood up over her head. She looked back the way she had come. As the cool spring rain pattered off her cloak, she considered turning back and trying again tomorrow—if the sun was out. She had waited this long to hear anything about her parents. One more day wouldn't hurt. Besides, Michael would be upset she hadn't listened to him and waited.

"No," she said, "I can't do that to Meghan, or Danny for that matter. Anyway, I'll be back before Michael knows I left." Branches crackled in the wind. Ethelwynne jumped and unconsciously adjusted her sleeves. Michael had been so worried about her when the tree fell. *I can just tell him someone came with me. He doesn't have to worry about my safety.*

The thought of lying to him made her feel a little ill, but she told herself it was for his benefit. If he didn't think she was being reckless he wouldn't panic and be more forceful with her than normal. Then, once he realized she was more capable of managing things on her own than he thought, she could readdress his previous over-reaction. *Although*, she thought as she ran her thumbs over her wrists, *it might be better if I leave this in the past.*

The rain stopped around noon. Ethelwynne shook the raindrops off her cloak and paused in a small clearing to eat a bun, some spiced cheese, and an apple. As she packed up her small picnic, a large shadow passed overhead. Ethelwynne looked up and gasped as a magnificent winged horse flew by.

"Evlayar," she breathed and stopped to watch the blue roan evlayar as it flew further away from the manor. Its black wings stretched wide on either side of it. Its hooves barely seemed to clear the tree tops, but the rider—she assumed they must be an elf—sat confidently upon its back.

She'd never seen an evlayar in the human realms before, though she heard King Kellan and a few other nobles had a couple. Most of the creatures lived in the realm of the elves. When she could no longer see the horse and its rider, she began walking towards Heatherfield again.

Soon the trees' shadows started stretching across the road as the sun dipped lower in the sky. Ethelwynne rubbed the back of her neck and ran her hands down her braid. Maybe she was mistaken, and it was longer than a day's trek to the manor, after all.

Ethelwynne shuddered at the idea that she might have to spend a night in the forest by herself. "I should have waited for Michael." She rubbed her arms. "He'll be so upset when he finds out about this."

Up ahead the road curved. Ethelwynne picked up her skirt and jogged to the corner. "The manor has to be around this bend."

No candles flickered in the distance. All she saw were dark trees, bushes, and the outsides of petals closed up for the night lining the road until it disappeared around the next corner. Her skirt slipped from her hands and swished back down around her ankles. Her heart began to race, and she felt sick. She stared at the road in front of her. "No," she moaned. She couldn't sleep outside. The tent, the blankets, everything she would need to campout in the forest—all of it belonged to Michael. It was all with him in the caravan.

She blinked back tears and took a deep breath to calm herself. "Maybe it's around the next bend?" she said out loud to make it seem like she was less alone in the fast-approaching night. "Or maybe, if it's not, there will be a place to sleep around it? You know, somewhere sheltered in case it starts to rain again."

Nothing looked like a good place to sleep as she approached the second bend. Clasping her hands together, she continued down the road. "I can do this," she whispered with much less confidence than before. Her eyes widened as she tried to see in the growing darkness to find a sheltered place to sleep.

When she was almost to the third bend, a small pathway leading off to the side of the road appeared beside a tree. Ethelwynne quivered as she looked down the dark and foreboding path. The sparse moonlight barely reached through the branches. It was much safer to stay on the path where she wasn't likely to become lost. "I'd feel rather foolish if the manor was around this corner and I stopped right here," she told the trees swaying indifferently around her.

She approached the corner. "Please, please, please be there," she whispered over and over again. Clouds covered the sky sending her into absolute blackness. The trees formed one solid wall on either side of her as their trunks blended into each other. Her heart raced. Waves of nausea swept across her. Ethelwynne raised her hands in front of her face and haltingly moved forward. She willed the clouds to open up so she could see the road or the edges of the trees. Her hands brushed the rough bark of a tree in front of her, she turned to look down the road. The manor sat in a small halo of light off the roadside. Candles flickered in the manor's many windows and lamps twinkled along the wet walkway.

Ethelwynne placed a hand on her chest and took a few shaky breaths to steady herself before she walked towards the front door. She rapped on the door and waited. Ethelwynne heard a muffled yelp and someone shuffling on the other side, but the door remained shut and soon silence echoed from within the building.

CHRISTINA VAN STARKENBURG

.

— CHAPTER FIVE —

Into The Storm

Ethelwynne knocked on the main door of Heatherfield Manor a second time. Still no one answered. She sighed. This was not going the way she planned. She withdrew from the door and glanced at the windows to see if she could spot movement within. Nothing.

Frowning, she walked back down the steps to try to find a servants' entrance. "They might not be seeing any visitors, but they'll still need to purchase food," she muttered as she walked along the path circling the building. She needed to know what happened to the gates and why her parents never returned from their trip to the elven realm.

Thunder rumbled in the distance and she glanced up at the starless night sky, "Or perhaps they'll shelter a beggar; they are known for their generosity." Ethelwynne pulled her cloak tighter as the wind picked up.

When she approached the back corner of the manor, she heard some voices speaking elvish in the garden. If she had been a child, she would have danced. Now, she didn't even need to get them to answer the door. She veered off the pebble path and cut across the grass towards the hedge marking the edge of the gardens.

The closer she got, the more apparent it became that two elves were arguing about something. Rather, it sounded like one of the elves was very angry about something and the other was attempting to appease him. Though since she wasn't able to make out the words, she couldn't be sure.

Ethelwynne looked back at the manor and considered trying her luck at the servants' entrance. She took a step towards it before changing her mind. She had heard a servant behind the door the first time she knocked, and since they refused to answer, the elves in the garden were her only chance of learning about her parents.

The elves' words grew clearer the closer she drew to the entrance. "Nothing?" demanded the first. "Your rangers, who are supposed to be experts at their jobs, have found nothing?"

"Well, Your Majesty, given the time of year and the spring run-off, it's to be expected that we haven't found anything yet. But, I assure you, it's only a matter of time."

Prince Damien scoffed. "Only a matter of time?" He paused. When he spoke again, he drew out each individual word. "We. Don't. Have. Time. My brother also has his rangers searching for the key. If we don't find it before him, everything will be ruined, and we will be forced to spend the rest of our lives under his reign. Or worse, if he finds out what really happened, we will be executed for treason."

The two elves walked past the gap in the hedge. The prince was dressed in rich robes that looked almost black in the lamp light. The spun gold thread making up the embroidery glittered like stars as his movement sent them rippling in and out of the light. The other was dressed in the garb of an elven officer.

"I know, milord, but—"

"No," Damien snapped. "I don't want to hear excuses, Akimos. I want results."

Ethelwynne tried to flatten herself into the hedge. Dots darted across her vision and her head spun as she waited for them to disappear behind the leaves again. This was stupid. How could she have thought that coming here would help her learn when the gateways were going to be opened? She should have listened to herself when she convinced her brother not to come. She told Danny that Prince Damien wouldn't have time for their questions. What had possessed her to think that maybe one of the servants would?

"Rest easy, Your Majesty," said Akimos. "With your quick thinking in moving us here, your brother has no idea where the key was lost. As far as he knows, it was stolen from the Keeper of the Keys' bedchamber in the humans' capital..." The elves walked further away, and their voices blended with the wind once more.

Ethelwynne melted to the ground and let out the breath she'd been holding. She rubbed her hands along her skirt to smooth it as she waited for her knees to stop shaking enough that they could support her.

She should just go home. Prince Damien said the key was missing. The elves were still in the human lands. Clearly her parents were trapped in the elven realm, and they would not be getting out until the key was found. She had her answer. Perhaps not the one she would have liked, but at least she knew the truth about the key. No longer would she have to listen to the rumors or imaginings of traveling merchants. Ethelwynne took a few breaths and put her hands down to steady herself.

Footsteps thudded down the path. Ethelwynne froze still crouched on the earth as an elf ran right past her towards Prince Damien and Akimos. Ethelwynne shut her eyes and prayed desperately that this elf also wouldn't notice her.

"What is it, Heotene?" asked Akimos. He sounded closer; Ethelwynne assumed he and the prince must have walked back to the opening when they saw Heotene enter. Ethelwynne opened her eyes. Heotene stood feet away from her in the garden's entrance. If Ethelwynne hadn't valued her life so much, she could have reached out and touched her. Ethelwynne willed that each breath she took would be silent and not betray her.

"I have news from the River Ems, Your Majesty," said Heotene.

The prince hissed.

Ethelwynne's heart threatened to break free of her chest. Her ankles and wrists shook from supporting her in such an awkward position. *Please move further into the garden.*

"Never say the place out loud," said Damien. "You don't know who might be listening."

Heotene nodded curtly. "We found the thief, Your Majesty."

The prince stepped into Ethelwynne's view. A broad smile stretched across his face as he held out his hand expectantly. "Excellent. Perhaps I spoke too hastily."

The runner shuffled nervously in front of him. "We didn't find the key on his body, sir."

Prince Damien roared and backhanded her. "What do you mean, you don't have the key?" He grabbed the elf's collar and shook her. "We cannot get back to my kingdom without it."

Heotene stammered something Ethelwynne couldn't make out before Akimos spoke up, "Your Majesty, we knew using magic to find the key was a long shot. Our magic has always been unstable in the human realms."

"Did you have any good news? Or did you just come to waste my time with tales about not finding the key?"

Heotene shook her head.

Prince Damien dropped her and stalked back along the hedges. "Is this truly how you serve me, Akimos? By leading fools such as this?"

Akimos tried to defend his guard, but what he was saying was lost as the trio disappeared further into the garden.

Ethelwynne shifted her weight so she wouldn't fall over. When she couldn't hear them anymore, she stood up and looked at the gap in the hedges. No one walked past. Slowly Ethelwynne backed up. Heartbeats passed. She still didn't hear anyone. Her white-knuckled fingers held the edges of her skirt tightly.

She looked around her. She couldn't head towards the house. If she were seen, she wasn't sure she could lie away the panic on her face, and they wouldn't let her in anyway—not with what might be discussed within its walls. The forest. She could slip into the forest surrounding the grounds and sneak back to the road. It would be dark, but if she stayed close to the tree line she could use the candles in the windows to guide her. She ran towards the shelter of the trees.

The storm rumbled closer. Halfway to the forest, Ethelwynne glanced behind her. The elves were coming out of the garden. She stumbled over a root and fell to the ground. The elves yelled. Ethelwynne pushed herself up and ran across the grass and into the forest. She stumbled again and almost collided with a tree. She propelled herself off of it and looked back to see Heotene running along the hedge towards her. A branch slapped Ethelwynne across the face and reminded her to watch where she was going.

Her heart dropped out of her throat, and she ran through the trees without any thought about where she was heading. Ethelwynne prayed the elf was still winded from her last run—the River Ems was a long way from Heatherfield—that would be the only way Ethelwynne would ever outrun her.

The forest grew darker and more menacing the further in she went. Large fat raindrops splashed on her forehead and dripped into her eyes. She blinked them back and swept a hand across her face.

The storm quickly picked up and soon Ethelwynne was drenched. Tears mixed with the raindrops pouring off her cheeks. Her mind was racing as quickly as her feet. Prince Damien was planning on trapping King Orrin here. What about the humans who were stuck in the elven lands? What about her parents' trading routes with the elves? She needed to warn the king. He had to find the key and reopen the route.

The rain pasted Ethelwynne's hair to her face as she ran through the forest. Her braid was destroyed, and her head ached from where strands of her hair had snagged on branches and been ripped out. The sound of her shoes smacking the mud drowned out the sound of her gasping for breath. Her hands stung from slapping tree branches out of the way.

Ethelwynne stared out into the dark, rainy forest with wide eyes. She frantically tried to see the trees so she could avoid them. Lightning flashed across the sky and lit up a tree right in front of her. She threw her hands up in front of her face and scraped her palms as she lunged around it and darted into the blackness once more. Her heartbeat competed with the thunder as it pounded in her ears.

The next time lightning cracked across the sky, she looked behind her as she fled. The elf was not in sight. It was a small and momentary comfort. She had no idea where the road was, or even which direction she was running in. She could have run right across it and never even known in this storm.

Crack! A tree gave out under the force of the wind and slammed into the ground in front of her. Ethelwynne skidded through the mud and uselessly waved her hands to try and stop herself from falling. This storm was going to kill her. Mustering her strength, Ethelwynne rose from the ground and fled. She needed to find shelter. As much as she wanted to keep running from the elves, getting away from them was not worth her life.

Thorns raked across her legs as she barreled through a bush she didn't see. The plant held her skirt fast. She pulled it free with a yank. The fabric ripped as she continued to run.

She tripped over a rock and crashed to the ground. Her blood mixed with the mud on her knees, but she barely felt it. She needed to get away from here. She pushed herself up and kept going. Her lungs screamed at her for more air, but she couldn't stop.

Thunder boomed shaking the ground beneath her. The trees around her bowed under the force of the wind. Branches snapped and fell to the ground. The wind howled in her ears. The rain pounded her.

Ethelwynne tripped over a branch from another fallen tree and collapsed to the ground by its trunk. Her breath came in fast, ragged gasps. She tried to stand, but her legs gave out. She yelped and collapsed into the mud. Ethelwynne's whole body trembled and shivered.

She crawled closer to the trunk to take shelter under its fallen canopy. The tangled branches of this broken tree were not what she had in mind when she decided to look for shelter, but she no longer had a choice.

She wrapped her arms around herself and buried her face in her knees. Why had she ever thought that talking to the prince's attendants would be a good idea? Ethelwynne gasped for air as she cried. Her one consolation was that Heotene would not be able to hear her sobs over the roar of the storm.

Ethelwynne squeezed her eyes shut and tried to make herself as small as she could underneath the tree. The leaves bent inwards with the wind and the constant raindrops. Cold wet droplets ran off the branches and down her neck. Ethelwynne shivered. Lightning flashed across the sky again. Still, she saw no one. Maybe the elves had turned back in the storm and she was alone out here in its path.

Another tree succumbed to the storm and slammed into the one Ethelwynne was hiding under. She screamed and ducked, covering her head with her hands as the vibrations of the impact echoed through her body.

The branches of the two fallen trees mingled together, sheltering her from most of the rain, and leaving her in a tight cocoon. Her pulse was racing as she looked around blindly. Was another tree going to fall on top of her and squish her? Her chin trembled and she whimpered as she listened to the storm rage on until it had nothing left to terrorize her. Exhausted she fell asleep for the final few hours until dawn.

*   *   *

The first rays of sun peeked into the forest and revealed the full extent of the damage to Ethelwynne's wide and weary eyes. Her rigid muscles ached from being so tense for the entire night. She crawled out of her nest and looked around. Branches, needles, and leaves covered the ground. Several trees lay down waiting to become homes and food for new plants and animals. The weak sunlight shimmered off pools of waters inside the cupped fallen leaves. She carefully picked up a few and poured the water into her parched mouth.

Her achy knees sank into the soft earth as she paused there trying to get her bearings. After a few moments, she pulled herself onto one of the fallen logs to sit. The cuts on her body burned. She winced.

Ethelwynne didn't know which direction she had come from. Grabbing a twig, she spun it on the trunk. When it stopped, she started walking in the direction it pointed. *Please don't be back to the manor.* She looked around her to see if there were any elves nearby, but there was no sign of anything living in the wrecked forest behind her.

The ground beneath her feet vanished and she fell. Branches crackled and snapped as she landed in a thorn bush. The force of her stop knocked the air from her lungs.

Tears streamed down her face as she lay there gaping.

Then, the air rushed in. She gasped and cried as air filled her lungs over and over again. She tried to stand, but she couldn't find adequate support in the thorn bush. Ethelwynne crawled out of the thorns, wincing as they scratched her face. She pushed herself up and stood on wobbly legs.

Ethelwynne studied the hill while she tried to gather enough of her self-resolve to overlook the pain emanating from her entire body. There was no way she ran up that slope the night before. Her heart lifted slightly with the knowledge she was not heading back towards the manor. But even though she didn't know precisely where she was, she knew this place was still too close to Heatherfield to be safe. She had to get back to town. Grimacing, she slowly walked away from the hill.

The sun shone through the gaps left by fallen trees, branches and leaves. The rays warmed her back as she continued to walk. All was quiet around her. She occasionally saw a bird fly past, or some rabbits race out in front of her. But, for the most part, she was alone in the woods with her thoughts.

What was she going to do now? She didn't know where she was, or where she was going. Meghan was going to be so mad at her for not making it home on time. How could she have been so stupid? Hot tears started to trickle from her eyes and drip off her chin. She wiped them away on her dirty sleeve.

"Maybe the elves will find me." She laughed bitterly. This was not what she pictured when she left Sweet Briar. She should have told Danny what she intended to do. He would have come with her, and he would not have let this happen. Danny was always so sure of himself. He would have known how to get the elves to speak with him. He would have called out and gotten the elves' attention before they overheard something they shouldn't have.

A red fox darted past her. She jumped and stubbed her

toes as she stumbled over a root. Her heart raced for a few seconds before she caught herself. Ethelwynne hobbled over to the tree and leaned against it closing her eyes. This was ridiculous, even foxes were scaring her.

She started walking again, carefully picking her way through the woods. She had to keep going. The sounds of a brook babbled up in front of her. Warily she approached it stopping by the edge of the trees to look around and check for elves or bears or anything else she did not want to run into at the water's edge.

A deer was standing between her and the brook looking at her. Ethelwynne sighed in relief. If it was here, chances are predators were not. The only thing she would have to worry about were the elves. She used the trunk she was beside to support herself as she knelt in the soft moss and cupped her hands to catch the water as it burbled past. The cool water soothed her sore throat and quenched her thirst.

The deer gradually disappeared into the trees as she washed some of the mud off of her scrapes. Then she pushed herself up off the ground and started walking along the creek.

Ethelwynne laughed when she saw a stone bridge materialize out of the forest ahead of her. As she approached it, she heard people talking and wagon wheels rumbling across the bridge.

Ethelwynne hobbled forward as fast as she could. She scrambled up the bank and onto the road. "Hey! Help!" Ethelwynne waved her arms and hollered after the wagon. The woman sitting in the back looked at her and pulled the children with her closer. The wagon didn't stop. "No! Please." Ethelwynne tried to run after them, but her legs burned with exhaustion. The wagon disappeared around the corner leaving her standing there on the road.

Ethelwynne's shoulders slumped. "Thanks for the help," she muttered sullenly as she continued to walk behind the wagon. She sighed. At least she knew what direction to travel now. There had to be a town over there. And maybe, if she had any luck at all, and she was pretty sure she was due for some right about now, it wouldn't be too far.

Her stomach ached as she continued to walk. Next time, not that there would ever be a next time, but next time, she'd pack food and water just in case something went wrong and she was separated from whomever she was traveling with. She would also stay with her traveling companion.

Walking did not help the pain. She stopped more and more frequently as the day wore on to rub her legs and ankles and try and give her body a bit of a break. No other wagons passed her as she plodded along. By the time she was ready to sleep for the night, she came across a large hill in the road. A soft light glowed from the other side and as she climbed it, the smells of fresh bread and stew wafted through the air to greet her.

"I can do this," she told herself, as she started to climb. The hill wasn't steep, but every muscle in her body ached. She wasn't sure how much strength her legs had left; they practically begged her to stop. "It won't be long now." She continued to talk to herself as she progressed up the hill one step at a time. Then, after what seemed like several hours of agony, she reached the top and saw a city spread out before her.

Ethelwynne whooped at the sight of it. Candles flickered in the windows of the small houses that dotted the roads spiraling out from the center square where all of the farmers would set up their shops once they had something to sell. From where she stood, Ethelwynne could just make out people coming and going from several large buildings.

Beyond the houses and inns stood three towers that dwarfed every other building in the city. Bridges connected the towers high above the tops of the houses, and several skyships were moored to some of the spokes that stretched outwards from the towers.

"Sky ports!" she squealed. "This has to be Helmsville. This is perfect. I can spend the night with Michael's parents." Ethelwynne smiled wearily. A small part of her hoped she wouldn't see him, but she tamped the thought down as she started to walk down the other side of the hill towards the city and the shadows of the towers. He cared about her and her safety. Before he could say something, she would simply apologize for not listening again.

First, she needed to tell the city guard about the elves' plot. They could pass along the message to the king. Then, after a restful night, she could return home as though this had never happened.

A large ship cut across the last rays of the sun as it came into dock on the left tower. Although she couldn't see it in the dying daylight, she knew the ship's hull was covered with intricate paintings. It always amused her that the owners of the ships went to such lengths to decorate the bottom of their boat, presumably because that's what the people beneath them could see.

Ethelwynne's mouth opened in awe as she watched as the workers scrambled to furl the sails. She gripped her hair and twisted it nervously as the ship glided closer to the towers. It looked like it was moving too fast to stop in time. What would happen if it crashed into the tower?

Ethelwynne pulled her hands from her hair and winced as she snagged a knot. "Ouch." She massaged her scalp and started untangling her hair. As she watched the ship dock at the tower, it dawned on her that this was going to be the first time she met Michael's mother. Ethelwynne wanted to make a good impression.

She stepped off the road and leaned against a tree. She worked her fingers through her hair patiently. As she watched the ship, she gently pulled out the twigs and leaves. By the time the ship was moored, she had managed to get all of the knots out and redone her braid. She glanced down at the small pile of twigs and leaves by her feet and laughed. "Maybe that's why the wagon driver kept going. They weren't sure if I was human or a bush monster." Now that she was feeling slightly more respectable, Ethelwynne walked down the path into the city.

CHRISTINA VAN STARKENBURG

— CHAPTER SIX —

Thief in the Night

With the exception of a few stragglers, the streets were vacant when she arrived. The smell of supper and the sounds of laughter and fighting wafted out of the houses she passed. The people who were still out on the street looked at her with disdain and clutched their purses a little closer.

She gritted her teeth. She had hoped that redoing her braid would convince people that she wasn't just a vagabond. But after several people outright ignored her or merely acknowledged her to assure her that under no uncertain terms would they be giving her any pennies, she had to admit that her tattered gown was thwarting her attempts.

Two more people approached the spot where Ethelwynne was standing. The woman—who was wearing a powder blue hat—looked over at Ethelwynne. She gasped and clutched the arm of the young man she was with. From the horrified expression on her face, Ethelwynne was sure her knuckles would have been white underneath her gloves.

The man brandished his cane in front of him like a sword. "The stables or the sky-moorings always need extra hands," he spat. "If you don't back off this instant, I will be forced to call for the guards. They know how to deal with your sort." He pulled his partner in a wide circle and glared over his shoulder at Ethelwynne. "Disgusting rabble." He turned to his partner. "I'm sorry you had to see that, my dear. This part of town is usually safe."

Ethelwynne yanked on her newly done braid and muttered angrily to herself as she walked through the street. "This is ridiculous. I'm just trying to get help."

On the next street, Ethelwynne saw two guards patrolling. She bit her lip and walked towards them. They would listen to her message and help her. After all, helping those in need was their job. Then she could leave this dreadful city, go home, and be done with this nightmare. "Excuse me," she called out furtively.

"Beat it rat."

"But I need your help," she pleaded.

"Help?" The other guard cackled. "Sure, we can help you. I'm sure the jail cells are nice and comfortable."

Ethelwynne jolted backward.

The first guard smirked. "Not the kind of help you want? Then, scram." He advanced towards her with his hand on his cudgel. "If we see you again, or if we hear you've been bothering the nice folk who live here, we will throw you in jail and you can live there with all your rodent friends."

Ethelwynne backed away and threw her hands up in resignation. She stopped trying to speak to people and wandered the side streets and alleys. Maybe she would get lucky and stumble across Michael's shop on her own.

Ethelwynne turned around a few times in her aimless wanderings to avoid running into more members of the town guard. Clearly, they would not believe her until she had a bath, so it would be best not to get thrown in prison before she had a chance to do so. Michael could pass the message along for her.

Tears ran down her cheeks as she resigned herself to

spending a night on the streets. She wiped her eyes and rounded another corner to look for somewhere that seemed safe, sheltered, and secluded for the night. The narrow alleyway opened up onto another main road. As she approached the end of the alley, she saw something that warmed her heart: Michael's store. The sign with the Brown family crest painted on it creaked every time the sparse breeze nudged it. Her stomach fluttered. If anyone would help her, it would be them. She floated down the alley towards the street.

No lights flickered in the shop's windows, or even in the rooms upstairs. Given the late hour, that made sense, but she assumed he lived in the apartment above it. Or at the very least his parents did, and they just had the shutters closed. They could point her in the right direction.

Ethelwynne paused. *Is he home?* She bit her lip. He was planning on coming here after he dropped her off in Bewdley. Had he already returned to the village to bring her to Heatherfield Manor? She rubbed her arms where his fingerprints blended in with the bruises from the forest. *He's going to be so disappointed when he finds out I didn't wait for him.* A heavy weight formed in the pit of her stomach as she stared at his shop.

She looked down at her tattered dress. What would he think of her if she showed up at his house looking like this? Ethelwynne shuddered and wiped off some of the dirt on her cheeks and tried to brush the dried mud off of her dress the best she could. *I should have waited. None of this would have happened if he was there.*

"No," she said with more confidence than she felt. "He loves me. While we were traveling together, he talked about supporting me and taking care of me. He was just… concerned, and he overreacted, but he apologized." She took a steadying breath. "If he sees me covered in bruises and limping, he'll want to help me. Even if there is some mud in my hair." She nodded and started walking again.

A man swore as he approached the entrance of the alley. Ethelwynne jumped.

"We should have arrested her on the spot. I knew she was trouble when we saw her," he continued.

Ethelwynne recognized his voice as one of the guards who threatened to arrest her earlier. Her pulse raced as she slipped further into the alley and squatted down behind several of the barrels.

From where she hid, Ethelwynne watched through a small gap between the barrels as the two men walked in front of the alley entrance. The one on the left spat on the ground and said, "Stole from the elves. What an idiot. Let's hope that brown-haired wretch gets what's coming to her."

She closed her eyes and hoped it was dark enough in the alley that they wouldn't see her.

"Shh," said the other, "if you stop mentioning we've seen her, we won't be blamed if we can't find her again."

She clutched her bag closer as their words buzzed in her mind. The elves accused her of stealing. She had not expected that, though she had to admit it made sense. They would need to justify their need to capture her somehow, and calling her a thief would ruin any credibility she might have otherwise had with the guards.

The guards wandered into the alley. Ethelwynne's heart formed a knot in the back of her throat. The light from their lamp cast long eerie shadows on the wall behind her. Ethelwynne tried not to breathe. The two men stopped in front of the barrels closest to the entrance.

She squeezed her eyes shut and prayed they wouldn't find her. *Please don't come any closer.* One of the guards started walking again. The sound of his shoes hitting the cobblestone got louder as he came closer to Ethelwynne's poor hiding spot. He kicked the barrel she was behind. The one stacked on top of it barely missed Ethelwynne's head as it fell over, rolled across the alley, and came to a rest beside a broken barrel.

A small squeak escaped from Ethelwynne's lips. She covered her mouth with her hands and tried to disappear into the barrels' shadow. Both guards stopped talking.

"Did you hea—" said the one towering above her.

A rat scampered over her foot and disappeared through a hole on the other wall. She closed her eyes and bit her lip. Tears trickled down her cheeks. This was not happening. She should never have left home.

"Damn rats," muttered the guard closest to her as he kicked the barrel again.

The second grunted in reply.

"Let's get out of here." The two men turned back around and walked towards the main road again, their footsteps thudded away from her.

Once she couldn't hear their footsteps anymore, Ethelwynne stood up as fast as she could and darted away from her hiding spot. She had no intention of sharing the ground with that rat, or any friends it might have, any longer than absolutely necessary.

She leaned against the opposite wall of the alley and breathed heavily and reminded herself the guards had not seen her. She still had a chance to make it out of this mess, maybe, hopefully, before Michael heard she'd been accused of robbery. As a shop owner herself, she knew he considered thieves worse than the rats living in this alley.

She crept back down the alley towards the main road. Ethelwynne prayed she would make it to Michael's before someone saw her. At the corner, she stopped and peeked out. The road was empty. She dashed across the street and stumbled into the alleyway beside his house. After catching her breath, she went back and checked to see if anyone was coming for her. The street was still deserted. She breathed a sigh of relief and rested against the side of Michael's shop.

When her legs had stopped shaking, Ethelwynne headed around to the door in the back. Her hand was poised to knock when she realized she had a problem. She couldn't ask Michael for his help anymore. It was the prince of the elves who accused her of thievery. Michael's family could lose their business if the authorities learned they'd helped her, even though she hadn't done anything wrong. She groaned. Her parents would lose their trading license if she was discovered before this could be fixed.

She looked down at her tattered and mud-stained outfit. *I still need something new to wear.* She looked at the dark shop behind her and put her hand on her purse. She might not be able to ask him for help, but she could still pay him for some clothes. She'd just slip in through the window, take some clothes and leave the money on the counter. Their prices wouldn't be that much different from her own; she could guess the right amount to leave. Once she got this thing sorted out, she could come back and pay the rest if she guessed wrong.

"Okay." She wandered towards the front of the shop where there was a window on the building's side. Ethelwynne felt ill as she scanned the alleyway and listened for footsteps. Silence greeted her. She put her hands on the pane and tried to push it open. It was locked. She bit her lip and looked around. There was nothing in the alley that could help her.

She edged towards the road again. There was still no one in sight. She ran across to the rat-infested stack of barrels and grabbed one of the broken boards.

When she made it back in front of the window, she squeezed the jagged edge into the tiny gap between the window and the wall beneath it and pushed down. Her feet lifted off the ground. There was a crack as the lock broke and the window creaked open.

Ethelwynne heard footsteps approaching. She pulled the

board out of the window and darted behind the building. From where she hid, she peeked around the corner at the main road. Two more guards strode past.

They didn't stop, and they didn't look down the alley. Ethelwynne breathed a sigh of relief. As their footsteps disappeared into the night, she went back to the window and tried again. Now that the lock was broken, the heavy window creaked open. She took a deep breath as she slipped into the shop. *Michael will never forgive me if he finds out. But at least if I pay them, they'll never have to know it was me.* She closed the window behind her in case any guards did wander down the street and padded across the floor towards the dresses.

She froze with her hands on the first one. *I can't pay him. The whole point of breaking in was to avoid incriminating him in all this. What would the guards think if I left behind money?* She moaned. It was too late to turn back now. She was already inside. Besides, she didn't know where any other clothing shops were.

Ethelwynne took a deep breath and turned away from the dresses. The guards were looking for a strange woman. If she wore pants, she might be able to walk past them. She bit her lip and began to rifle through the men's pants and shirts until she found something that would fit her. The instant she found something that might work, she quickly undressed and changed into the pants and shirt.

She pulled her braid out of the neck-hole as she examined herself in the dark. She had no idea what color anything was—hopefully, it was all some version of brown so she wouldn't draw attention to herself—but the garments fit her. They were loose enough to hide her figure, but tight enough that she didn't have to worry about the pants falling off.

Ethelwynne looked up at the table before her, perhaps if she refolded the clothes Michael's family wouldn't even notice something missing.

That done, she shoved her dress into her bag. She'd have to get rid of it somewhere else. The bag bulged and the seams stretched around the tear, but it held. She prayed it would hold just long enough.

She spun towards the window and opened it. The gentle breeze swirled some of her hair in front of her face, but Ethelwynne brushed it aside. *My hair! The length might give me away.* Her breath hitched as she stepped away from the window and went back to the table. She eased opened a drawer and fished a pair of scissors out of it. Squeezing her eyes shut, she cut off her braid.

Blinking to keep her tears at bay, Ethelwynne stuffed the braid into her bag too. She put the scissors away and slipped out of the store, shutting the window behind her. She caught a glimpse of herself in the dark glass. She supposed she looked boy-like—at least in the dark. Hopefully, the perception would last long enough for her to get safely out of the city.

But where could she go? She couldn't lead the elves to her home, and going home wouldn't get her parents back anyway. The king. She needed to tell King Orrin, his brother wished to overthrow him if she wanted to live and see her parents again. King Orrin was likely in White Shield at King Kellan's palace.

Ethelwynne glanced up at the towers looming above her. With a bit of good fortune, she could hop onto a skyship. Helmsville was the only sky port on this side of the lower arm of the Greisgebied Mountains. Since it wasn't winter, the chances of the ship heading away from the mountains towards the sea and tiny villages were slim, which meant that these boats would most likely head back over the peaks.

As she walked down the alley, Ethelwynne pulled the braid out of her bag and undid it. Tearfully, she scattered stray strands on the ground for the rats to use in their nests.

As Ethelwynne walked towards to the towers, she tried to figure out how she was going to get up to the ships. She'd never actually been on an air dock before, but the ones she'd seen always seemed to be well guarded. As she neared the tower grounds, she came across some crates piled in an alley.

She considered hiding in one of the crates; perhaps they would be loaded onto a ship tomorrow. She ran her hand through her hair—then blinked in shock when her hair suddenly stopped. She took a steadying breath, clasped her hands in front of her to stop herself from running them through her hair again, and tried not to think about it.

In the end, she kept on walking towards the towers. It was too risky to wait and hope that these crates would be loaded onto the ship. Plus, she didn't really have a way to open them. As she approached the towers, she felt like she might throw up.

Two guards headed her way. She tried to swallow, but her mouth was too dry. She looked at the alleyways behind her and considered running into them, but that would definitely look suspicious.

Her stomach lurched as they walked past her. The guards didn't even look at her. Ethelwynne breathed a sigh of relief and kept walking through the open gates. She brushed off her pant legs, in case there were any stray pieces of hair there.

While the rest of Helmsville was settling down to sleep for the night, the towers still buzzed with activity. Men and women scurried to and fro getting crates on and off the moored boats. Guards inspected the crates and barrels that were carried and rolled over to the middle tower.

Something banged and clattered beside her. She jumped and turned to see a crate busted open with fruit spilling out of it. A large burly man started yelling at the smaller man in front of him for dropping it. "You, there," he pointed at Ethelwynne, "come clean up this mess."

Ethelwynne looked around furtively. She hoped the man

wouldn't decide to blame her for this mess, and nervously walked over.

"Well come on, boy, I don't got all night for this."

Ethelwynne nodded and picked up some of the spilled fruit and put it back into the crate. One of the other men hammered it shut.

The leader wrinkled his nose as he studied her. "You're a scrawny little thing; can you even carry one of these things?"

She nodded and he shoved a crate into her arms as the other men chuckled. Her eyes widened fearfully. She staggered, but she didn't fall.

The man turned back around and picked up a different crate and walked towards the tower.

She bit her lip and took a tentative step forward. She didn't fall. *Okay*, she thought, *I can do this.* Slowly, she followed the other men towards the tower. A small gasp of surprise escaped her mouth when it dawned on her that she was going to get up the tower. She didn't have to find a way to sneak in; she just had to make it to the tower and ride up on the dumbwaiter with this ship's crew. Not only that, but judging by the man calling her "boy," her disguise was working.

"Here, this one looks to be more your size." The one who dropped the crate grabbed it out of her arms and handed her a smaller one before continuing towards the tower.

"Thanks," Ethelwynne mumbled. She tried to make her voice sound lower than it was so her disguise would hold.

But he had already moved on. "Tryin' to squish the boy, Bart?" he called to the man who'd given her the crate.

"Build up his arms, is all. Scrawny thing like that'll never survive in this work." The other men chuckled as Bart put one of his crates down to sign the paper the guards waved in his direction.

Ethelwynne's stomach constricted as the guards studied

the men entering the tower. But they seemed to trust that Bart knew his crew, and she was able to slip in with them.

"Don't forget to take the stairs," said one of the guards as he skimmed the paperwork. "The dumbwaiter's still broken."

"Yeah, yeah, we know," Bart replied, impatiently tapping his fingers on the crate he held over his shoulder. Then he picked up his other crate off the table and began to walk up the stairs with the rest of the men and Ethelwynne following behind.

She prayed that her legs would make it all the way up the stairs. The climb didn't seem to bother anyone else. The crew teased each other good naturedly as they climbed flight after flight. Ethelwynne tuned out their banter and focused on taking one step after another. She couldn't fall behind. She wouldn't know which ship they were from, and she had to get to the capital. Slowly the men's chatter died off as they too focused on climbing the stairs. Ethelwynne panted and wheezed. *No wonder Bart doesn't care that he picked up a new helper, these stairs are horrible.*

At last they made it to the top. Ethelwynne leaned heavily against the wall and tried to catch her breath while Bart spoke with the guards in front of the doors. Once the guards were satisfied with Bart's answers, they let them through and shut the door behind them.

Ethelwynne breathed a sigh of relief when she realized the guards stopped watching the crew when they were on the platforms. Now all she had to do was get onto one of the ships unnoticed. She followed the crew onto their ship and placed her crate in the pile. There were too many men milling about for her to slip off somewhere on this ship without being seen, so she disembarked and went to look for a different ship.

Alone on the platform, she picked a boat to hide on, but the first ship she walked onto was bereft of crates. *Probably not leaving in the morning*. Ethelwynne crept back to the gangplank. A group of men clomped past while she was hiding behind the ship's wall. She waited until she heard the door back into the tower thump shut before peeking out. The way was empty once again.

She considered trying a third ship to check if they were leaving in the morning, but her whole body begged for rest. She knew the ship she helped load was filled with fresh fruit. They had to be leaving first thing in the morning. She waited a few more moments to see if any other crew members walked past, then she slunk back to the first ship. It was deserted. Sighing with relief, she snuck back on and crept below deck to find a secluded corner to hide in.

She slipped into a gap under the stairs in the storage room and leaned against the wall. Moonlight peeked through the porthole beside her. Exhausted, Ethelwynne plumped up her bag to use as a pillow and went to sleep.

*   *   *

Ethelwynne jolted awake when her head collided with the beam in front of her as the boat lurched. She yelped. When she remembered where she was, she clapped her hand over her mouth. Her eyes widened as she waited for someone to come and investigate the noise. No one did.

Slowly, she began to relax. Footsteps thudded continuously overhead and she heard people constantly calling out to one another. Perhaps, when she called out, it had blended into the din. She leaned back into her little alcove and looked out the porthole. The early morning sun was casting long shadows across the town. The skyship lurched again and steadily turned away from the tower, soaring higher into the sky.

Ethelwynne clutched her bag closer as her stomach gurgled. She should have pocketed some of the fruit before it was hammered back into the crate last night, but she'd been too scared that Bart would recognize her and alert the guards. There was no way she could open the crates now without being heard, she'd have to try and find the galley later to get some food.

Ethelwynne looked out the porthole again and gasped as she stared down at the tops of the trees rustling in the breeze far beneath her. A bird flew past her window. She brought her hands together in awe, but they fell limply to her lap when the ship turned away from the mountains. It wasn't heading to the capital.

How would she get to White Shield before the prince found the key now? She moaned softly and tried to console herself with the thought that the elves probably wouldn't suspect she was on this ship since it was sailing closer to them instead of over the mountains.

Dread filled her heart as the ship stopped a few hours later. There were only a few places it could have gone. She looked through the porthole. Blood drained from her face as her fears were confirmed. They were over Heatherfield Manor.

CHRISTINA VAN STARKENBURG

— CHAPTER SEVEN —

Stowaway

Footsteps thudded down the stairs into the storage room. Ethelwynne squished herself as far back into the shadows as she could. Through the gap between the boxes, she watched as a woman dressed in emerald green clothes tapped different crates. Other crew members pried the crates open and the woman inspected the fruits and placed a variety of different ones into a basket.

Ethelwynne's stomach grumbled at the sight of the food. She squeezed her eyes shut and prayed no one heard, but the sound of the men thumping around drowned out any sound she made. The men tromped back up the stairs with their collection of fruit and Ethelwynne was on her own again.

Her mouth watered as she realized they had not resealed the crates. After briefly weighing the risks of leaving her spot, she darted to the nearest two crates. Hoping the crew wouldn't notice anything missing, she grabbed a couple of apples and peaches from each. Then she dashed back to her hiding place and frantically shoved them into her overflowing bag. More of the threads around the hole snapped. She was going to have to fix that soon.

The sounds of people yelling rang through the ship as it

lurched again, knocking Ethelwynne into the wall. Several of the fruits fell out of her bag and rolled around. Ethelwynne scrambled to gather them up and shoved all but one peach back inside.

She hoped the peaches wouldn't be too bruised when she opened the bag for another one later. Maybe, once things settled down and the ship wasn't swaying as much, she'd turn her old dress into a second bag to carry the fruit.

After the ship leveled out, a crew member came downstairs to put back the fruit they had grabbed earlier and hammer the crates shut. Ethelwynne froze with the peach in her mouth.

The woman in green and Bart had followed him down. Gone were the plain clothes Bart was wearing the night before. Today, he was dressed in rich purples and blues with elaborate embroidery work up the legs of his pants. Ethelwynne wondered if this was his normal wear, or if he was wearing this outfit in honor of the elf prince.

The woman stopped on the other side of the room and watched as the plain-clothes crew member went from crate to crate and sealed them shut. Bart followed him around and checked each crate. As soon as he was finished hammering and the woman cleared him, the crew member darted up the stairs.

Peach juice dripped down Ethelwynne's chin. It tickled, but she was too scared to move to wipe it off her face.

"Blasted elves," snapped Bart, as soon as the crew member had left the hold.

The woman shrugged and spread out some papers on one of the crates. "As long as the wind holds, it'll take us three or four days to get to White Shield. We can offload there."

Ethelwynne's whole chest felt lighter. They were going to the capital. She could warn King Orrin and be done with this mess.

"Let's hope it holds," grumbled Bart. "Darn elves not

thinking our food is good enough to even open the blasted door. Let 'em starve then."

The woman chuckled and continued to examine the papers in front of her as she absentmindedly tapped a pencil against her cheek. She licked the pencil and wrote something on the page in front of her. "There."

Bart did an exaggerated bow and moved aside to let the woman lead the way up the stairs. He climbed up after her, leaving Ethelwynne alone again.

Before taking another bite of the peach, Ethelwynne wiped her face on her tattered dress and stuffed it back into her bag. She hoped they would fly straight to the capital without stopping at Helmsville or anywhere else, along the way.

When her heart stopped racing from her fear of being discovered and returned to Heatherfield Manor, Ethelwynne peaked out of her porthole again and watched the trees swaying beneath her. Birds fluttered en masse from one tree to another.

I wonder if this is what it's like to sail on the ocean? This was faster than walking. She shifted in her small hiding space to try and see the front of the ship. From where she sat she could see the Greisgebied Mountains looming ahead.

Some of the white peaks vanished into the misty rain that surrounded them. Even though she was now hiding aboard a ship to try and get away from the elven prince, Ethelwynne was grateful she was inside and would not get wet this time. She'd gotten drenched enough running through the storm two days ago. She had no desire to be soaked to the bone any time soon.

The rest of the first day passed uneventfully. When she felt confident that crew members were not going to wander down to her hiding place, Ethelwynne emptied her pack. Pulling out her sewing kit, she patched up the seam. After she carefully folded the clothes, they fit into the bag much more easily.

Succumbing to her boredom, Ethelwynne dozed a bit. The sound of footsteps woke her as people came into the hold a few more times. No one discovered that they had an extra passenger. One of the times people were down there, a crew member mentioned that they should reach the mountains the next day. Then she was left alone in the growing darkness.

That night, when she figured most of the crew would be sleeping, Ethelwynne crawled out of her hiding spot to stretch her legs. She was so stiff from sitting in her spot all day, but the pain from yesterday's mishaps had dimmed to a subtle throb. Stretching it helped, and Ethelwynne sighed with relief.

As long as she didn't become careless, she was sure she could avoid being caught, although she wasn't entirely sure how she was going to get back off. What if the towers in White Shield were as well guarded as the ones in Helmsville? Surely the guards would notice if one lone person exited the ship when it was supposed to be empty, and she was pretty confident she could not climb down the sides of the tower, nor did she want to try. She'd always avoided climbing trees when she was a child.

Ethelwynne groaned as she squished herself back into the space. She wrapped her arms around her knees and rested her head against them. From what she heard earlier, she had at least two more days to figure out how she was going to get out of here.

Could I join the crew in the confusion and bustle as they unloaded their wares? Afterall, I did join the crew to load the ship. Ethelwynne looked out the window at the shadows of trees rippling below. *No, that wouldn't work. Bart and the other guy called too much attention to me. Someone would recognize me.*

She shifted her weight so her legs wouldn't fall asleep.

Maybe I can bluff my way past the guards after the rest of the crew is gone? She bit her lip. *We will be in White Shield, so perhaps I could tell them the truth and get brought right to the king? That might work.* She paused to consider it further before groaning, *At least, it might work, as long as they haven't received word to watch out for a brown-haired thief.*

*   *   *

The next morning Ethelwynne woke with a horrible crick in her neck. These were going to be a long two days. She prayed it wasn't three. She looked out the window and watched the trees rustle in the wind. It was blowing towards the peaks. In theory, that should help the ship make it to the mountains easily.

The door banged open. The boy who took the crate from her thudded down the stairs, followed by the woman who'd been wearing green yesterday. She placed her hands on her hips. "Which one?"

The anger in her voice made Ethelwynne cringe. She was super thankful she was not on the receiving end of the woman's ire.

The boy looked around. "I don't know, ma'am."

She swore. "Open all of them then." She poked him in the chest. "Your ineptitude will be noted. Do yourself a favor and try and salvage what you can before we sell off a crate of bruised fruit. The loss of our reputation will come from your wages."

"Yes, ma'am." He responded weakly.

"Well?" She gestured to the stacks of crates in the room. "Find it." Then she stalked back up the stairs.

The boy collected himself and wandered over to the corner to start unstacking and opening the crates.

After he finished the first corner, the door opened again, and a man who looked remarkably similar to him came down the stairs. "Well, Cephas, Emily tells me the bruised fruit made it into the hold unmarked."

Cephas nodded. "Sorry, Sher."

Sher shrugged. "Mistakes happen. Just don't let it happen a second time." He picked up the hammer and shut the lid of the crate Cephas had just looked through.

"Thanks." Cephas pried open the next crate to inspect it for the bruised fruit. As he moved onto the next one, Sher hammered the lid shut.

The closer they came to her hiding spot, the further Ethelwynne shrank back into it. Her heartbeat pounded in her ears and rose up her throat with each step they took.

Cephas knelt down beside her alcove to grab the crate beside her.

She closed her eyes. *Please don't let him see me. Please, please, please don't let him see me.*

A hand wrapped around her arm.

Her eyes shot open and her stomach clenched into knots as she stared into Cephas's face.

"I wondered what happened to you." The exasperation and disgust in his voice was palpable as he yanked her out of the alcove.

A small part of Ethelwynne that was more angry than worried about the consequences of being found out wanted to yell that if he found this inconvenient, he should try living her life for the past few days. Getting in trouble for a few bruised fruits and letting her out of his sight—assuming he'd be blamed for that even though the man named Bart was the one who originally gave her the crate—was nothing. His captain wasn't likely to kill him for messing up. She however, did face that fate.

Sher put down his hammer and looked her over. "You'd better run and tell the captain we've got ourselves an unexpected guest on this trip. I'll bring her up."

Cephas dropped his crowbar on the nearest crate and

darted up the stairs, effortlessly taking two at a time, to go and find the captain.

Ethelwynne grabbed her bag off the floor and squished it to her chest. She blinked quickly to try and avoid crying. This could not be happening. They were so close to the mountains and White Shield. Why couldn't that fool have put the damaged crate somewhere else? They never would have noticed her then.

Sher roughly grabbed her arm, and pulled her towards the stairs. She struggled to escape his grasp, but he held her firmly. "We're in the sky. There's nowhere for you to run, girl. You might as well face the captain with some dignity about you," he said as he pushed her up the stairs. When the door at the top opened, the force of the wind almost knocked Ethelwynne over, but Sher seemed to expect that. Before she even had a chance to stagger under the gust his hands were on her back pushing her forwards and onto the deck.

Cephas met them at the top. "Captain Marino is in her cabin, sir."

Sher nodded to him and pulled Ethelwynne towards the captain's cabin.

Ethelwynne blushed as the crew members all stopped what they were doing to stare at her as she was dragged past.

Cephas knocked on the captain's door.

"Enter."

He pulled open the door and Sher pushed Ethelwynne inside.

The captain was sitting at her desk studying some papers. Her black hair was cropped close to her scalp and a gold chain dangled from her right ear. Her blue shirt was loosely laced over the front covering a white one underneath. Underneath her desk, Ethelwynne could see her black boots. They were so well polished, Ethelwynne was sure she would be able to see herself in them once she walked over.

Ethelwynne fidgeted.

"So, Sher, your nephew tells me we have a guest," she said without looking up from the papers.

Sher pushed her ahead of him. "Yes, ma'am."

She finally looked up and fixed her gaze on Ethelwynne. "What are you doing on my ship?" She rested her elbows on the desk and steepled her fingers in front of her chin.

Ethelwynne flushed and looked down without answering.

"I don't have time for this, girl. Answer the question or you will be locked in a closet until we arrive at White Shield. The guards there might have more time for this type of nonsense."

Sher cleared his throat.

"Yes?" the captain asked without taking her gaze off Ethelwynne.

"Apparently there was some noise in Helmsville about a thief."

"And so, your nephew just decided to let her walk onto my ship to save himself a few extra steps?"

Out of the corner of her eyes, Ethelwynne saw Cephas straighten and tense. She wondered if he was going to mention that it was actually the man named Bart who enlisted her help. "I'm sorry, ma'am," he said. "We didn't hear about the thief until after the ship was loaded, and because it was dark, none of us realized she was a woman."

"I'm not a thief," Ethelwynne interjected indignantly.

Captain Marino arched an eyebrow. "Your clothes and the peaches I suspect I'll find in your bag suggest otherwise." She reached out one of her hands.

Cephas yanked Ethelwynne's bag from her arms and passed it to the captain.

"Hey," Ethelwynne protested and tried to grab it back, but Sher held her fast.

The captain opened the bag and rifled through the contents. She pulled out the fruit and placed them on the desk in front of her.

Ethelwynne's cheeks prickled. She wished she could vanish into the walls behind her. "Well, that was, that's different. I can pay you for that."

Captain Marino dumped out her money pouch. She counted the coins and scraped them off her desk into a drawer. "But not for the ride." She dropped Ethelwynne's bag on the floor beside her desk and studied Ethelwynne for a few more moments. "Sher, can you see to it that this one has some useful tasks to perform for the duration of her stay? She can work off the rest of her debt on our way to White Shield." The captain turned her attention back to the papers on her desk. "Pity we didn't discover you before Heatherfield."

Ethelwynne blanched.

"Of course, Captain. I'm sure Bartholomew has lots of uses for a scrawny thing like her." Sher pushed her towards the door.

Ethelwynne put her hand on the doorframe to stop herself from being shoved out of the room. "What..." she bit her lip for a moment before she started again, "what will happen to me once we get to White Shield?" She felt ill as she waited for the captain to respond.

"Oh, I don't know," responded Captain Marino looking up from her work. "We will turn you over to the guards and let them know what we suspect. The rest is up to them. They could ship you back to Heatherfield, or, if King Orrin is still staying with King Kellan, they might bring you to him."

Ethelwynne straightened up a bit. She could meet the king's elves, pass along her message, and free her family.

"I wouldn't look too excited about that," Captain Marino laughed dryly, noticing her hopeful expression. "King Orrin is as foul-tempered as his brother and his guards are not known for leniency."

She dismissed them with a wave and Cephas shoved

Ethelwynne out of the room. He ushered her to the front of the ship where Bartholomew was inspecting some sailors' knots.

"Bart, the captain wanted me to tell you something," Cephas called.

"Untie them and try again," Bart barked before walking over to them.

Ethelwynne's cheeks flamed and she wanted to hide as Cephas explained who she was to Bart. The man's scowl deepened as he listened. "We've got lots of things to keep you busy on this ship," Bart said after sizing her up. "What's your name girl?"

"It's Ethelwynne," she said before it occurred to her that she probably should have made one up to prevent the elves from discovering who she was.

"Well, Ethelwynne, you can scrub the deck." He pointed to Cephas, "Make sure she doesn't miss a spot."

Cephas nodded and started to pull Ethelwynne back towards the center of the ship.

Bart turned his attention to Ethelwynne for a moment before he walked away, "Welcome aboard *The Passerine*."

The Greisgebied Mountains loomed ahead of *The Passerine*. The ship zigzagged through the air as she slowly moved through the oncoming wind. As Ethelwynne washed the decks, she heard other crew members complaining about how all of the tacking was costing them time. No longer were they optimistic that they would make it to White Shield in two more days. Now they were simply hoping they would make it to the mountains before it was too dark to navigate them.

When she was halfway finished, Sher came and traded places with Cephas. He sent his nephew back to the hold to finish up with the crates. Sher casually leaned against the railing while he watched her work.

Her knees ached from kneeling on them. Her fingers

were completely wrinkled. Between Cephas and Sher, this ship's deck was going to be cleaner than her parents' shop. And she thought her mother was a stickler when it came to dirt. She sat back on her heels and wiped her brow. The wind whipped her short hair around her face. She wished it were still long enough for her to tie it back and keep it out of her eyes.

"Are you done, girl?" asked Sher when he noticed her pausing. He strode up to inspect her handiwork.

She shook her head.

"Good, 'cause you missed some spots." He pointed at a part of the deck she had already scrubbed. Shoe prints marred her hard work. Her gaze followed the prints to where Sher was currently standing.

"If you really want this deck clean, you could learn to fly," she retorted.

"My dear girl, we are, in fact, already flying." He spun a slow circle with his arms outstretched to the sky, leaving even more shoeprints on the deck.

Ethelwynne groaned. Her shoulders dropped as she stared at the dirty deck.

"Oh, don't worry, girl. I'm only teasing you. The deck looks fine, but it is time to eat and the food is delicious."

Ethelwynne looked up at him hopefully, "So, I can be done?"

"For now," he shrugged. "I suspect you'll need your energy to help get all them dishes done afterward." He pointed up the masts to where sailors were furling the sails. "These boys and girls use a lot of dishes when they eat."

Ethelwynne sighed and threw her cloth into the bucket as she stood up. She walked over to the edge of the ship. As the sails were tied up the ship sank lower and out of the shipping lanes to where it would stop for the night. Ethelwynne leaned over the edge to dump out the waste water. The trees were almost scraping the bottom of the boat. Her stomach felt as though it were turning into knots. Now that she was outside of the ship and not behind her porthole, Ethelwynne did not like looking down at the ground far below. Her knuckles turned white against the bucket's handle. She took a step back and shook her head. She couldn't do this.

Sher put his hand on the bucket's handle. "I got this."

She turned to look at him. Her hand still clutched the bar.

"Come on, let go. I'm not so terrible that I'd make you dump the bucket over the edge when you're clearly afraid of heights. Just let go." With his other hand, he started to peel her fingers off before she let go and backed away from the edge.

He fished the cloth out of the bucket, wrung it out, and tossed it to her. "Be careful with this, or else you'll have to make a new one from that tattered dress of yours." Then he swung the bucket out over the edge and let the water rain down to the ground below. He handed the empty bucket back to her and showed her where she could put it and the cloth away before they walked down to the galley together.

*   *   *

The next morning one of the female sailors shook Ethelwynne awake as she lay in her hammock in their cabin. As the woman untied her, Ethelwynne thought about how even though she had been bound, this was still more comfortable than lying under the stairs.

After breakfast Bartholomew shoved Ethelwynne into a corner of the deck beside the stairs leading up to the quarterdeck. "Do not move from this spot or I will personally toss you overboard. Elves be damned."

Ethelwynne pressed her back into the wall and nodded.

Bart spun on his heel and began to order around the rest of the crew. The newer and younger members of the crew darted around with eyes that grew wider with each passing moment, while those, like Bartholomew and the crew members who had sailed this route before, buzzed around like cool collected chaos.

Ropes were checked twice. Ethelwynne overheard Emily say she was heading to the secondary steering mechanism in case the first one broke. No one wanted to lose their ability to steer in the mountain pass.

A vein in Bartholomew's forehead bulged as he yelled at one of the younger crew members who wasn't holding a rope correctly. She jumped and the rope slipped a bit before she tightened her grasp. Another crew member darted over and grabbed the rope from her to ensure it was secured properly.

The ship slowed down as the crew readied to enter the pass. Ethelwynne stumbled as the wind jostled them around harder than before. She held the stair railing beside her and closed her eyes. They were going to crash.

Someone tapped her on the shoulder.

Ethelwynne opened her eyes to see Sher standing in front of her.

"I need into the room behind you."

Ethelwynne looked nervously at Bartholomew before stepping aside. Bart was yelling at the woman with the ropes again, so maybe his crew would keep him busy enough that he wouldn't notice that she wasn't exactly where he put her.

Sher stepped back out with axes, swords, bows, and quivers filled with arrows.

Ethelwynne's stomach muscles tightened. "What are those for?" she squeaked.

Sher shrugged. "This is the only known pass through this part of the mountains, so pirates sometimes like to hang out here, if the King's Guard hasn't cleared them out recently." Then he called out to his nephew and few other crew members, including the woman Bartholomew was berating again.

"You want her?" yelled Bart. "She's going to kill us all."

"Which is why I don't want her anywhere near anything that has something to do with guiding us through the mountain pass," said Sher. "Maybe she'll be more useful as a lookout." He handed the men and women he had called over the weapons he'd pulled from the room under the stairs. Each individual received a bow and some other weapon should the pirates become close enough for them to be necessary.

"If not, we can always toss her off and be done with it," grumbled Bart.

Ethelwynne decided that was his favorite threat, and she sincerely hoped it was an empty one. From her spot, she watched as the blushing woman climbed up the mast.

The ship slowly swayed her way through the narrow passage. Everything seemed to be holding its breath. All Ethelwynne could hear was the creaking of the ship as it inched along. She felt like she'd been standing in the same spot for hours. She tentatively shifted a bit to loosen some of her muscles. Bartholomew noticed and glared at her. She froze again.

Lunchtime came, but no one stopped to eat. Bart motioned Ethelwynne over to him and had her run down to the galley to bring the crew members buns that they could eat while keeping the ship on course. Only one person at each station ate at a time.

Ethelwynne shut her eyes every time the ship swayed close to the mountain walls. It was so different traveling through the mountains on a ship than it was on a wagon. Not less terrifying though, but at least when they were on the ground the wind didn't threaten to dash them upon the rocks or knock their vessel off the cliffs to the rocks down below. She shuddered as she remembered the steep hills she and her father had driven up and down and the sheer cliffs that hugged the trail.

Finally, after an excruciating amount of time, some of

the veteran sailors called out that the end of the pass was only about an hour away. A few let loose wary cheers.
Ethelwynne felt herself relaxing. Her muscles ached from being continually tense. They were going to make it.

"Ship!" called the woman from the crow's nest. Moments later, the ship she had spotted drifted in front of them and blocked their path. A second ship drifted in behind them from its hiding place in between two of the mountains and closed off their retreat from behind.

CHRISTINA VAN STARKENBURG

— CHAPTER EIGHT —

Out on a Limb

Ethelwynne's face paled as she saw the dragonhead flags that the two ships were proudly displaying. She backed up into the wall behind her and tried to vanish into the hardwood.

Sher ran past her, yelling orders at the men and women he had tossed the weapons too. His teams split in two so they could cover the bow and stern of *The Passerine*. He ran to the front with the first team while Cephas went to the back with the second.

The pirate ships advanced.

Sher's teams lined up to face them.

Ethelwynne watched with a mix of curiosity and fear as the pirates wheeled a metal contraption to the front of their ship. As the boats floated closer to each other, she could see the form more clearly. The metal dragon matched the ones on their flags.

"Back!" yelled Sher as he darted away from the front yanking one of the men back with him. "Get me water!"

Fire spewed from the dragon's mouth and razed the front of *The Passerine*.

Screams erupted from the two crew members who were

not fast enough to heed Sher's call.

Bartholomew knocked into Ethelwynne and shoved her in the direction of the human chain that was forming to throw water on the flames.

Ethelwynne grabbed a bucket from Bart and handed it to the person in front of her. Water splashed on her arms and ran down her shirt.

"Careful, girl!" yelled Bartholomew as he grabbed another bucket from someone else. "We want the water on the fire, not you."

The ship turned abruptly and knocked Ethelwynne and a few other crew members off their feet. It picked up speed as it raced towards a small gap between the mountains.

"I thought this was the only pass," Ethelwynne said as she stood up and retook her place.

"It is," said Bartholomew. His voice flat and hard. He handed her another bucket before he moved towards the front of the line. Other crew members stepped forward to fill the void he left.

With her eyes wide, she continued to pass buckets of water. Ethelwynne prayed desperately that the fire would go out before they ran out of water and that they would find a new way through the mountains.

The Passerine dipped down sharply. Ethelwynne screamed and grabbed the railing beside her with one hand to keep from sliding to the bow of the ship. Trees and rocks rushed towards them as the ship dove.

Her eyes watered as the wind rushed past. She blinked and looked towards the captain. Captain Marino was holding onto the wheel calling out orders to people around her. Behind her, Ethelwynne could see one of the pirate ships. It was almost on top of them.

The Passerine tipped and swayed as it careened between the mountains. Buckets clattered past as people dropped them in an attempt to grab the guard rails and stay standing. The

114

pails disappeared into the smoke with small hisses as their remaining water hit the fire.

Ethelwynne yelped and grabbed the foot of a crew member to stop herself from sliding down the deck. Grunting she pulled herself up to the railing and attempted to stand on the sloped deck. She looked up at the pirate ship. The men and women on it were lined up at the front with bows pulled taut.

"The fire's out," yelled Bart over the cacophony. "So, stop pelting me with buckets. If I find out who dropped theirs, I'll tie them to their hands next time."

Yelps of pain echoed off the canyon walls as crew members were struck with arrows from the pirate ship that was descending to their level. One arrow thunked into the wood beside Ethelwynne's hand. She pulled her hand away and looked for shelter. She couldn't die. She had to warn the elven king so her family could come home.

Sher darted past as the ship leveled out. He stopped and took a few steps backward. "Here," Sher said as he handed her a few throwing knives.

Ethelwynne swallowed hard to try and loosen the lump in her throat. "I have no idea what to do with these."

"Don't stab yourself." He turned and continued to rush towards the back of the ship hollering at his crew to meet him there.

Ethelwynne's eyes widened in horror. The pirate ship was now flying level with *The Passerine*. Something metal clattered on the top deck.

"Hooks," spat Bartholomew from behind Ethelwynne. She jumped.

He pushed her towards the back of the ship and pointed to the hooks. "Make yourself useful. Cut the ropes."

Ethelwynne stared at him. Her eyes and mouth were perfect circles. She turned to look up the stairs to where the clattering was coming from. Arrows still rained down.

"Move!" He pushed her harder.

Ethelwynne stumbled a few steps before running towards the stairs leading to the top deck. In front of her, she heard Captain Marino yelling orders at the crew members who were helping her steer the ship. She was determined to outfly the pirates.

Ethelwynne paused at the bottom step and swallowed hard. She darted up the stairs, wobbling like a drunken fool as the boat lurched and bobbed in the wind and around the mountains. She grabbed onto the railing to help steady herself and cut through the rope tied to the nearest hook.

Arrows thudded into the deck around her.

Ethelwynne ducked down behind the top deck's outer wall. The next hook was nearby. She promised herself she could make it.

A large crash echoed through the canyon followed by desperate screams.

Ethelwynne ran for the next rope. While she was standing, she caught a glimpse of the pirate ship that was further away. It had collided with the cliff-face. Bits of wood smeared across the mountain face. The mast tipped over the side and tumbled to the rocks below.

Ethelwynne sawed through the rope with her dagger. The ship swung around another corner knocking Ethelwynne from her feet and saving her from some arrows that nearly found their mark.

The passageway widened as the captain spun *The Passerine* back onto the main trail.

The remaining pirate ship was still with them. More grappling hooks embedded into the top deck's railing.

Cephas appeared at her side and chopped through some of the new ropes with his hatchet.

Their efforts weren't enough and the pirates' corvus slammed down on *The Passerine*. Pirates streamed across as though they weren't sailing above the treetops.

Metal rang out against metal as the pirates clashed with the ship's guard and crew.

Cephas shoved the ax into her hands and drew his sword. "Keep cutting." He turned to fight the closest pirate.

Ethelwynne bit her lip as she swung the hatchet. The metallic taste of blood filled her mouth.

Cephas bumped into her as he grappled with another pirate. The ax slipped through her sweaty fingers and clattered to the ground.

Ethelwynne tried to grab it, but the ship lurched and dipped again, sending the weapon skittering across the deck.

Wood crunched as the ship's bottom scraped a mountain.

Ethelwynne pulled out a knife again and began sawing through the ropes once more.

"I got it, girl," Sher said after he'd knocked another pirate towards a waiting guardsman, and slammed his ax into the rope, severing the last rope from the ship.

"Now, the plank." He turned and darted towards the corvus.

Ethelwynne sheathed the knife and followed behind him. The ship tilted again. Ethelwynne grabbed the edge to keep from sliding across the deck. The corvus slipped from the edge as *The Passerine* leaned away from the pirate ship. The pirates screamed and struggled to pull it in and stop it from clattering to the ground beneath them.

Tree branches scratched Ethelwynne's fingers as she clung to the edge. "We're going to crash!"

"Not yet," yelled Sher, as the ship righted itself again. He quickly regained his footing on the mostly level deck and swung his ax at an incoming pirate.

Cephas also dove back into the fight and the two men tag-teamed the pirates who got close. Cephas swung his sword at another pirate. The ship leaned again, and his swing went wide as he stumbled back to the boat's edge. Ethelwynne grabbed onto Cephas as he toppled over the edge beside her. She screamed as his weight pulled her over the side and the two of them tumbled to the trees below.

Ethelwynne grabbed out for something to hold onto. Her eyes watered as the wind whipped past her face. Branches slapped her face and pine needles scratched her limbs as she fell. Her heart raced. The pounding sound of her own blood was deafening.

The first branch her hands grabbed snapped from the force of her falling. Her screams became silent when the air rushed from her lungs as she slammed into a different branch. Another branch scratched the side of her face. She tried to grab onto one. Her fingernails bent and tore as it slipped through her fingers.

Ethelwynne landed on another branch with a thud. She wrapped her arms and legs around it and gasped for air. The branch began to creak and splinter underneath her. She turned her head frantically to find another one that was close enough to grab onto. There was a thicker one to her right. Biting her lip, she stretched out and grabbed hold of it with one hand. The branch beneath her snapped off the trunk and tumbled to the ground below.

Ethelwynne yelped as she swung out under the new branch. It bent under her weight. She tried to grab it with her other hand. Her fingers started slipping as she swung wildly beneath it. Her foot touched a different branch and she was able to use it to steady herself enough to grab the branch above her with both hands. She tiptoed along the lower branch and inched her hands along the upper one to get closer to the trunk. Pine sap and needles stuck to her. The smell was overwhelming.

She hugged the tree close and shook. Her breathing came in coughing hiccups as she started to full-on cry. She squeezed her eyes shut, terrified to look up to see how far she'd fallen, or down to see how far she still had to go. She wasn't even sure she could climb down at this point.

Branches rustled around her. "Hey, you made it," said Cephas. His voice was ragged and out of breath. Ethelwynne turned and looked at him with wide eyes as he placed a hand on her shoulder. His face and hands were bleeding from where the branches had got the best of him. A watery smile was pasted onto his face. Pine needles stuck to his hair and clothes.

She didn't respond.

"Come on, we can't stay here." He started to climb down, but when Ethelwynne didn't follow he stopped. "Trust me, you'll be happier with your feet on the ground."

Ethelwynne's whole body shook, her knuckles turned white from clutching the tree so hard. "C-c-can y-you promise my feet w-will t-touch the ground w-without me falling anymore?"

The wind rustled the branches. Ethelwynne flinched. She squeezed her eyes shut and hugged the tree with all her might. Sobs pulsed from her body.

"Depends on how far up the bottom branches are," said Cephas. "But yes, most likely you won't have to fall. And if you do, well, I'll go first and catch you." She opened one eye a little and looked at him.

He ran one of his hands through his hair. "Come on, it's climb down now, or fall down later."

Ethelwynne nodded. "Okay," she whispered weakly.

Cephas began to climbing again, testing each of the branches as he went and guiding her to the branches that would support her weight.

Ethelwynne's hands shook as she grabbed the branches. The pine needles rustled against each other. Sap oozed out of the tree and coated her fingers with a smelly brown glue.

The tree was tall, and even though Ethelwynne was sure they'd fallen thousands of feet, it took them much longer to climb down than she thought it would.

Cephas patiently coached her down the tree. Halfway

down, he picked up his sword from where it had become tangled in the branches. He grunted as he inspected the damage from its fall. "Better than nothing," he muttered as he sheathed it. He continued down the tree. "Let's keep going, it's not much further now."

Ethelwynne glanced down. The ground was visible beneath the thicket of branches that surrounded them. It was much, much farther down than she anticipated after Cephas's comment. Ethelwynne moaned and leaned her head against the trunk. A wave of dizziness threatened to overtake her. She distantly heard branches move.

Cephas's hand rested on her back. "Breathe. You cannot faint up here. Just breathe."

Ethelwynne focused on his voice. She shivered as her vision cleared. "Thanks," she whispered.

"Better?" he grunted.

Ethelwynne took another shaky breath and nodded.

"Good. I can't carry you."

"Okay," Ethelwynne whispered and weakly reached out for another branch.

"Careful," said Cephas curtly. His hand firmly closed over hers causing the bark to bite into her skin, but effectively strengthening her grip on the tree. For all that he had said about not being able to carry her, he came pretty close as he guided her the rest of the way down. His hand covered hers on every branch. Ethelwynne relied on his strength, more than she wanted to admit, to help her hold on.

"Last branch," Cephas remarked after a little while. He swung down underneath it and dangled for a moment before dropping to the ground. "Your turn," he hissed to Ethelwynne.

She clung to the branches and took a few breaths to steady her nerves.

"Come on, we don't have all day. There might be pirates around."

"I can do this. I can do this. I can do this," she whispered as she also swung beneath the branch.

Cephas's hands grabbed onto her thighs. "I've got you. You can let go now."

Ethelwynne squeezed her eyes shut and squeaked as she released the branch. As Cephas slowly brought her to the ground, Ethelwynne grabbed him and held onto him as tightly as she held the tree and shook uncontrollably. Behind her closed eyes, all she could see was herself falling through the trees. She opened them. "I'm never flying again," she whimpered.

At last, her shivers calmed down enough for Cephas to extract himself. He held her out at arm's length and looked her over as though assessing whether or not she was going to fall the instant he let go. Apparently satisfied, he released her and held out his hand expectantly. "Now for those knives Sher lent you. I want all of the ones that survived our fall."

Ethelwynne gaped at him as she checked her pockets for the blades. To her surprise, two of them remained.

Cephas took them from her and put them inside the loose jacket he was wearing. Then, he turned and looked around them before picking a direction and setting out. They had barely cleared the tree when he grabbed Ethelwynne and clamped a hand over her mouth as he pulled her to the ground beside the trunk.

Her eyes widened again as two pirates, who also had the unfortunate experience of plummeting to the ground, walked past them. They were covered in scratches like she and Cephas were. One was limping. The other was rubbing his shoulder. They both looked angry. One kicked a rock as they walked past. It skittered over the ground and pinged off a tree. The two men yelled obscenities as they shook their fists at the sky.

Ethelwynne followed their gaze. The skyships were no longer overhead. Would Captain Marino and the rest of the crew come looking for her or Cephas? Or would they assume that the fall had killed them? She didn't know which she would prefer.

On one hand, if everyone thought she was dead, the prince's elves would stop looking for her and she might actually make it to the capital alive, so she could give her message to the king. On the other hand, she no longer knew how to get to the capital, and she knew she didn't do too well surviving in the wilderness. Just walking along the road at night to Heatherfield Manor had terrified her.

The two pirates vanished into the forest. Ethelwynne inched Cephas's hand off her mouth. "Do you know how to get out of here?" she whispered.

She felt Cephas nod his head over her shoulder as he put his hand more tightly over her mouth. His whole body was tense, and she felt him use his other hand to half draw his sword while they waited.

Her body tensed as she realized he didn't think the pirates were gone. She could have led the pirates to them by speaking. She squeezed her eyes shut. Ethelwynne tried to concentrate on the fact that Cephas said he knew the way out. All she had to do was let him guide her out of the forest, find a road that led to the capital, and she could leave him and his accusations of thievery behind.

At last, Cephas relaxed and released her. "This way," he murmured, tilting his head in the opposite direction of the pirates.

Relief filled Ethelwynne. She stood up and followed him away from the tree. As they walked, she kept looking behind them to see if the pirates had heard them and decided to follow. Something stepped on a branch. She turned to face it and froze. Staring back at her was a deer assessing the danger.

Cephas pulled her arm. "Come on," he whispered.

Ethelwynne tried to brush her hair out of her eyes, but

the strands were too short to catch behind her ear. She winced as some strands of hair joined the needles on her palms. As they continued going through the forest, she tried to ignore the strand of hair poking her eyes as she peeled off the needles pricking her palms and wrists.

Eventually they came to a creek. Ethelwynne dipped her hands into the water to wash away needles and grime.

Cephas kneeled beside her and rinsed briefly before wading into the shallow water to gather up some cattails. "Hungry?" he asked.

Ethelwynne made a face as she shook her head. There had to be better things to eat in the forest than cattails.

Cephas shrugged. "When I make them later, you should eat some. I am not carrying you when you get too tired to walk."

She wrinkled her nose at the plants and wondered if Cephas would know how to prepare them better than her mother did. Her mother could cook many wonderful meals. Something with cattails was not one of them. "Won't the ship come looking for you?" Ethelwynne bent down and dipped her hair into the water to try and rinse out some of the sap.

"Not likely." He continued to snap off more cattails.

Despite the fact that she didn't want to ever ride on a flying ship again, Ethelwynne looked up at Cephas in shock. "What if you were hurt? What about your uncle, Sher? He wouldn't try to find you? That's horrible."

Cephas put his collection of cattails down on a rock and studied her. "My uncle knows I can take care of myself in the woods, even if I was injured. And even if I couldn't, they can't risk everyone on board to save one unlucky crew member."

Ethelwynne shook her head. "I would never abandon my family like that."

"I've heard some thieves think they're honorable," he eyed her as he picked up the cattails and began to walk through the woods again. He paused before the trees hid him from view to look back at Ethelwynne and make sure she was up and following him again.

As they walked Cephas would occasionally stop to grab some more reeds or fiddleheads to eat. By the time they stopped for supper, he had gathered a small feast of greens.

"Can we have a fire?" Ethelwynne shivered in the evening breeze. She should have waited until summer.

Cephas studied the forest around them. "Just long enough to cook the things that need to be cooked," he said at last. "We don't know where the pirates went, and I don't want to fight them again."

Ethelwynne gathered pine needles, a few twigs, and branches from the forest floor while Cephas tried to light a flame. Soon, a tiny fire was crackling, and their meal was roasting. Ethelwynne quietly watched the flame while Cephas prepared the food.

He handed some of it to Ethelwynne, "Eat." He put out the fire and leaned back to follow his own advice.

Ethelwynne ate it without really even tasting it, which she supposed was a good thing, because it meant she wasn't going to gag.

An owl hooted in the treetops as the crickets sang their lullabies, but beyond that, the forest was silent around them. "You should go to sleep," Cephas said as he sprawled out on the ground. "We have a long walk ahead of us."

Ethelwynne nodded and lay down on the ground underneath the canopy of trees. Rocks poked into her sides. She moved to a different spot to try and find a comfortable position. After a while, Ethelwynne settled for a position with the least number of rocks poking her.

She looked up at the stars and listened to the cricket song as she tried to figure out what she was going to do now. She had no idea where they were or how they were going to get out of the woods. Tears silently ran down her nose and cheeks.

Cephas started to snore.

She turned to face him. Could she even trust him? Wouldn't he just dump her with the authorities as soon as they were out of this mess? She considered getting up and leaving him in the forest to try and find her own way out. But she immediately rejected that idea. She had never been over these mountains before, and she wouldn't know how to get back. Not for the first time, she wished she had never heard about the missing key.

After a while, Ethelwynne fell into the deep sleep of the emotionally spent—the kind that left her with no dreams to remember and no feelings of rest having happened. So, even though the sun was now up when it hadn't been moments before, she questioned whether or not she had truly fallen asleep at all.

Cephas didn't appear to have had the same issue. Once the sun woke him, he quickly ate some of the leftover food, gathered up his meager belongings, and harried her so they could set out as soon as possible.

Ethelwynne nibbled at the food he had passed to her as she walked beside him. She knew she would need the strength, but it remained tasteless.

A light rain began to fall as they slowly made their way through the never-ending trees. Ethelwynne sighed. She scanned the forest to see if there were any stray pirates near them, but they seemed to be alone minus the occasional rabbit and deer. At one point, they came across a bear with its nose in a berry bush. Cephas put his hand in front of her as he backed away so they could give it a wide berth.

"Keep walking along this cliff," Cephas told her after a while and vanished into the trees before she could respond.

Ethelwynne swallowed and forced herself to keep walking forward. There was a cliff face beside her; she could not get lost. The elves had no idea where she was. They were not going to jump out in front of her and kill her. She tried to tune out the sounds of the forest by focusing on her breathing. She was going to make it to the capital, warn the king, and save her family. She was going to make it.

Someone touched her shoulder. Ethelwynne jumped and spun around.

Cephas was looking back at her. Concern briefly flashed across his face. "I didn't see any traces of pirates near us, so you can stop checking over your shoulder as we walk."

"Oh." Ethelwynne noticed Cephas was still watching her. She flushed and turned around to continue walking. "What are you going to do with me once we're out of this mess?" She played with the edges of the shirt she was wearing while she waited for his answer.

"Bring you to the guards in White Shield," he said as he stepped past her and took the lead again. "It's what I would do with any thief. Don't assume the plan changed because I saved your life."

"I'm not a thief. I didn't steal anything..."

Cephas turned around and arched an eyebrow in her direction.

"... except for the fruit, which I paid for."

"And?"

Ethelwynne sighed. "And the clothes, but I didn't have a choice and I intend to pay for them later. So, it's not really stealing."

"You want me to believe you're not a thief, but you just admitted to stealing on at least two occasions in just as many days." He looked at her over his shoulder, "If you want to convince the guards to let you go, you're going to need to learn to lie better."

"I'm not a liar and I'm not a thief, and I don't want to be one," she snapped. "I should never have gone to Heatherfield. But, unlike you and your uncle, I can't just abandon my family when they're in danger or trapped on the other side of the gates. You might not think I have honor, but at least I care for my family."

Cephas stopped walking and turned to face her. "What does your family have to do with this? Do you somehow think it makes it better that you stole from the elves to help feed your family?"

"What? No. That's not what I'm saying at all." She threw her hands up in the air. "I was just... It's just that... You know what, just forget it. You wouldn't believe me anyway." She stormed past him. Maybe if they came across a road, or she somehow figured out where they were, she would leave him behind. The experience in Helmsville had shown her how much the guards in a town would listen to her if they thought she was a thief, and since she doubted there was any way to convince Cephas that she wasn't one, she could not arrive in White Shield with him beside her ready to hand her over to the prison guards.

Cephas fell into step beside her. "You're going to get yourself lost if you're not careful. It's this way." He veered away from the cliff face, down a steep and rocky hill that led to an even thicker-looking forest.

CHRISTINA VAN STARKENBURG

— CHAPTER NINE —

Thunder and Elves

Ethelwynne and Cephas walked in silence for a bit. Clouds started to roll in and block the sun. Ethelwynne groaned, "More rain. I hate rain." She kicked a shrub to emphasize her point.

Thunder rumbled in the distance. Ethelwynne flinched. Memories of the last storm she spent outside in the forest flashed through her mind like the lightning that ripped across the distant sky. "Can we find some sort of shelter?" She looked up at him pleadingly.

Cephas sighed as more thunder rumbled. "I want to get a little bit farther from the base of this hill, so we don't have to worry about mudslides."

Ethelwynne paled at the thought of being buried by mud.

"Come on," said Cephas. "It's not much further, and the sooner we start climbing down again the farther away from the mountain we can get."

Ethelwynne nodded and scrambled down the hillside as quickly as she could without breaking anything. Soon the ground began to level out.

"Let's gather up any branches we see," said Cephas when they were far enough from the mountain.

A storm like the one that nearly killed Ethelwynne had hit this side of the mountain recently, so it was not hard to find fallen tree limbs. They gathered their branches in silence. The thunder rumbled louder and closer. A crack of lightning flashed through the trees. Ethelwynne jumped. She hugged her bundle close as she watched the sky and shivered.

"Here," called Cephas from in front of her.

She ran to him and watched as he wedged a small log between two trees that were spaced fairly close together.

"We can use the shorter branches to make sides," he said as he picked up a branch and rested it against the log he'd propped up. Ethelwynne nodded and put down her pile to help. Soon they had a small triangular frame to cover them. As the rain began to fall, Ethelwynne and Cephas covered their shelter with twigs, leaves, needles, and dirt from the forest floor to make it waterproof. Once Cephas was satisfied with it, they crawled inside.

"This is much nicer than the last place I weathered out a storm," Ethelwynne mumbled as she watched the water pour over their entrance. She hugged her knees. Spots danced in her eyes as lightning flashed across the sky.

As her vision cleared a shadow appeared in front of the entrance. "Do you mind if I join you?" asked a feminine voice with a thick elvish accent. The elf knelt down and looked into their shelter. Her thick cloak shimmered in the lightning flashes from all of the water running off of it.

Ethelwynne's eyes widened as she realized it was the elf from the manor. She felt her stomach muscles tighten and she drew her legs in even closer to her and tried to disappear into the darkness at the back of the hut.

Cephas moved towards Ethelwynne in the tiny space to try and make room for the newcomer. "Of course."

Heotene ducked inside and shook off the raindrops. Surprise registered on her face when she looked at Ethelwynne. She smiled. Ethelwynne supposed Cephas might assume it was a friendly smile, but to Ethelwynne, the look was anything but warm and comforting. "It's fitting that I found you in one storm since I lost you in another," Heotene remarked as she idly twirled a dagger in her hand. "But rest assured, I will not lose you a second time."

Ethelwynne shivered. Her eyes darted from Heotene to the downpour. But even if she could convince her legs to support her, Ethelwynne doubted she could outrun the elf a second time. Heotene did not look winded.

"You don't need your knife out to prevent her from leaving," Cephas remarked. His hand slipped inside his jacket. "She doesn't know where she is. She has nowhere to go, except to White Shield with us."

Heotene laughed. "I have no intention of taking her to White Shield. My prince has given me his blessing to carry out her punishment immediately, and her crime demands death."

Blood drained from Ethelwynne's face.

"We don't kill thieves here." Cephas pulled out a knife and shifted his body, blocking Heotene from Ethelwynne's view. "I will bring her to White Shield and hand her over to the authorities. You are welcome to travel with us, but I will not let you kill her."

"You don't honestly think you can stop me, do you?" Heotene sighed. "Then I will simply kill you both." She thrust her knife at him.

Cephas blocked her with one arm and slammed his knife into her thigh and pushed her through the branch wall. "Run Ethelwynne!"

His voice jolted her into action and she burst out of the collapsing shelter and ran into the rain. She was soaked instantly.

Cephas caught up to her. "Faster," he yelled and grabbed her arm to pull her along in his wake.

Ethelwynne stumbled as she looked back to see the elf

leaning against a tree, nocking an arrow.

"Arrow!" Ethelwynne yelped and pushed Cephas behind a tree. The arrow whooshed past and thudded into a trunk. They wove through the forest as fast as they could until the storm clouds cleared and their lungs would take them no further.

"We've lost her," Cephas gasped between breaths. "We must have lost her." He leaned against a tree and panted.

Ethelwynne shook her head to save her breath for breathing and continued to stare back the way they came.

Cephas caught his breath much sooner than Ethelwynne did and pulled her forward. "Come on, we have to keep moving."

She wheezed and stumbled after him.

Cephas slowed his pace long enough for Ethelwynne to catch her breath before racing away again. It felt like they continued that pattern for hours: sprinting when they had the breath to do so, and walking slower when Ethelwynne's lungs felt like they would explode. The two walked until Ethelwynne's legs would carry her no further.

Ethelwynne collapsed to the ground. Her legs felt like jelly. Her arms seemed all rubbery. Stray water droplets splattered on her head and back as she struggled to push herself up off the ground.

"Come on," Cephas said as he pulled her to her feet. "I want to get further away from her." When he released her, Ethelwynne wobbled forward a few steps and stumbled over a root tumbling to the ground again.

"Well," said Cephas with a sigh after the third time Ethelwynne fell, "I suppose we'll spend the night here."

Ethelwynne wearily leaned her head against the trunk behind her and looked up at Cephas with heavy eyes.

He was staring back the way they came. After a few moments he sat down beside her. "With that leg of hers, she can't follow us right now anyway."

Ethelwynne nodded sluggishly and with her last conscious thought, she hoped that was true. She dreamed that the elf caught them and woke up with a jolt when Heotene was about to stab her. The only thing she heard was Cephas's soft snoring. Ethelwynne tried to settle back into the quiet night, but she jumped every time a night creature moved in the dark. Heotene didn't reappear, but Ethelwynne was so wound up that she didn't think she'd be able to sleep anyhow. Long after the moon set, she finally felt tired again. She closed her eyes and drifted back to an uneasy sleep.

Early the next morning Cephas woke a very sleepy Ethelwynne up. "We should keep moving" he whispered. "I know the elf was pretty hurt, but she might have a bit of magic ointment with her, so I'd rather have as much distance between us as possible."

Ethelwynne blinked groggily and nodded. She yawned and stretched as she stood up. Once she was sure her legs would support her, they raced further away from where they last saw Heotene. Ethelwynne's thighs and calves ached from the run the day before, her arms burned from climbing down the tree, and she was hungry.

She couldn't keep up the pace for long. "Wait. Please," she called out as loudly as she dared.

Cephas stopped running, and looked back at her. "We can't stop yet."

Ethelwynne nodded. "I just need to walk for a bit."

He sighed and started quickly walking through the forest in front of her. Ethelwynne still had to jog at times to keep up. Cephas kept glancing behind them. Ethelwynne flinched whenever the wind rustled the leaves. The sooner they were far, far away from the elf the better.

Ethelwynne tripped on a rock and fell to the ground. An arrow zinged into the tree right above her.

"Come on!" yelped Cephas as he pulled her to her feet. They fled into the trees, ducking under branches. They heard

Heotene following behind them, but she didn't sound like she was getting closer. The wound in her leg must still be hampering her, which gave them a chance to get away.

Soon the roar of a waterfall drowned out the sound of their steps and that of their pursuer.

The trees stopped and they ran out in front of the bottom of a waterfall. "This way," called Cephas as he ran into the shallow river avoiding the bowl in front of the waterfall where the water was much darker and deeper looking and splashed across to the other side. When they were hidden by the trees again, Cephas turned to follow the river downstream. "That river will take us to Stormont. My family lives there," he said.

Ethelwynne nodded and followed him through the brush. The thunder of the waterfall soon disappeared into the trees behind them.

Ethelwynne and Cephas suddenly found themselves without cover again as the trees parted for the river once more. Cephas stopped. Ethelwynne's heart raced and her stomach felt like a stone as she skidded to a stop, colliding with Cephas's back.

She almost fell, but he caught her with one arm and pointed with the other. "That boat…"

Ethelwynne followed his gaze to a logging boat floating on the river. The workers were poling the logs into position.

"Maybe we can get on that boat," he finished and started running again for the water, dragging Ethelwynne behind him.

One of the loggers noticed the two of them and called for the ship's captain.

A bald man walked off the boat and approached them as they arrived on the shore. Two burly men flanked him. "Whatever trouble you're looking for, you best be gone before you find it."

"Please," gasped Cephas. "We need to get to Stormont.

We're both strong and we will work on your ship if you help us."

The captain spat on the ground. "She certainly don't look it. Got any money to offer?"

Cephas looked at Ethelwynne who shook her head. Captain Marino had taken everything Ethelwynne had when she'd been discovered hiding on *The Passerine.*

Cephas groaned and held out his sword. "What about this? You'll get a decent price for this, but it's the best I can do. We lost everything else when we fell off our skyship during a pirate attack."

"Skyship? Pirates? Ye brought pirates to me ship?" hollered the captain. "Blast it all. Men get ready to leave now. Forget what ain't tied to the ship."

"Sir?" asked Ethelwynne. She glanced over her shoulder and shivered. Heotene could pop through the trees at any moment. She doubted the elf was that far behind them.

He glowered at them, then gestured for them to get on the ship. "Me wife would never let me hear the end of it if she heard I didn't help some people in need. Keep your sword."

Ethelwynne breathed a sigh of relief as she and Cephas followed the captain across the ramp and onto his boat.

"But, know this. If either of you causes trouble, I'm not stopping the ship to let you off. I'll toss you overboard and you can try to dodge the logs on your way to shore."

Ethelwynne glanced towards the trees that were hiding Heotene and gulped. But at least this time she could swim if she fell off.

Cephas held out his hand. "Thank you, sir. I'm Cephas Merrilin by the way."

The captain clasped Cephas's hand in both of his own and shook it vigorously. "You can call me Captain Amos."

"We're ready Capt'n," called out one of the crew members.

Amos clapped his hand on Cephas's back, "Well, let's get you two to Stormont. Welcome aboard *The Backcut*."

As the boat floated down the river, Ethelwynne turned back to face the way they came. Heotene limped out from the trees. Ethelwynne felt the blood drain away from her cheeks as the elf raised her bow. But it seemed like she decided the boat was too far away, or perhaps she wanted fewer witnesses, for she lowered her bow and disappeared into the forest again.

"Ethelwynne?" Cephas tapped her on the shoulder. The tone of his voice suggested that this was not the first time he'd tried to get her attention.

She turned and faced him, giving him a weak smile.

"You don't look too well," remarked Cephas as he studied her. The concern etched into his face almost allowed Ethelwynne to believe that perhaps their encounter with Heotene changed something. Perhaps he finally believed her when she said she never robbed the elves.

"If you're going to be sick girl, get it all over the railing or clean it up yourself," said Amos as he wagged his finger in her direction. "Now I've got a boat to steer, so stay out of the way."

He walked into the cabin to take over steering as the boat bobbed towards the city of Stormont. Logs thumped and bumped into each other as the ropes corralled them and pulled them along in the boat's wake.

"The captain was hoping we'd join him so we stay out of his men's way. But we can stay out here for a bit if you think you're going to be sick."

Ethelwynne shook her head. "I'm fine," she said.

Cephas furrowed his eyebrows and frowned. "You look like you're about to keel over."

"I'm fine," Ethelwynne reiterated and tried to sound like she meant it. "I saw…" she tried to find a way to describe Heotene without tipping any of the workers off to the fact that it wasn't pirates that pursued them, in the end she decided that the simplest description would be the most truthful "…her. She's gone now."

Cephas's eyes widened. He looked up and scoured the shoreline for any signs of the elf. "I should have brought you inside right away." He grabbed her elbow and followed after the captain.

"I'm pretty sure she's gone," said Ethelwynne.

Cephas nodded and scanned the treeline again as he shoved her into the cabin.

Captain Amos glanced over at the two of them as they entered the cramped space. "You're not going to throw up in here, are you?"

Ethelwynne shook her head. "No, sir."

The captain nodded curtly. "Good. Now sit there and stay out of the way." He pointed to an empty spot on the floor. Ethelwynne and Cephas made their way over to it and plopped themselves down.

Ethelwynne leaned her head against the rough wooden wall. She closed her eyes to shut out the world around her. She was safe for now, but how long would that last. Heotene had found her in the middle of nowhere during a storm. She would find her in Stormont too. She opened her eyes minutely, Heotene would kill Cephas too now that he sided with her—even if he didn't fully believe her version of events. She couldn't stay with him, but how would she make it to White Shield without him? She sighed and let herself feel the boat moving over the gentle river waves.

*   *   *

Cephas shook her sometime later. "We're almost there."

Ethelwynne rubbed her eyes and stood up to look out the front of the ship. The ship rounded the final bend and the city's river watchtowers came into view. A guard walked out onto the dock and waited for them to sail up and stop so he could inspect the merchant's wares.

Ethelwynne's stomach fluttered at the sight of the guards. There was no reason they should be looking for her. Ethelwynne was almost positive Heotene wouldn't be able to beat them to Stormont and warn the guards to look out for her. But what if Heotene wasn't the only elf hunting her. If she was the prince, she probably wouldn't leave this mission up to one person alone.

Her heart was in her throat the entire time Captain Amos chatted amiably with the guards. He gestured back up the river and Ethelwynne caught the word "pirates."

The guards followed his gaze and nodded to each other before marking down he had arrived with his load of lumber. "See you in a while," they called out as Captain Amos guided the boat away from the dock.

Amos steered *The Backcut* to the lumberyards. As his men worked to bring the logs to shore without injuring themselves or damaging their product, he walked Ethelwynne and Cephas to the gate. "Feel free to travel with us anytime," Captain Amos said as he clapped Cephas on the back as Cephas disembarked. "You did good for a first-timer."

"Thank you, sir."

Captain Amos beamed and headed back to his ship.

"He let you help after all," Ethelwynne said as she watched him bark orders to his crew.

Cephas nodded and left the lumberyard. Ethelwynne followed him through the bustle of the port city. They walked through the dingy area down by the docks, up past the nice area of town and back out into the rundown outer ring of the city before stopping in front of a building with a distinct lean and herbs hanging in the windows. Cephas knocked on the door.

After the third try, a woman about Ethelwynne's age opened the door. Ethelwynne was startled by how much she looked like her brother. From her curly dark brown hair to her nearly black eyes, to the way she carried herself, there was no way to deny that these two were related. "Cephas!"

"Hello Xiamara."

She threw her arms around his neck. "Uncle Sher got here yesterday." She released her brother and wiped away the tears forming in her eyes. "He said you fell off."

She hugged him once more and beckoned them inside as she wandered into the kitchen area. "Mother isn't home right now. She's off meditating and whatever else they do during the Festival of the Painted Lady. She just left a couple of days ago for the monastery so she doesn't think you're dead. She won't be back for about a month. Drinks?" Any trace of her tears vanished when she turned to face them holding a pitcher and a couple of cups.

Cephas accepted the cup offered to him. "This place is looking a little rough. We just sailed here on a logging ship. Perhaps I can get us some lumber to fix the place up?"

Xiamara shrugged. "Mother can, and has, traded her services in exchange for some work to stop the roof from leaking and to replace the rotting stairs, but it would be easier if my brothers stuck around long enough to help out sometimes." She poked Cephas in the chest and turned towards the table to knead the dough. "Are you going to be staying?" She paused and looked up at him.

Cephas looked down. "Not for long," he whispered.

Xiamara frowned and mumbled something Ethelwynne didn't catch as she went back to kneading. "Uncle Sher and Talman are planning on stopping by for supper later. Can you and the lovely lady you've failed to introduce stay for that at least?"

"That's the plan," Cephas said. "We'll even stay the night—just for you."

"Mmhmm. I'm sure it has nothing to do with you needing something from the shops that are shut."

Ethelwynne took in the humble house as she listened to the exchange. The rough-hewed table and chairs, the moth-eaten curtains, the dusty vials and shockingly spotless bandages on a shelf by the door, and the comfortable air. Love held this building up. She turned to face the sibling duo.

Xiamara was looking at her. When their eyes met, she turned her gaze on Cephas as she finished rolling the dough into balls and placing them in a pan. "Were you planning on introducing your friend?" Xiamara asked as she carried the buns over to the fire to rise.

Cephas smiled and laughed.

Xiamara put her hands on her hips covering her skirt in flour and stopped talking long enough for Cephas to introduce Ethelwynne to her.

"Nice to meet you." She dusted off her hands and picked up a knife to chop some vegetables for the soup. "Do you want a dress to wear or are you happy in that?" She waved the knife at Ethelwynne's pants and shirt.

Ethelwynne looked down at what she was wearing. It felt like ages since she'd worn a dress. She missed the way they swished when she walked, but running through the forest was much easier when she didn't have to hold up her skirt to do it. And if Cephas let down his guard, she would have to do that again. In fact, she was a little surprised that he had chosen to bring her here instead of bringing her to jail. "I'm fine."

Xiamara nodded and went back to chopping up the vegetables. She put the knife down and shoved the buns in the oven.

There was a knock on the door, but before any of them could move to open it, Sher walked in and looked around. Confusion and relief splashed across his face when he spotted Cephas. He ran over and swept his nephew up in a hug. "Glad to see you're alright boy. But uh," he glanced over Cephas's shoulder at Ethelwynne, "I would have thought you would have gone straight to White Shield instead of coming here."

"I would have thought the same for you," said Cephas.

"Nah, ship was too damaged to make it that far." He shrugged. "Captain Marino is right ticked about having to limp here instead, but at least we were able to sell the goods to a local merchant, so the food won't spoil and the rich people of Stormont will eat like kings."

"Well, we know of a logger who would be willing to sell Captain Marino some wood at a decent price."

Ethelwynne smiled but didn't bother letting him know that that wasn't how it would work unless Captain Marino also knew someone who would be able to plane the wood for her.

"And the girl? Why is she here?" asked Sher.

Cephas glanced over at her.

Ethelwynne flushed and kicked the ground lightly. What she wouldn't give to have someone see her as a merchant instead of a thief again.

"We ran into an elf who's hunting her," he said after a moment. "She wanted to kill Ethelwynne. But since that's not the punishment for thieves here, I refused. The elf didn't appreciate that very much, so we ran."

"And you came here?"

Cephas shrugged. "It was closer and we ran into a lumber barge that was heading this way."

Sher stroked his beard. "The girl still has to get to White Shield, but we don't want to fight every elf on the way there—"

"She could wear a disguise," Xiamara piped up. She walked over and pinched her brother's cheek, "Look at you being all rebellious and helping thieves."

Cephas swatted her arm away.

"Xiamara," Sher interrupted before Cephas could

respond, "do you know if your mother left behind any charms that could help Ethelwynne change up her appearance a bit?"

Xiamara picked up the vegetables and plopped them into the pot that was starting to boil. "You don't need a charm for that. We can get you everything you need in the market." She turned and studied Ethelwynne for a moment and opened her mouth to begin talking again "for instance we'll need—"

The door opened and a curly-haired young man entered. As the door swung shut behind him, his jaw opened and he stopped in his tracks as he took in Sher and Cephas standing in the kitchen.

"Talman!" bellowed Sher walking over to embrace him.

Talman looked past him and arched his eyebrow in Ethelwynne's direction. "Who are you? And what's with the pants?"

Sher shrugged, "It's easier to work on a ship in pants. Can you imagine trying to tie up some rigging in a dress? This is Ethelwynne by the way. Like you, she has a knack for getting into trouble."

Talman winked. "Sounds like fun."

"Don't get too attached," said Cephas as he sat down at the table. "I'm taking her to the guards in White Shield."

Talman sighed and joined his brother at the table. "I should have known you'd be no fun." He sniffed. "What smells like it's burning?"

"The buns!" yelped Xiamara and rushed to pull them from the oven. She fanned the black tops frantically and bit her lower lip.

"It's fine Xia," said Sher. "They're just extra crispy. That's all."

Cephas and Talman nodded their agreement and each grabbed a bun from the tray she placed them on, bouncing the hot buns from one hand to the other before setting them down with a clatter on their plates.

"Speaking of being no fun," said Talman waving a fork-speared carrot in Cephas's direction, "if you want to just let the girl go, the guards here need to fill some spots—a bunch of them are retiring." He elbowed Ethelwynne then lay his hand over his heart. "I promise not to let her get into too much trouble. Besides, if you have a guard's income, maybe you can convince mom to move before the roof falls on her head."

"She's never going to move," said Xiamara. "She's worried that a change of location would put off her poorest clients. So if you guys do end up sticking around, you'd better get good at using a hammer." She looked at her brothers pointedly as she spoke.

"If Cephas does that, you could take his place on *The Passerine*," suggested Sher.

Talman shook his head. "I like my feet flat on the ground."

"Or rooftops," Xiamara said smiling sweetly.

Talman laughed. "Houses are still on the ground. Besides, I'm thinking of joining a logging crew."

"You do realize that logging boats don't float on the ground, right?" said Xiamara. "There's this thing called water."

Talman tossed his burnt bun at her.

*　　*　　*

When the meal was finished Talman went out with some friends and Xiamara showed Ethelwynne to the room they would share for the night. "It's not the most comfortable, but I can go get a few more blankets. Make it a bit more cushiony." As she went in search of more blankets, Ethelwynne walked back to the main room to speak with Cephas. She wanted to know why he hadn't immediately brought her to the town guards. She slowed her steps when she heard Sher and Cephas talking.

"I won't let Captain Marino know I saw you, so you can come and join us when you're done," said Sher.

Cephas sighed. "You don't want to trade places? I'll go help fix the ship and you can bring her to White Shield."

Sher laughed. "No can do. If the captain sees you, she'll demand that you ditch the girl with the local guards or lose your job with her." The door thumped shut.

"Hey, here you go." Xiamara handed Ethelwynne an extra blanket. "We can head to the market in the morning to grab the make-up and stuff."

Ethelwynne nodded and looked over at Cephas who joined them in the hall. He leaned against the wall and studied her.

Xiamara followed her gaze, "See you in a few minutes, Ethelwynne. Good night Cephas."

"Good night Xia."

Xiamara hugged her brother and disappeared into her room.

Ethelwynne played with the corners of the blanket. "Why aren't you turning me in?"

"If the elf told the guards here that the Prince of the Elves wanted you for theft, they would give you to her. In White Shield, you will get a trial. However," he said stepping forward—any trace of levity from an evening spent with his family vanished from his face, "if you run, I will find you, and I will dump you with the first town guards I find, even if I know they'll pass you off to her."

Ethelwynne swallowed and nodded. "I won't run," she whispered. "I promise." Cephas stepped back and she walked past him into the room she was sharing with Xiamara.

— CHAPTER TEN —

On the Rooftops

Cephas did not join them for breakfast. Xiamara mentioned that he had already left for the day. Ethelwynne's heart raced as she ate the burnt fish and bread. Even with Cephas's threat still ringing in her ears she considered slipping out when Xiamara was distracted. She didn't think it would be too difficult to find her way to White Shield from here.

The door opened and Sher walked in and swept his niece up in a hug. Ethelwynne shoved her fork into her mouth to stifle a sigh. She doubted he would let her out of his sight.

When the last of the food had been eaten or tossed, Ethelwynne and Xiamara cleared the table. "If you would like I can make the next meal," Ethelwynne offered as they did some dishes. "Your family has been so kind, it's the least I can do."

"Oh, you don't have to do that. What kind of people would we be if we didn't help you?" Xiamara said as she put the last of the bowls away. "Alright then, let's get you dressed to go out."

"Out?" asked Ethelwynne as she followed Xiamara back to the room the two of them had shared the night before. Ethelwynne couldn't believe that they were going to let her leave the house.

"How else are we going to get you a disguise?"

Ethelwynne bit her lip. "Your brother is okay with me leaving the house?" She hoped the question wouldn't change Xiamara's decision to leave, but she didn't really want to risk running into Cephas while they were out and have him assume she was running. Ethelwynne wasn't sure she was prepared for that yet.

Xiamara opened her closet and pulled out a green dress as she shrugged. "Well he's not here, so..." she held up the dress to Ethelwynne, frowned, and pulled out a pink floral one instead. "I get that pants make a lot of sense if you're working on a ship, but here in the city, you'll stick out like a sore thumb especially with that horrible haircut. Looks like someone cut it while wearing a blindfold."

Ethelwynne gently patted her hair as she blushed.

Xiamara handed her the dress then walked over to the vanity. Sitting down she opened up a myriad of vials that were filled with makeup and began to paint her face. "Because of the festival, no one is going to look twice if we have our faces decorated today. So, no one will recognize you, and I can do something with your hair so it doesn't look like a rat's nest."

"It's the morning," Ethelwynne looked at Xiamara quizzically. "Where I'm from, we usually only paint our faces when we're heading to the bonfire at the end of the festival."

"You are missing out," Xiamara laughed. "What a waste to spend all that time decorating your face to only show it to people after dark. I mean sure the lights of a flickering fire can be romantic and all that, but I want people to see this masterpiece." She circled her face and turned back to the mirror to continue painting it. "Get dressed while I'm finishing. It'll be easier to deal with your hair and makeup then."

Once Xiamara was finished putting on her own makeup, she began to work on Ethelwynne, yanking and pulling what remained of Ethelwynne's hair into a braid interwoven with flowers. Ethelwynne flinched with each tug. Her eyes watered from both the pain on her scalp and the realization that there was no way she could walk to White Shield in this getup. The only chance she would have to survive was if people and elves didn't notice she was there.

"Perfect. Now it looks like you've got long hair again." Xiamara took a step back to marvel at her handiwork. "Well, almost perfect. Remind me to fix up your hair for real when we get back."

She bit the end of her thumb as she studied Ethelwynne. Then she picked out a few jars of makeup, grabbed some brushes, and began covering Ethelwynne with the creams and powders.

"This is amazing," said Ethelwynne. The black and orange butterflies Xiamara painted across her face looked like they were flying over to land in the flower field that was her hair. The goddess should be pleased by the details and devotion Xiamara put into capturing the likeness of the creature chosen to represent her. "No wonder you dress up like this for the whole day. No one around me is this good."

"Perhaps they are, but since you only see them in the firelight you don't really get to appreciate it." Xiamara grabbed Ethelwynne's hands as they hovered over her cheeks. "Don't touch it. You might undo all my hard work, and we do not have time to fix it. All of the best items will be gone if we don't leave now."

Sher was leaning against the table when they came in. He handed Xiamara a purse with some change in it for the disguise. Xiamara giggled and handed Ethelwynne a basket as she pulled her out the door. "This way," she said as she hurried down a few blocks and across the bridge that divided the lower class from the upper class.

Ethelwynne tried to memorize all of the twists and turns they took as they wove their way to the market. She was positive Cephas would keep his promise and turn her in to the closest town guard if she ran away and he was able to find her, so she wasn't intending to run. But if she thought he was changing his mind about bringing her to White Shield instead of turning her into the guards here, or if she discovered that Heotene was in the city, she wanted to know a way out.

As they approached the town square, they slowed down and wandered through the market. Almost all of the women were wearing costumes like Ethelwynne and Xiamara. Although Ethelwynne noted, few of the other women looked as exquisite as the two of them.

They stopped at a variety of vendors to look at their wares. Xiamara picked up several different items and showed them to Ethelwynne. At several different booths, Xiamara asked the vendor about the price. Each time the amount given made Ethelwynne blanch and turn down the necklaces or earrings Xiamara was holding. There was no way she could spend someone else's money on something so expensive and unnecessary.

"What do you think of this one?" Xiamara held up her hand which now sported an extravagant silver ring with an emerald on it.

"I don't know. Can we go now?"

Xiamara sighed, took the ring off and put it back on the table. After thanking the vendor for his time, she walked away with Ethelwynne and pulled her into the nearest alleyway. Then, with an exasperated tone that one might use on a mischievous child, Xiamara remarked, "If we just went and got what you're looking for, someone might notice and think it suspicious. I'm merely making this outing look more normal."

"Fine," Ethelwynne snapped. "But that was the sixth

stall we've stopped at, and we haven't purchased a single item that I might actually need."

"Besides," Xiamara continued, completely ignoring Ethelwynne's outburst, "you aren't currently wearing any jewelry, perhaps it would throw them off if you suddenly started."

"You do realize your brother wants to throw me in prison, right? A bracelet isn't going to do me any good there."

"No, but it might help you not go to jail."

Ethelwynne threw her hands in the air. "How? How exactly will it help me?"

"Because I know my brother." Xiamara put her hands on Ethelwynne's shoulders and continued speaking. "Look, my brother loves to protect people, but with the pants and the hacked off hair, you don't really look like a woman who wants to be kept safe. If you're not going to wear a dress, maybe something shiny will remind my darling brother that you are a woman who desperately needs his help." She turned around and started walking back towards the market. "And who knows, maybe once he decides you're someone worth taking care of, he'll decide that means keeping you safe from the horror and shame of prison."

Ethelwynne stared at her agape. "Do... do you believe me?"

Xiamara looked back at her and shrugged. "I like you, but what I think doesn't really matter. Cephas, is who we need to convince."

Ethelwynne threw her hands up in defeat and followed Xiamara back into the square. "Alright, but can we at least look at something I might be able to afford. It would take forever for me to be able to pay you back for this."

"But that stuff's not as pretty," Xiamara moaned as she walked away from the jewelry booths close to them and towards one where the jewelry was significantly less fancy with much smaller gemstones. She looked back wistfully at the vendor with the green ring, "That ring was so lovely." Xiamara sniffed. "You don't know what you're missing."

Ethelwynne rolled her eyes and picked up a simple silver chain with a small flower pendant dangling from it. "What about this?"

Xiamara made a face. "You might as well not even wear jewelry if you're going to choose that one."

Ethelwynne sighed and put the necklace back on the table.

The scowl on the vendor's face grew as Xiamara continued to disparage all of the simpler pieces he had on display, especially when Ethelwynne also turned down all of the more exquisite items. The two women decided to leave before he called the guards to remove them for wasting his time.

"I'd feel bad spending your family's money on something like that," Ethelwynne explained as they headed to a different table.

Xiamara rolled her eyes.

"Besides, I like plain jewelry."

"You have no style." Xiamara poked her in the center of her chest.

"When my life is normal, I make and design clothes for people. I have style."

Xiamara's eyebrows eked up on her forehead. "I bet they're all practical."

Ethelwynne pursed her lips and chose not to answer.

"That's what I thought." Xiamara shook her head and muttered about how "There's no magic in that" as she walked to a stall that didn't sell jewelry. "Regardless of whether or not you want jewelry, you will need these," she said picking up a variety of plant leaves, flower petals, and oils for Ethelwynne's disguise. "I'll show you how to make the dyes and makeups later so that you can bring some with you and keep up the disguise until you're sure you're safe."

Ethelwynne looked at all of the items that Xiamara had put in her basket. "I don't really wear makeup," she said. Her insides tightened with each new jar or bag Xiamara added. She would never remember how to use them all.

Xiamara looked over at her and rolled her eyes. "It's not that bad. I'm sure you can put up with it for a little while. I mean it's this, or being found by someone who wants you dead." She grabbed Ethelwynne by the arm and led her to yet another stall. "Let's go grab some small jars for you to keep the powders in once they're made, and then I need to get some bread." She stopped in front of the stall and selected five small jars. After she checked to make sure the corks created a good seal without being impossible to pull out, she paid for them and carefully place them in the basket. Then she walked towards one of the buildings that ringed the market stalls.

Ethelwynne toyed with the jars they'd purchased as she followed Xiamara towards the bakery. "Do you think I'll be able to convince Cephas to help me?"

Xiamara stopped in the middle of the street and looked at her. Several other shoppers almost ran into the two women before she continued towards the bakers. "It's possible. Like I said, he does enjoy helping people out..." she paused at the entrance of the shop, "but we can talk about this at home."

The scents of loaves of bread and buns wafted through the air as they stepped inside. "Mmm..." Ethelwynne took a deep breath.

Xiamara handed her a few buns. They were still warm against her fingers. Ethelwynne held one close to her face and closed her eyes as she inhaled its scent. Her mouth watered. Ethelwynne shoved it in her basket and covered it with the cloth so that she wouldn't be tempted to eat one or more of the buns right here.

The bell on the door jingled. Ethelwynne looked up from

her basket and watched with wide eyes as Heotene walked to the counter to buy some food. Her heart stopped. She struggled to fill her lungs. Ethelwynne bit her lip and reminded herself that there was no way for the elf to recognize her in this outfit. She looked nothing like herself with the face paint.

She glanced down to make sure the cloth covered everything in the basket and prayed that the soft buns would cushion and muffle the sounds of the vials and jars gently bumping into each other. Ethelwynne felt the panic rising within her as she forced herself to look away from the elf. If Heotene hadn't recognized her yet, there was no way she was going to make it easy for her by openly staring at her in horror.

She walked over to Xiamara who was still hemming and hawing over what bread she should buy and tugged at her sleeve. "We need to leave now," she whispered as softly as she could while desperately trying to keep the look of panic out of her eyes.

Xiamara turned to face her and her expression changed from annoyance to concern. "I'm almost done," she answered, then she turned back to the assistant who was helping her and pointed at a loaf. "That one Patrick."

Patrick nodded and wrapped up the bread and a few extra buns for them as Xiamara counted out the change.

Ethelwynne watched the elf out of the corner of her eye. She was still haggling with the baker. Ethelwynne closed her eyes and focused on breathing. Since Heotene had not attacked them in front of the loggers when they were in the middle of the forest, she wasn't likely to kill her here in the bakery where there were even more witnesses. She started bouncing on the balls of her feet as she waited for Xiamara to finish up.

"Okay, we're done," said Xiamara once Patrick handed her the package. "Let's go home." She waved to Patrick over her shoulder as they walked from the store. Xiamara looped her arm through Ethelwynne's and wandered down the street. "We can't run or we'll draw attention to ourselves," she whispered as they walked through the market.

Ethelwynne chanced a peek behind her. The elf was leaving the store and lazily strolling in their direction flitting from one vender to another. Heotene's gaze trapped Ethelwynne's as the elf glanced their way. "I'm pretty sure it's too late for that."

Xiamara licked her lips. "He's here?"

Ethelwynne shuddered. "She, and yes. She was in the bakery."

Xiamara's eyes widened. "The... the elf?" She looked behind them to where the elf was trailing them. Her face paled. "What now? What are we going to do? We need to get home. Guards? Will the guards help...?"

Ethelwynne shook her head. "We can't ask the guards for help."

Xiamara whimpered.

"I think we need to find Cephas or Sher." Ethelwynne peeked behind them again. The elf was nowhere to be seen.

Xiamara nodded. "Yes, you're right. One of them can help." She nodded some more and shook herself. "Right. Yes. We need to find my brother or Uncle Sher, but we can't go straight home." She started walking again. The fear she'd expressed moments before melted away with each step and soon confidence oozed out of her. Ethelwynne wished she knew how to replicate the woman's sense of calm. "Let's try to lose her in the market first." Xiamara pulled Ethelwynne through the busy market.

Ethelwynne prayed that they would soon blend into the colorful crowd out celebrating the festival, but, since this was now the second time Heotene had found her, Ethelwynne wasn't sure their ruse would work. The words of the elf captain flashed through her mind. What if Heotene was using magic?

Without warning, Xiamara turned and pulled Ethelwynne down a narrow road. "This way. Don't drop the basket," Xiamara warned before she broke into a run and sprinted down the alley and pulled Ethelwynne around the second corner.

Ethelwynne's heart started racing faster than her feet. She wondered if she would ever get used to running for her life. As her feet pounded against the cobblestones, she decided that she hoped the answer was no. With the goddess's help, this nightmare would be over long before she became accustomed to the fear.

Xiamara pulled her down another alleyway and up some wooden stairs on the side of a building. The steps creaked in protest and Ethelwynne was sure at least one was going to splinter beneath her feet. Xiamara ducked through a window on the top floor and pulled Ethelwynne inside. "We can lose her through here."

"We're in someone's house," Ethelwynne whispered with wide eyes as she looked around the bedroom. The blanket was crumpled on the foot of the bed, and a change of clothes was draped over the back of a chair.

Xiamara opened the door and disappeared into the room across the hall. "Yes. So there's a good chance she won't think we went this way. Shut the door behind you."

Ethelwynne gaped like a fish but did as she was told. The other cleaner-looking bedroom had double doors that opened up onto a balcony.

Xiamara hopped over the railing and onto the roof beside it. She ran across the sloped surface and agilely jumped to the next roof where she paused to make sure Ethelwynne was following.

Ethelwynne hesitated on the balcony. *It's this or go back to the elves*, she reminded herself, but it didn't make her feel any better. She bit her lip and hopped over the railing. Her feet slipped on the roof tiles as she stumbled across it.

"Don't slow down," Xiamara called back to her and reached out to help her make the leap.

Ethelwynne yelped as she left the roof. Her feet touched the tiles on the other house and she flopped forward into Xiamara's arms.

"Alright. Good job. No more stopping or she might see us." Xiamara took off again.

Ethelwynne followed her and tried her best to keep up as they moved from rooftop to rooftop. Several of the buildings had flat roofs with gardens growing on them, but unfortunately for Ethelwynne, most of the roofs they darted across were slanted.

"We're almost there," whispered Xiamara as she got down on her stomach and slipped off the edge of the roof feet first. Ethelwynne lay down beside her and watched with relief as Xiamara dangled from her arms and dropped a foot to the ground. Ethelwynne spun her body around and dropped down beside her. The two women leaned against the wall to catch their breath.

When they had arrived at the market earlier this morning, Ethelwynne had been sure she would have been able to find her way back to the house. Now she had no idea where they were. All she knew was they still had to cross the river. "How are we getting across the bridge without anyone seeing us?" Ethelwynne asked between gasps.

Xiamara shook her head and held her sides. "We can't," she said when she finally had enough air to spare. "But we'll try to act natural and hope she doesn't speak to anyone who's seen us."

"There's no other way across?" Ethelwynne rubbed her arms and rocked back and forth as she furtively looked out of the alleyway and saw the bridge looming before them. She tried to swallow to add moisture to her dry mouth but she wasn't able to.

"We could hop across those boats and logs," said Xiamara pointing to the floating pathway beside the bridge, "but that would definitely be noticed." She fixed her dress and headscarf. "Okay. I'm ready." Xiamara turned to face Ethelwynne and touched up the flowers in her hair. "There. Good?"

Ethelwynne curled her hands tightly around the basket's handle. She closed her eyes for a moment to steel herself for this walk. It felt so exposed. Her nails pressed against her palms. When she released the handle with one hand, small half-moon shapes showed her where each of her fingers had been. She nodded at Xiamara.

They linked elbows and casually walked out of the alley. Xiamara tried to engage Ethelwynne in a conversation, but neither woman really felt like speaking. They kept looking behind them or down the roads beside them to see if the elf had found them already.

They stepped onto the bridge with a soft thud. The wooden boards creaked beneath them. The water rippled past them underneath. A stray log clattered into the channel's wall. "One... two... three..." Ethelwynne faintly counted her steps as they crossed the exposed expanse. "Twenty-six... twenty-seven." Her foot touched the cobblestone on the other side.

"Just a little further," murmured Xiamara as she walked stiffly to the houses that lined the road and would hide them from the bridge.

Once the two of them cleared the houseline, they broke into a run and didn't stop until they burst through the door of Xiamara's home. Xiamara slammed it behind them and the two women collapsed on the floor.

At the sound, Sher and Talman looked up at them from their Game of Shala. When they saw the panic on Ethelwynne's and Xiamara's faces both men stood up and abandoned the game. Talman reached for his scabbard on his chair. Sher dropped his black tower piece on the table as he reached for his ax. It landed on the table with a clatter and knocked the other tokens over. One of the white egg-shaped pieces rolled off onto the floor.

Ethelwynne watched it spin around before coming to a stop. She tried to blink back her tears, but they fell off her cheeks anyway. "She's here." She pulled the flowers out of her hair. "She saw us."

"Who saw you?" Talman asked, confusion spreading across his face.

"Are you sure she recognized you?" asked Sher. "I don't recognize you."

Ethelwynne glanced at the door behind her and pictured Heotene's casual stride as she walked towards them. "I'm sure." She wiped her eyes and decided not to tell Sher her theory about Heotene. She wouldn't make it out of town without their help if Heotene was using magic. "I don't know how. But I'm sure."

"Who saw you?" Talman repeated.

"Well, we can't stay here anymore," said Sher. He looked around to assess what they would need to take with them. "Even if she didn't follow the two of you back from the market, she knows you came here with Cephas. All it would take are a few well-placed questions and she'd learn he lives here."

Talman slammed his empty hand down on the table. The other three looked at him. "Who saw you? And why does that mean we have to abandon our home?"

"Ah, well..." started Ethelwynne before trailing off.

"An elf is hunting Ethelwynne," Sher answered.

Talman swore and punched the wall. Dust and splinters fell to the ground from the hole he created.

Ethelwynne jumped.

Talman angrily shoved his sword back into its scabbard. "When you said she liked to get into trouble, I didn't think you meant someone wants to kill her." He stormed over to Ethelwynne and Xiamara and yanked the two women back onto their feet. "Let's get going then. I have some friends who could hide us, but," he looked pointedly at Xiamara and Sher, "Cephas can't know about them or where they live."

Ethelwynne shuddered as his scowl rested on her for a moment.

"No," said Sher. "Cephas needs to know where Ethelwynne is. We need a different option."

"I know where we can stay," said Xiamara, "but we'll have to go after dark. Do you think we'll be safe here until then?"

Sher nodded. "Grab everything you're going to need. We won't be coming back here any time soon," said Sher. As he waved them through the doorway to their sleeping quarters, he tossed Ethelwynne a bag. "Here. You can put your things in this."

"Thanks." Ethelwynne followed Xiamara into her room and dumped their purchases into the bag Sher had just given her. Then she changed back into pants. If she was going to be running across roofs again, she did not want to have a skirt waving about her legs threatening to trip her and knock her to the ground far below. Not when she could help it.

"You'll also need the mortar and pestle," said Xiamara as she packed her own things. She picked up a gold necklace with a purple pendant and hugged it close. "There's one in the front room by the locked cabinet that you can take. Shoot. The herbs, I'll need those." She got up and walked out of the room with Ethelwynne following behind her.

In the front room, she put down the necklace to hand Ethelwynne the mortar and pestle for her bag, and pulled out the contents of the cupboard and wrapped them in clothes before placing them in a separate basket with a different mortar and pestle. "We have spares," she answered when she saw Ethelwynne's confused look.

"Hey Xia? I'm hungry, can you grab me some food," called Talman.

"Yeah, sure," said Xiamara. She wandered over to the kitchen area and pulled out some cheese before going to her room to grab the bread they purchased for lunch. With the simple meal prepped, Xiamara looked over everything she had packed. "We're ready."

Sher looked at them, then shook his head and smiled as he circled his face with his fingers. "You should take that off. Since you know, she's seen you in it."

Ethelwynne flushed under her make-up. Talman went outside and filled a bucket with water so the two women could wipe their faces clean. Then they waited. Cephas didn't return, but Ethelwynne was too scared to ask them where he was. After a tense and silent afternoon, the sun vanished below the horizon and it was time to leave.

CHRISTINA VAN STARKENBURG

— CHAPTER ELEVEN —

Xiamara's Necklace

The four companions slipped out of the back door and began their trip through the alleyways and up along roof-top paths to Lady Kiran's house. As they ran, Xiamara stayed beside Ethelwynne and quietly explained to her that Lady Kiran was a woman whom most people didn't know she and her family had any connection to because of the Lady's high status within the city.

"Several years ago," Xiamara whispered as they crept along, "her three sons nearly died from a fever. The other healers in the area that the wealthy tend to visit, weren't able to do anything. So she came to Mother." She stopped talking as they came close to a road.

Sher leaned into the wall behind him. He put his finger up to his lip to silence them as he listened.

All Ethelwynne could hear was their own breathing. She shivered and rubbed her arms that were covered in goosebumps despite the warmth of the night.

Sher nodded and turned to them. "Just act casual." He paused to look at each one of them in the eyes. "Don't run, just walk. I'll go first. Count to twenty, then follow." He turned around and strolled across the street. As he

disappeared into the alley on the other side Ethelwynne heard
Xiamara counting under her breath. When she reached
twenty, she took a deep breath and walked across the road
behind her uncle.

Ethelwynne felt sweat beading on her forehead as she
internally counted to twenty. Something clattered behind her
and she lost her place. She looked around frantically but saw
nothing.

Talman shoved her towards the road. "Move."

Her pulse pounded in her ears. Mindless of what Sher
said she ran across the road and collided with him as he
waited for her.

He looked around over the top of her head. "I don't see
anything," he whispered. "I think we're still good. Let's keep
moving." He let go and walked down the alley.

Ethelwynne nodded. Her legs felt wobbly as she
followed him. When this was over, she was never leaving
home ever again. Her parents could travel to the elven lands
on their own, or her brother could if he needed a break from
the farm. But whatever happened, she was staying put.

Talman pushed her forward. "Move it," he hissed.

She bit her lip and started walking faster.

"Anyway," continued Xiamara interrupting
Ethelwynne's thoughts, "Lady Kiran said she would lend us
whatever aid we needed should something happen. Being
hunted by someone seems like a good reason to call in the
favor."

A walled manor loomed in front of them. The four
companions walked around to the back gate where the
servants' entrance was. Xiamara knocked. After a few
moments, the gatekeeper arrived and she spoke quietly to
him.

The gatekeeper put his hands up in front of himself to
stop them. "Wait here," he whispered. Then he ran across the
courtyard and into the house. Moments later he reappeared

and unlocked the gate. He looked out down the alley as he waved them towards the house.

Talman whispered something to Sher before turning and walking back down the alley. Ethelwynne watched him leave and wondered if he was going to go find Cephas and let him know what happened and where they went. The gate clicked shut behind him, and the gatekeeper relocked it.

Once inside they were ushered into a quaint sitting room. A stern-looking woman in a deep maroon dress sat in one of the chairs waiting for them. She waved her hand and gestured for them to sit down.

"Hello, Xiamara. Welcome to my home. Samson tells me you have a problem."

"Yes," Xiamara started but Lady Kiran put up a hand to cut her off.

"I don't need to know why you're hiding if you do not wish to tell me. However, I do need to know who you are hiding from so my guards can be alerted to any potential danger." She turned to study each of them in turn.

Xiamara glanced at Ethelwynne and her uncle before continuing. "There's an elf ma'am."

Lady Kiran nodded and tapped her finger on her chin as she listened to Ethelwynne and Xiamara describe Heotene. "I shall inform my guards." She rose and glided to the door. Lady Kiran paused in the arch and turned back to face them. "Please make yourselves at home while you are here. You may stay as long as you need to. I will forever be in debt to your mother." Then she called one of her servants over to show them to the guest rooms where they would be staying.

*   *   *

Ethelwynne shut the door behind her and Xiamara and crumpled to the floor. She felt exhausted by her fear and the flight. "I shouldn't have gone to the market."

Xiamara murmured something in response as she walked over to the vanity. The bare surface was immediately covered in jars with what seemed like every color of cream or powder as Xiamara meticulously spread out all of her supplies. "Of course this would happen during the festival. Couldn't be any old time when I don't need all of my makeup and dyes and whatnot."

She gave the arrangement a satisfied smile and turned to her bag again. She pulled out her clothes and hung them in the closet. Then a few pieces of jewelry were carefully laid on the vanity before she began to rifle through her bag.

"Heotene won't stick around forever," said Ethelwynne. "After a couple of days—"

"Who?" Xiamara stopped digging through her bag and tilted her head to face Ethelwynne.

"The elf, her name is Heotene."

"She just told you her name? Hi, I'm Heotene, and I'm here to kill you?" Xiamara upended the remainder of her bag's contents on the bed and frantically sorted through them.

Ethelwynne sat down on the other bed and sank into the mattress ever so slightly as she nodded. She figured it would be safer if Xiamara didn't know the real reason why the elves wanted to kill her, so she remained silent. "What are you looking for?" Ethelwynne asked getting up off the bed. "Maybe I could help you find it?"

Xiamara looked up at her. Her eyes welled with tears. "I can't find my necklace," she sobbed. She blinked rapidly and ran her fingers under her eyes to stop herself from crying. "I don't know where I put it."

Ethelwynne picked up the bag. "Maybe it got caught in here. What's it look like?" She felt along the entire inside of the bag and its pockets. When she didn't find it, she turned to her own bag in case the necklace had been dropped into the wrong bag. It wasn't there.

Xiamara sat on her bed and cried.

Ethelwynne sat down beside her and hugged her. "Let's get some sleep. We're probably both so tired that we're just missing it."

Xiamara nodded and curled up under the blanket without changing into her nightgown.

Ethelwynne changed and slipped under her own covers before blowing out the lantern. She listened to Xiamara's subdued sobs humming in the darkness. After a while, the sounds from the other bed stopped and Ethelwynne rolled over to try and get some sleep herself.

When she was almost asleep, Ethelwynne heard the gentle tingle of jars as Xiamara cried out softly when she bumped into the vanity. Several bottles clinked together as they fell over. Ethelwynne opened her eyes in time to see Xiamara catch one that rolled over the edge. "What are you doing?" she mumbled.

"Sorry. Didn't mean to wake you." Xiamara put the vial back on the vanity and walked over to the window. "I'll be right back, don't worry."

Ethelwynne sat up. "Are you crazy? It's the middle of the night. Can't this wait until morning? Or could you send Talman when he gets back? Heotene saw you with me."

Xiamara stopped opening the window and turned to face Ethelwynne. The moonlight shimmered off of her tear-streaked cheeks.

"I forgot the necklace Uncle Sher gave me after my dad left." She wiped her eyes. "I thought I grabbed it, but I must have put it down when Talman asked me to help him with the food and then I forgot to pick it back up."

"And the men wouldn't understand." Ethelwynne reached over and hugged her. "Okay. Let's go get it then."

"What? No. I can't ask you to do that."

"I'm not completely useless," said Ethelwynne as she threw on her clothes. "At the very least I can watch your back."

Xiamara was silent for a moment, then she nodded, "Thanks." She reached inside her cloak and handed Ethelwynne a couple of daggers, "You might need these." After Ethelwynne pocketed the blades, Xiamara crawled out into the night and landed in the courtyard below.

Ethelwynne hopped down to the ground beside Xiamara. The two of them leaned into the wall behind them and listened to see if anyone else in the manor was still up. Safe in the knowledge that their departure was still hidden from those who would stop them, they darted to the outside wall. Ethelwynne pointed to some barrels that were leaning against the wall by the stable and the two young women used them as steps to hop over the wall.

Ethelwynne wasn't entirely sure how they were going to get back in to Lady Kiran's. But that was a future problem so she tried not to dwell on it. After all, they could just knock on the gate again. Right now, they needed to focus on crossing Stormont without being seen, grabbing the necklace, and returning unscathed.

Ethelwynne scanned the black path behind them to see if anyone noticed their descent, but the alleyway they landed in was empty. This was a good start. No one to bother them, and no one to alert the authorities that they saw two people leaving a building in this part of town by hopping over the wall instead of going through the gate.

Xiamara started running for the road, but Ethelwynne grabbed her and pulled her back further into the shadows before she reached the road. She leaned into the shadows and listened for the sounds of shoes padding across the cobblestone.

"We're trying to be quick," whispered Xiamara.

"True, but I'd rather not have someone panic and call the guards because they think they're going to be robbed."

"Oh." Xiamara looked at her feet. If it had been brighter

in that alleyway, Ethelwynne was sure she would have seen her blushing. "I hadn't thought of that."

Ethelwynne shrugged and leaned against the courtyard's wall so she could see further down the road. "That way's clear." Xiamara mimicked her movements to check the other direction. "Same."

The two women slipped out of the alleyway and started walking down the road keeping close to the shadows just in case someone looked out an upper window at Lady Kiran's place.

They came to the river that split the city in half. Some guards were leaning on the bridge's banister, joking with one another before they split off to continue their patrol of the city's mostly empty streets. It was only a few moments before the two men split off in opposite directions, but Xiamara was bouncing on the balls of her feet by the time they were far enough away from the bridge for the women to cross unnoticed.

"They're not doing a very good job," Xiamara mumbled when they were across the bridge and the guards were no longer preventing her from getting to her necklace.

Ethelwynne rolled her eyes and smiled at the young woman's change in opinion. "I'm sure they'd be more vigilant if they had something specific to watch out for. Besides, it's not like we're not allowed to be out at this hour, we'd just prefer not to have any questions asked about why we are."

Xiamara muttered something that Ethelwynne took to be agreement as they continued to wind their way through the city streets. At Ethelwynne's urging they stuck to the roads. Jumping from roof-top to roof-top in the middle of the day or earlier that night when the moon was full and bright was difficult enough. Now that the moon was playing-hide-and-seek behind wispy clouds she was sure she would miss a ledge and fall to the ground.

As they got closer to the house the two women couldn't help but feel more anxious. They spent more time looking over their shoulders to see if anyone was watching them. The last thing they wanted was for Ethelwynne's tail to catch them without anyone knowing where they were.

Xiamara stealthily unlocked the backdoor and slipped into the dark house. Ethelwynne followed her inside. The floor creaked as they walked through the kitchen. Both women jumped.

Xiamara shook her head. "Sorry," she whispered, "that was me. I forgot the floorboard was loose there."

"It's okay," Ethelwynne whispered back. Xiamara got on her hands and knees and felt around the floor in front of the herb cabinet while Ethelwynne ran her hands purposely across the tables. The moon appeared from behind a cloud and cast an eerie glow into the abandoned home.

Something glinted in the soft light by the cabinet. "There." Ethelwynne pointed at it and walked over to where the necklace lay. "Is this it?"

Xiamara walked over and took the necklace from her. "Yes, she said, smiling slightly.

"Perfect. Now, all we need to do is get back," Ethelwynne said as she turned towards the door.

No footsteps followed her. She turned around and watched as Xiamara tried to put the necklace on. Xiamara fumbled trying to put it on in the dark. Ethelwynne walked over and helped her.

They heard a soft thud on one of the nearby roofs as they left the building. They both darted into the relative safety of the shadows and waited. No more sounds followed them. Breathing a shared sigh of relief Xiamara and Ethelwynne slunk back towards Lady Kiran's home for the second time that night.

They crossed the river and slipped into an alleyway. Several guardsmen walked past.

The two women slowly backed further into the shadows. Ethelwynne's heel bumped into something solid moments before arms wrapped around their waists and hands clamped over their mouths.

Xiamara flailed and her elbow connected with her attacker's chin.

He grunted and shoved Xiamara into the wall. Xiamara let out a muffled yelp, as her attacker pressed her into the stone.

Ethelwynne's attacker lifted her off the ground. She squirmed and kicked at her attacker's legs as he turned and walked deeper into the alley. Ethelwynne could no longer see Xiamara, but she could still hear her struggling. They had to get away. When Ethelwynne and her attacker neared one of the alley walls, she stopped kicking at her attacker and placed her feet against the stone and pushed as hard as she could.

Her attacker cussed as he lost his balance. He stumbled but managed to stay on his feet and hold onto her.

Ethelwynne bit his hand. She tasted the dirt and grit on his palm.

He swore and threw her to the ground.

Her palms burned as they scratched along the stones. She bit her lip to stop from crying out and tried to stand up.

His boot rammed into her side digging the point of one of her knives into her.

Tears filled her eyes as she stood up. Ethelwynne reached into her pocket and pulled out one of the knives from her damp pocket. She tried to see where Xiamara was without taking her eyes off of the man in front of her. They needed to get away. Xiamara was struggling with her attacker. Ethelwynne saw her knee him in the groin. He dropped and she scrambled out of his reach.

The man in front of Ethelwynne lunged towards her. She lashed out at him with her knife.

He yowled as she connected with his hand and drew

blood. The man grabbed her wrist with his bloodied palm and forced the knife from her hand. It landed on the ground with a clatter.

Ethelwynne twisted her arm and managed to slither out of his grasp. Her foot connected with the knife and it skittered towards the entrance she and Xiamara had come from.

Her attacker tried to grab her again.

Ethelwynne skirted around his arms and ran towards where Xiamara was. They both turned to flee to the road.

Three more men blocked their path. One was clapping deliberately. Another slapped Ethelwynne across her face.

The metallic taste of blood pooled in her mouth. She rubbed her hand across her lips. It came back wet and dark in the cold moonlight.

"Well done ladies," said the clapping one. Ethelwynne noticed he had a scar running across his left eye, "but I've had enough of this. Grab them."

Ethelwynne and Xiamara turned to run the other way, because there were only two men behind them. The one who had been fighting Xiamara was smiling wickedly, the one Ethelwynne cut was scowling at them.

A gag choked Ethelwynne and jerked her head back as she tried to get away. Her arms were tied behind her. Her fingers began to feel cold and tingly. A bag was thrown over her head slamming her into pitch darkness. One man searched her for more knives as she continued to struggle. After he triumphantly pulled them from her pocket someone else picked her up and threw her over his shoulder like a sack of potatoes.

She heard the thud of their footprints as they ran through the city. Occasionally they'd stop and she'd feel the cold damp of a wall against her arms.

She heard Xiamara's muffled cries, a thump, and then silence. Ethelwynne wiggled frantically. She called

Xiamara's name, but the gag stifled her cry. Her arms ached from their bindings. She had no idea what she would do if she fell down, but she had to try.

The man holding her tightened his grip on her waist and legs. Someone else slapped her. "Stop moving or you will regret it," warned the man with the scar.

Ethelwynne was fairly sure she would regret it more if she didn't struggle.

She heard a door open. The place smelled of smoke and sweaty socks. Stairs creaked. Her head cracked against a wall as the man turned. Ethelwynne yipped. He chuckled. Another door opened. Something thumped in the dark. She heard Xiamara groan. Then the man carrying Ethelwynne dropped her with a thud.

The bags were pulled off of their heads. The man with the scar leaned down in front of them and grabbed Ethelwynne's face, forcing her to look at him. "Short-haired girl with green eyes, who likes to hang out with a brown-eyed local lass. I'd say we found ourselves the right pair boys." The other men laughed.

He released Ethelwynne and ran his rough hand along Xiamara's jawline. "My, my, my, what pretty things we have." Scarface took her necklace and stood up. "Don't get too comfy ladies. That elf'll pay a pretty penny for you in the morning." He smiled as he slammed the door behind him and his men.

Ethelwynne heard the lock click sealing them in. She struggled against her bonds. The gag fell off. Ethelwynne shifted so she could look over at Xiamara. "You alright?"

The other woman shook her head and sobbed. She rolled away so she was laying on her other side. "Just leave me alone," she cried.

Ethelwynne stared at Xiamara's heaving back as she continued to struggle. Her wrists burned as the rope bit into them, cutting them open. But the knot wouldn't give.

By the time the sun shone through a large crack in the boarded-up window, Ethelwynne's wrists and the ropes that bound her were red, but she was no closer to being free. She squinted and shuffled her bound body so that the light was no longer directly in her eyes and looked around the room to see if there was anything she could use to free herself, but with the exception of her and Xiamara the room was bare. While she was shuffling around, she bumped Xiamara who groaned.

Ethelwynne vowed to learn how to defend herself better. Having knives was useless if she didn't know how to use them. The man had disarmed her so easily it was embarrassing. *At least I managed to cut one of them* she thought indignantly.

Ethelwynne looked over her shoulder at Xiamara. "Xia?"

The woman looked tired but had the same look of determination Ethelwynne had come to recognize from her brother. "Think the knots in the ropes are as poorly done as the ones in the gag?"

"No." Ethelwynne sighed. "I spent the better part of the night trying, but maybe there's something in here that we can use to cut them." The floor squeaked as Ethelwynne rolled and shuffled around to try and see every corner of the room.

"Shh. Stop fidgeting before they come and check what all the racket is."

"How else are we supposed to find something to cut the ropes with if we don't move?"

Xiamara sighed with relief and swung her hands in front of her. She rubbed her wrists. "I thought you were supposed to be a thief. Isn't untying ropes second nature to you? Clearly you need to work on it." She smiled briefly and started untying the ropes binding her feet together.

Ethelwynne's mouth dropped open. Xiamara shrugged. Once she finished her own feet she got up and walked behind Ethelwynne and untied her hands. "Can you get your feet now that you can see the knot you're working with?"

Ethelwynne looked at her raw wrists and nodded.

"Good. I'm going to check that crack and see what it looks like outside. Hopefully, I'll recognize the part of the city we're in. Who knows, maybe we'll get really lucky and this will be the first floor or there will be some sort of roof close enough for us to jump on or some sort of trellis for us to climb down."

Ethelwynne nodded as she focused on the knot. It seemed to simply give when Xiamara had undone her own binds, but Ethelwynne's hands shook as she struggled to get the ropes to come apart. Eventually, she was able to get the knot to loosen and slipped her ankles out. The ropes had been so tight there were red dents embedded into her skin. Ethelwynne rubbed them and winced. She wiggled her feet. Her toes prickled as blood began to flood unhindered through her feet again. Once she was sure she could, Ethelwynne stood up and tip-toed to where Xiamara was standing.

"We have to go downstairs," Xiamara said so softly that Ethelwynne barely heard her.

Ethelwynne glanced at the boarded-up window. "Why? You don't think we could break the boards?"

Xiamara blinked slowly and tilted her head as she stared at Ethelwynne. Then she sighed. "You haven't been listening to a word I've said. We could get through the window, but there's no way to get down without breaking a leg."

"Okay, but we'll need a plan. It's not like we can just fight our way past."

"Yeah, but last night we weren't expecting it. Now they won't be expecting it."

Ethelwynne raised an eyebrow in her direction and gave her a skeptical look.

"Okay, okay. Well, do you have any ideas? It's not like we have a lot of time."

Ethelwynne paused at the door and listened. "Bring the rope and gags. Maybe we can trip them with it and then tie them up?"

"Works for me." Xiamara went and gathered up the ropes and rags, then joined Ethelwynne at the door.

Ethelwynne stared at it. She leaned down to try and see underneath the door. She couldn't see anything, so she leaned against it to try and hear if there was someone on the other side. She didn't hear anything either, so she turned the knob slowly and pushed. It didn't budge. "Worth a shot," she muttered.

Xiamara pushed her to the side as she pulled out some of her hairpins and knelt down in front of the door. She slid the pins into the keyhole and began to jimmy the lock while she softly coached herself through the process.

Time seemed to stand still as Ethelwynne watched her struggle to open the lock.

At last, they heard a click. Xiamara turned the knob and the door gradually swung open. She smiled. "The benefit of having a brother who's always up to mischief."

Ethelwynne held her breath as more of the hallway came into view. Her stomach clenched as she waited for someone to notice them and to come running to rebind their hands and feet. The hallway was empty. She let go of her breath and heard Xiamara doing the same thing. Ethelwynne ran her fingers through her hair as she stood up and forced her shaky legs to step into the hallway. Their room was at the end of the hall, three other doors lined the walls and the stairs were at the far end. She took another step out away from the door and listened. Nothing.

Xiamara stepped out behind her. The floor creaked.

Ethelwynne's heart stopped. She turned her head to look at Xiamara.

Xiamara's mouth was open and her eyes were wide as she stared at the end of the hall.

Ethelwynne licked her lips and took a slow shaky breath as she turned towards the stairs. She took a step backward in case they had to run back into the room. No one came up the stairs. Cautiously she took another step forward.

"Before we run downstairs and get caught, let's check these rooms," Ethelwynne whispered as she gestured to the doors and looked at Xiamara. "Maybe there's a trellis or stairs underneath the window."

Xiamara nodded and quietly shut the door to their prison behind her. The two women tiptoed over to the first door. Ethelwynne could almost touch the doorknob when the floor creaked again.

They heard wood splintering downstairs. Men started yelling. Metal clashed against metal. Ethelwynne no longer cared if someone heard them as she turned the knob and pushed the door open.

Footsteps thudded up the stairs.

The two women ran inside and shut the door behind them. Ethelwynne held the knob with white-knuckled fingers as she swiveled her head around looking for some way to block the door. A table stood in the middle of the room with a notebook, vial of ink, and several strands of jewelry strewn upon it. Xiamara snatched her necklace from the table. "Help me push the table in front of the door."

The door in the room next to them slammed open.

"No time," called Ethelwynne racing to the window. Xiamara joined her and the women grunted as they pushed it open.

Ethelwynne leaned out to see if there was any way for them to get down. She spotted an awning beneath them. "It's a bit of a drop, but I think we can make it."

The door to the room swung open and banged against the wall.

CHRISTINA VAN STARKENBURG

— CHAPTER TWELVE —

Deep Wounds

"Look out!" They turned at the sound of the familiar voice and saw Talman in the doorway, his back to them as he tried to block one of their captor's swords. Talman yowled when his efforts merely deflected the blade into his side.

Sher stepped into view and pushed the thug back. "Xiamara! Ethelwynne! You're alive!" Sher yelled as he parried another thrust. Even in the chaos Ethelwynne could tell there were more men here than there were last night.

Talman staggered back through the door. Sher followed him in and Cephas brought up the rear.

As he stood on the threshold, Cephas swung his sword out and caught the man who stabbed his brother under his arm and across his chest.

The man's shirt turned red as blood ran down it. He staggered to the far wall and collapsed to the ground.

Cephas backed fully into the room. The wind from the door whipped his hair around as Talman slammed it shut.

"There's more coming," Talman gasped clutching his side where blood dripped between his fingers. He leaned heavily against the door groaning.

Xiamara squealed. "You're hurt." She ran towards

Talman.

"Not now." Talman waved her off with his other hand. "Get her out of here."

Ethelwynne opened her mouth to tell Talman to go with her when someone slammed into the door. Talman grunted and staggered forward.

"Go!" yelled Talman. He stumbled further into the room as the door swung inward pushing him away from its support.

Sher nodded and pulled Xiamara towards the window.

"No!" Xiamara yelled and grabbed onto the window frame. "I'm not leaving without you."

Cephas spun around to face the next onslaught.

The man Ethelwynne had slashed the night previous entered the room holding an ax in his other hand. With a howl, he swung his ax at Talman.

Talman barely stepped aside in time. But as the man finished his swing, Talman slashed his blade out over the lowered ax and caught the thug across his waist. The thug crumpled to the floor holding onto his stomach.

The man with the scarred face walked into the room.

Cephas turned his attention to the gang's leader. The ringing of their swords clashing reverberated through the room.

Ethelwynne shivered at the sound.

The scar-faced man swung his blade at Cephas's head but Cephas blocked it and forced him back towards the door.

Heotene walked into the room.

"I thought you said you had them under control," said the elf. Ethelwynne watched in horror as Heotene turned to face Talman. He raised his arm to strike her, but in one fluid motion, she caught his arm and ran him through with her rapier.

He crumpled to the ground. Blood began to pool on the floor around him.

"Talman!" Xiamara screamed.

Out of the corner of her eye, Ethelwynne saw Xiamara let go of the frame and tried to run to her brother. But, before she took a step, Sher wrap his hands around Xiamara's waist and pulled her out of the window with him. Her screams reverberated through the room.

"Fortunately for you, she's the right one," The elf continued completely unaffected by Xiamara's cries. She stepped over Talman's body. She ran towards Ethelwynne leaving bloody prints behind her.

Cephas spun out of the scar-faced man's grasp and slammed his pommel into the back of the man's neck. The man's head thudded off the wall and he slumped to the floor.

Cephas ran towards Ethelwynne. He jumped and skidded across the table so he could be between the woman and elf. "We did not come here to rescue you fools only to have you caught again," he snarled without turning around.

The elf laughed and casually ran her blade along his from where she stood on the other side of the table. "Are you sure you're up for this little boy? A real fight without any tricks to help you?"

Cephas looked behind her to his brother's fallen body.

The elf's smile grew as she followed his gaze. "I suppose that pathetic attempt at valiance was someone important to you. I'm terribly sorry, but you already used up my one time offer of leniency."

Ethelwynne saw the scarred man stand up and rub his head. He picked up his sword from where it fell. She yelled, "Cephas look out!"

Cephas spun towards Ethelwynne and grabbed her as he dove out the window.

She screamed.

Cephas wrapped his arm around her head and pressed it against his chest as they somersaulted through the air.

She heard the awning tear as his shoulder landed on the

material. They rolled towards the edge, but the canvas couldn't hold them and they crashed through.

Cephas grunted as he slammed into the ground with her on his lap. Sher pulled Ethelwynne to her feet then offered Cephas a hand.

"Talman!" Xiamara shrieked at the open window.

The elf appeared at it and scowled when she looked down at the broken awning. She disappeared inside.

Cephas grabbed Xiamara and pulled her towards the gate. "Move."

Tears blurred Ethelwynne's vision as she ran after him.

*　　　*　　　*

A reserved silence filled Lady Kiran's sitting room as Ethelwynne, Cephas, Sher, and Xiamara sat there. Each individual stared blankly in front of them as they were lost in their own thoughts.

"I can't... believe... he's gone." Xiamara eyes fluttered constantly in a fruitless attempt to keep her tears in them. She drew her knees up into her chest. "I wish mother wasn't at the monastery right now. What are we going to tell her?"

Ethelwynne got up from where she was sitting and perched on the arm of Xiamara's chair and rubbed her back. She had no words to offer. Talman died saving their lives. She and Xiamara had been so stupid to think that they could go back to the house and get a necklace without anything bad happening. Everything bad was happening. Nothing had gone right since her parents first left for Grahamadon.

Xiamara's sobs filled the room.

Cephas stood and stared out the window. His cup of water hovered in front of him, but it never quite made it to his mouth.

Sher rested his head on his clasped hands as he sat in one of the overstuffed chairs. He looked over at his nephew and

180

his niece. "Do you remember when he tried to show us how he could fish without a net?" Sher said. "He fell right into the stream and all of the fish swam around him."

"Some even jumped over him," whispered Xiamara. She rubbed tears off of her cheeks and took a few breaths to try and compose herself.

Sher laughed sadly. "He nearly caught one of them when it got stuck in his shirt."

"He was so mad," Xiamara chuckled softly.

The bottom of Cephas's cup clicked sharply as it hit the table beside him. The water sloshed all over the wooden surface. "This is his own fault. If he had just listened, he would never have been injured in the first place."

The other three turned to face him. Ethelwynne couldn't meet his eyes. She focused on the clear liquid as it dripped off the table and pooled on the wooden floor.

"And you!" He rounded on Xiamara and Ethelwynne. "What were you thinking? Going back to the house like that?"

"You didn't have to come for us, we were escaping just fine without your help," Xiamara snapped.

"And how did you plan to make it across the yard with all of those thugs? There was a window beneath the awning."

Xiamara flushed and burst into tears again.

Cephas pointed at Ethelwynne. "This is your fault. If you weren't here, none of this would have happened." He stormed out of the room, slamming the door behind him.

Ethelwynne, Xiamara, and Sher all stared at the door as the echo of the slam reverberated through their ears.

"He doesn't mean that—at least, that's not the only thing going on," Sher grunted, avoiding Ethelwynne's tear-filled eyes. "He's probably just upset that he's the one who wants to be a guard—the one who wants to be a hero—and when the time came, he wasn't able to save everyone."

Ethelwynne blinked back tears and nodded. She wanted

to believe that Sher truly meant what he said, but she was more inclined to agree with Cephas. There were so many decisions she wished she could go back and undo. If she had never left home, or if she went her own way after she fell off the ship, or if she escaped while Xiamara got the supplies, then the elf would never have had a reason to bother Cephas's family in the first place. Xiamara wouldn't have had to leave her home, the necklace wouldn't have been forgotten, the two of them wouldn't have been caught, and Talman would still be alive.

She rubbed Xiamara's back absentmindedly and tried to smile when Sher told them other stories about Talman. As she listened to him, Ethelwynne decided that she would try to make it to White Shield on her own, after all, the elves did say their magic didn't always work. There was a chance she could avoid Heotene. Her gaze drifted towards the door Cephas had walked through. *Maybe Cephas will be so thankful I'm gone, he'll leave me alone,* she thought. Then she shuddered. *Or maybe he's out there right now, trying to track down a guard to report me too.*

Sher ran out of energy to tell stories, and the room fell into a muted silence. Ethelwynne excused herself to go pack. A small amount of relief bubbled up inside her when she passed Cephas's door and heard him moving around within. She quickened her steps lest he should exit, and slipped into her room.

He hasn't reported me yet, she thought as she dumped the contents of her bag onto the bed. There was nothing there that looked like it might be useful on her trip. Ethelwynne held up a jar of blush and considered putting it and the few other cosmetic items that she recognized back into the bag. "No," she mumbled, "there's no way I could transform myself into someone unrecognizable. They'd just take up space." She put them with the rest of the jars on the vanity.

Ethelwynne looked up when the door opened and

desperately hoped it looked like she was settling into the room instead of packing to leave.

Xiamara entered hugging a bundle to her chest. She wiped her red eyes and handed it to Ethelwynne. "Take it. I know you're thinking about going on your own."

Ethelwynne opened her mouth as she saw the food inside. "Thank you."

Xiamara nodded again and sank gloomily on the bed. Tears began to trickle down her cheek again. She took her necklace off and dangled it from her fingers. "Cephas was wrong. It wasn't your fault. I should never have gone back for this."

Ethelwynne sat down beside her and rested her hand on Xiamara's knee.

"Talman used to tease me about my infatuation with jewelry and other pretty things." She curled into a ball on the bed. "He was right." The necklace clinked dejectedly as it landed on the floor. Ethelwynne sat impassively beside her as the woman poured out her heart into her sheets.

Xiamara's sobs ended abruptly. She wiped her eyes on her sleeve and stood up. "Come on," she whispered as she moved to the vanity, "we have a lot of work to do to create a good disguise for you before you leave." She picked up some scissors and dye and turned to face Ethelwynne. "You ready?"

Ethelwynne nodded. She doubted the disguise would help. After all, Heotene had recognized her when she was entirely covered in face paint, but she figured having something to do might help Xiamara feel better.

"Good." Xiamara sniffed and pulled a chair over with her foot and motioned for Ethelwynne to sit down.

As Xiamara concentrated on cutting Ethelwynne's hair and blending the dye to color it, her sobs grew less frequent and she started to smile some more.

In much less time than Ethelwynne expected, her shaggy

brown hair was trimmed into a smoother bob and dyed the deepest black she could imagine. Ethelwynne gently touched her hair and marveled that it was actually hers when there was a sharp rap on the door.

"Our caravan leaves in two days," Cephas called through the wood.

Xiamara, who looked a little lighter now, walked over to the door and swung it open. "What do you think? Pretty unrecognizable huh?"

Cephas glared at Ethelwynne. "It'll have to do." He turned to face his sister and his expression softened, "Good work Xia."

Xiamara hugged him and he awkwardly patted her back before gently pushing her back into the room. His gaze quickly assessed Xiamara, before he turned away to focus his attention on Ethelwynne, "I have to leave the manor for a couple of hours. Stay put and don't do anything stupid while I'm gone."

Ethelwynne nodded. She managed not to glance at her packed bag that was partially hidden by the bed and prayed she didn't look overly guilty.

Cephas wilted slightly as he turned and walked down the hall.

Xiamara shut the door and walked back to the vanity to clean up the supplies.

Ethelwynne nudged the bag further out of sight in case Cephas decided to come back. "Do you think he suspects anything?"

"If he thought you were going to run for it, he wouldn't leave. At least not without tying you up and asking one of Lady Kiran's guards to sit on you while he's gone." Her hand closed around one of the jars when she gasped and spun towards Ethelwynne with wide eyes, "We never got the knives back."

"It's not like I know how to use them."

"If you're going by yourself, you need something to protect you." She grabbed Ethelwynne's arm and pulled her towards the door. "We'll make sure Cephas is really gone, then you can keep watch while I slip into his room to grab some of his knives."

They padded to the window at the end of the hall that overlooked the street and watched as Cephas strolled away from the manor. Ethelwynne settled herself into the corner, and leaned against the wall to keep watch out of the window and down the hall. Xiamara slipped away and opened Cephas's door.

Ethelwynne tried not to fidget as she waited for Xiamara to emerge. She figured if anyone asked, she could say she was enjoying the view from the safety of the shadows. Since this window overlooked the city and the river and forest beyond it was a spectacular view, so she assumed the servants or Sher would believe her.

Xiamara came out of Cephas's room. As she closed the door behind her, she motioned with her head that they should return to their room. Ethelwynne left the window and joined her. Once their own door was closed, she handed the knives to Ethelwynne. "Cephas is still gone, so now's probably the best time for you to leave."

"It's the middle of the day, how will I get out of the manor?"

"Go out the servant's entrance. Since we went over the wall last time, I don't think they'll expect you to just walk out the door."

Ethelwynne considered the idea and nodded, "You're right." She gathered up her bag and placed most of the knives in one of the pockets. The last knife she hung from her belt. Then she turned to say goodbye just in time to watch Xiamara sink heavily onto the bed and burst into tears.

"I'm such a horrible sister. Talman should still be alive."

Ethelwynne sat down beside her and hugged her until the

tears subsided. "We made a mistake, but that doesn't make you a bad sister."

Xiamara sniffed and nodded. "I'm going to miss you." She turned and hugged Ethelwynne tightly. "I'll tell everyone you wanted some time to yourself to read."

"Thanks."

"Be safe." She hugged Ethelwynne one more time and left the room.

"I'm sorry," Ethelwynne whispered to the place Xiamara had stood. Then she turned and picked up her bag. After one last look around the room, she draped her cloak over her arm and leaned against the door to listen. Everything was quiet. She opened the door a crack and peeked out. No one was there. Taking a deep breath, she stepped out into the hall, down the servants' stairs, and out the backdoor.

She forced herself to walk through the city. With every step, she reminded herself that she looked different and that running would draw unnecessary attention to herself. Her whole body shook as she made her way slowly through the streets. She started counting her steps to try and give her mind something else to focus on.

As she neared the edges of the city, she saw Cephas exit a stone building beside the road that led to White Shield. She gasped and darted into an alley. Nervously she peeked around the corner. Besides two passersby who gave her concerned and confused looks, no one noticed her abrupt departure from the street. She watched as a guard patted Cephas on the shoulder as he spoke. Cephas nodded in response. Her chest felt tight as she wondered if he was reporting her. The guard walked back inside leaving Cephas alone. Cephas lingered in front of the door for a moment before he turned and slowly walked away from the building.

Ethelwynne ducked into a doorway as he walked past. She counted to twenty, but he didn't stop. She edged out of the doorway and peeked around the corner. Cephas was nowhere in sight. Ethelwynne sighed in relief. She took another second to gather herself up before continuing on her journey.

She walked through the crowded city to the forest that surrounded it. When she moved far enough down the road to the capital that she wouldn't be easily recognizable from someone standing in the city she breathed a sigh of relief. She thumbed the knife on her belt as she headed for White Shield. If there was anyone she could deliver her message to, they would be there.

The city was barely hidden behind the towering trees when she heard someone galloping down the road. Her stomach rose to her throat as she rushed into the bushes. Her heartbeat pounded in her ears. A messenger raced past her without taking his eyes from the road.

When he was out of sight, she let out a slow breath while she waited for her legs to stop shaking. Then Ethelwynne climbed back onto the road and continued on her way.

The sounds of horses and wagons drove her into the bushes and behind the trees five more times before noon. Each time her heart felt like it was going to pound its way out of her chest. She wondered how no one else could hear it thundering. And each time she wished that she had someone with her who could fight. Part of her believed going out on her own was a mistake, the other part was thankful she wasn't putting anyone else in harm's way.

The sixth time she dove off the road she stumbled into an almost invisible path leading away from the road. "I might as well have some lunch," she murmured as she walked far enough down the deer path that she was sure she wouldn't be heard from the road. Ethelwynne placed her hands on the trees as she passed them to steady herself until she came to a large rock jutting out of the ground. She climbed on it and sat down.

Ethelwynne opened the bag and pulled out an apple and

polished it on her sleeve. "When this is over, I'm never leaving home again," she assured the apple before she took a bite.

"Good," came a very annoyed voice from behind her.

Ethelwynne jumped and fell off the rock. Her arm caught the bag straps and pulled it off with her. She choked on the apple and floundered as she tried to untangle the straps from her arms and pull out a knife.

Cephas emerged from the trees by the deer path and crossed his arms. "I can only imagine you won't be any trouble for me if you're there."

"How'd you find me?" Ethelwynne wheezed between coughs. She rolled onto her knees and pushed herself up. She tried to tamp down the panic bubbling inside of her. He hadn't decided to let her go. Was he going to drag her back to Stormont and hand her over to the guards? She picked up her apple from beside a large shrub and inspected it for dirt, as she tried frantically to think of a way to get passed him. Maybe if she made it to the road, she could run and if a wagon passed by the driver might assume Cephas was a bandit and choose to stop and help her.

Cephas glared at her as she brushed herself off and picked up her belongings. "You pay as much attention to your surroundings as Xiamara does. No wonder the two of you got caught."

Ethelwynne crossed her arms and glared back at him. "I look around," she snapped, choosing to ignore the fact that he snuck up on her because she wasn't paying attention. "And, you shouldn't have come." She brushed more dirt off her apple, grabbed the knife she dropped and marched past Cephas to the road.

Cephas followed her. "I'm bringing you to White Shield."

"What?" Ethelwynne stopped in the middle of the road and spun around. "I thought…" She snapped her mouth shut and decided against reminding him of his promise to dump her with the next guards they met should she run. "Just leave me alone. I can make it to White Shield on my own." She turned back towards White Shield and ran.

"You don't honestly expect me to believe that you'd walk up to the city guards and surrender yourself to them for stealing from the elves and your role in my brother's death?" Cephas called from behind her.

Ethelwynne's steps slowed and she looked back at Cephas as he approached her. "I'm sorry about Talman. I never meant for someone to get hurt."

"Of course not," Cephas snapped. "You thought you could get away with stealing whatever you wanted and that no one would be harmed. After all, it was the elf prince, he's rich. He's not going to miss it."

Ethelwynne blinked back tears. "I am not a thief. I didn't steal from the prince. I just..." She bit into the apple to stop finishing that thought. He'd never believe her anyway, and knowing the prince was committing treason would just get him killed too. The apple tasted like dirt. Ethelwynne threw it into the forest and watched it disappear into the shrubs.

They walked in silence. A pang of hunger gnawed at her stomach, but she figured she deserved it and didn't stop to grab something else to eat. She heard a wagon coming up from behind them, it was still hidden by the trees. Now was her chance. She tore away from Cephas.

CHRISTINA VAN STARKENBURG

— CHAPTER THIRTEEN —

Michael

Cephas grabbed her around the waist and covered her mouth with his hand as he yanked her off the road. Her heart raced as a wagon rolled past. Through the branches she watched as the kids in the back of it giggled as they bounced along. Their mother yelled at them to sit down before they fell out. She squirmed and tried to get out of Cephas's grasp, but he was immovable.

He released her when the wagon was out of sight. Ethelwynne avoided looking at him as they climbed back up on the road and continued their trek, but he didn't say anything about her attempted flight.

They walked down the deserted road for a few hours until the sun began to set. "We should make camp," said Cephas as he stepped off the road. He pulled Ethelwynne behind him into the trees and looked around. "These bushes should give us enough coverage for the night. We can wrap our cloaks tight to stay warm." He crouched down to crawl under the branches.

"I know. This isn't the first time I've slept outside."

Cephas looked up at her and shook his head. "Coming? Or are you intending to wait out in the rain?"

Ethelwynne sighed and pulled her hood up as the first raindrops started to patter onto the fabric. Then she crouched down and crawled in beside him. If she curled up into a tight ball, she could just fit without any part of her being exposed to the rain, but she was fairly certain Cephas was going to get wet. *Maybe it'll make him change his mind and he'll just go home.*

Branches crackled as he shifted his position. "If you didn't steal from the elves, why are they chasing you?"

She looked over at him and considered her answer while she listened to the soft patter of the raindrops on the leaves. "I overheard something I shouldn't have."

"What?"

"I can't tell you." Ethelwynne flushed as she felt the weight of her pathetic answer. It was true, but still, it seemed weak and like she was avoiding the truth. "They'd kill you if you knew."

Cephas arched an eyebrow in her direction and she felt her blush deepen as her stomach turned in knots. "That elf intends to kill me anyway. I think I deserve to know why she's willing to kill me and Talman to get to you."

Ethelwynne squeezed her eyes shut and buried her head in her arms to avoid looking at him. "Heotene will only kill you if you're with me. If you stayed in Stormont, she'd leave you alone."

Cephas scoffed. "You can't honestly believe she'll let me live if I leave, can you? She'll assume you told me what really happened."

"I'm sorry. I can't."

"You're sorry about a lot of things."

After a few moments, Cephas spoke again, "Aspen Grove is the next town we'll hit. When we get there, we'll join a caravan."

She lifted her head up and looked at him. "What?"

"We'll look far less suspicious if we're traveling in a

192

group," said Cephas in a low voice.

Ethelwynne continued watching him in the deepening dusk as she tried to figure out whether or not he believed her, or, more importantly, if she could trust him.

He studied her then answered her unspoken question. "Just because I'm willing to believe that there is more to your story than that elf is saying, doesn't mean I don't intend to hand you over to the King's Guard." He shifted his body to get out from under the steady drip that found its way through the leaves. "And, in case you think about slipping off in the night, you're not all that good at covering your tracks. I'll find you again."

Ethelwynne tried to shift under the branches so she didn't have to face him, but it didn't work. The space was too small for her to turn around in, and she wasn't going to crawl back out simply to crawl into it backward.

The rain never got any heavier, it just remained a constant light rain drizzling down on top of them. Combined with her traveling companion it was enough to make it a miserable night. Ethelwynne longed for an inn or better yet, her own bed above her family's store.

She wondered how the store was doing without her there. By now Meghan would have had to return to helping her mother run their business. Was Danny managing the store? But he would be needed at Annie's family farm. Was Annie his wife now? Would he have gotten married with her missing? He didn't want to get married when it was just their parents missing. She groaned.

By now Danny probably thought she was dead on top of their parents being trapped in Grahamadon. Tears trickled silently down her cheeks and she buried her face in her arms again so Cephas wouldn't see. She wished there was some way to send Danny a message to let him know that she was alright. Ethelwynne shivered and adjusted her cloak trying to get warmer.

Cephas grunted and crawled out from their pitiful shelter. When he crawled back in, he pulled his cloak overtop of Ethelwynne. Ethelwynne lifted her head and watched him from inside her cozy cocoon as he lay down beside her on his stomach. His legs were sticking out of the shelter and the raindrops that managed to navigate the leaves and branches covered him in tiny wet dots.

He appeared to fall asleep much faster than she would have imagined possible when one is wet. She sighed and fingered his cloak. Knowing he was getting wet didn't feel as satisfying anymore.

*   *   *

The rain continued to fall gently as they got up the next morning. Ethelwynne handed Cephas back his cloak. "Thank you," she murmured.

He nodded and draped it over his shoulders before bending down to grab his bag and setting out down the road.

While they walked, the sun came out. Ethelwynne looked up and smiled as the heat caressed her face and dried her off. After they were on the road for a few hours, she paused and studied Cephas.

"What are you doing?" Cephas asked scanning the road behind them.

"Cephas, I intend to go to the capital. You don't need to bring me there. Go home to your sister; it's where you want to be."

"No."

"Why not?"

Cephas spun to face her. "Because you know nothing about surviving in the wilderness on your own, and the only way my brother is going to get justice, is if you do."

"This isn't my first time away from home." She shook her head and marched past him, ignoring the small voice in her head reminding her that it was the first time she was on the road without either of her parents. "I know what I'm doing."

He pointed to the side of the road. "That plant. Can you eat it?"

Ethelwynne looked at the plant with clusters of small white star-like flowers on it. "Uh, yes?" She looked over at Cephas. He crossed his arms as he frowned at her. "No?"

He threw his hands in the air. "See? Nothing."

"Well, it doesn't matter. Because I can just carry food and sleep in towns and under bushes on my way there."

"And with what money do you intend to buy food? I thought you weren't a thief. Besides, do you even know the way to the capital? Do you even know how to get to Aspen Grove?"

"It's this way, and I would work. Where I'm from inns aren't opposed to giving someone room and board in exchange for a night of labor. I'm not useless."

"What happens when we reach the fork in the road? What happens if you leave the road?"

"There are signs, and I'd travel beside it like I was before."

"Yeah, and leave glaring trails behind you. You might as well sit in the middle of the road and wait for Heotene to find you. Maybe she wouldn't kill you right away since you're being so agreeable."

She glared at him and stalked down the road. Despite her defiant attitude, the silence made Ethelwynne antsy. The sounds of the forest amplified. Wide-eyed she looked around. She bit her lip and considered asking Cephas if he was sure they were still safe. She shook her head and kept walking in silence. He'd just think she was crazy. As the wind rustled through the trees, she thought she heard someone walking. She spun around to look behind her and backed up into Cephas, a mixture of frustration and confusion was blended on his face. She blushed and darted past him keeping her eyes on the road. Now he probably thought she was crazy and a klutz.

She realized he hadn't started walking right away when she heard him jogging to catch up to her. She looked up at him, but her cheeks still prickled with embarrassment and she turned her focus back to the dirt beneath her feet.

He fell into step beside her. "The elf isn't here. You're still safe."

Ethelwynne grabbed her bag's straps weakly as the heat spread from her cheeks down her neck and up to her ears. She nodded weakly and wished there was somewhere for her to hide, that it was raining so she could justify putting on her hood, or that her hair was long enough to hide what must be horribly bright red splotches on her cheeks.

Cephas didn't say anything about them or her irrational behavior as they walked towards Aspen Grove. Michael would have. He and Danny would have teased her about it endlessly. "Do you think we're going to make it to Aspen Grove tonight?" Ethelwynne asked to distract him from her foolishness.

He shook his head. "No, but we might not have to sleep outside tonight. There's a couple of farms on the way, maybe one of them will let us spend the night in the barn in exchange for some chores."

She rubbed her arms and nodded. "That would be nice."

Soon they came to a fork in the road. A rotten sign with the names of the various towns down the roads was laying in pieces on the ground. The arrow with the letters A-S-P on it was resting against the post and pointing up to the sky. Ethelwynne blushed again as Cephas motioned for her to take the left path.

Dark clouds drifted across the sun as they continued to walk down the path towards the town. Ethelwynne hugged her cloak closer and prayed that they would reach the farms before they were soaked.

As they crested a hill a small farm came into sight. Ethelwynne heard the thrumming behind them. She looked over her shoulder and watched with a mix of marvel and horror as a wall of water pouring from the sky moved towards them. "Come on," she tugged Cephas's arm. They broke into a run as the rain chased them down the road. They were drenched the moment it caught up to them.

They ran to the farm. Cephas knocked on the door. It opened a crack and an elderly woman peeked out at them. "Can we spend the night in your barn?" asked Cephas after he introduced himself and Ethelwynne.

She pursed her lips then nodded. "I suspect it's alright, but you'll have to ask Al. He's in there now." The woman looked at the mud forming just past the stoop. "Maybe you could help him?"

"Of course," Cephas said. The woman smiled and shut the door. The two of them ran to the barn and darted through the door. A solitary cow looked over at them and bellowed from her stall on the far wall, and chickens clucked and screeched as they scattered. Cephas called out "Al? Your wife sent us to see if you needed any help."

Al stood up from where he was sitting beside the cow. "Darn that woman. I can handle myself," he grumbled, but the smile that spread across his face and crinkled his eyes stole all the mirth from his grumbling. "Well, what are you waiting for? Grab a pitchfork and give them poor critters some food so they can keep feeding us." He pointed to a bag in the corner that was sealed up tight. "There's some food for the birds in there. But make sure you close it good or they'll dump the whole thing out and they won't get no more food 'til harvest."

Ethelwynne nodded and went to feed the chickens while Cephas grabbed a pitchfork and answered Al's questions about where they were going when they got caught in the storm. All the birds squawked over to her as soon as her hands touched the bag. She scattered the food away from her so that the birds would give her enough space to reseal the bag properly.

"Thanks for your help," he said grinning. "You can sleep in the barn if ye'd like, but I bet Val has some good food for us first." He grabbed his cane from where it was leaning beside the cow's stall and waved at the two of them to follow him back to the house.

In the short time, she knew that she was going to be having guests, Valerie had prepared a delicious meal of roast chicken, boiled potatoes and carrots, and apple pie to warm their hearts and bodies. As they sat at the table, Valerie piled the food high on Ethelwynne and Cephas's plates. Ethelwynne tried to argue that it was too much, but Valerie insisted she would need all of that food after the long day she must have had. Ethelwynne didn't realize how right the older woman was, until all of the food was eaten.

As the meal ended, Al pulled out his citole to play some music. "Either of you play?" he asked after the first few songs.

Ethelwynne and Cephas both shook their heads.

"You're missing out," he said with a mock frown as he strummed the first few notes of another song. The rain had lessened a bit when he finally put the instrument down. "Well, we best be getting to bed. I suspect you folks will want an early start in the morning." He handed them the lantern that was flickering on the kitchen table. "Just make sure you put it out before you fall asleep," he said as Valerie handed the two of them a few quilts.

In the barn, Ethelwynne and Cephas climbed into the hayloft to sleep. She draped her cloak over the railing to dry and stifled a sigh when she noticed Cephas lie down in front of the ladder. As she snuggled into the thick quilt Valerie had given her, she fumed. She hadn't tried to run since that first time. Now that she knew the signs weren't reliable, it's not like she knew the way to White Shield. As long as Cephas didn't turn her in, she wasn't going to run.

She closed her eyes and listened to the sound of the rain pattering on the roof. Instead of reminding her of her night trapped under the trees, the sound reminded her of Al's music. She focused on the peace the music had brought her after the meal and soon drifted off to sleep.

The next morning, they woke up when Al crept in to start his chores for the day. After apologizing for waking them he offered them a ride to town. "I was planning on heading into Aspen Grove today, so it wouldn't be a bother. The missus is hoping to sell some quilts at the market, and I've a few vegetables I'd like to get rid of."

"Thank you," said Cephas as he climbed down the ladder to help. Ethelwynne packed up their belongings and went inside to help Valerie fold the quilts she was hoping to sell. After a quick breakfast, the trio climbed onto the wagon and headed towards town.

Soon other wagons began to join them on the road as other farmers from the area set out to town for the market. Al waved to the ones he knew and liked and warned Cephas and Ethelwynne to avoid the ones he couldn't stand.

Once they arrived in Aspen Grove, Ethelwynne and Cephas offered to help Al set up his booth, but he waved them off. "I'm sure you've got more important things to do than to help me some more."

Thanking him, the pair set off through the village to try and find a merchant caravan to join. Aspen Grove was much smaller than Helmsville or Stormont, and the houses were smaller and spread further apart and many of them were covered in thatch. No one would be running across the roofs here. It reminded Ethelwynne of home.

"There's a caravan we might be able to join," Cephas pointed to a wagon down one of the roads.

Ethelwynne followed his gaze. Her eyes widened as she saw a man with the jacketed bear patch on his sleeve throwing a package onto the wagon. She grabbed Cephas's arm and pulled him back behind the building they just past.

He arched an eyebrow in her direction but didn't resist her tugging. "What now?" he asked once they were out of sight from the wagon. Then he lowered his voice, "If there was an elf in the town she would be swarmed by people trying to look at her. And the guards would've paid us more attention. She's not here."

"It's not that," Ethelwynne moaned and peeked around the corner at Michael's caravan.

Cephas squeezed his eyes shut and rubbed his forehead. "The elves are trying to kill you, and now you have a problem with someone over there. How much more trouble can you be in?"

"No, it's not... it's just..." Ethelwynne rubbed her arms where Michael had grabbed her as Cephas leaned against the wall and waited for her to gather her thoughts in a coherent manner.

"We can't travel with that caravan," Ethelwynne whispered. She kicked at some of the dirt beneath her shoes.

"Fine," snapped Cephas. The anger and annoyance in his voice were impossible for her to miss. "We won't take that caravan. But, as soon as we have the chance you are going to tell me everything."

Ethelwynne hung her head and nodded.

Cephas stalked off in the direction of the inn they had passed. "Maybe we'll get lucky and find a different caravan owner in there."

Ethelwynne sullenly followed him. The hairs on the back of her neck prickled as she walked. She glanced behind her, but there was no one there. She rubbed her neck and hurried to catch up to Cephas who was opening the door.

He held it open for her. She took a quick step in, then

stopped and backed up into Cephas. What if Michael is inside?

"Too late now," whispered Cephas as he pushed her inside and walked up to the counter. As he haggled for rooms and information from the innkeeper, Ethelwynne scanned the crowded room. Tension poured from her body when she didn't recognize anyone.

Cephas looped his arm through her and walked over to a booth, pulling her down into the seat beside him. "Well my dear, we might be in luck." He flicked his gaze over towards the counter.

Ethelwynne reflexively buried her face in her hands. It didn't occur to her that he might tell the innkeeper they were married to save money. She wondered if Al and Valerie thought they were married too. She tilted her chin and looked over her fingers at Cephas. "In luck? How so?"

"Wesley, the innkeeper, was telling me that they are expecting a few more caravans to roll in today, but they might be late because bandits have been attacking everyone."

"Everyone?"

He nodded. "We got lucky on the way over. I hope Al is just as lucky on his way home."

Ethelwynne looked towards the market where they left him and nodded. While she was looking up, Michael walked into the common room from the hallway leading to the rooms. *He's here. He's staying in the same inn.*

Michael walked over to the counter and sat down.

Ethelwynne wracked her brain for a way to get passed him and out the door. She glanced over to the hall and wondered if it would be easier to sneak past him to their room.

Cephas cupped her chin and forced her to look at him. He was clearly a better actor than she was, because his expression mimicked the one Danny wore whenever he spoke about Annie. He didn't let her turn her head as he looked over her shoulder. "Thank you," he said as Wesley placed their cups of red wine and bowls of beef stew before them.

"Not a problem you two. Will you be needing anything else?"

Ethelwynne and Cephas shook their heads and Cephas lowered his hand. Ethelwynne turned and watched as Wesley wandered nonchalantly back to the counter to flirt with Michael.

Cephas stirred his soup briefly before taking a bite. "Are you alright?"

Ethelwynne nodded and took a sip of the wine. She prayed Michael wouldn't turn around.

"Okay," said Cephas. He took a few more bites before speaking again. "After we eat, I was thinking we could put our bags in our room and then go see if any other caravans rolled in yet."

Ethelwynne nodded and tried to eat her meal. She watched as Michael finished his drink and stood up. She turned her head and tried to say something to Cephas to make it look like they were having a conversation, but nothing came out. She drank more of her wine. Michael walked out of the common room without looking in her direction. Ethelwynne relaxed back into the chair. She looked towards Cephas. "Eat faster," she whispered before she turned to her own meal and tried to eat it as quickly as she could.

When their bowls and cups were almost empty, Wesley walked over again. "Either of you want a refill?"

"No thank you. We're fine," said Ethelwynne for the both of them.

"Alright, enjoy yourselves then," said Wesley as she smiled and walked back to the kitchen.

After a few more bites and sips they went up to the room Cephas had rented for them. Ethelwynne sank onto the bed, or at least she would have if it wasn't as hard as a rock.

"I'll take the floor," Cephas said as he dropped his bag by the desk and leaned against the door. "So, about that caravan we can't take."

Ethelwynne rapped her knuckles on the mattress and wondered if he had the better deal sleeping on the floor. She glanced around the room they would be sharing. Xiamara would call it functional. There was a bed, a desk, an armoire, and nothing else. "Did you really say we were married just so no one would bat an eye when you cornered me in a room like this?"

"One room is cheaper," said Cephas, the light tone he'd used in the dining room was completely gone. "You not being able to run away again was an added benefit."

"I'm not going to run. I've come to terms with the fact that I won't make it there on my own."

"The caravan?"

Ethelwynne stood up and placed her bag on the desk and fiddled with the few items inside it as she gathered her thoughts. "It's Michael's caravan." She wished that explained it all, but she doubted Cephas would be satisfied with just a name. He didn't know who Michael was to her. Ethelwynne pulled out a jar of red powder that had somehow made its way back into her bag. She thought only the items needed for the hair dye were put back. A brief smile touched her lips as she wondered why Xiamara thought she would need this jar.

"And Michael is?"

She sat down on the edge of the bed again and studied the jar. "He..." She stopped and started a few times as she tried to figure out how to explain Michael to Cephas. As she stammered along in her story, Cephas moved from the door to the window.

"I'm going to pay him back," she finished and looked up at Cephas for the first time since she started talking. He was staring out the window as he leaned against the window casing with one shoulder. She couldn't keep the desperation out of her voice as she spoke. She needed Cephas to believe that she wasn't a thief. "I wanted to pay him right away, but his family would lose their license if it was found out they willingly helped me after the elves accused me of stealing. And I couldn't do that to him. I couldn't... I couldn't take away his livelihood."

Cephas looked over at her for a moment then turned his attention back to the street beneath the window. "Tell me about the elves."

She shook her head even though he was no longer looking at her. "Not here. It isn't safe."

"Neither was the middle of the forest."

His voice cut her and she blushed. "I'm sorry. But I can't."

Cephas took a deep breath. "Fine." He pushed off of the trim and walked back towards the door. "Another caravan has pulled in. I'll go see if I can get us a ride. Perhaps the bandit attacks can work in our favor and they'll hire us as guards." He pointed at Ethelwynne and grabbed his sword. "You. Stay here. We can talk about the elves when I get back."

He rested his hand on the doorknob and he turned back to Ethelwynne. "Stay. I am not in the mood to hunt you down, again."

Ethelwynne put her hands up and promised to remain behind.

Cephas eyed her suspiciously before shutting the door.

Ethelwynne stared at the door for a few moments. What could she tell him? She sighed and decided to leave that problem for another time. She might not be able to put it off forever, but at least for a little while longer.

She picked up her bag and rummaged through it for the paper Xiamara wrote the hair dye directions on. She flipped it over and grabbed a stylus from the room's small desk and began sketching out a dress design.

She drew with Xiamara in mind. "Not everything I make has to be practical," she muttered as she redrew a line. Making something nice for Xiamara was the least she could do to thank her. She had no idea how she would eventually get the gown to Xiamara, especially since she didn't intend to leave home ever again, but perhaps if she was able to patch things up with Michael, he'd bring it for her.

She was still working on the dress design when Cephas returned. He walked over to the desk and rested his sword on it. "The caravan was willing to hire us. They'll pay me upfront and you once we get there if they think you were worth it."

She put the stylus and paper down so she wouldn't accidentally mark up the page. "Worth it?" Cephas opened his mouth to say something but Ethelwynne held up her hand to cut him off. "You know what, never mind." Ethelwynne stood up and undid and redid the bed sheets and wished that she wasn't stuck in a room with nothing to do. It didn't matter that the owner was probably right, because she still didn't know how to fight. She was sick and tired of people not trusting her. After she smoothed out every last wrinkle on the bed spread, she sat down and stared at her drawing. Unwilling to risk damaging the image with her ire, she planned out the design in her mind until she thought she was calm enough to not tear the paper.

CHRISTINA VAN STARKENBURG

— CHAPTER FOURTEEN —

Wagon Fire

When they arrived at the caravan the next morning, Axel told them Cephas was to be part of the crew walking around the wagons so he could react to different attacks faster. Ethelwynne would be sitting on the back of the rear wagon to keep watch.

While they waited for the last few new guards to arrive, Ethelwynne watched as Michael and his crew got ready and rumbled passed them. She breathed a sigh of relief once he had left without noticing her.

"Let's move out," yelled Axel once the last two guards arrived. With a few clicks and whistles to get the horses moving, the caravan started off. When her wagon passed the last of the houses, Ethelwynne turned her attention to the trees around them. She was going to show Axel that she was worth his money. She'd need it to help her get home after she delivered her message to the king.

The company rounded a bend and creaked to a stop. Ethelwynne looked around the edge of the wagon to see what was happening. Michael's caravan was blocking the way. He was standing beside the wagons. She dug her fingernails into her palms to avoid covering her eyes and watched as Michael waved to Axel before he hopped back onto his wagon. The two caravans began to roll down the road together. "Oh no," she whispered as she sat back down on the seat.

Ethelwynne tried to focus on the trees and shadows around her, but she kept taking furtive glances around the canvas top towards Michael's wagons. By the time Cephas finished his first cycle and was walking beside her, her throat was tight and she felt ill. "How long did you say it was going to take to get to the capital?" she asked.

"Five days." He studied her and glanced towards the front wagon. "Relax, you look nothing like yourself and even if you did, I doubt he'd notice."

"What's that supposed to mean?" she hissed.

"Besides, you're supposed to be a guard," said Cephas ignoring her question and the look she gave him. "If you look this nervous when we're barely beyond Aspen Grove, they'll probably fire us before we reach the next village. Have you seen anything worth checking out further in the forest?" He shifted and scanned the forest edge around them.

"No."

Cephas nodded and continued walking.

She tried not to let her nerves distract her from her job. But while she didn't look to the front as much as she had been, she couldn't help glancing in that direction a few times as the wagon rumbled along.

That night she and Cephas sat around the fire eating when it wasn't their watch. As she munched her food, Ethelwynne tried to figure out the best way to ask Cephas what his earlier comment about Michael meant, but before she found the words some of the other off-duty guards came and sat down with them.

"Pretty unusual for a woman to know how to fight," remarked one as he sat down right beside her.

She shrugged. "It's no big deal."

"Well," he said leaning in, "if you want a few pointers, I

can teach you a thing or two."

Ethelwynne moved over to give herself more room. "No thanks, I can handle myself."

Several other of the guards chuckled. "Of course you can sweetie," one of them remarked with a wink.

Cephas gestured towards the edge of the camp with his head and stood up. "She's not lying gentlemen. But you'll have to continue this conversation without us because it's our watch." He held out his hand to Ethelwynne to help her up. Together they walked away leaving behind the laughing guards.

"Thank you," Ethelwynne said once they were far enough away not to be overheard.

Cephas nodded. "Stay sharp, and prove to them how capable you can be." He stopped after they passed the first few trees, "If they catch you, slice their hands—they won't be able to hold you or their weapon."

Ethelwynne nodded and swallowed to try and get some moisture back in her mouth.

"Now come on, I have no intention of being late to relieve the other guards." He turned and continued to walk towards the meeting spot.

Ethelwynne and Cephas waved to the other guards as they approached them. After a succinct exchange about the quiet evening, the other two guards wandered back towards the fire and left Ethelwynne and Cephas standing on the dark forest edge.

As she stared into the night, the darkness seemed to close in around her, sending shivers down her spine. She was not good at this being a guard thing. Her chest tightened, and her throat felt so tight she wasn't sure she'd be able to yell out any alarm should she see something. She took a deep breath and began to circle the camp. She and Cephas were walking in opposite directions.

Around the half-way point, she met up with one of the

other guards on duty. He was one of Michael's guards. Ethelwynne prayed he would not recognize her in the dim light. They waved, assured each other that they had not seen anything out of the ordinary, and turned around to head back the other way. Ethelwynne breathed more easily the farther away from him she got. Perhaps Cephas was right about no one recognizing her.

The wind whistled through the trees as she walked towards where she would meet up with Cephas again. A branch snapped. Ethelwynne jumped and spun in the direction of the sound. Her eyes saw nothing. As she tried to get control over her unsteady breathing, she pulled out one of the knives and walked towards the sound. She bit her bottom lip to silence her breathing. She was not going to be found a coward if this was one of the other guards, and she certainly didn't intend to raise the alarm for a badger.

Her wide eyes tried to make out every tree, every leaf as she walked in some desperate attempt to not trip and to not let everyone down. She definitely preferred traveling in these caravans as the merchant, not the guard.

A hand clamped over her mouth as an arm wrapped around her waist pulling her behind a tree. Her body tensed as she stabbed her attacker's leg with her knife.

Cephas swore softly and released her. Ethelwynne looked from him to the blade. In the moonlight she could see a sliver of blood on it. She opened her mouth to apologize but he covered her mouth again and whispered, "I'm fine, but they're looking for you. Stay here. Do not fight. And, if anyone spots you, run, remembering your life depends on it. I'll find you when I can." Then he released her and vanished into the still and silent darkness.

Ethelwynne counted her heartbeats as she waited for something, anything to happen. She took a few deep breaths to try and calm herself. The seconds stretched. Was he playing a cruel trick on her? Despite what he said earlier about her being able to take care of herself, she knew he agreed with the other guards that she was useless in a fight. *Why hasn't he called out a warning if there are bandits around?* She hugged herself and imagined him laughing this over with the other guards later. Her cheeks burned as she stepped out from behind the tree to continue her route to their meeting point.

"To arms! We're under attack!" Cephas called from the other side of the camp.

The night erupted into noise. Ethelwynne leaned back into the tree she was standing beside. Several torches flickered through the trees near the camp as men yelled and weapons clashed. Suddenly she could see how close she was to the camp when one of the wagons burst into flames.

She inched around the tree so that the light wouldn't catch her and reveal her. Standing there she clutched two knives. She didn't really know how to use them, but it made her feel safer. She would not go down without a fight. This time she was determined that she would do better than when she and Xiamara were kidnapped in town.

One man ran past her. By the symbol on the back of his tunic, she knew him to be a guard from Michael's caravan. Axel followed him. He was limping as he ran towards the darkness. Arrows caught them both in the back, they yelped before collapsing to the ground motionless.

The guard who offered to teach her a few pointers passed her as he backed away from the wagons and fought off one of their attackers. He called for help when he saw her.

Ethelwynne tried to signal to him not to draw attention to her. She'd watched helplessly while Talman died in front of her. There was nothing she could have done to save Axel or the other guard, but maybe she could help this one.

Once the two men were past her, she ran out from her hiding spot and slashed the bandit in his left arm with her knives. He howled in pain and spun to face her.

She darted out of the reach of his ax.

He smiled and turned back to face the guard, swung his ax with his right arm and chopped deep into the guard's leg. The guard dropped to his knees, and the bandit finished him off with another strike then he turned to face Ethelwynne again.

"Well, well, well, a short-haired woman in pants. You're gonna make me rich." He started walking towards her and hooked his ax back onto his belt. "Let's do this nice like. I don't want to kill you. So you can put those knives away before you hurt yourself. All you have to do is come with me. I won't hurt you, and I'll tell my men to leave the rest of the people alone too."

Cephas's warning to run rang through her head. She stepped back and tried to circle around him.

"No?" he sighed and ran towards her.

Her heart rose to her throat and her legs forgot how to move. Forgetting about the knives in her hands, she threw her hands up to try and push him away from her. There was a sharp intake of breath as the blades sunk into him. He looked at her stunned. The knives remained embedded in his chest as Ethelwynne backed away horrified by what she'd done.

The man didn't fall.

Ethelwynne ran.

Brittle branches and twigs snapped underneath her feet. She glanced behind her but she didn't see him. She darted behind a tree and listened. No branches snapped once she stopped moving. She pulled out another dagger in case he was just adept at sneaking through the brush undetected. She peeked behind the tree. Orange light glowed from the direction of the wagons. The yells of men fighting and clang of their weapons rang through the air.

Nothing moved near her, but she feared she was still too close so she started running once more. The sound of the crackling flames spurred her on and she used the firelight to guide her through the forest.

She splashed across a wide stream and tripped on the slick rocks. Ethelwynne dropped the knife as she tried to stop herself from going under water. Her hands scraped on the ground leaving tiny bits of flesh behind. A spark fizzled on the water beside her. Wide-eyed, Ethelwynne looked behind her. The trees had caught fire. Ignoring the pain in her knees, her hands, her lungs, and her legs, Ethelwynne stood up again and ran through the knee-deep water and away from the flames.

The smoke blocked out the sky. Ethelwynne prayed that Cephas made it to safety and that the shallow stream was wide enough to keep the flames from her. Her panting turned into coughing as the smoke reached her.

She put her hand on a tree and doubled over as she coughed. The smoke stung her eyes. Through the tears she saw a bandit rush past her. He stumbled over some rocks and collapsed to the ground. The man looked behind her with fear in his eyes. He tried to stand but a dagger flashed through the air and sliced through his neck.

Ethelwynne reached for another dagger as she turned around.

Cephas stood behind her in the haze. Blood was smeared into his shirt, and dripped freely from slashes across his arms. Smoke stained his cheeks and forehead. She watched with dread as he approached the fallen bandit and retrieved the blade. He wiped the blade on the other man's shirt. "The elf prince got tired of waiting for Heotene to kill you," he said as he stood and walked towards her. "He put a bounty on your head and spread the word to every bandit or pirate he could. We need to move." He handed her three of her knives.

She wondered how he had the time to find all three blades, and interrogate some of the bandits while fleeing from the flames.

Cephas grabbed her arm and pulled her along in his

wake.

She squeezed her hand around the blades and they bit into her palm, but the pain didn't compare to the fear. "The fire." She felt the heat of it on her back. The ash in the air scratched her throat. "We won't outrun it."

Cephas looked at her without stopping and she saw the blaze burning in the reflection on his eyes. It was too close. "The stream was wide enough to stop it, and it's rained enough that the ground and plants aren't too dry."

Deer and rabbits raced past them, as though they too were unconvinced by Cephas's claim. Ethelwynne put the knives away and tried to move faster, to catch up with the animals that were leaving them behind. Cephas coughed and continued to lead her away from the flames, the wagons, and the man she killed.

The smell of burning leaves and wood traveled with the smoke, but whenever Ethelwynne glanced behind them, the flames seemed no closer. Cephas kept a firm grip on Ethelwynne's arm as he guided her through the woods.

She tried to swallow to ease the ache in her throat. But her parched mouth offered no relief. "Where are we going?" she braved the pain in her lungs to ask.

"There's another road this way," Cephas said, his voice hoarse.

The heat died down the further away from the flames they moved, but they didn't stop going. Eventually, the red sun crept up and burned Ethelwynne's tired eyes. Everything looked odd in the hazy-orange air. It was eerily silent. Not even the birds seemed interested in singing this morning.

The treeline broke before them and Cephas and Ethelwynne stepped out onto a pebble beach beside a lake far too wide for them to cross. The two of them wearily sank into the waves and drank the cool water deeply. The water relieved some of the pain in Ethelwynne's throat. She sat in the water and turned to face the way they came. The lingering haze made the fire seem closer, but the billowing smoke was far enough away for her to feel safe for the moment.

"Let's keep going," said Cephas.

She ached everywhere, but she gritted her teeth and forced herself to stand and keep going. *If Cephas can walk further, so can I.* "What about your cuts?" Ethelwynne asked gesturing to his arms.

"They're not deep. When the ashes aren't stinging my eyes anymore, I can wash them better, but we weren't the only ones fleeing from the fire. I don't want to stay here in case any of the bandits make it too."

Ethelwynne gulped and nodded. Her hand dropped to the sheath on her hips. She fingered the handles. "The man..." Tears pooled in her eyes and she wiped them away smearing soot and ash across her face. "Did I... did I kill..." She choked on the words.

Cephas walked back to her and lifted her chin so she had to look at him. "No, I did. You just slowed him down."

She closed her eyes and nodded.

Cephas sighed and hugged her. "You had to do it."

She opened her eyes and looked up at him.

"He would have killed you or captured you and brought you to someone who would have killed you. Either way, you would be dead," Cephas said and stepped back to hold her at arm's length. "Next time hide better and leave the killing to me. This is what I train for."

Ethelwynne mouthed the word "Okay."

Cephas squeezed her shoulders. "Come on, we need to keep moving."

* * *

At the end of the day, they set up camp on the lake shore. Cephas stood in the shallows and caught a few fish with a makeshift spear. The scabs on his arms proved to Ethelwynne that his cuts hadn't been serious.

She started a small fire on the rocky beach to cook their meager meal. He'd been hurt because of her, but instead of being sorry she was just mad. "You lied," she said as she glared at him.

Cephas stepped out of the shallows and knelt down on the rocks to clean his catch. "Did you get any leaves?"

"Here." Ethelwynne dumped them at his feet and stalked back over to the fire to put another branch on. "You said we were heading to another road." She sat down and began to massage her feet.

Cephas dipped the leaves in water and wrapped them around the pieces of fish. He carefully placed the bundles in the coals before looking at Ethelwynne. "The elves have both city guards and bandits looking for you," Cephas replied calmly. "We wouldn't make it if we took the road."

"Shouldn't I get some say in that?" She threw one of her shoes at him. "I have to get there quickly. If I don't, my parents are going to be lost forever."

"What do your parents have to do with any of this? The only thing you told me is that the elves mistakenly think you stole from them and now they want to kill you."

"Xiamara was right about you."

"Shouldn't I get to know the truth?" he asked, ignoring her statement. Then he added, "It's not like I'm risking my life for you or anything."

"You don't care about me or getting me to the capital," Ethelwynne continued. "You just hope this makes you look good when you apply to be a town guard. Well guess what, I don't want to be the reason you get hired." She got up and stamped out a spark that had landed on a root. "I don't need you to protect me."

"Yes, I can see how you don't need me to protect you. I mean I've only had to rescue you from being sold by slavers a few days ago, bandits yesterday, and a murderous elf how many times now? You're clearly perfectly capable of taking care of yourself."

"We would have gotten out without your help, and if you hadn't gotten in the way with your noble can't-do-anything-wrong attitude, I would already be in White Shield and Heotene wouldn't be a problem."

"Of course you would have. Because once you and Xiamara dropped out of the window, the front of the building would have been completely empty of slavers. Oh wait," he tossed her shoe back to her, "that just happened because the three of us showed up."

He turned his attention to the fish in the fire and reached in to grab the leaf packages out with a stick. Sparks flew as he disturbed the coals and landed on his hands. Cephas swore and tossed the stick to the ground as he slapped the sparks from his hand. Pieces of burnt fish and leaves spread across the rocks.

"We would have come up with something," Ethelwynne spat clenching her shoe. "We did get free from our bonds, and get out of the room we were trapped in. But this isn't about me. It's about you, not trusting me. Why couldn't you just say 'Hey Ethelwynne, because both guards and brigands are trying to catch you, I don't think the roads are the safest way to go'?"

"You were barely able to put one foot in front of the other." Cephas dipped his hands in the lake and looked at Ethelwynne over his shoulder. "I didn't want to stress you out with the thought of everyone who wants you dead."

Ethelwynne glared at him and considered throwing her shoe at him again. "I can handle it." she said, walking towards him. "I have been through a lot lately. That was not the first time someone tried to kill me these past couple of weeks." Cephas stood up as she advanced. "I've come to terms with the fact that the elves want me dead, and that

Heotene is willing to work with both guards and thugs to find me. Hearing that we can't travel on the road wouldn't have driven me over the edge of despair." She slapped his chest with her shoe. "But you don't care about that, because pretending I'm just a little girl who needs to be protected feeds your desire to be a hero."

"And you're not pretending to be one? Why do the elves want you dead? What do your parents have to do with it? Why is it so important for you to get to the capital that it couldn't wait until I had time to mourn my brother?" He turned away from Ethelwynne and walked towards a tree where he rested his forehead on his arms. "I'm the oldest. I should have protected him. Just like I should have protected Xiamara. What a great job I'm doing."

Ethelwynne's shoe slipped from her fingers and splashed into the lake. "I'm so sorry Cephas."

"Just tell me why I'm doing this," he answered. The weight of his time with her bled out of his words and burdened his posture.

Ethelwynne stared at his back and nodded. She bent down to pick up her shoe and walked back to her cloak to sit down. "I didn't steal from the elves."

"So you've been saying."

Ethelwynne took a deep breath as she sat her shoe down near the flames to dry. "I went to Heatherfield Manor to find out why the gates were still closed because my parents are trapped on the other side. But when I got there, no one would open the door. So I went around to the servants' entrance to see if they'd let me in that way when I heard some elves talking in the gardens. It was the prince and the captain of his guards." She looked up from the flames and over to Cephas. He had turned around to face her as he listened, but his expression was unreadable. "The two of them were talking about the key and how they had stolen it from the king to trap him in our realm. But, before they were able to cross back into Grahamadon, someone stole the key from them. The prince's men killed the thief, but he fell into Ems River. And before I was able to get away, they saw me."

The rippling waves and the small pops and crackles from the fire became the only sound when Ethelwynne stopped speaking.

"We're going to need help," Cephas said after a moment.

"If we make it to the capital, I can pass the message along the next time the king holds an audience in the throne room."

"King Orrin hasn't ousted his brother, so he might not know," said Cephas as he picked up the spear to try and catch new fish. "If you just show up there, there's a good chance the guards will arrest you on sight." He looked up from the water. "You will not be able to pass along your message from prison."

"I could tell the jailor."

"The jailor won't believe you without proof. By the time you find someone who does believe you, Prince Damien will probably have found the key and locked his brother out of the kingdom, and then we'd have to deal with an angry elf king who can't rule Grahamadon taking his frustration out on all of us."

"I don't think King Orrin would react that way. He has to be the more rational of the two. Besides, how will we find the key? The elves have been looking for months, and they have magic, and they can't find it."

"My mother can help us, or she'll know someone who can," Cephas threw the spear into the water, and ran over to retrieve it. A fish writhed on the end. "And," he said as he walked back to the shore to clean the fish, "the elves' magic might not work as well in the human realm. At least, I think I remember mother saying something about that."

"Why wouldn't it?"

He shrugged. "I don't know. Ask my mother when we get there."

219

CHRISTINA VAN STARKENBURG

— CHAPTER FIFTEEN —

The Painted Lady's Order

The next morning, they skirted the woods by the lake. Before the sun had reached its zenith, the body of water narrowed into a river and they came upon a dirt road with a rickety wooden bridge. They hovered behind the trees and listened.

"I don't think waiting is going to make it any less risky," Ethelwynne whispered. Cephas nodded and stepped out onto the road. Ethelwynne toyed with the edges of her sleeves as she followed him onto the bridge. The hollow thuds seemed to echo down the corridor between the trees.

"Don't run," whispered Cephas as he looked around. "If anyone sees us, we'll look less suspicious if we're not running."

Ethelwynne nodded and rubbed her arms as a shiver swept through her. Sher had said the same thing when they were fleeing to Lady Kiran's place.

Once they were on the other side, Cephas glanced around them one more time before pushing Ethelwynne off the road and back towards the lake. "We'll cut through the forest. It'll be faster and safer."

Ethelwynne sighed and began following him through the trees.

They left the water when the sun was at its highest point. The forest grew denser the further in they walked. "Ow," Ethelwynne yelped as she scraped her leg across the rocks jutting out of the hill they were climbing down. "I swear, you are choosing the most difficult path through these trees." She ducked under some branches as she followed him.

Cephas looked at her with pursed lips and shook his head before he continued trudging through the trees.

"I know that walking along the road isn't safe for us, but…" she paused, afraid to give voice to her concern. She followed Cephas in silence for a few minutes, before she decided that Cephas deserved to know. "Cephas? What if Heotene is using magic to find me?"

She looked at Cephas, but he didn't turn to face her and his speed didn't slow.

"I mean, she found us in the middle of the mountains, and then she found me in the market when I was covered in so much make-up I didn't recognize myself."

Cephas stopped to help her over a fallen log as he responded: "I've thought about that, but I'd rather face just her instead of all of the guards in a town or the brigands on the road." Once she was over, he started walking again, ducking under branches, stepping around animal burrows, and climbing over mossy rocks.

Ethelwynne glanced back the way they came and yelped as she stepped in a small hole. "They might be able to find us anyway. I'm not the most graceful."

As she moved forward again, she focused on where she was placing her feet and walked into Cephas who had stopped. He rubbed the back of his neck as he stared at the path behind them. After a moment he threw his hands up in the air. "If it's that bad, I can go back behind us once we find a safe place to spend the night and see if I can disguise our path." He turned back around and continued walking into the forest until he found a suitable spot.

While he was checking their path to make sure it wasn't an obvious trail right to them, Ethelwynne decided to practice throwing her knives. She kept vowing to learn how to use them. It was time. She picked a tree and threw five of them in that direction. Two landed closer to her than the tree, the third clattered uselessly against the tree to the left of her target, the fourth one landed in the shrubs behind the tree she was aiming at, and the fifth landed at its roots and slid across the ground to bump into the trunk.

"Really?" She stamped her foot in frustration and lined up her shot for the sixth time.

"You're throwing them wrong. Stop bending your wrist."

Ethelwynne jumped and spun around to face Cephas holding the knife out in front of her. "You shouldn't sneak up on me like that. I could have hurt you. Again."

Cephas surveyed their campground and her knives littered around it. "The only person you're likely to hurt is you." He walked over and grabbed the knife from her hand and threw it at the tree. It stuck. "See? If you don't bend your wrist, you can actually aim." Cephas went and retrieved the knife from the tree. He also gathered up four of the other knives. "Where's the sixth one?"

Ethelwynne blushed and pointed towards the bushes it had landed nearby. "Over there somewhere."

Cephas rolled his eyes and got down on his knees to look for it. After a few moments, he got up, brushed the dirt from his pants and handed the knives back to her. "Try again, and remember, keep your wrist straight."

Ethelwynne's cheeks prickled as she took the knives and tried again. None of the knives went anywhere near the tree she was aiming for. She wished he wasn't watching her. This was humiliating.

"You're still bending your wrist," said Cephas.

"Don't you have something better to do?"

223

Cephas snapped a stalk off of a rhubarb plant and began to tear the leaves off it as he leaned against a tree. "No." He bit into the stalk and gestured with it to show Ethelwynne that he thought she should try again.

Ethelwynne sighed and tried to ignore him as she went back to practicing. After a few more tosses she was pretty sure she wanted to turn around and throw the knife at him. As she picked up her knives from the ground in front of the tree yet again, she had to admit that because of his advice the blades were actually going in the direction she was hoping for now. "He could be nicer about it," she muttered as she walked back to her starting point and dropped the knives on the ground beside her. She turned around to face her tree and lined up another shot.

"Try stepping into it to give yourself some more strength," Cephas called from the sidelines as he snapped off another rhubarb stalk.

With one last glare in his direction, she lined up her shot again. Reminding herself that he was just trying to help, she stepped forward as she let go of the blade. The knife arched through the air once and embedded itself into the trunk.

"Ha!" Ethelwynne yelped and clapped her hands together. She smiled and turned to face Cephas. He handed her another knife.

"Again." He pointed to a different tree.

Ethelwynne groaned, and sighed and took aim. This knife did not stick to the tree he pointed to. Neither did the next one. But the fourth knife stuck again for a moment before the hilt dropped and the knife thudded to the ground below it.

After a few more tries, Cephas told her to stop so he could sharpen her blades before it got too dark to see.

"I can sharpen them."

"Have you ever done it before?"

"No."

"Then no, I don't feel like having to teach you that too, and I'm not letting you ruin my knives by trying to figure it out on your own."

Ethelwynne sat on the ground and started to massage her hands and shoulders. Then, while he sharpened the blades Ethelwynne grabbed one of the rhubarb stalks to eat. "Thanks."

He nodded without looking up from the knives.

Ethelwynne watched as he sharpened them. He might not want to teach her but perhaps she could learn by watching.

He held up the final knife to inspect it before handing it back to her so she could put it in the pouch. "It might be worth your time to learn hand-to-hand combat too."

An image of the man she stabbed invaded her thoughts. Ethelwynne opened and shut her mouth a few times while she tried to find the right words to say no, but all she managed to come up with was a whispered "Not tonight."

Cephas put his hand on her shoulder. "People and elves are trying to kill you. I will do my best to keep them away from you, but I won't always be able to protect you." As she nodded in response, Cephas laydown on the ground to sleep.

*   *   *

Around lunchtime, the forest began to feel different. The air felt moist and heavy, like she was trying to breathe through a thin veil of water. The trees and plants seemed lusher, in deeper and richer shades of greens, purples, and reds.

"Stay close," Cephas cautioned as they walked deeper into the dark trees.

Ethelwynne had every intention of doing just that, in fact, she had been purposefully getting closer as the air became thicker around them. She had no intention of telling

Cephas that though. Although, since she'd bumped into him twice already, she would have been surprised if he didn't suspect that.

Ethelwynne was worried that if she lost him for only a moment, she would never find him or her way out of the gloom. The stray beams of sunlight that did penetrate the canopy of the old forest didn't seem to add much light to it.

She heard water rushing down a river near to them. Suddenly the deep greens and dark shadows opened up to a waterfall. From where she was standing, she couldn't see where the water went after it tumbled down the rock face in front of them. Curious she moved closer.

"Careful," Cephas grabbed her arm to stop her from walking forward.

"Where does the water go?" Ethelwynne asked and stood up on her toes to try and see farther. "I can't see the river. We should be standing in it."

Cephas pulled her further back and circled wide around the waterfall. "It goes underground. You'll see when we get to the top." He continued to pull her towards the rocks and gestured towards them when he stopped. "You first."

They climbed up the slippery rock face pulling on roots and low hanging branches to yank themselves up to the top of the rock face. The moss felt cool under her fingers and the rocks slick from the constant splashing of falls.

At last, she made it to the top. She pulled herself over and spun around while she was still lying on her stomach to offer a hand to Cephas and gasped. The waterfall disappeared into a hole. Pitch black swallowed up the white frothing currents and stray leaves that had the misfortune to blow over the pit.

Cephas pushed her hand aside and heaved himself up onto the top. He sat down beside her and dangled his legs over the edge and leaned on his arms. "I once chucked a candle with an enchanted flame down there. I still couldn't

226

see the bottom." After a moment he stood up, "Come on, it's not far now."

They followed the river to a stone wall that was almost hidden in the vines and flowers that crept up its sides. Cephas led her around to the thick wooden door. He picked up the brass knocker and rapped it hard against the door. A few moments later, a woman about the same age as her mother opened the door and silently glared at them.

"We're here to see Idra," Cephas said apparently undeterred by her ire. After staring at them for a few moments more she stepped aside and motioned them in. Then as the door slammed shut behind them, she led the way up to the main building.

Inside the walls, there was a stone pathway that wound through the gardens up to the front door of the monastery. Red, purple and pink flowers dotted the pathway. The sun seemed to actually care about this spot and shone in brightly. Women also dotted the garden sitting quietly, soaking up the noonday sun as they meditated.

Their guide ushered them across the cloister, through the refectory and into the dormitories where she unceremoniously abandoned them in a windowless room. Ethelwynne looked around the room. Candles burned along its edges, sending flickering shadows dancing across the walls, but beyond that the room was empty. "I wonder what they use this room for."

Cephas sat down and closed his eyes as he leaned against the wall. "Some of the women live here all year round. If any of them have children, this room is turned into the school."

Ethelwynne dropped to the ground beside him. "How do you know that?

"This is where I learned to read," said Cephas without opening his eyes. "Why don't you work on that dress you were sketching? It might help the time pass."

"I don't have a stylus."

Cephas was silent for a moment. He walked over to her. "Pull out two of your knives. I might as well teach you how to use them while we wait."

Ethelwynne groaned but did what he asked. He showed her the correct way to stand and how to effectively use the knives to cut the other person should she ever find herself in a close-up battle.

When several of the candles had completely burned out Ethelwynne asked to stop. She leaned against the wall breathing heavily. "Do you think our guide left us here to be forgotten until the end of the festival?"

Before Cephas answered, the door creaked open and a woman whose looks proclaimed her to be his mother entered. "Cephas," she said with the exasperated sigh of a woman whose child has once again done something he should not have, "what are you doing here? Couldn't this have waited for one week? You know I'm not supposed to be interrupted." She opened her arms to him and Cephas embraced her.

"We need your help," Cephas said before summing up Prince Damien's plan and how they were involved.

Idra put her finger to her lip as she considered what he had told her. "I must speak with the head of my order. I will return shortly." Then she turned and slipped back out of the door leaving Ethelwynne and Cephas alone once more in the growing darkness.

Cephas stared at the closed door for a moment before he turned to Ethelwynne. "Again?"

Ethelwynne gulped some air and nodded as she walked to the center of the room and readied herself. Cephas took the other knife out of his pocket and lunged at her. She stepped back to avoid the blade.

"You didn't mention Talman."

Cephas grunted and swung the knife at her. The flat of the blade slapped her arm and left a red mark just above her wrist. Her knife clattered to the floor and Cephas took a step back. He wiped his eyes while she picked up her blade and prepared herself again. "I will before we leave," he said softly and stepped forward again.

One by one the candles burned out. When only five remained, Cephas handed Ethelwynne back her knife and the two of them wandered over to the wall to rest and wait. Ethelwynne shut her eyes. When she opened them, only two of the candles remained lit.

The door opened and a young woman burst in with an armful of new candles. She jumped when she saw that the room was occupied and dropped her burden. Some of the small white candles rolled across the floor, others snapped where they landed.

Ethelwynne and Cephas bent down to help her pick them up, but she slapped their hands away, and after gathering up her candles left the room as quickly as she came into it.

"Great," muttered Cephas. "Couldn't even leave us a candle."

"Perhaps they were worried you'd throw these ones into a waterfall too."

Cephas laughed.

Ethelwynne smiled and held out two candles. "I picked them up before she noticed I was trying to help, but she never took them from me."

Cephas smiled and took one of the candles from Ethelwynne. "Thief." He walked over to one of the still burning candles and lit his, then he hovered it over top of the old one so that the wax would melt and it would sit in the stand. Ethelwynne lit the one beside it with hers.

Now, no longer in danger of being left in the dark Ethelwynne and Cephas walked over to the door and leaned against the wall beside it and waited for Idra to return.

*   *   *

The two candles that she and Cephas had lit were almost burned down when the door swung open, blowing out the candles. Cephas and Ethelwynne were momentarily thrown into complete darkness before a new candle was lit by the regal woman coming into the room. Idra followed her in wordlessly.

Cephas stood and bowed before her. "Reverend Mother."

The woman sighed much like Idra had done the first time she entered their room and clapped her hands on his shoulders. "Idra explained your situation to me. I'm sorry this burden has fallen on your shoulders."

The Reverend Mother looked at Ethelwynne over Cephas's shoulder. "I can give you an amulet that will guide you to what you seek. But know this, if you let your thoughts become clouded, it may not be the key that the amulet guides you too." She nodded towards Idra. "Idra will bring you to your rooms for the night, and I will have the amulet ready for you in the morning, along with some supplies and a ride for your journey." She released Cephas and turned to leave.

"Wait," Ethelwynne spoke up. The Reverend Mother stopped and turned to look at Ethelwynne. "The elves have been using magic to find the key, but it isn't working." She shuffled nervously and felt her cheeks flush. "What makes this amulet different from their magic?"

"There is not enough time for me to fully explain the reason their magic is not working," said the Reverend Mother. "However, I can say this: if the elves were using a magic object, they brought with them from the Grahamadon it would work in our lands, but our realm is not suited to their style of magic. Any spells they cast here, will likely fail or only work in part. The same can be said of our magic. Because the amulet was created in the human realm using human magic it will work. If you took the amulet with you into the elven realm it would work. If, however, I tried to create it there, the magic would likely fail." She brushed Ethelwynne's hair from her face. "Do not let your worries bother you. The amulet will work. Now it is time for you to rest." Her gown swished softly as she left the room and walked down the hall.

Idra silently waved for the two of them to follow her. She led them down the hall away from the Reverend Mother. They climbed some stairs and entered a hall that was lined with doors. She stopped at the second one and turned to Cephas as she opened the door. "You may sleep in here my son, and I will return with some ointments to heal your wounds."

Cephas pulled the door closed and sighed. "Let's show Ethelwynne where she'll sleep. I have something else to tell you."

Idra studied her son's face. Worry crept across her features when he looked away. Idra hugged her son tightly before continuing down the hall and stopping at the final door. "You may sleep here."

She held open the door as Ethelwynne slipped past her. Someone had already been in there to turn down the sheets. The light from a single candle flickered in the water from the wash basin.

"Thank you," said Ethelwynne. Idra moved to shut the door, but before she was able to, Ethelwynne hugged her.

Idra brushed her hair with her hand. "Sleep well child. I will see you in the morning."

Ethelwynne nodded and stepped back into her room shutting the door behind her.

CHRISTINA VAN STARKENBURG

— CHAPTER SIXTEEN —

A Poisoned Swim

The next morning Ethelwynne was woken by someone rapping on her door. "One moment," she called out groggily as she got up to rinse her face.

When she opened the door the young woman who had dropped the candles the night before, was waiting for her. Without saying a word, the woman began to walk down the hall towards the stairs. She waved for Ethelwynne to follow her and continued to guide her to the refectory for breakfast. Cephas arrived with his mother as Ethelwynne was sitting down. His wounds from the fight with the bandits were completely faded. But his mother's pain from hearing about Talman was visible in the vacant expression on her face as she sat down heavily.

Ethelwynne wished there was something she could say to help Idra feel better, but if she had never met the Merrilins, Talman would still be alive. Ethelwynne turned and studied the table in front of her. It was covered in platters and bowls of pancakes, oatmeal with cream and strawberries, sausages and gravy, fried potatoes, apricot turnovers, and apple pie. Her mouth watered in spite of her grief.

The Reverend Mother entered the refectory. Cephas and

all of the other worshippers stood up. Ethelwynne blushed and rose to her feet. When the scuffling of chairs stopped, the Reverend Mother raised her hands as she prayed to Satia and blessed the food. The rest of the meal was conducted in silence. As Ethelwynne ate a turnover she wondered if that was because of the festival, or if they always ate their meals in silence here, but there was no way she could ask.

As the meal ended, Idra stood up and motioned to Cephas and Ethelwynne to follow her. She led them to the office and knocked on the inner door. After a few moments, the Reverend Mother opened the door and let the three of them inside. The center of the room was dominated by a dark brown desk that had an ornate forest scene with fairies and other fantastical creatures dancing carved into the front.

The Reverend Mother walked around her desk. As she sat down, she pulled open a drawer and took out a small wooden box and set it on the center of the desk. "This will help you find the key should it still be in our land."

Ethelwynne opened the box and pulled the silver chain out. A dark green stone with fine silver wires twisted into images of butterflies, dahlias, and roses hung on it. Awed by the beauty of it, Ethelwynne gently ran her thumb across the bumpy surface.

Remember," continued the Reverend Mother, "this charm will only work if you are able to quiet your mind and focus on what you are looking for. Should your thoughts stray to your family, or friends who have helped you along the way, the amulet will guide you to them instead."

"Thank you," said Ethelwynne as she put the necklace on.

The Reverend Mother nodded and rose. "Food has been prepared for you. It is waiting in the stables. Idra can take you there now. Take care, and may Satia bless your efforts."

Idra, Cephas and Ethelwynne bowed as they left the room and headed down to the stables. There were three stables built into the shape of a horseshoe. The remaining side was blocked with a gate to keep the young animals contained. Ethelwynne breathed in the smells of the animals and hay as Idra lifted the latch and let them into the barnyard. As Idra shut the gate behind them, two other women stepped out of the barn leading evlayar.

Ethelwynne gasped and took a few tentative steps towards the winged horse-like creatures. They were magnificent. Sunlight danced in the mane, tail and wings of the chestnut one. The black one seemed to absorb all of the light around it with the exception of the white star-shaped pattern on its forehead and the three white feathers on each wing that were blinding by the contrast. Ethelwynne ran her fingers through her hair and wondered what she was getting herself into.

"It's just like riding a normal horse on the ground," Idra said as she came to stand beside her.

Ethelwynne nodded but couldn't help but think that Idra was forgetting to add the fact that if you fell off this horse you wouldn't break a leg; you'd die.

"Come now, you don't have all day, and I need to get back to the celebration."

Ethelwynne looked back out of the stables to where the women were meditating. She shook her head, Idra and the rest of the women here had an odd idea of what celebrating looked like. She steeled herself as she approached the evlayar. She reached out her palm and gently touched its nose. It snorted. She jumped.

"Oh come on girl, this is not the first time you've touched a horse, is it?"

She straightened her shirt and closed her eyes while she took a deep breath. The scent of oats, hay, horses, and evlayar filled her nostrils. "It is for a winged-one," she muttered as she opened her eyes and reached out and petted the evlayar again. She could do this.

Idra rolled her eyes and pulled Ethelwynne beside the black one. "Come on, let's get you on her. This is Starblade. She's very sweet."

Ethelwynne stepped onto the mounting block and put her foot in the stirrup. Idra explained how to get on without hurting the evlayar's wings. With a final deep breath for courage, Ethelwynne pulled herself into the saddle and leaned back while Idra fastened the straps that would keep her there.

"Comfortable?" Idra asked as she finished up and gestured for Ethelwynne to sit straight again.

Ethelwynne awkwardly patted the evlayar's neck. "No." Her fingers vanished into Starblade's silky main. The evlayar shook her head and neighed as though to say that she too was not comfortable with this arrangement. Ethelwynne pulled her hand away and gingerly wrapped both of them around the bar on the front of the saddle.

Idra nodded and turned to walk over to her son.

"Wait."

Idra looked up at Ethelwynne. "Yes?"

"I just... I wanted to..." Tears welled up in Ethelwynne's eyes as she recalled Talman's sacrifice. "I just wanted to say I'm sorry about Talman."

Idra squeezed her leg, unshed tears briefly swam in the bottom of her eyes before she blinked them away. "Thank you. And know that I don't blame you. Now dry your eyes or you won't be able to see where you are going." With that, she patted Ethelwynne's leg and walked over to Cephas.

The two of them embraced. Ethelwynne watched as Cephas half-heartedly tried to push his mother away before sighing, hugging her tightly once more, and then unwrapping her arms from him.

"Good luck," Idra said as her son easily swung into the saddle. Reading was clearly not the only thing Cephas learned when he was here.

"Which way?" he asked steering his evlayar towards her.

Ethelwynne took a few deep breaths and closed her eyes as she tried to concentrate on the gateway's key. Nothing happened. Her cheeks prickled, she wondered what Idra, Cephas, and the other two women must think of her. She must look like a fool to them.

A hand touched her leg. Ethelwynne opened her eyes and looked down at Idra. "Relax child. Don't think about us. Don't think about your parents. Do think about why you are doing this."

Ethelwynne sighed. "How do I not think about all of that?"

Idra was silent for a moment. "When we teach new recruits to meditate, we get them to count for every breath in and every breath out. It gives them something to concentrate on, until they are able to sit in true silence. Why don't you try that, but instead of numbers, think 'key to the realms'?"

"Okay." Ethelwynne wrapped her fingers around the cool amulet and close her eyes again as she tried Idra's advice.

"Don't give up if nothing happens right away," said Idra. Ethelwynne heard her footsteps as the older woman walked away. "Be patient with yourself and it will happen."

Ethelwynne concentrated once more. She consciously slowed her thoughts and her breathing as she thought *key to the realms* every time air filled her lungs and every time she released the air. Still nothing happened. Ethelwynne tamped down her frustrations and continued to breathe in and out. Suddenly, the knowledge burned within her. Ethelwynne swivelled in her saddle to point behind them to the east. "The key is that way."

Idra stopped stroking Starblade's nose and gazed in the direction Ethelwynne pointed. "The evlayar will only take you as far as the edge of the forest," she said as she led the Starblade through the barnyard gate.

"Why?" asked Ethelwynne, even though she was fairly confident she wouldn't want to ride the creature beyond the forest's edge.

"They do not like the marsh beyond, and while the Reverend Mother could compel them to cross it, I doubt anyone else could." She stopped and rubbed Starblade's nose. "Now go." As Idra released Starblade the evlayar began to move.

Ethelwynne leaned forward and squeezed the bar until her knuckles were white. The evlayar galloped down the walkway and spread its wings. Ethelwynne couldn't breathe. Starblade cleared the outer wall. The wind choked Ethelwynne as they rose above the trees. Her chest ached. She felt dizzy and nauseous. Black spots marred her vision. She clenched her eyes shut to block out the spots and tried not to think about falling off.

She whimpered. *I can do this. I can do this. I can do this,* she told herself over and over in hopes that she would somehow believe it.

Her muscles tensed and her body froze in the pose for the entire flight. When Starblade's feet once again touched the ground. Ethelwynne gasped and climbed off before Starblade had fully stopped. She backed away from the evlayar and fell to the ground behind her.

Her whole body shook. She was never, ever going to do that again. From now on her feet were going to stay firmly on the ground. No more flying horses or ships. If she was ever given the option between a skyship and a flying horse, she'd walk. At least that way if she fell, it wouldn't be far.

"Ethelwynne." Cephas walked over and squatted in front of her, the two evlayar were munching grass behind him.

"I'll brush down the evlayar and get them ready for their flight home." He held up a hand to silence her, "Starblade and Celosia know the way. In the meantime, can you make sure we keep going in the right direction?"

"How... how did that not bother you?" Ethelwynne willed her body to stop shaking, but to no avail.

Cephas shrugged and stood up, "It's not my first time. Besides, I've been working in the sky for a few years now." He walked away to tend to the evlayar and left Ethelwynne to attempt to calm herself.

She grabbed hold of the amulet. Her shudders became less frequent as she focused on the key. The magic's warmth filled her. They still needed to go straight. The Maudinmere Marsh lay before them with the River Ems and the northern arm of the Grahamadon Mountains beyond. "I really hope the key is on the other side closer to the mountains and not in these waters," Ethelwynne said as she rose to her feet and walked over to Cephas.

Cephas whispered something to Starblade and Celosia. Celosia nudged his cheek with her nose then turned and ran. Starblade followed. The two evlayar spread their wings and rose into the sky.

It was much easier to admire their grace and beauty from the ground. Ethelwynne's hair whirled around her face as the evlayar turned back towards the forest. She held it back from her eyes as she watched the creatures soar over the trees. "Ready?" she asked after a moment.

Cephas nodded and handed her one of the bags. He shouldered the other and the two of them headed towards the marsh. Ethelwynne gagged as the smell from the Maudinmere reached her. She buried her nose in her cloak. "I hope it's not as far across as it looks."

Cephas scrunched up his face. "Maybe we'll get used to it."

Ethelwynne doubted that, but there was little they could do about it. They needed to get the key and the elves had a huge head start to find it. They stepped into the soft, oozy ground.

The silence hung heavy in the air the further away from

the edge they traveled. Ethelwynne's skin prickled as she felt the cool assessing gaze from unseen eyes. She shivered and stepped over some thin purple vines to be closer to Cephas.

Cephas looked over and smiled. "We'll make it through," he said.

Ethelwynne nodded and watched the ground. Green vines draped the mossy surface and covered the few fallen logs that littered the soft earth.

"Careful," Cephas said and put his hand on her shoulder to stop her from stepping on one of the logs. He nudged it with his foot and it rolled forward and disappeared beneath the algae-covered water.

Ethelwynne shuddered as an air bubble popped on the surface of the ooze where the log had disappeared. She watched as the green liquid ceased rippling and looked like the ground once more. "How do we get around?" she asked softly?

Cephas pinched the bridge of his nose.

Ethelwynne squeezed her eyes shut. There had to be a way across. "Do you think the amulet could guide us?" She peaked over at Cephas.

Cephas shrugged. "We can try, or else we'll have to test every step before we take it."

Ethelwynne closed her eyes and concentrated on her breathing. It was easier to think about a safe path then it was for her to focus on the key, perhaps because the path was more immediately important. She opened her eyes as the warmth washed over her. "This way," she said and cautiously took a step to her right. The ground beneath her feet was firm though still very damp and her foot sank into it. Cephas stepped into the impression her foot left behind as she moved further into the Maudinmere. In some places patches of water showed through in the center of wide algae-covered pools, but most of the water was hidden beneath the green carpet.

Ethelwynne ducked under a dead branch and stepped

over one of the weird purple vines that seemed to writhe on the ground. She paused and turned to look at Cephas. "Do you think it's s—" Her voice hitched as Cephas tripped over the thin purple vine. She watched motionless as it wrapped around his leg and he fell into the marsh.

"Cephas!" Ethelwynne cried when he didn't surface. She dropped her bag and ran towards the water to try and pull him out. Weeds wrapped around her legs as she struggled to reach him. Her heartbeat pounded in her ears as she fought off the weeds. She had to reach him. He couldn't drown in this diseased water. She couldn't be alone here; she'd never make it. She took a deep breath and dove under the water.

Ethelwynne couldn't see well underneath the murky surface. She was too worried about Cephas to be surprised by how deep it became so quickly. Her hand brushed his sleeve in the gloom. She grabbed hold of his arm and tried to pull him up, but he was hopelessly tangled in the weeds.

Her lungs screamed at her to go back up for air, but Cephas didn't have the time. She pulled one of the knives off of her belt and tried to cut him free of the plants. The water seemed to thicken around her limbs. She moved so slowly.

At last, Cephas lifted free of the plants. Ethelwynne tugged him towards the surface. She struggled to find the strength. Black spots filled her vision, as she watched the stream of bubbles escape from her mouth. Her legs floundered uselessly behind her. Ethelwynne reached up in desperation hoping to touch some of the grasses that dipped into the water. There was nothing for her to grab. They were going to drown.

A dark object dipped down through the mire towards them. Ethelwynne wondered if the plants had decided to save them after working so hard to kill them. Solid fingers wrapped around her own and pulled her and Cephas towards the surface.

Ethelwynne gasped as they broke through the water into

the air. She scrambled up the mossy bank and pulled Cephas behind her. The one who saved them helped her pull Cephas further out of the water. Ethelwynne kept her eyes focused on Cephas who hadn't moved. Ethelwynne shook Cephas. "Breathe. Come on breathe." She nearly drowned herself trying to save him, but it still wasn't enough.

The elf shoved Ethelwynne out of the way, and poured a dark liquid into Cephas's mouth. Ethelwynne watched her with wide-eyes, but her mouth wouldn't work. *She saved us. Did she not recognize me? Does she not work for the prince? Has he changed his mind about killing me on sight?*

"What are you doing to him?" she asked when she found her voice.

The elf began pushing deeply into his chest over and over again. "The creature that pulled him under can stop him from breathing air," she said without taking her eyes off Cephas. "The medicine will hopefully counteract that curse."

Murky water oozed up out of Cephas's throat as the elf worked. Her posture relaxed and she turned him on his side to let it spill down his cheek. "I take it you've never been to the Maudinmere," said the elf as she looked over at Ethelwynne for the first time since pulling them out of the water.

Ethelwynne shook her head.

The elf pushed Cephas onto his back and pressed on his chest again until more green liquid filled his mouth. "It isn't safe to stay in one place for long. If he doesn't start breathing on his own when the liquid stops, I can try and help him bring up some more of the liquid, but then we'll have to move him somewhere safer and hope he survives." She looked back at Ethelwynne after she rolled Cephas to his side. "If you're the praying type, now is the time to hope your Goddess hears you."

At last, the murky water stopped trickling out of Cephas's mouth. He coughed and rolled over onto his hands and knees and violently hacked up the remaining water from his lungs.

He moaned and sat back on his heels as he rested his head on his arms.

"Cephas!" Ethelwynne yelped and scrambled over to hug him. "We can't stay here. Can you walk?" He nodded weakly. She and the elf pulled Cephas to his feet and draped his arms around their shoulders to help him get further away from the water's edge.

"Let's not do that again shall we?" the elf said once Cephas began walking on his own. "Try to watch where you're stepping next time, these waters are poison."

Cephas coughed and stumbled forward. "Who are you?"

"My name is Jocasta. I am one of the King's Guard." She paused from her constant scan of their surroundings and faced the two of them. "My turn. Who are you and what are you doing out here? Besides trying to kill yourselves?"

Ethelwynne looked at Cephas. What should they say? All she knew was the necklace was telling them to go east. "We are heading to the mountains. My aunt lives over that way and I wanted to visit her so we decided to take a shortcut through the marshes."

"I see," Jocasta followed her gaze to the distant peaks. "As it happens, I am headed in that direction as well. Allow me to help you make it there alive."

"Oh no, as one of the King's Guard I can only assume you must be incredibly busy. I, we," she gestured to include Cephas in her statement "wouldn't want to keep you from your tasks."

"It's no trouble." She looked up at the sky as they approached a knoll, "Come. Let us rest here. We can head out at first light."

Ethelwynne looked to Cephas for help, but his head was already drooped to his chest as he sat and leaned against a gnarled tree trunk.

"I'll be back, I'm going to go scout ahead for a bit," said Jocasta as she walked off the hill and back into the muck. "Stay on this hill."

Ethelwynne watched Jocasta walk away as she removed her shoes. She dumped out all of the water and then set them aside to dry, as she let her wrinkly toes dry out as much as they could in a place like this.

"What do we do Cephas?" she whispered. But the only answer she received was his soft snoring. *Maybe she doesn't know who I am,* Ethelwynne thought as she untied Cephas's cloak and draped it over some of the finger-like branches of the trees he was leaning against. *After all, she hasn't tried to kill us yet.*

Just before the sun vanished behind the distant trees, Jocasta returned. "Why don't you take the first watch? I'll take the second and we can let him sleep."

Ethelwynne nodded. "Did you see anything I should know about while scouting?"

"Nothing you need to worry about," murmured Jocasta from where she had curled up.

Ethelwynne's skin crawled as she scanned the marsh. As she stared out over the bleak lands, the sky clouded over, but, mercifully, the rain stayed away as did whatever dangers lurked in the algae-covered waters and in the tall grasses.

— CHAPTER SEVENTEEN —

Creature of the Deep

The next morning it was even worse. When the clouds let out a constant drizzle, the sharp grasses clung to their legs and left little cuts across their legs whenever they found a gap in the travelers' clothes. Their feet were perpetually damp from the thick mud. Their bodies were chilled by the rain.

The hairs on the back of Ethelwynne's neck prickled as she ran her fingers through her matted mane. "I keep thinking we're being watched," she mumbled.

"We are," Jocasta said.

Ethelwynne shivered and looked around more carefully but still didn't see their watchers.

"If we are lucky, they will simply continue to watch us, but the creatures who live here do not like to be disturbed. And when the two of you decided to dive deep into the first lake, you alerted more of them to your presence than any of us would have wished."

An eagle screeched overhead. Ethelwynne jumped. She rubbed her arms to try and warm them up as she continued to follow Jocasta. She might not trust the elf, but she was grateful she was here. They would be dead if not for her.

Cephas snorted and huffed about how they didn't intend

to go swimming, but that the path was awful. "We should have just taken the evlayar to the other side of this place." He swatted a branch out of his way. The water droplets sloshed into Ethelwynne's face as it swung back to its original position a hand's breadth from her eyes.

Ethelwynne yelped, ducked, and decided against reminding him what his mother said about the evlayar. When he reached the next branch, he came out of his miserable, wallowing self-pity enough to hold the branch so Ethelwynne could pass by without being slapped.

The patter of the raindrops on the water was constant melancholic music beside them. Ethelwynne heard a plop and splash. She paused and turned towards the lake on their left. Wide ripples spread out from a place not too far off the shore.

Ethelwynne looked at Jocasta, she had her bow out and was stringing it in spite of the rain. "Keep walking Ethelwynne," she said without ever turning around to look at her.

Ethelwynne nodded and continued to walk behind Jocasta along the narrow muddy path, but she took out two of her knives and held them in the palms of her hands. She glanced behind her and saw that Cephas also had unsheathed his sword.

They walked in silence, each trying to keep both eyes on the water while still watching where their feet were going so they didn't end up in the lake again. The clouds overhead grew darker and the rain began to fall more heavily. Soon Ethelwynne could only see misty shadows where her companions stood. She tried to see the ground in front of her or the water where their watchers waited.

Ethelwynne bit her lip. Her hands clenched around her daggers' hilts so firmly that her fingernails left red crescents in her palms. She raised one hand to shield her eyes from the rain so she could see Jocasta.

A long, dark purple tentacle rushed through the reeds and wrapped around her leg. Ethelwynne screamed as it pulled her down and across the muddy earth.

Cephas yelled her name.

One of Jocasta's arrows pinned the tentacle to the ground.

The dorsal fin and head of a giant three-eyed fish crashed through the surface. Two large tentacles flanked its head with a few smaller ones writhing on top. The monster screeched in anger deafening the trio. Two more tentacles rose from the water, outlined by a white halo of raindrops that pounded off its skin.

Ethelwynne slashed her daggers without any precision or care and hoped she made contact. One of her knives cut deep into the tentacle that was dragging her through the mud. Dark blood splashed out across her as the creature shrieked in pain. The limb released her.

She scrambled back from the beast. Cephas stepped in front of her and fought off the tentacle that was coming back to claim him and the other that was vying for Ethelwynne again.

Jocasta loosed several arrows at its other arms as they approached.

Undeterred by the arrows two of the creature's arms shot towards Jocasta.

She dove out of the way, dropping her bow. As she stood, she drew her sword, and cut off one of its limbs.

The creature screamed. Ethelwynne desperately tried to cover her ears to block out the sound, but it was no use. The sound was inside of her mind.

Fighting for control, Ethelwynne glanced towards the others. Cephas stood frozen, but the creature was ignoring him. Jocasta was being pulled towards the water. Her sword was not in her hands. Ethelwynne ran over and stabbed down on that tentacle with both of her daggers.

The monster shrieked again. The tentacle under her blades lashed out and threw Ethelwynne into a dead tree. The tree cracked from the force and toppled down. Branches scratched her cheeks, hands, and sides as she tried to untangle herself from their snare.

The beast disappeared back into the waters.

"Move!" Jocasta yelled as she picked up her weapons.

Ethelwynne shoved the branch from her body and grabbed Cephas's arm and pulled him with her. When she reached Jocasta, the elf looked at Cephas's glazed expression, swore, and shoved him in front of them. As they raced through the mire, Jocasta grabbed his arm to turn him. Ethelwynne followed as fast as she could, struggling for air. The three of them slipped in the mud and splashed in the shallows as they ran from where the creature was lurking along a path that only Jocasta could see.

Ethelwynne's heart pounded in her ear as they ran. Her lungs felt like they would burst. She stumbled over a root submerged in the shallow water. Her legs gave out and she fell into the murky liquid. "Wait... please," she gasped.

Jocasta slowed her pace to a quick walk, "We're not far enough away yet. Up ahead the path veers away from this lake and into the marshes that connect it to the other ones. It's too shallow for that creature there, but it can still get us here."

Ethelwynne's stomach sank as she pushed herself up from the muck to keep going. Cephas fell into step beside her. His eyes looked clearer. "You can do it Ethelwynne," he said.

She looked up at him as she stumbled along the trail. He seemed very frail after the poison of the lakes and the fight with the monster. He gave her a small smile and turned his gaze towards to Jocasta's back. Ethelwynne promised herself that if he could keep going, so could she.

They continued to slosh through the water that

sometimes went up to their waists. The further they went from the lake the more Cephas lagged behind. The rain started falling harder again. It pounded in Ethelwynne's ears, drowned out any sound from the waters, and prevented her from seeing beyond her small halo of vision. Jocasta's form was almost indiscernible in front of her. The elf slowed down minutely to stop the other two from losing her.

Ethelwynne turned around to check if Cephas was still following her. Her foot snagged something under the water, and down she went. Weeds wrapped around her limbs. She thrashed and panicked as though the plants were alive and the creature had gotten her and was trying to pull her to her death.

Cephas reached down and yanked her up out of the water. She coughed and gagged as he ushered her in the direction Jocasta had gone. "Come on, we'll be away from these waters soon and we can rest then."

After a while, they still had no sight of Jocasta. They tried calling out to her, but the wind whipped their voices away. They had no way of knowing if Jocasta could even hear their calls. What if they went too far and missed the path? This was not a place they would want to be lost without a guide. Ethelwynne stumbled again and Cephas grabbed her elbow to steady her.

"Thanks."

When he didn't release her arm, Ethelwynne looked over at him. His hair was plastered to his face, and he wore a pained grimace on his face. She wondered if he was still holding onto her to steady her or to steady himself.

They trudged forward and nearly collided with Jocasta as she stood in front of a tree. "Good," she said. "I don't have to go back and find you. This way." Jocasta turned to the south and started leaving the waters behind them. Soon their feet didn't disappear completely beneath the mire with each step. It almost felt like they were walking on solid ground again, but Ethelwynne knew that if it weren't for the drumming of the rain, they would still be able to hear the squelching of their steps in the soft earth.

Jocasta didn't stop until they left the lake far behind. As they climbed a rocky outcropping, the rain let up, revealing the moon high above them. "We'll sleep here for the night. The rocks can hide and protect us from any creatures that might serve the zonkenwae." The elf looked at Ethelwynne and must have seen the confusion on her face. "That tentacled fish-like creature. It can compel other creatures to serve its will." Her gaze flicked towards Cephas who had dropped to the ground and fallen asleep, "Sometimes it drags creatures it deems more useful to its home beneath the surface."

Ethelwynne followed her gaze and shuddered. "Do you think—"

"We'll have to watch him. But the sooner we are away from here, the better things will go for him."

Her wet cloak gave no warmth against the cold night air or the thoughts that tumbled through her mind, so Ethelwynne huddled next to Cephas in an attempt to share some of his heat. Rest did not come easy to her that night. Every time she started to drift off, she felt the slimy tentacle wrap around her leg again and jolted awake.

*   *   *

The next morning when Jocasta and Ethelwynne woke up, Cephas continued to sleep, shiver and sweat. Ethelwynne placed her hand on his forehead. He was burning up. "He's getting worse," she said, turning to Jocasta in alarm. "Can we—"

"Wake him up," said Jocasta as she finished rolling her blanket. "We can move a bit slower, but we can't stay here."

Ethelwynne nodded and put her hands on his shoulder to

shake him.

He moaned and opened his eyes a little. Coughing, he sat up. A thin line of green liquid dripped down his chin before he wiped it away.

Ethelwynne stood up and offered him a hand to pull him to his feet. Once he was standing, she put his arm over her shoulders to help support him.

Jocasta grabbed his bag and added it to her own. "We can trade in a while if you would like."

Ethelwynne nodded and followed Jocasta through the marsh. She prayed that they would make it out alive and before Cephas grew too weak to walk or fight off the lingering effects of the zonkenwae.

Cephas rested heavily on Ethelwynne's shoulder as they trudged through the marsh. As the day approached noon, he stumbled and fell. His weight pulled Ethelwynne down with him. Again and again, the two of them ended up in the muck. Jocasta stopped scouting ahead and wrapped his other arm around her shoulder. Even with the elf's help, his legs gave out and Ethelwynne found herself struggling under the added weight.

"Not here," said Jocasta in response to Ethelwynne's unasked question. That became the only phrase Jocasta would say as the hours trudged on. Every time Ethelwynne glanced in her direction, the elf would shake her head or say "not here" without ever taking her eyes from the path she seemed to instinctively know.

Ethelwynne stopped wondering when Jocasta would think they were far enough from the lake to be safe and decided the only safe place would be the other side of the Maudinmere. She didn't notice at first when Jocasta stopped walking on top of a grassy knoll and took an extra two steps before Cephas's weight held her back.

"It's getting darker and we wouldn't want to trip and dunk him in one of the streams that run through these lands."

Ethelwynne sat him down and then spread out his blanket and helped him into it. He was out long before Jocasta got the campfire started so they could make something warm to eat that night and keep the chill at bay.

"Don't wake him," Jocasta said when Ethelwynne leaned over to shake him and give him something to eat. "We can try and get him to eat something in the morning, but right now, it's more important for him to rest." She finished her meal and began walking around the edges of their small camp.

Ethelwynne nodded and watched him warily. He began to shiver, so she placed her blanket on top of him and moved closer to the fire to keep warm herself. She stared up at the sky. Stars blinked down at them every so often as clouds moved through the sky. "How much further until we're across?"

Jocasta, who had been looking out across the marsh, turned around to face her. "At his pace? I don't know. Normally I'd say two days at most."

"Is he going to make it?" Ethelwynne whispered looking over at his sleeping form. He seemed so peaceful right now.

Jocasta followed her gaze and shook her head. "I don't know."

Ethelwynne wrapped her arms around her legs, hugging them close. This was her fault: first Talman, and now she was going to lose Cephas too. She wished, once again, that none of this had ever happened. Why, oh why did she think going to that manor was a good idea? What did she expect to learn? As she cried, the rain started falling once more.

*   *   *

The rain relented in the early morning hours. Ethelwynne lifted her cloak from her eyes and peered out into the bleakness. Jocasta had wandered off again, searching for whatever it was that she was hoping to find out here or scouting to make sure that creature or any other creature wasn't following them through the muck.

Ethelwynne turned to check on Cephas to see if his fever had broken at all. His blankets were in a soggy pile. He was not in it. *Maybe he's gone to relieve himself?* She packed up her belongings while she waited for him to return. After a few moments she softly and tentatively called out his name.

There was no answer. *What if the creature sent minions to come and claim him?* Ethelwynne rung out his blanket and rolled it as she yelled a little louder. She wondered if yelling disturbed the creatures in the marsh—or did they only dislike it when people stepped in their waters?

No response.

Ethelwynne rushed to gather up the rest of Cephas's items and bundled them together. Her heart was pounding in her chest and she felt her throat constrict. She desperately wished Jocasta would come back. She tried to console herself with the possibility that Cephas was actually feeling better and went to scout with Jocasta; it would be good practice for when he became a town guard. But, as she hurried to put everything into the bags, she knew in her heart it wasn't true.

She shouldered both bags. It was awkward to carry all of their gear, but without Cephas's added weight, it didn't feel heavy. After adjusting the straps, she began searching the damp soil for clues. She didn't know how to track, but surely she could recognize boot prints in the mud and follow them. Their campground was pretty mushed with footprints. After searching for what seemed like forever, she found a single print leading away from the camp. She put her own foot beside it. The boot print was much larger than her own. She didn't think Jocasta had feet that big.

Perfect. Now she needed to find a second one. She called for him again as she searched. Still nothing. She kept turning around towards their campground to make sure she knew how to get back to it, Jocasta would be returning there. She was torn between going back to wait for Jocasta and trying to find Cephas before it was too late—that is if it wasn't too late already. She didn't really know how she would find him, especially since she couldn't seem to find another footprint.

She wove her way through the marsh slowly, trying to avoid stepping into the waters. She called his name again, louder this time.

"Where did you lose him?"

Ethelwynne jumped and spun. The weight from the bags knocked her over and she sat down hard in the mud. Jocasta walked over and helped her up.

"I found a footprint this way," Ethelwynne pointed and walked back towards the print.

Jocasta thoroughly examined the print and the plants around it. After a moment she stood up and set out veering in a different direction than the one Ethelwynne had tried. Hours slipped by as the two women wove their way through the marsh. They stopped frequently for Jocasta to check some unseen clue. After she did so, they would start walking in a different direction, only to change to a new one a little ways away.

"It feels like only a drunk person would have gone this way," Ethelwynne remarked as the trail lurched and jerked in the oddest of directions.

"He is ill, and he isn't thinking clearly," said Jocasta absentmindedly as she bent down to study yet another plant. "This way." She stood up and changed course again.

"At least he's walking away from the other lake," Ethelwynne said, trying to sound hopeful and optimistic.

Jocasta nodded as she knelt down again and examined a leaf. "The waters here are all interconnected."

Ethelwynne bit her lip. "Do you think—"

Jocasta held up her hand to silence Ethelwynne. Ethelwynne tried to hear what Jocasta was listening to. But all she heard were the birds and frogs that somehow lived in this poisonous land. She made a mental note to ask Jocasta how they could survive in this deadly place. Even though the marsh wasn't in Grahamadon, the elf seemed to know a lot about it.

Jocasta put her hand down and started to run towards a small hill they could see up ahead. Ethelwynne ran along behind her. Her progress was hampered by her desire to watch where her feet were stepping so she didn't fall flat on her face and slow Jocasta down.

The top of the hill overlooked another lake. This one looked much cleaner than the first. The sun sparkled off the brilliant blue surface. Green reeds swayed on the water's edge. Ethelwynne bit her lip and spun in a slow circle to see if she could spot Cephas from up here.

"This way," Jocasta called. Ethelwynne turned around and saw Jocasta rushing down the steep embankment on the other side of the hill towards the lake. The elf disappeared into the tall reeds.

Ethelwynne followed along the path left in Jocasta's wake. Up ahead she heard Cephas grunt. She raced forwards. Cephas was lying in a shallow pool of water on top of a mound of flattened reeds. Jocasta was pinning him down as he struggled to stand.

"What is going on?"

"He was heeding the creatures call." There was no emotion in Jocasta's voice when she spoke, but Ethelwynne's heart began to race just the same.

Careless of the moisture, Ethelwynne dropped the bags on the ground and went to kneel beside his head. "Cephas wake up," she called and tapped him on the cheek. He stared back at her blankly through glassy eyes.

Panic tinged her voice as she continued to call his name. She didn't know if it would help, but he had come back to them when she'd fallen in the marsh and when she'd nearly been slapped by a branch. Perhaps they have been traveling together long enough that her voice would pull him back from the creature's mental clutches.

Minutes stretched. He coughed and blinked. Recognition shown through his expression. "Ethelwynne?" He moaned.

Jocasta released him from her hold. He sat up and looked around them. "Where are we?"

"Too close to the water," said Ethelwynne as she stood up and offered her hand. His grip was faint as she and Jocasta hoisted him back to his feet.

"We'll camp on top of the hill," said Jocasta as she guided Cephas back along the path they had crashed through. Ethelwynne gathered up the bags, then struggled to follow the two of them back up the steep slope. Jocasta wove back and forth along the climb to try and ease their journey.

"What about the creature's call?" Ethelwynne asked when she had enough breath to do so. Her feet slipped. She grabbed some reeds and grunted when the sudden stop jarred her arms.

Jocasta glanced back at her but didn't come to help. Ethelwynne scrambled back to her feet, she could tell Cephas was struggling more than the two women. He needed all of Jocasta's attention.

"We'll keep watch and not trust his safety to wards tonight."

"Wards? You've been using magic?"

Jocasta nodded as she continued the ascent.

Ethelwynne thumbed the amulet around her neck and glanced towards the Greisgebied Mountains. *Has Prince Damien found the key yet?* The amulet dropped from her fingers as she slipped on a moss-covered rock. She could focus on saving her parents and opening the gateways when the surface beneath her feet was no longer sloped.

Cephas collapsed as the ground leveled out. Ethelwynne stumbled to the ground beside him and pointed to a small group of trees. "That looks like a good spot to camp." Cephas moaned and crawled the rest of the way before crumpling into a heap and falling asleep.

Jocasta took a drink from her waterskin and looked around. "I'm going to take a quick walk around our camp to make sure we are safe here, and to see if I can find us a shorter trail out of Maudinmere." As she reattached the skin to her belt, she walked away from the copse.

Ethelwynne watched her leave as she put down the bags. Then she sat down beside Cephas and rested her back against the tree. Her gaze and thoughts drifted towards the mountains looming in the distance. Her stomach churned as she thought about her parents and her brother. The familiar sensation of warmth ringed her eyes, but she blinked back the tears before they could form and focused on the amulet. She traced the floral designs with her fingers and slowed her breathing.

Cephas coughed in his sleep.

Ethelwynne turned to regard him. "You should have just gone home," she whispered and leaned over to check his temperature. He shivered as his forehead burned her palm. *Or let me stick with my original plan of trying to speak to the king during one of his sittings.* She leaned back against the tree with a sigh. *We should have trusted the evlayar's instincts and stayed as far away from this place as possible.*

The late evening sunlight sparkled off of the clear blue lake. From her place on top of the hill, Ethelwynne's blood ran cold as a large fin broke the surface of the water. She put her hand on Cephas's chest to prove to herself that he was still there. The creature surfaced and seemed to looked at her and Cephas. The zonkenwae screamed. Ethelwynne's eyes squeezed shut as she tried to block out the pain of the sound. Her forehead pressed into Cephas's chest as she curled up. He stirred. "No Cephas," Ethelwynne yelled to make herself heard over the monster, "stay here with me."

The shrill sound stopped. Ethelwynne panted and slowly

lowered her hands from her ears.

Cephas moaned. "Ethelwynne?" His voice was barely audible, but Ethelwynne wasn't sure if that was because her ears were still ringing from the zonkenwae's cry, or if he really was that silent.

Wearily, she turned her face towards him. His hand flopped on her back. He patted it a few times before his hand fell to the ground. "We'll make it out of this place."

"I hope so," she whispered in response, but his eyes had already shut and his breathing had slowed again.

Ethelwynne turned as Jocasta ran into their campsite. "Is he?" Her gaze shifted from Cephas to Ethelwynne. "Are you alright?"

Ethelwynne pushed herself off of Cephas and collapsed against the tree. *No. My parents are probably still trapped. My brother and all of my friends think I'm dead. A horrible monster is trying to drown Cephas, or force him to serve it. It feels like everything is trying to kill me right now. The only good thing that's happened lately is we haven't seen Heotene, but that's probably because she's too smart to follow us in here.* She studied Cephas and sighed. "We're still alive. Did you find a way out?"

Jocasta sprawled out beside her. "I think so. With any luck we won't have to backtrack to our last campsite. Though, I don't know what waits for us at the end of this path. We might end up wishing we did take an extra day to go back the way we came."

Ethelwynne let Jocasta sleep and took hold of the amulet once more. She tried to still her thoughts and focus on the key. The wind whistled through the branches. Creatures splashed in the lake. Her thoughts drifted to her family, to Cephas's family, to Michael. The amulet remained cold in her hands. Ethelwynne smacked the ground in frustration. She needed to concentrate. She needed to get out of here. With a long sigh, she let the amulet drop back around her neck and hugged her knees as she stared out into the night.

CHRISTINA VAN STARKENBURG

— CHAPTER EIGHTEEN —

The Marsh's Edge

As the sun rose, Ethelwynne rolled over and placed her hand on Cephas to wake him. His body was drenched as though he had run through the rain or swam in the lake. Her mind came fully awake instantly and she sat up. "Jocasta?"

Jocasta crested the hill.

Ethelwynne pointed at Cephas. "He's soaked."

Jocasta nodded. "His body has been fighting with the water's poison. I believe he's winning."

"So he didn't..." she swallowed and took a deep breath to slow her racing heart. "He didn't go anywhere last night. It's just the fever."

The elf nodded as she knelt beside Ethelwynne to examine Cephas. "I haven't left the camp, and neither has he," she put her hand on Ethelwynne's shoulder and stood up again. "If he did leave, he would not have returned."

Cephas began to shiver so Ethelwynne draped another cloak over him. She opened her bag and pulled out a cloth from within it so she could wipe some of the sweat and moisture off Cephas to help him avoid freezing. As she mopped his brow his eyes flickered open. He pushed her hand back and sat up. Moving quickly, she shifted her weight to help support him as he wavered in the air. His back rested against her shoulder. "Morning." His voice rasped.

Ethelwynne stretched out her foot and hooked it around the strap of his bag so she could pull it closer and offer him a drink.

Water dribbled off of his chin as he took shaky sips. "Thank you," he murmured as he handed her back the waterskin before he lay down once more.

"Perhaps we should stay for one more day to give him a chance to get his strength back," Ethelwynne said as she packed up their supplies after eating a small breakfast of bread and cheese. She thumbed through their rations. There was still plenty of food—probably because Cephas hadn't been eating—so they wouldn't run out if they were careful.

Jocasta looked up from where she was rolling up her bedding. "No, the further we get from the waters the safer we will all be."

A soft moan drew her eyes to Cephas who was struggling to sit once more. "I'll manage," he said. His head swayed back and forth as he spoke. His eyes barely seemed to be open.

Wincing, Ethelwynne looked back at Jocasta pleadingly, but the elf didn't turn her way. With an inward groan, Ethelwynne returned to packing up the supplies. She could tell this was going to be a long day.

She shouldered both bags and helped Cephas to his feet. Jocasta supported him on the other side and the trio slowly climbed down the hill towards the mountains. The deceptively clear waters of the Maudinmere twinkled on their left.

Cephas's legs gave out as they neared the bottom and he slid the rest of the way down with Ethelwynne and Jocasta scampering to catch him and prevent him from getting hurt. They rested there for a while, munched on some bread, and let Cephas take a short nap, before heading out again.

The base of the hill was still in sight when Cephas sank to his knees again. "I'm sorry," he mumbled.

"It'll be dryer there," said Jocasta, pointing to a grassy knoll in front of them much like the one Cephas had disappeared from. She handed Ethelwynne her pack and half carried, half dragged Cephas to the bump as Ethelwynne stumbled along behind. Once Cephas was lying on solid ground, Jocasta came back and helped Ethelwynne with the supplies.

In the short amount of time it took the two women to reach him, Cephas had already fallen asleep. "We should have waited a day," said Ethelwynne as she dumped the bags beside him.

Shaking her head, Jocasta pointed behind them. "Look how far we've come. There's no guarantee he'll be stronger tomorrow. He needs to get out of this place and away from these waters. Only then will he truly recover. We'll go slow, but we will keep moving." She turned and pointed in the direction of the mountains to where Ethelwynne could see a small cluster of trees. "We'll stop there next. It's also out of the mud."

Ethelwynne tried to focus the amulet on the key again, but her thoughts kept drifting to Cephas and the long journey they had before them. As he stirred, she let the amulet drop around her neck again and picked up the bags once more. Once Cephas had something to drink and another piece of bread, they began to slosh through the shallow water and mud to the next dry area.

When they got there Cephas napped while Jocasta pointed out their next resting place. "That is as far as I have traveled this way. When we reach there, I will go and see if I can find another resting place while he naps."

Ethelwynne nodded as she sat against a tree facing the mountain. *One, two, three, four...* Ethelwynne thumbed the amulet as she counted her breaths. Once her breathing slowed, she closed her eyes and switched to thinking *key to the realms* with each breath in and out. Warmth radiated from her body as she focused on the key. Their path would need to go south if they were going to find it, but, the elves had not yet taken it through the gateway. There was still a chance she could see her parents again.

Cephas's coughing tore her from her thoughts. Shuddering in the cold void left by the sudden dispersal of the amulet's magic, Ethelwynne opened her eyes and looked at Cephas. He was sitting leaning against a tree. Unlike her, he was facing back the way they came. Ethelwynne wondered if his gaze was tracking the lakes with the zonkenwae within it, or if he was looking passed it to the monastery and his mother.

"Ready?" asked Jocasta from where she was waiting. Her gaze never stopped scanning the horizon.

Even though the elf wouldn't see it, Ethelwynne nodded as she stood up and shouldered the bags once more.

With a groan Cephas pushed himself off the ground and moved to join the elf. Ethelwynne noted that his steps looked less wobbly than they had before and smiled. Perhaps Jocasta was right and the further away they moved from the creature the healthier he would get.

A thick fog overtook them as they squelched their way to the next rest area. Ethelwynne squeezed Cephas's hand on her shoulder and looked passed him to Jocasta who was supporting his other side. *At least we can't lose each other.*

Ethelwynne yelped as the ground beneath her gave way to water. Her grip tightened on Cephas's hand, and she felt herself being lifted to safety by him and Jocasta. Her clothes were soaked from the waist down and she could feel the algae dripping down her legs. She shivered in the fog.

"We're almost there," said Jocasta. Ethelwynne could barely see her in the fog even though the elf was once again supporting Cephas as they walked. "Make sure you test the ground before you step. We'll slow down some more."

Slowly they trudged forward, pushing down into the ground before each step to find a safe foothold there. Ethelwynne's foot scraped against a root. "There's a tree in front of me." She heard Jocasta and Cephas sigh with relief.

"We made it," said Jocasta.

They moved a bit faster as they climbed onto the dry ground. Two trees stood on the cusp of the water and marked their camps' eastern and western borders. The three travelers sat in a line between the trees, unwilling to see how far their dry land stretched in the other directions.

*　　*　　*

By morning the fog cleared. "Shall we continue?" asked Cephas, after they'd eaten. His skin and his eyes looked healthier.

Smiling, Ethelwynne picked up the first bag. "Yes."

"I can take one of those," said Cephas.

With a shake of her head, Ethelwynne picked up the second and started walking. "If you're feeling better tomorrow you can take them, but for now save your strength for the mud and mire."

Sighing, Cephas fell into step behind her and Jocasta. Once again, the journey was slow, but it wasn't Cephas's constant need to nap that held them back. They had to test each step because Jocasta didn't know the way. As they walked, Ethelwynne's gaze flicked from watching the water, to watching the sun overhead. When it reached its zenith, they stopped to eat and let Cephas rest.

With a slight nod to Cephas's sleeping form, Jocasta left their dry patch and went to try and find them a safe passage through the muck. She returned before Cephas woke. "There seems to be a way. I didn't travel the whole path, but it is far to the next dry area." She looked at Cephas. "Wake him."

Ethelwynne reached over and shook Cephas awake. He looked at her groggily for a moment before nodding and standing up. He swayed for a moment and rested his head in his hands. Ethelwynne felt her heart jump, but he quickly recovered and held out a hand to help her up. She didn't accept it out of fear that she might pull him back down. Turning away from him, she grabbed the bags before she stood.

They walked through the marsh once more. Reeds bushed against their thighs. Bugs drank their blood. The sun cooked the decaying animals that lost their way in the mire. *But*, as Ethelwynne constantly reminded herself, *there is a path for us to follow. We needn't worry about falling into the algae-covered waters as long as we step where Jocasta does.*

Cephas began to pant as the day wore on.

Jocasta stopped in a dip where the water was up to her waist. "This is as far as I made it."

In the distance Ethelwynne could see a lone tree. There were no leaves. The black branches jutted up to the sky in harsh angles as though to ask the goddess why it alone was left in this forsaken place. By the time they made it to the knoll the dead tree was standing on, dark clouds rolled across the moon.

"If it wasn't this dark, I suspect we would be able to see the edge of the Maudinmere," said Jocasta. "Even at this slow pace, we should be out of here by the afternoon."

"Good riddance," said Cephas. "I can't think of anything that would possess me to ever come back to this place."

Ethelwynne whole-heartedly agreed with Cephas, but as she looked towards the edge of the wetlands, she didn't say anything. The amulet was in her hands and her thoughts drifted over the lands to the key. The magic still tugged her east. The prince hadn't found it and retreated to the elven lands yet.

Something splashed in the water behind their camp.

Ethelwynne let go of the necklace and it dropped to her chest as she spun around to face the water. Her hands grabbed for a couple of daggers.

As she studied the water for the center of the ripples, she saw Jocasta string her bow out of the corner of her eye.

Carefully, Ethelwynne took a few steps away from the shallows towards Jocasta.

Something giggled to her right.

She spun on her heels.

An arrow whooshed past her cheek.

Ethelwynne turned in time to glimpse a tiny sharp-toothed creature as it shrieked and dove back into the waters. Many tentacles undulated behind it, propelling it deep enough to avoid the arrow.

"Nacomins," Jocasta wrinkled her face in disgust.

"What are they?" Ethelwynne scanned the waters as more of the giggling and shrieking creatures surrounded them.

"Thieving pests," snapped Jocasta. She traded her bow for her sword. "I am not wasting arrows on them. Watch our supplies. We don't need to have them taking our food and replacing it with river plants."

Two jumped from the waters and scrambled up the shallow slope to Ethelwynne. She hopped over the first and tried to sidestep around the second, but it spun and grabbed her leg with its tentacles pulling her to the ground.

The first giggled with glee and bared its teeth to bite her.

She slashed it with one of her daggers.

It chomped down on the blade and pulled it from her hand.

She kicked it backwards with her free foot.

It snarled and disappeared into the reeds.

The other nacomin released her leg with a pitiful squeal after Cephas slammed a stick down on its limbs. It hissed and lunged at him, but Cephas caught it with the stick and tossed it. The creature screamed as it flew through the air until it landed in the water with a splash.

Ethelwynne grabbed her dagger and pulled herself up.

Cephas handed her the stick he'd been using. "Better than your daggers."

Ethelwynne took it and swatted another one. The stick thunked against the creature as Ethelwynne flung it out into the deeper waters.

The creatures' giggles reverberated through the dark, becoming louder and louder as more of them joined the hunt. They circled the knoll. Cephas, Ethelwynne, and Jocasta stood with their backs to each other and the bags. The swarm closed in around them as the clouds parted to let the moon shine through. Ethelwynne batted away one or two that raced out in front of the others, and she heard the whistle of Cephas or Jocasta's blades as they battled the creatures in front of them. Her heart raced as she swung the stick back and forth to try and keep the creatures at bay.

Ethelwynne turned when Jocasta yelped and stumbled into her. A nacomin was stuck to her side. Ethelwynne bashed it with the stick. It shrieked and leapt off Jocasta towards the waters taking clothing and flesh with it.

The waters writhed with all of the nacomin darting in and out of them. Jocasta stood up with an agonized moan and slashed more of the creatures with her blades.

"There's too many." Ethelwynne kept swinging her arms as she swivelled her head to look for somewhere they could run.

The creatures stopped laughing and froze.

The sudden silence caused shivers to run down Ethelwynne's spine. "Jocasta?"

The nacomin' heads swivelled as one to look off into the deep waters.

"We need to get out of here," said Cephas.

Ethelwynne felt him bend down and grab the bags, but

268

her eyes remained transfixed on the distant spot the nacomin all seemed to be looking. She squeezed her stick and stepped backwards.

As quickly as they appeared the nacomin dove into the waters. Ethelwynne watched the white foam trails zipping away from them.

Silence echoed through the marsh.

Large ripples created a wake behind an emerging fin.

"It followed us," yelled Jocasta, "Run!"

"This way!" yelled Cephas.

Ethelwynne followed his voice. When the clouds unburied the moon again, she saw the hill he was leading them to and ran to it, praying that no deep pockets of water were in front of them.

Three long purple tentacles snapped out at them. Ethelwynne whacked one with a stick as Jocasta and Cephas hit the others with their swords. The zonkenwae ripped the stick from Ethelwynne's hands as she ducked underneath the creature's tentacle. She pulled out her knives and lashed out at the creature. Dark blood rained down on her head.

The ground became firmer as it began to rise. The creature wrapped a limb around her leg. She screamed and stabbed it with her blades as it tried to lift her from the ground. Cephas spun and stabbed it with his sword as well. The zonkenwae released her and shrieked. Ethelwynne, Jocasta, and Cephas covered their ears with their hands and let the creature's cries urge them forward.

At last, the zonkenwae stopped screeching. The tentacles no longer swayed around them. Ethelwynne collapsed to the ground atop the hill. Her body trembled as she kneeled in the cool grass. In the dark night she saw trees before them. A sigh of relief escaped her mouth. The creature wouldn't be able to grab them from the other side of the hill. At least for the night, they were safe.

Jocasta's groan roused Ethelwynne. She turned to face

the elf who was clutching her side as she fumbled feebly with the ties on her bags. Ethelwynne pushed herself up and went to help.

Jocasta lifted up her shirt. The cut was long and deep in her side, the cloth she was using to try and clean it was entirely red from her blood.

"I come from a family of cloth merchants, but we also sell clothes to individuals who don't have time to make their own." Ethelwynne wrung her hands and hoped Jocasta wouldn't sense how nervous she was. "I could try to sew up your side if you would like."

Jocasta closed her eyes and nodded. "Here." She handed Ethelwynne a little black bag with a silver evlayar embroidered onto one side.

Ethelwynne opened it up and found a needle and thread. Her stomach tied itself in knots, but she tried not to show it as she wove the thread through the elf's side. Jocasta flinched ever so slightly every time the needle pierced her skin, but said nothing as she lay limply on the grass. The last stitch in place, Ethelwynne twisted the thread into a perfect knot, snipped it off with her dagger and wrapped a bandage around Jocasta to keep the stitches in place.

"Thanks," mumbled Jocasta as Ethelwynne dripped the waterskin over her hands to clean off the blood. "How'd Cephas make out?"

Ethelwynne turned to find Cephas sitting overlooking the marsh. "I'm fine," he called in response without turning around. "I'll stand watch while you get some rest. I've gotten more sleep than anybody else in the past few days."

Jocasta nodded weakly again.

They camped for the night, and even though Jocasta said that they should be safe, she didn't argue when Ethelwynne and Cephas said that they intended to take turns watching during the night. Wearily she told them to wake her for her turn and turned in for what remained of the night.

The next morning the three companions groggily greeted the sun and assessed their injuries by the light of day.

Ethelwynne helped Jocasta rewash her cut, and apply a new bandage over the wound which was still seeping blood. "Those nacomins are vicious. You wouldn't think something so small could do so much damage."

Jocasta winced in reply as the freshwater touched her side. "You did a good job with the stitches."

Ethelwynne smiled as she wrapped the bandage around Jocasta. "I suppose you have to continue doing whatever it was you were doing before you stopped to help us across?" Ethelwynne tried to sound nonchalant as she knotted the bandage in place. She held her breath as she waited for Jocasta to answer.

Jocasta shook her head. "No. I was looking for someone who was supposed to be in this area, but I'm fairly confident that if he is in there, I will not find him. Instead, I'll make sure you at least make it to civilization alive and in one piece before I head back to the capital."

"Thank you," Ethelwynne said as she turned to repack the bandages. *How are we going to get the key with Jocasta here? True, she said she worked for the king and not the prince, and she hasn't tried to kill us, but...* Ethelwynne looked over her shoulder at Jocasta who was trying to stand up without stretching the stitches in her side. *Can we risk getting the key? What if she recognizes what the amulet does and is just waiting for us to find the key before killing us?*

Biting her lip, Ethelwynne turned to face Cephas. He seemed to be doing better, but she was still worried about him and all of the poisonous water he had consumed. She didn't want to wait in a small hovel of a town for Jocasta to leave. All she wanted was for this journey to be over so she could see her family and Cephas could go home and be safe with his.

She sighed. She wanted to trust Jocasta. After everything

CHRISTINA VAN STARKENBURG

they'd been through, it no longer felt dangerous to be close to her. Besides, even though the elf was injured, Ethelwynne figured it would be better to have someone like her with them, then to go it alone with just Cephas who was still weaker than he cared to admit. *Unless we run into Heotene and the two of them team up against us.* She sighed once more and stood up.

Taking a slow breath, she let the amulet guide them towards the mountain.

*   *   *

They reached the Ems River before noon. The wide river trickled lazily passed them. Fish broke the surface occasionally to eat the flies buzzing across the surface. "We need to get to the other side," Ethelwynne said to Cephas.

He nodded and started walking south along the river's edge. "Wait here, I'll see if I can find a way across."

"Wait—"

"Sit by this tree so you'll be hidden," Jocasta said as she pulled Ethelwynne to the ground near the tree's roots. Then she took off running to the north.

"You're both injured," Ethelwynne protested, but Jocasta didn't stop. Ethelwynne threw her arms across her chest. *Unbelievable.* She glared at the water and gasped. Jocasta was gone. Watching the direction Jocasta had gone, Ethelwynne stood up. The elf didn't reappear. She ran after Cephas.

He spun to face her with his sword raised as she caught up to him, but his blade dropped as she came through the trees. "What—"

"I thought that maybe we would be able to find a way across and get the key before Jocasta finds us again." She started walking alongside him and looked through the trees at the river. No rocks or sand jutted out of the water.

"You don't trust her?" Cephas grabbed her arm and turned her to face him. "After everything she's done?"

Ethelwynne silently floundered before the words tumbled out. "I want to. But, can we?"

He stared back in the direction they had left Jocasta and sighed. Dropping Ethelwynne's arm he continued to walk along the bank.

A boat bobbed in the shallows on the far bank in front of a small house. As they stepped out of the trees, they saw that the house was on the outskirts of a small village. No one came outside as they waved and called out for help crossing the river.

"Where is everyone?" Ethelwynne lowered her arms and frowned.

"Maybe they have some sort of town meeting today," said Cephas dropping his arms. He looked upriver. "The water is just getting deeper this way,"

Ethelwynne's stomach twisted in knots as she looked back the way they came.

"Maybe Jocasta had better luck." Cephas squeezed her shoulder and gestured for her to lead the way. "We'll find a way to keep the key from her."

Ethelwynne wilted and started walking to the tree where she was supposed to be waiting. Neither said anything as they trudged back along the river. Ethelwynne stared out over the water and hoped they had missed a way across the first time they passed, but it all looked the same.

"Come on," she said when they reached the spot. "I don't want to wait here. We can walk along the river and find her."

Cephas nodded and continued to follow her.

A twig snapped in front of them. Ethelwynne and Cephas darted behind trees and drew their weapons.

"It's just me," Jocasta said stepping into view.

Ethelwynne relaxed her grip on her daggers and moved

to join her. "You stepped on a twig. I thought you were more careful than that."

Jocasta smiled. "I wanted to give you some warning. See how you react."

Ethelwynne studied her suspiciously, but she couldn't decide whether or not she believed the elf.

"There's a low water crossing back that way," the elf continued and turned to walk back the way she came.

As she followed Jocasta, Ethelwynne watched the river. Soon the water began to bubble as it flowed around rocks.

"Here." Jocasta stopped on a dirt path that dipped in to the water. On the far side, Ethelwynne could spot wagon wheels climbing the other bank. "Careful," the elf cautioned as she stepped into the water.

Ethelwynne paused. "This isn't... There's no way that the zonkenwae could be here, right?"

Jocasta looked back at her. "The bodies of water are completely separate. It's the rocks you need to be careful of—they are slick."

Ethelwynne stepped into the riverbed as she rubbed her stomach to try and ease the tension nested there. With her other hand raised to balance, she began to ford the Ems River. When she was about halfway across, she moved her hand from her stomach to her throat and thumbed the amulet. For the first time the key didn't call to her from the east. Ethelwynne looked up the river. Heotene had said they found the thief's body in the water. The key was somewhere in the river. Her throat constricted at the thought of diving to the bottom of the water. *Satia, please let it be on the shore.*

Once her feet were on the far shore she started heading back towards the village with the boat with Jocasta and Cephas following close behind. As she slowly walked along the shore she wondered if what she felt would change when she was beside the key. Right now, she just knew with a resounding sense of surety that the key was in front of her once more.

The amulet seemed to radiate heat as she squeezed it. She stopped and let it thump against her chest. Her gaze dropped to her feet as fast as her body dropped to the smooth pebble beach. Ethelwynne began picking up stones and moving them aside. Thoughts of Cephas and Jocasta vanished from her mind.

The key was here.

Distantly, she heard Cephas ask "here?" She nodded without looking up from her task.

"What exactly are the two of you looking for?"

Ethelwynne's head snapped up as she remembered the elf. "Um…" She tried to remember the lie she told Jocasta about why they were heading this way. "My grandmother collects smooth rocks and shells…"

Jocasta's arms crossed over her chest as she frowned at Ethelwynne.

The amulet cooled as Ethelwynne flushed under Jocasta's disappointed stare. Her gaze flicked off of the elf as a black and white bird swooped down to the ground and grabbed something gold from the pebbles. Ethelwynne focused on the twinkling light as the bird struggled with the weight.

"The key," Ethelwynne whispered and started running after the bird. She chased it off the beach and into the trees. The bird disappeared when she tripped over a root and looked down to stop from falling to the ground.

"No, no, no, no, no, no." Ethelwynne grew frantic as she looked around for the bird.

Cephas grabbed her shoulders when he and Jocasta caught up to her. "It's ok."

"No, it's gone. The bird…"

"Ethelwynne, look at me," Cephas said as he cupped her chin and raised her face towards his. "We can find it back, if you calm down." He dropped his hand and wrapped hers around the necklace.

Ethelwynne took a few breaths to calm herself down. He was right. They were so close, but they could find it again. She nodded.

Jocasta gestured to a tree in front of them and remarked dryly, "I'm sure you'll find what you're looking for. They say hearing a magpie sing is good luck."

Ethelwynne pushed away from Cephas and spun to look at the tree Jocasta was pointing to. High in the branches she saw a tangle of thin twigs and grasses. Something glittered on the top edge of it as the small black and white bird hopped around the rim. "The nest." Ethelwynne smiled. *Good luck indeed.*

She looked at Cephas. "Can you climb—"

Leaves rustled and twigs snapped. Ethelwynne clamped her mouth shut as Cephas pulled her behind a tree. Out of the corner of her eye, Ethelwynne saw Jocasta hiding and resting an arrow on her bow.

Heotene stepped out of the brush.

Ethelwynne shuddered. *She can't be here right now. We're so close to saving my parents.* Ethelwynne shifted her head to look at Jocasta. The elf didn't completely draw her bow, but she also didn't reveal herself to Heotene. Jocasta was watching Heotene with the same dedicated focus she had witnessed on Cephas's face before the bandit attack and on her own father's face one of the rare times he took her hunting. Relief washed over Ethelwynne; the two elves were not friends.

Ethelwynne turned her attention back to Heotene. There were three of them. They could beat her and then grab the key. If Heotene's clumsy gait was any indication, she wasn't paying attention to her surroundings anyway. The elf was staring at something in her hands.

Ethelwynne lowered her hands and drew her daggers.

Heotene stopped at the base of the bird's tree.

"No," Ethelwynne whispered and stepped forward. *Heotene found it. The elves finally got a magic item to work.*

Cephas clamped his hand over her mouth and held her tightly.

Ethelwynne watched as Heotene shimmied up the trunk, grabbed the key from the nest and dropped to the ground. She put the key in her pocket and darted away.

Ethelwynne yanked Cephas's hand away from her mouth. "We need to stop her Cephas, she has it." She pulled away from Cephas and started after Heotene. "We can't let Heotene get away with the Key to the Realms. If we don't stop her, my parents are lost forever."

Jocasta stepped in front of her. Her bow was pulled taunt. "What do you know of the key?"

CHRISTINA VAN STARKENBURG

— CHAPTER NINETEEN —

The Key Thief

Ethelwynne shivered under the intensity of Jocasta's gaze. "The prince intends to lock the king out of the elven realm when he has the key." She gestured in the direction Heotene ran. "She is helping him."

Jocasta lowered the bow fully. "The prince wants to do *what*?"

"Lock the king out of the elven realm."

"And your proof of this treason is?"

Ethelwynne switched to elvish, "I overheard him say so when I was at Heatherfield Manor. I went there to try and find out why the gates were still closed—my family is stuck on the other side—when he mentioned his plan."

"Come," said Jocasta heading after Heotene. "One of the gates is too close to let her keep the key should you be speaking the truth. If you are lying, I will stand before my king and accept the consequences."

Cephas and Ethelwynne followed her. Since Heotene had a substantial lead, they crashed through the trees without caution. But, before they were able to catch up to her, Jocasta pulled up short at the base of a hill and stopped Ethelwynne and Cephas from continuing. She lifted her finger to her mouth to silence their protests before creeping forward. Carefully they crested the hill and hid behind some of the low bushes growing with abandon on its slopes. A small town of tents spread out before them. Elves dressed in livery darted from tent to tent. Armored elves practiced their swordplay and archery off to one side. Evlayar and horses were munching grass and oats in their pens on the other side. In the middle of it, Ethelwynne spotted Heotene saluting to Captain Akimos before following him under a large pavilion.

Jocasta swore under her breath when Ethelwynne pointed the pair out and motioned them back down the hill to the forest.

"We need a plan," Cephas said, looking towards the camp. "We can't just walk in there."

Jocasta nodded. Concern etched across her brow. "I can't go in either." She touched the crest on her shirt, "If what you say is true, they will likely kill me on sight."

Ethelwynne ran her fingers through her hair. "I could try and slip in."

"No," Cephas said. "If we need to sneak in, I'll go."

With a shake of her head, Ethelwynne rejected his idea. "You've never seen the key before. I have. We can't risk you grabbing the wrong one."

He frowned as Jocasta sighed. "It could work," she said, "but how will we get away once you have the key?"

"Could we race them through the mountains and go through the gate ourselves?" Cephas suggested. "It wouldn't be so bad if we were to do it since we don't intend to close them forever."

"No," said Jocasta at the same moment that Ethelwynne remarked, "It wouldn't work."

"Why not?"

Ethelwynne glanced over at Jocasta to see if she was going to explain it, but the elf was watching her intently. Ethelwynne sighed. "The key only works at certain times, and I haven't been paying enough attention to the moon to know how close we are to a time when the key would work. But even if we got there at the right time, and found the keyhole, the key wouldn't shut the gate right behind us. We'd have to get through it first, find the keyhole on the other side and then shut it and hope no one was in the passageway as it's shutting because they could still get through."

"You know a lot about how the key works," remarked Jocasta. "I was under the impression that most humans thought it was fickle elvish temperaments that decided when the gateways were to be opened."

Ethelwynne shrugged, "I've been going through them since I was born, and I asked a lot of questions as a child. Any other ideas?"

"There was that boat," said Cephas. "We can use it to sail upriver and closer towards the capital."

Jocasta nodded, "It won't get us all the way, but it'll be faster than trying to flee on foot."

"What about their archers?" asked Ethelwynne. "Won't they be able to pick us off if we're just floating in the middle of the river?"

"It gets wider, a bit south of here," said Cephas. "We can just row closer to the other side of the water, it should be far enough away. At the very least make it more difficult for them."

"Okay," said Ethelwynne with about as much confidence as she felt. "What about the evlayar?"

"I can untie them and scare them off," said Jocasta. "I do know the command for 'go,' and it would be the perfect distraction for you to get into the camp and get the key. But you'd have to be quick about it, while they might send everyone to catch the horses and evlayar at first, sooner or later, and you'd better assume sooner, someone is going to realize that this is a distraction to steal their attention away from the key."

Ethelwynne bit her lip and nodded. She could do this.

Cephas disappeared to see if the boat was still there, and if necessary to barter with the owner for their chance to use it.

Ethelwynne paced around their hiding spot, practicing walking without making a sound. Jocasta dozed on the ground nearby, occasionally muttering "I can still hear you" sluggishly.

When Ethelwynne saw Cephas approaching she stopped circling the camp. Jocasta opened her eyes and propped herself up with her elbows.

Cephas looked at the two of them and nodded. "We can use the boat. The paddles are inside."

Ethelwynne bounced on the balls of her feet. Eventually, Cephas patted the ground beside him and offered her something to eat. Sighing, she sat down and took the bread and cheese. *We're so close. This has to work.*

As they ate, Jocasta described where Prince Damien's tent would be. "Unless he is inside of it, his tent shouldn't be guarded," she said breaking a chunk of bread off of her loaf. "We won't be able to see it from the pens so we can't plan our distraction around him being gone, but at least you'll know if it's safe to try."

Ethelwynne listened and tried not to squirm. She could do this. Glancing over her shoulder she watched the shadows draw long lines up the hill. They would have to wait until the sun was completely set or risk being silhouetted on top of the hill.

As darkness fell, the three of them started to move towards the camp. After a while, Cephas whispered "good luck" in Ethelwynne's ear before he and Jocasta slunk off to the north to create a distraction and silence the guards if need be.

Ethelwynne squeezed his hand and gave him a small smile before she crawled up the hill, darting from bush to bush. She reached the top of the hill unbothered by the guards. Elves strolled around the camp nonchalantly, although there were noticeably fewer of them this time than earlier.

She took a few breaths to steady her breathing and studied the camp in the flickering light of the lanterns hanging by some tents and carried by servants going about their chores. Prince Damien's tent was on the opposite side of the camp from the horses and evlayar. It was larger and more ornately designed than the others. Satisfied that she found her target she waited for the clouds to drift over the moon before she slipped down to the outer tents.

She crept closer. Guards flanked the entrance. Ethelwynne groaned inwardly and wondered if the prince would leave his tent to investigate the commotion.

The tent flaps of the prince's tent flew open as he exited it. With a practiced air, the guards caught the flaps and held them out of Damien's way. A second elf dressed in similar armor to Jocasta followed him out.

"Tell my brother that I have been unsuccessful locating the key as of yet. But we were finally able to get that tracking charm to work, so it shouldn't be long now," said Prince Damien. "My scouts have informed me that they suspect its mired deep in the mud at the bottom of this river. Thus far no one has been able to hold their breaths long enough to find it."

"Of course, my lord." The elf bowed deeply. "Do you require further aid?"

"No," snapped Damien. He clenched his fists and Ethelwynne was sure he was about ready to strike the elf. From where she was crouched, she could see his knuckles whiten and his hand vibrating as he continued in a calmer tone, "No, that won't be necessary."

The elf bowed deeply again and headed towards the animal pens—Ethelwynne hoped he got to his evlayar before

Jocasta and Cephas freed them. While her thoughts followed him, she kept her eyes on the prince. Now that he'd dismissed the king's ranger, she wondered where he would go and prayed that it would not be right back into his tent.

The prince glared at the departing elf before stalking off towards the interior of the camp.

Ethelwynne bit her lip and waited for the prince and his guards to move far enough away from the tent. As she watched their retreating backs, she glimpsed the king's ranger behind them. *Maybe Jocasta will be able to get his attention. If he has an evlayar we can give him the key and he can return it to the king while we get away. This whole thing could be over tomorrow.*

Shaking her head, Ethelwynne admonished herself for getting distracted. This would be over immediately if she was seen. She returned her attention to the prince; he and his guards disappeared behind a tent. As the guards' cloaks drifted behind the tent, Ethelwynne turned and looked the other way. There were no elves. She darted to the tent and slipped in.

Hopefully, the prince didn't have the key on him. She figured that's what she would have done had it already been stolen from her once, but the prince did seem arrogant. Perhaps that arrogance would play in her favor. She looked around and rooted through Prince Damien's belongings.

Yelling drew her eyes to the tent's entrance. She licked her lips and tried to swallow to moisten her mouth. The flaps stayed closed. She ran her hand through her cropped hair and looked around the tent. *Where could it be?* Ethelwynne knew she didn't have much time. Soon one of the elves would realize this was a distraction.

She played with the amulet as her thoughts drifted from the key to Cephas. *Were they able to free the horses and evlayar unseen? Would he and Jocasta get away? What if the prince did have the key on him? What will I do then? Will I have to hide in his tent and wait for him to fall asleep? He'd definitely find me.*

She shook her head. These stray thoughts were going to get her killed. She took a deep breath as she clasped the amulet in her hands and cleared her mind of everything but the key. It was close, but was it too close for the amulet to guide her to it? She closed her eyes and took a deep breath. Trusting its pull, she walked to the far side of the tent and knelt down—the key was in a boot.

She reached inside and pulled it out. Flames danced in her eyes and she dove backwards. It was warded. They weren't as arrogant as she thought or hoped.

She ran out of the tent without stopping to check to see if someone would see her leaving and fled the camp. Arrows embedded into the trees beside her as she ran.

"The key set off a trap," she said as Cephas and Jocasta came into view.

"This way," Cephas called and took off before her. Jocasta waited for her to catch up and then fell into step beside her letting Cephas lead the way to the boat. Shouts followed them as they ran towards the shore. "Watch out," said Cephas as they came to a dip in the ground that they had to jump over. They skidded down the rocky embankment to where the boat was hidden below. Cephas made it first and began to untie it. Jocasta hopped in and the two of them gave it a bit of a push off the shore and reached out their hands to catch Ethelwynne as she jumped. The force of her landing on the boat pushed it out into the water. Cephas and Jocasta grabbed the paddles to start working their way across the lake and upstream.

They heard yelps and splashes from the shore behind them as the elves tripped in the dip of the earth and fell down the rocky shore into the water. Ethelwynne clutched the key to her chest and ducked down as Cephas and Jocasta paddled furiously to get out of reach of any arrows. One arrow pinged into the side of the boat. Followed closely by a second. A third splashed into the water behind them.

"Stop!" yelled a voice in elvish. "We can't lose the key to the water a second time."

Ethelwynne could hear the elves running along the shore, but the current was lazy so it wasn't hard for Jocasta and Cephas to row against it, and soon they outpaced the runners. When her hands stopped shaking, Ethelwynne laced the key onto her necklace beside the amulet and took over rowing from Cephas while he dozed in the bow. Then once he rested a bit, he relieved Jocasta, so she too could take a break after the initial sprint.

They carried on like that, snatching short rests and switching out rowers until the black sky began to brighten and herald in a new day. They rowed to shore and climbed out. Cephas pushed the boat back into the current and they watched it float sluggishly back down the river.

"What about the boat's owner?" asked Ethelwynne. "Surely he'd want his boat back."

"The low-water bridge should stop it," remarked Cephas as he rolled his pant legs back down once he stood on the shore.

Ethelwynne folded her arms in front of her chest and frowned.

"What?" asked Cephas. "It was the owner's idea. Said the current would most likely bring it to shore near where he normally stores it anyway, and if not, the bridge should stop it."

Ethelwynne sighed and turned to walk through the trees. "How far is it to the capital?"

"Close enough that there is a chance we could make it," said Jocasta as she moved passed Ethelwynne. "We should take the mines beneath the mountain; the evlayar will not be able to follow us there."

"Lead the way," said Cephas as Ethelwynne nodded and

stepped quickly to walk beside Jocasta.

"Did you see the other ranger at the camp?" asked Ethelwynne.

Jocasta nodded. "He was too well guarded for me to risk signalling him."

After a while, they came to the edge of the forest. A huge meadow and long grasses stretched out before them to the base of the mountains.

Ethelwynne spun the tips of her hair through her fingers as she watched the sky for any evlayar. "What do we do now?"

"Pray," said Cephas as he stepped out into the open.

The mountains loomed above them as they walked along the meadow. Ethelwynne's eyes constantly slipped upwards as they rushed through the plain. Every once in a while, the shadow of a bird flying overhead would dart across them. Ethelwynne's heart would stop as she dropped to the ground. She knew it wouldn't help if an elf was flying overhead because chances were they would have already spotted the travelers on the ground. But she did it anyway. It made her feel better when she noticed that Cephas and Jocasta also ducked instinctively. But it was never elves.

"Where are they?" she wondered out loud. "I mean, I'm glad they're not here, but you'd think they would have figured out which way we went by now."

Jocasta looked back towards Prince Damien's camp. "Maybe Cephas and I were more successful than we could have imagined when we shooed the evlayar away."

"Maybe they figured we took time to sleep," said Cephas.

"Either way, let's not waste this opportunity," continued Jocasta. "The mines are ahead. The adit should be under that rocky outcropping over there."

Ethelwynne looked in front of them where Jocasta was pointing. Large slabs of rock were leaning against each other forming the mine's triangular entrance a little ways up the mountain. She shuddered. What would it take for those rocks to fall down?

They reached the base of the mountain without encountering any elves.

"Shouldn't there be some miners around?" asked Cephas as they began to climb towards the entrance of the mine.

"You would think so." Ethelwynne grunted as she pulled herself up onto a small ledge. She leaned back against the mountain face. "You'd also think that there'd be a better path leading to the entrance." She panted. The exhaustion from only dozing for a short time in the boat and all of the walking and climbing was beginning to wear her down.

She brushed some sweat off of her forehead with the back of her hand. She could feel the dust and grit smearing across her face. What she wouldn't give for a clear stream to wash off in. Or better yet, a bath in a house that she never had to leave.

"We can't stop here," Jocasta called down to her.

Ethelwynne groaned. She turned around and continued to climb up the mountain face. "Just a little further. I can do this. It's only a little further."

"I've figured out why there are no miners," Jocasta called from the entrance of the mine.

"That doesn't sound good," Cephas called up to her.

Ethelwynne looked over to him. His face wasn't as flushed as she was positive hers must be. She was sure he could have easily kept pace with Jocasta climbing up the rocks, but she appreciated that he had chosen to stay beside her instead.

Ethelwynne and Cephas continued up the mountainside to the adit. Ethelwynne crawled under the leaning rocks to get out of the sun and hide from anyone who might be looking for them. Her heart raced as she saw what Jocasta was talking about. The entrance to the mine was caved in.

"The miners..." Ethelwynne looked at Cephas, they couldn't stay to help them.

"Looks like it happened a while ago." Cephas pointed to some moss growing on the rocks.

Ethelwynne studied the stone and tried to control her heartbeat. "Now what?" she asked.

Jocasta looked up the rocky path before them. "We go over the mountains. It should take us two days as long as the path is passable and we're not... interrupted."

Ethelwynne groaned.

*   *   *

The cold wind burned Ethelwynne's cheeks as they trudged towards the mountain pass. Trees and shrubs lay behind them, no longer offering any scant protection from unfavorable eyes. She gripped her cloak tightly closed with one hand and shielded her eyes from the sun with the other. Before the light forced her to look away, Ethelwynne spotted an evlayar and its rider being buffeted by the wind. "Hurry," she called over the gale's roars.

At least the evlayar won't be able to make it through this. Ethelwynne looked around for a hidden way down. Up ahead there was a rocky outcropping. It would hide them from the elves' eyes, and perhaps the wind would be lessened that close to the cliff face. She let go of her cloak and grabbed Jocasta's shoulder as she pointed.

Jocasta nodded and tugged Cephas's arm to get him to change directions. They slid under the outcropping and walked along the edge of the mountain face. The wind whistled as it raced off the rocks above their heads, but the trio no longer needed to lean into it to make any progress forward. Sighing with relief, Ethelwynne followed the outcropping as it wound around the mountain and revealed a very narrow path on the face of a cliff.

The wind whipped Ethelwynne's hood off as she stepped around the corner. She gasped and pulled it back on in a futile attempt to get it to stay. As they worked their way down the mountain, she had to let go of her hood and let the wind take it so that she could use her hands to keep her balance on the narrow ledge.

The mountain dropped away beside her. The height scared her almost as much as flying had, but she couldn't stop. They had to keep going. The elves were filing down the pass behind them, making slow and steady progress. Ethelwynne assumed the only reason they weren't moving faster was they didn't know who held the key, and if they attacked and that individual fell, the key would be lost again.

Jocasta eventually said that she would hold them off. She flattened herself into the mountainside so that Cephas and Ethelwynne could squeeze past. "I can see the exhaustion in your eyes, you still haven't fully recovered from the poison," she said to Cephas when he protested that it should be him since he was in the back.

Ethelwynne squeezed Jocasta's hand as she slipped around her on the narrow path, and tried not to dwell on the fact that this could be the last time she ever saw the elf. Her heart raced and she risked a glance backwards as she continued down the rocky trail. Rocks skittered out from under her foot and she slammed into the mountainside to avoid falling.

She and Cephas kept walking even when they heard the sounds of Jocasta clashing with the elves behind them. The night was fast approaching and they could see the flickering lights of White Shield in the distance.

After talking about it, they decided to risk climbing down the mountain after dark. They didn't want to be left here, so close with the key still in their grasp. But the dangers of the mountain got the better of them and the ground beneath their feet gave way. Ethelwynne and Cephas slipped off the ledge.

Cephas managed to grab a ledge to stop his descent.

Ethelwynne's fingers closed around his boot.

He groaned as the weight of their bodies jarred his shoulders.

She clung desperately to him and tried to find a hold on the cliff face before her.

But the wind was cruel and cold on Cephas's fingers and the two of them tumbled down into the dark when he couldn't hold on any longer.

The drop wasn't far. Ethelwynne hit a shrub and reached out to grab it. Branches scraped her arms and face as she tumbled further down the gentle slope.

When she looked up where Cephas landed, he wasn't moving. "No. Not again," she murmured as she scrambled back up the hill to him.

His face looked pinched in the pale moonlight. He groaned as she reached him. "My leg," he gasped. "When we fell, my leg hit a ledge."

Ethelwynne bit her lip as she looked at his leg. His knee was off center. If only she'd held onto both legs, then they'd be away from the wall. "Let me see if I can get something to splint it with. It'll be hard to get off the mountain, but—"

"No." Cephas shook his head. "You need to get to the capital."

Ethelwynne's eyes filled with tears as she handed him her bag. "There might be some bandages still left in the bag."

Cephas took it. "Go," he whispered and leaned back heavily. His eyes closed as he rested against the rock face.

Ethelwynne shook as she backed away. She knew he was right, but she couldn't pull her eyes from him. Twigs snapped underfoot and rocks skittered away from her heels as the wind kissed the wet trails running down her cheeks.

"Run Ethelwynne."

She was too far to see the expression on his face, but the

pained twinge in his voice compelled her to turn and scramble down the mountainside. If she lingered any longer, she would never leave, and all would be lost.

The moon was still high above her when her foot touched the cobblestone road leading up to the city gate. She stopped.

Ethelwynne realized she had a problem. *Without Jocasta, how am I ever going to get an audience with the king to tell him about the key and Prince Damien's plot?* She looked at the city's lights twinkling in the distance. *Maybe I can convince the guards at the gate I have a message from one of King Orrin's rangers.*

She started to run towards the city.

Heotene stepped out onto the road before her.

"How do you keep finding me?" Ethelwynne asked as she stepped back and pulled out a couple of knives.

"I am not losing you again," Heotene spat. She ran towards Ethelwynne with her sword.

Ethelwynne dodged the first attack and blocked the second.

"You will pay for all of the problems you have caused me."

The two combatants were so close, Heotene's breath ruffled Ethelwynne hair. As Ethelwynne studied her opponent she noticed that the elf was wearing an amulet that looked very similar to her own. It was not made with elvish magic. She prayed that the women at the monastery were alright.

Pulling away, Ethelwynne tried to circle around the elf, but Heotene cut her off again. Ethelwynne narrowed her eyes and clenched her knives; she had battled giant swamp monsters, nacomins, and Cephas. She was no longer defenseless. She was no longer afraid.

She stepped forward and tossed her first dagger. As Heotene swung her sword to swat it away, Ethelwynne threw her other one.

Heotene screamed in pain as the blade lodged into her left shoulder. She pulled it out and dropped it. The blade hit the ground with a clatter. The elf closed the distance between them as Ethelwynne pulled out two more blades.

She dodged and slashed one knife across Heotene's left arm the way Cephas showed her. The elf yelped and released her sword with her left hand. Awkwardly she raised it using only her right.

"Just let me go," said Ethelwynne as she backed up. She ran off the road and into the bushes, where she circled around the elf.

Heotene's blade thunked into the trunk beside Ethelwynne.

Ethelwynne yelped and ducked around it. She continued her spin and before Heotene was able to pull the blade out, Ethelwynne stabbed her in the back with both daggers.

Heotene screamed.

Blood pooled on the back of the elf's shirt and dripped off the knives as Ethelwynne pulled the blades out. Ethelwynne stared at the blood as it oozed towards her. She held the blades as far away from herself as she could and backed away.

Heotene fell to the ground.

The tears that burned her cheeks were the only thing Ethelwynne felt as she stared at the fallen elf. Ethelwynne forced her gaze from Heotene's body. Right now, she needed to live. She needed to get to White Shield. She needed to see the king.

Ethelwynne ran for the road. As her feet hit the cobblestones she stumbled and fell. Her hands smacked the pavement. Glinting in the moonlight beside her, were the first knives she had thrown. She grabbed the blades as she stood and ran. Her tears blinded her as she raced towards the city.

CHRISTINA VAN STARKENBURG

— CHAPTER TWENTY —

The Way In

Ethelwynne panted and dried her cheeks as she walked up to the gate of White Shield. It was closed against the night. She knocked on the small door.

After a few moments, a small window popped open and a surly looking guard sneered through at her, "What's your business boy?"

Ethelwynne cocked her head to the side, and opened and shut her mouth a few times before she remembered her appearance, which to be honest was probably quite disheveled looking on top of wearing pants with short hair. "My companions and I were attacked on the road and I lost my way and them. I'm hoping to come in to spend the night somewhere safe."

His eyebrows shot up once she started speaking and he gave her a second more studious look. Evidently, he was satisfied with his appraisal of her for he stepped back and opened the door a crack. "You may come in miss. Sorry for the confusion."

Ethelwynne nodded graciously as she strolled through the doors. "Where could I find an inn?"

The second watcher suggested a place called the

Hibernating Bear and called for a man named Tom to escort her there safely. Ethelwynne tried to assure them that she would be fine on her own and that she didn't want to disturb them or take them away from their duties.

"Nonsense," said the second guard, "you were just attacked on the road. While our city streets are safe for you to wander around on your own, you must be ready for some rest. Our roads are a bit confusing for a stranger." He turned towards the guardhouse a second time. "Tom!"

Tom skidded to a stop inches from Ethelwynne. His bedraggled hair and frumpy clothes gave him the appearance of someone who had just been woken up, which Ethelwynne assumed was the case from his wide eyes and the way he kept licking his lips. "Yes, sir?"

"She needs a guide to the Bear."

"Yes, sir." He looked at Ethelwynne and bobbed his head so much she thought it might fall off. "This way miss."

He waved her down the street, but not quick enough for them to miss the second watcher saying "We'll discuss your tardiness when you get back."

Tom turned around and bobbed his head again. As they rounded the first corner his shoulders slumped and he frowned.

Ethelwynne had been hoping to wander the streets a bit to see if she could figure out where the castle was and find the best way in. She didn't intend to spend the night in the inn, but she couldn't think of anything better to say when she was being confronted by the guards.

She stared at the boy leading her towards the Bear. Perhaps his carelessness could be useful. "Thank you for offering to show me the way." She smiled at him when he glanced at her.

He grunted in response.

"But," she continued, "I really am capable of taking care of myself. I don't need a guide. I'm told the streets of White

Shield are perfectly safe."

He shook his head. "Sarge told me to take you. I don't need him to ream me out about failing to do that too."

Ethelwynne sighed. Great. Now, what was she going to do? She really didn't want a lot of people to know that she was here. She walked in silence for a bit. As she and the underling walked towards the Bear, she decided to try and use his knowledge of the city to her advantage and learn more about the place. "How do you get to the castle from here? I've heard it's quite stunning to see, and since I don't know how long it'll take my friends to arrive, I thought I'd check it out in the morning."

"It's nice," the boy said with all of the enthusiasm of someone who was rudely pulled from their bed to run an errand they personally didn't think was important. "You follow the main road. You can't miss it; the castle is at the end."

"Oh perfect, thank you," said Ethelwynne brightly. She bit her lip and considered how to phrase her next question. "Have you ever seen the king?"

He shook his head.

"No? But can people see the king? I would have thought that actually getting to see him would be one of the best parts about living in White Shield."

Tom shrugged. "He does let normal people come and complain about things sometimes. But usually, the guards or lesser nobles deal with that sort of thing. I suppose you could see him in a parade or something."

"Do you know when the next time he'll let people petition him?"

Tom barked a laugh. "No. I've more important things to think about."

Ethelwynne bit back the urge to ask him what he considered more important because it clearly wasn't working as a city guard. In the short amount of time she had been with him, he had acted sluggishly, cowardly, and disrespectfully towards the individual he was supposed to be helping. Not one of those qualities was a good characteristic for a guard to have. Cephas would never have acted like that if he was working.

Instead, she let him guide her in silence. Her thoughts wandered back from where she was to where she abandoned her friends. She looked at the peaks that surrounded the city and rubbed her arms as she listened to the wind whistling in the distance. *Were Jocasta and Cephas alive?* She doubted Prince Damien would let Jocasta live after her interference. *If only we had made it to the mountains faster. Jocasta wouldn't have needed to stay behind to give us more time, and we would have been able to go slower down the mountainside and not fallen. Would Cephas survive his injury on the mountainside by himself?* She knew that he was right and that it was important for her to be here with the key safely inside the city, but she still felt awful leaving him in that position on his own.

They arrived at the Bear. Ethelwynne bid the young guard goodnight before she stepped into the cacophony. Men were singing off-key and clinking their glasses together. A bard was standing on a raised platform playing a lyre and singing the song properly; although, his cheeks were quite red as well. The barmaids expertly danced around their clients without spilling a drink or dropping a meal.

Ethelwynne paused a moment on the threshold to take it all in. She looked back out the door and saw the boy trudge back towards the gate. His shoulders slumped even lower and his feet dragged on the road. Ethelwynne's annoyance over Tom's earlier carelessness dissolved into pity as she watched him. "Poor guy." Evidently, he was not looking forward to his upcoming conversation with his sergeant. Still, she wished he would walk a little faster so she could step back outside and continue on to the castle.

"Welcome to the Bear. Don't let the noise scare you darling," boomed a plump woman in a dirty apron. Ethelwynne assumed she must be the innkeeper. She waved her spoon around ecstatically as she ushered Ethelwynne into the common room. "Come, enjoy a drink, spend the night, wash some of the dust off your skin." She shoved Ethelwynne into a chair. "Now tell me what you would like dear."

"Uh... I'm not sure," Ethelwynne said. She frantically tried to think of a way to get out of this. She didn't have money to spend, and even if she did, she didn't have the time to spend it. However, Ethelwynne didn't want to leave a lasting impression on this woman in case everything went wrong, which didn't seem too far out of the realm of possibility.

"Don't know what you want?" The woman waved the spoon in front of Ethelwynne's face with mock severity. "Well let me tell you, I have just the thing." She spun and hollered at one of the serving maids. "Gretchen!"

The girl jumped and sloshed some of the ale from the cup she was handling over her hands. She wiped the liquid off the table with her apron and placed the cup in front of the customer who was too drunk to notice that his cup wasn't as full as it should have been. Then she dried her hands and walked over to where Ethelwynne and the innkeeper were. "Yes, ma'am?"

"Get this girl a little something special to drink. Poor thing's too tired to know what she wants, so grab her some of the wine. That'll brighten up any night."

"Uh wait," Ethelwynne interjected and both of the two other women looked at her. "Before I have something to eat and drink, I'd really like to wash off a bit. You know, feel less grimy," she ran her fingers through her hair and pulled out a leaf that had apparently stuck around since the other side of the mountain, "and you know, stop shedding leaves."

She blushed.

The barmaid smirked as the innkeeper laughed, "Of course dear. Follow me. Don't worry, I'll have Gretchen send you a drink in the baths. Loosen you up while you're washin'."

Ethelwynne nodded and hoped Gretchen was quick and brought the drink before Ethelwynne was forced to strip and waste time in the bath.

The innkeeper turned to face Gretchen who hadn't budged. "Well, you heard the girl. Move."

The barmaid handily dodged the swinging spoon and sauntered to the kitchen to grab Ethelwynne her drink.

Ethelwynne followed the innkeeper deeper into the building to a large room where several steaming baths sat unoccupied.

After the innkeeper left the room, Ethelwynne unclasped her cloak. Wincing, she put it down on one of the chairs while she waited for Gretchen to come with the wine. She massaged her shoulders and arms as she tried to figure out how she was going to get into the castle.

She could, in theory, try to pass herself off as someone with money. The amulet around her neck was nice enough for a visiting merchant to wear. However, the clothes she was wearing were not. She sighed. There was no way for her to get an appropriate gown. She was not a thief.

Footsteps thumped along the wooden floor outside the bathroom, but Gretchen did not appear. Shrugging, Ethelwynne brushed her fingers through her hair and combed out leaves and untangled small twigs.

As she unknotted a particularly entangled twig, she wondered if she could somehow break-in. She shook her head. The palace would be better guarded than Michael's shop and she was not an expert. Ethelwynne pulled her hair. "Ouch," she muttered as the twig finally came out.

She rubbed her head to soothe the ache. *Is Michael*

alive? Even when Cephas thought she was a thief, he had been kind. She leaned against the wall. Her gaze drifted to her wrists. Michael wasn't like that. Still, he didn't deserve to die because of her. She hoped he was alright.

Ethelwynne walked over to one of the washbasins, rinsed the mud off her hands, and splashed some water on her face. She needed to focus, there would be time to think about Michael later. She wiped the water off with a cloth and looked towards the room's door again. At this rate, she could have been at the castle before her absence was noticed. Either that or she could have washed her whole body. She still could wash her whole body, but her clothes would be dirty and she didn't want to be clean and then slip into filthy clothes.

As she turned from the door to the shuttered window she wondered if she should wash her clothes. They wouldn't dry in time for her to see the king tonight, but if the king was holding court tomorrow, a clean outfit would help her get in. "No," she said softly as she picked up her cloak and moved towards the window. The prince's elves could be arriving at the city any moment. Her rather fast trip down the mountain would only buy her so much time. She had to see him before the prince was able to paint the same picture of her to the king as he did to the Helmsville guards.

Gretchen sauntered into the room with the wine. She rolled her eyes in Ethelwynne's direction, put the cup down on the counter, and left the room muttering about how impossibly slow some people are.

Once the woman left, Ethelwynne said a quick prayer of thanks to Satia that the baths were on the first floor, opened the shutters and flipped the lock. She rested her arms on the sill as though she was merely enjoying the breeze on her face while she looked around to see if anyone would notice a woman slipping out the window. The way was clear.

Ethelwynne swung herself over the sill and stepped outside. She walked to the back of the courtyard and stepped on a barrel so she could reach the top of the wall and pulled herself up. Once she was satisfied that the alleyway was also clear, Ethelwynne swung over the wall and dropped lightly to the ground.

"I am getting way too used to this," she muttered to herself as she slipped into the shadows and worked her way through the alleyway. Further away from the inn the alleyway wasn't empty. As she stepped over one man who was clutching a bottle in his sleep and darted around another who was relieving himself on a wall, she figured no one would really believe the men here anyway, even if they actually remembered seeing her. And why would they? From the way everyone avoided meeting each other's eyes, it was fairly obvious that no one here wanted to be seen any more than she did.

At the end of the alleyway, she wrapped her fingers around the key. Tom said to go straight up the main road, which was behind her. With any luck, this one would run parallel to it or connect with a road that was attached to it. She turned left and headed towards the castle.

Eventually, after she took more wrong turns than she was willing to admit, Ethelwynne found a road that connected with the main one. Soon the palace towered before her. Ethelwynne paused in the middle of the road. She knew it was big, but the size of it blew her away. Heatherfield Manor was dwarfed in comparison. She ran her fingers through her hair and let out a long slow breath.

Hoof beats clattered against the cobblestone road behind her. "Get out of the way!" A man yelled.

She spun around and dove out of the way as a man on horseback raced past her.

"Watch where you're going fool!" He called as he rode past.

"Seriously?" She pushed herself up off the ground and brushed some of the dirt off. "Like I'm the one who needs to pay attention? I wasn't moving."

She watched as he rushed up to the castle gates and spoke briskly with the guards who let him in. She bit her lip. They were not unilaterally denying people because of the hour. There was a chance she could get in. Ethelwynne sighed. It did not help her feel more confident.

She put her hand up to her neck and wrapped her fingers around the key then she slipped it back underneath her shirt. She could do this. Ethelwynne walked towards the palace.

"May I enter?" she asked the guards when she was close enough. "I have a message for the king."

They ignored her.

I should have washed my clothes if I wanted to get in this way. "Excuse me sirs, I have an urgent message for the king. I need to speak with him immediately."

"No. The king doesn't have time for the likes of you today."

Ethelwynne folded her arms across her chest. Having guards tell her to go away was getting old. She was not in the mood for their stuck-up ways right now. If they did not let her in, she would have to break into the palace, and that was not something she felt capable of or interested in doing. She bit down her annoyance and continued in her best shopkeeper voice: "Gentlemen, please, the message is from one of King Orrin's rangers, Jocasta. If not for an injury, she would be here now. You can ask the guards at the gate; they can assure you I lost my companions when we were attacked on the road." They couldn't vouch for any message, but she doubted the guards would actually send someone to check. "It's important that I tell the king now."

"Never heard of her," said the first one.

"What's the message?" asked the other.

"Do you know all of the elvish rangers by name?"

"No," he spat. "Now get out of here and stop wasting our time or we'll have you thrown in prison."

Ethelwynne threw her hands up in surrender and walked away. She wished Jocasta were here to let her in, or better yet, to be the one to pass the message along to her king.

Ethelwynne walked down the road that was beside the castle. Even without looking behind her she could feel the guards' eyes on her. But they didn't say anything else to her as she continued to walk away. She slipped down a side road that led away from the palace and counted to twenty before peaking around the corner. The guards were no longer looking in her direction.

Sighing with relief she strolled across the road down the alleyway that ran alongside a different palace wall. She held her breath as she walked. Guards would have no reason to tell her not to be here, but if they passed along a message that they saw someone matching her description here to the duo at the front... She shook her head. Better to not think about it.

She heard voices above her. Ethelwynne shrank back into the castle wall as the guards strolled above her. Her foot pressed against a metal bar. It creaked ever so slightly as it moved. Ethelwynne froze and prayed the noise would not alert the guards. The guards above her did not look down.

Ethelwynne bent down and looked at what she was leaning against. It was a tiny grate that had a few bars rusted off in the middle, plus a few more that were ready to go. The hole looked like it might be just big enough for Ethelwynne to squeeze through.

Ethelwynne glanced around her and confirmed that the road was still deserted. She sucked in her stomach to try and make herself as small as possible and squished her way into the hole.

The grate was covering the entrance to a small tunnel. The passage smelled of moss and spruce. Ethelwynne assumed it was designed to let the melted snow escape the grounds in the spring.

As she crawled through it, Ethelwynne prayed the other

side would not be blocked. Crawling forward was hard enough. She didn't want to have to try moving backward, and she desperately needed to get in.

When she got to the other side, she was greeted by the trunk of a spruce tree. It blocked part of the path, but there was no grate and she was fairly certain she could fit through the gap. She waited until she couldn't hear any guards nearby, then she put one hand on the trunk and the other on the wall and pulled herself free.

She ducked some branches and leaned against the trunk while she peeked out at the small walled garden before her. Her muscles relaxed a bit when she confirmed that there were no guards in it. Ethelwynne guessed the path she just came in on was forgotten because of the tree she was resting on. That definitely boded well for her entering unnoticed.

As she looked around the small space, she spotted an arched wooden door with a small window across from where she was hiding. Footsteps thumped along the wall behind her, and she heard the needles of the spruce brush across the soldier's armor. She peered through the branches and watched the castle guards walk further down the wall. When she could no longer see them or see any guards approaching from behind her, she ran to the door and pressed her ear to the wood. A continuous stream of people rushed back and forth on the other side.

Exhaling sharply, she dove back under the cover of the spruce. She would not be getting in that way. Her gaze moved along the wall to a darkened window with a hydrangea bush blooming beneath it. The branches rustled around her as she rose to a crouch.

"Hey, did you hear something?"

Ethelwynne froze. She glanced up and saw the guard's hands resting on the wall as he leaned over the garden. She counted her heartbeat as she and the guards waited.

The guard leaned back and began walking along the wall

again. "Probably just a bird."

The other guard nodded. "Probably, but we can still ask Thaddeus to make sure nothing has been disturbed when we see him."

Her eyes bulged. She did not want to meet Thaddeus. Swallowing hard, she slunk around the edge of the garden to the window and peered through the glass. In the pale light, she saw something that looked like a desk, but no people or lights.

Her gaze flicked to the wall and she wondered when the next set of guards would be by, or how quickly Thaddeus would reach the garden. She should have asked Xiamara to teach her how to pick a lock—she doubted jamming a branch into it and forcing it open would go unnoticed. She breathed a prayer and pushed up on the pane. The window moved. Before her nerves left her, Ethelwynne pulled herself into the room and shut the window behind her.

The room looked like it might be a study. There was a beautiful oak desk and the bookshelves that reached to the ceilings were filled with tomes. A quick glance told Ethelwynne that a lot of them were either written a long time ago or in a different language, for she couldn't understand what the covers said.

There were two doors in the room. One was painted to match the walls. Ethelwynne leaned against it and heard a lot of feet scurrying past. The other one was more ornate, and she assumed it led out to one of the halls that the servants only walked down to dust and sweep. As she leaned against it, she heard no one.

She opened the door a crack and peeked out. The hall was empty. Stepping out, she shut the door. Ethelwynne touched the amulet around her neck and focused on King Orrin. She sensed him distantly behind her, well beyond the castle walls. Frowning, she turned her attention to King Kellan. He at least was in the palace, but apparently, he was on the other side of the solid wall in front of her. Sighing, she dropped her hand and picked a direction to go.

It was amazing how deserted the palace was. When she was at home Ethelwynne often longed for her own space. It felt like she was constantly in her parents' presence. There was no escape from them. If she was angry with them, tired, or just wanted to be left alone she had to leave the house and go somewhere else. But here, in this hall listening to nothing but the soft padding of her own feet, Ethelwynne realized how much more she preferred being so close to her family. For something that was so stunning and majestic, the palace was also very cold and lonely. She clutched the key around her neck as she wandered through the halls. Maybe if she happened upon the king, she could hold it out to him before his guards tackled her for being where she shouldn't be.

The confident click of shoes echoed down the hallway towards her. Her heart leapt into her throat and her stomach constricted. She spun around and as quietly as she could slipped into the nearest room to hide. The key thumped against her shoulder before falling to rest at the base of her throat.

She backed up from the door. It was a study or a small reading room. Ethelwynne's inspection of the room was cut short when a camouflaged door, much like the one in the room she originally entered opened. Ethelwynne darted behind a bookcase and breathed a silent prayer of thanks that the door swung open so she was blocked by it instead of the person entering seeing her instantly.

Some maids darted in and tidied up the room and set out some tea and biscuits. Then they fluttered to the opposite side of the bookcase to wait. Ethelwynne leaned against the wood and willed herself to be invisible. If they were setting up for tea, she had clearly chosen the wrong room to hide in. She bit her lips and squeezed her eyes shut as she waited for whoever was coming to enter the room while she wondered why they were meeting at this hour of the night.

The door clicked open. Ethelwynne assured herself that as long as they didn't look in her direction, she should be safe, and there was no reason for them to look this way. The fireplace, chairs, table, and tea were all on the other side of the room. She opened her eyes and peeked at the men trailing into the room. The light from the hall silhouetted them, but once the door was shut, she could see that it was King Kellan who walked in with his entourage.

Ethelwynne couldn't breathe. Did she dare interrupt now? Even though she knew her mission was important she was too frightened to move and so she waited while the others in the group made their reports to the king.

One was talking about the food stores, another talked about the kingdom's finances. As they droned on, Ethelwynne practiced what she intended to say to the king once her feet and mouth would move again.

The voice of the third man pulled her from her reverie— it was the man who nearly trampled her outside the gate. "We don't appear to be any closer to locating the key, your majesty. And the elves are getting antsy. King Orrin has started calling his brother much worse things than a 'careless and unmitigated fool'."

Ethelwynne stopped rehearsing and listened. This was the moment to interrupt. She could even hold out the key and say "Here it is." But she remained paralyzed by fear.

After they were finished, they left. The king tapped his cup to get the maids to refill his drink and then he dismissed them too. Once the hidden door clicked shut behind them King Kellan rested his hands in his palms. He looked exhausted.

Ethelwynne undid her necklace and took the key off the chain. She pocketed the amulet and chain and held the key in her palm. Now was her chance. Before she could change her mind, she spun out from her hiding spot.

— CHAPTER TWENTY-ONE —

A Meeting with the King

Kellan looked up at her. Shock briefly registered through the exhaustion. His eyes flicked to the side of the room before he turned his attention fully on Ethelwynne.

Ethelwynne put her hands up to show him the key and that she wasn't armed and launched into her tale as fast as she could. Maybe she would be able to say her piece before he called the guards and had her hauled away to prison for the rest of her life. "Please don't arrest me and have me thrown in prison forever, I really, desperately need to speak to you, and the guards wouldn't let me in. I have the key to the realms and the Prince of the Elves is trying to kill me because I found out that he wants to trap his brother in our world so that he can be the king of the elves in their world." She gasped for breath and stared at the king wide-eyed as she waited for him to respond.

"I didn't catch a word of that milord. Did you?" asked a voice from behind the king.

Ethelwynne jumped back and tripped over a stool before landing on the ground. She looked behind the king and saw a man standing in the shadows, he was not one of the individuals who entered the room with the king. She wondered if he had been in there all along, or if he had slipped in through the servants' entrance while she was distracted. He was armed but looked rather relaxed considering he was in a room with the king and an intruder. From his uniform, she assumed he must be a guard's captain.

"No, Captain Henryk," said Kellan without taking his eyes from Ethelwynne. "I did not."

Ethelwynne took a few breaths to try and calm down and repeated her story a bit slower. This time she also mentioned Jocasta and Cephas, and how she would have come with them but Jocasta stayed behind on the mountains to slow the elves down and Cephas broke his leg while they were escaping. She held out the key again.

Henryk moved from his spot and took the key from her hand and placed it on the desk before pulling her to her feet. "How did you get in here?"

Ethelwynne blushed. "There was a rusted grate in the wall that led to a small garden." She bit her lip and toed the ground. "I don't know if I could take you there. I wasn't really paying attention to where I was walking."

"This is the key," said King Kellan. "Send for Orrin."

Captain Henryk nodded. Keeping an eye on Ethelwynne, he walked to the door and opened it.

A guard jogged over and saluted him.

"What is it, Thaddeus?" asked Henryk.

"I was just in the queen's garden, sir."

"And someone else had been there," finished the captain as he moved aside and gestured to Ethelwynne. "We've noticed and she's quite contained."

Thaddeus glared at her from behind Henryk. "I shall tell the guards to work the garden into their rotation until the grate is repaired."

"Thank you, Thaddeus," said Henryk as he dismissed him.

The guard turned and stalked down the hall towards the garden and guards.

Henryk turned his attention to someone else that Ethelwynne couldn't see and instructed them to send a rider to call back King Orrin before stepping back into the room and giving Ethelwynne his full attention once more.

Her cheeks burned even hotter and she looked away from him to find King Kellan had stopped examining the key and was also studying her over his steepled fingertips. "What is your name girl?"

"It's Ethelwynne Tregown, sir." Self-consciously she smoothed out her shirt and the tops of her pants. "Your majesty?" She scuffed the ground with her shoe. "Do you know if there's any way we can check and see if Jocasta and Cephas are okay?"

"That depends, Jocasta is probably beyond our reach right now. Perhaps we can send someone to check on your friend Cephas to see if he has made it somewhere safe in spite of his injuries." The king glanced over at Captain Henryk, who nodded and opened the door to tell someone to try and find Cephas.

"Where exactly did you leave your friend?" the man asked, leaning into the room.

Ethelwynne described the place the best that she could. The man nodded and headed out.

"Thank you," Ethelwynne murmured. With everything said she wasn't exactly sure what to do anymore. She hadn't really thought this far ahead, she'd only focused on trying to get the job down. She shuffled her feet and brushed off her shirt.

"Captain Henryk, can you show this woman to somewhere more comfortable? I suspect we'll have more questions in the morning."

"Yes, milord." The Captain of the Guard bowed to King Kellan. Then he firmly rested his hand on Ethelwynne's shoulder and guided her towards the door. He led her through the winding halls of the castle and to a sitting room with a couple of comfortable-looking chairs, some books, and two doors. The first door led to a bedroom, the second revealed a tub. The captain called for a servant and soon the bath was filled with steaming water and a nightgown was laid out for Ethelwynne.

"Good night miss," called Captain Henryk as he stepped from her room once he was satisfied that she would have everything she needed. After the door clicked shut, she heard him through the door directing someone to watch her. As the feet shuffled into place in front of her door, Ethelwynne figured she was probably more trapped here than she was in the kidnappers' room with Xiamara.

"At least it's more comfortable," she said as she unbuttoned her shirt and slipped into the bath. Finally, she could be clean. After she finished bathing, she let herself soak in the water.

Ethelwynne dozed off and her head slipped beneath the surface. Reeds and purple tentacles wrapped around her and pulled her deeper. Ethelwynne gasped and splashed water all over the floor as she sprang up. Coughing and shuddering she climbed out of the tub and wrapped herself in the bathrobe. She slipped on the wet floor and crashed to the ground with a yelp and then moaned as the abrupt stop jolted all of her bruised and battered muscles and joints.

"Miss?" The man, who Ethelwynne assumed was her guard, knocked on the bathroom door.

"I'm fine." The pain that was relayed through her voice didn't convince her of her statement, so she doubted it would work on the guard. She scrambled to her feet before he could decide to come in and check.

"If you're sure..." said the guard. She heard him take a step back before he stopped. "I could get one of the maids to help you..."

Ethelwynne leaned against the door. "That won't be necessary. I'm fine." Her voice sounded less pain-filled, but she didn't hear him walk away. Perhaps he needed some extra assurance. "I just, I fell off a cliff earlier today, and I just bumped my elbow on the tub as I was getting out. It's already bruised, so it hurt more than normal."

"A cliff? Do you need the surgeon?"

Ethelwynne glared over her shoulder at the door. Though, upon second thought she realized that if she wasn't so embarrassed about her nightmare or falling on the floor she probably would be quite touched by his concern. Sighing, she tried to tame the annoyance out of her voice. "No. I'm fine. I just need sleep."

"If you're sure," said the guard again. She heard him walk to the hall door and open it. "I will be here if you change your mind." The door thumped shut behind him.

Ethelwynne leaned her head back and breathed deeply. Slowly, so she wouldn't slip again, she moved away from the door and retrieved her necklace from her soiled clothes. Cephas would have responded that way; even when he thought she was a thief he made sure she made it down the tree safely, and that she had food, shelter, and protection.

She peered out the bathroom doorway. The guard was not in her sitting room. Shivering, she walked over to the bedroom to put on her nightgown where it would not get wet. The soft cotton felt cool against her skin. Her gaze drifted towards the windows. She couldn't see them in the blackness, but she knew the mountains were out there, hopefully hiding and sheltering Cephas, maybe even Jocasta. "They should be here too."

She sank into the bed as she sat. Tears sizzled on the flame as she leaned over to blow out the lamp. *What will I say to Idra if the guards don't find him?*

*   *   *

CHRISTINA VAN STARKENBURG

When she woke up, a white blouse, a wide wine-red belt with a golden rose clasp, and a brown skirt with gold thread stitched across it in a diamond pattern with a rose embroidered at each point were laid out on the chair beside her bed. Ethelwynne admired the needlework for a few moments before the smell of breakfast compelled her to sit. A tray holding soft boiled eggs, meat-wrapped asparagus, and scones rested on the vanity.

Ethelwynne moaned as she moved to the vanity to eat. Now that she was rested, she was starting to feel her mountain trip. The food was delicious. Ethelwynne pushed the empty tray away and turned to the clothes. Once her dress was on, she went into the sitting room to wait. Ethelwynne thumbed through some books indifferently as she wondered what would happen next.

Captain Henryk knocked on her door to escort her to the meeting. She gripped her skirt tightly as she walked along behind him. The painted designs on the walls which had delighted her yesterday, made her feel dizzy and ill today. The concentric square tiles on the floor only made her feel worse. "Will King Orrin be there as well?" she asked focusing on Henryk's back.

"He has not yet returned." Henryk opened a door and held it for her. "This way."

Ethelwynne gulped and stepped inside. It was the same study she had been in the night before, though the faces inside it were quite different from the previous day. Aside from the king, there were two women and three men. Ethelwynne recognized Lady Tamara, who was sitting under the window from one of the times she passed through Sweet Briar on her way to her manor. Her family was in charge of enforcing the king's rules in their area. Thankfully, there was no reason for Lady Tamara to recognize her, her mother always went to the manor with material whenever the lady required it and whenever Ethelwynne had gone along, they only ever spoke with the servants. Based on Lady Tamara's presence she assumed that the other individuals were also lords and ladies, though she didn't recognize any of them.

Henryk placed her in the center of the room then moved to the side, while the sensations of the nobles' gazes settled into Ethelwynne's skin. She resisted the urge to shudder, but felt her cheeks beginning to match the red of her belt. Letting her skirt fall from her hands, she clasped them together and faced the king.

The calm expression he wore the night before was once again on his face, but this morning it lacked all of the exhaustion it bore the previous time she saw him, and while she was infinitely grateful that he had loaned her a more presentable outfit to wear to this session, she prayed that she would not have to stand in front of his intense gaze for long. More than the other nobles, his gaze seemed to see right through her.

He broke off his examination of her and turned to address the lords and ladies in the room. "As you know, last night this young woman brought me the Key to the Realms. I have asked her about her journey, but I'm sure she'll be willing to share it once more for you to hear, and then if any of you have questions for her, you may ask. Miss Tregown?" he turned towards her and let her relay her story once more.

When she finished one of the lords scoffed. "How do we even know this girl is who she claims to be? And how would a peasant recognize the key anyway."

Ethelwynne turned to face him. But Lady Tamara who was seated beside him, raised her hand cutting off any words Ethelwynne may have spoken in her own defense.

"The girl is almost a spitting image of her mother, even with her altered hair I can recognize the connection." She pursed her lips as though the words tasted sour in her mouth. "As her family resides in one of my villages, I can attest that her parents never returned from the elven kingdom and that she went on some misguided quest to speak to a member of Prince Damien's household. The beginning of her tale, at the very least, is true."

"And the key?" asked a lady from behind Ethelwynne. "Like Lord Yole, I want to know how a simpleton like her came to see it."

Lady Tamara shook her head. "That I do not know Lady Layla; the girl will have to answer for herself."

Ethelwynne shifted her attention towards Lady Layla, "I've traveled to Grahamadon with my father many times. Though I was there to learn the trade, I also had time to myself. As a child I spent that time exploring and asking questions of anyone who would listen to me." She turned to look at Lord Yole, "One of those individuals was the Keeper of the Keys. He showed me the key and explained to me how it worked."

"Why would he show you the key?" asked the lord who was standing beside Lord Yole.

Ethelwynne shrugged slightly. "I don't know sir."

"Of course you don't," said the lord on her right. His lip curled up in disgust as she turned to face him. "That would be too convenient."

"I don't know Lord Dariel," said the lord who asked the question. "That may have actually been too convenient if she knew the answer. I find liars are so adept at answering questions they don't know; they seldom admit they do not know the answer."

"And that is why your province is overrun with criminals, Lord Pierson, while mine is perfectly safe for travelers."

"Safe? Your towns—"

"Gentlemen," interrupted the king and gestured to Ethelwynne, "shall we return to the issue at hand?"

The two lords glared at each other for a few moments, before turning their ire and annoyance upon her. Their questions were relentless. Every time Ethelwynne began to answer a question a different noble would pipe up with one they thought was more important or pressing. She fought for composure while she tried to explain that she could speak elvish without being given the opportunity to demonstrate. But the nausea that swept over her in the hall was creeping up again, and she could feel her hands begin to tremble as she tried to explain that Jocasta was not part of a plot against the elven king. And, even with the occasional support from Lady Tamara, by the time the nobles were finished questioning her about her life, her family, her companions, and her unwanted connection to the prince, she wanted to do nothing more than find a hole somewhere to crawl into and cry.

Finally, King Kellan leaned back into his chair. "I have no more questions. Thank you for your honesty Ethelwynne." He looked to the men and women with him, and they all shook their heads signaling that they too were done with their questions. King Kellan turned to face her once more. "Henryk will you show her back to her quarters?" The captain nodded. "Very good. Enjoy your afternoon."

Captain Henryk beckoned for Ethelwynne to follow him out of the room then led her back down the halls.

"Here we are," said Captain Henryk, directing her towards her room. "I'll send someone up to fetch you when King Orrin arrives. Try not to stress about it too much. Now if you'll excuse me, I have some important matters to attend to, like that grate you crawled through." Then he left.

Soon a young woman bobbed into the room. Her red hair bounced around her shoulders with every step. "You got some smudginess on your nose," she rubbed her own nose to show Ethelwynne where the spot was on her own face.

Ethelwynne flushed and wondered how it survived the bath. She winced. "It's not dirt. It's a bruise."

"Well, I suppose we'll need some makeup then. My

name is Abby. Missus Marsha said I was to teach you how to properly address nobility before the elf king arrives. Apparently you bungled it up a bit this morning." With that she launched into a lecture about the proper way to curtsey, how deep to go for a baron or a countess, and what to call them.

Her explanation finished, Abby said, "I'm going to find you some makeup to cover those bruises." With that, Abby bounced out of the room. She giggled as the door shut behind her. "Oh Stewart, I'm glad it's you guarding this here door." Abby giggled again, then Ethelwynne heard the soft padding of her feet as she darted down the hall.

Ethelwynne paced while she waited. She glanced out the window. Captain Henryk had not chosen this room at random. It was on the third floor, and there was nothing near the window that looked like it might be useful for her if she decided to climb down. The vines growing up from the courtyard below barely made it to the second floor. Not that she was intending to run away, but after being chased for so long not having a way out made her feel nervous.

A short time later Abby returned with a woman, whom she introduced as Missus Marsha. Missus Marsha's white hair was pulled into a tight bun, and her equally white apron was spotless. She gestured for Ethelwynne to step forward.

Ethelwynne grudgingly left the windowsill, and stood before the woman.

"Well then, let's see what you've learned," said Missus Marsha. "Show me how you curtsy when addressing an earl."

Abby curtsied from where she stood by the door.

"None of that girl," said Missus Marsha without turning around. "If you've done your job properly, she shouldn't need you to demonstrate now." She folded her arms across her chest. "I don't have all day. Let's see it."

Ethelwynne dipped into what she hoped was a passable curtsy for a noble.

"This is a palace not some rabble-welcoming inn. You will learn how to curtsy before you meet the elven king. I will not have you disgracing the good name of King Kellan with your uneducated ways. Understood?"

Ethelwynne nodded.

Marsha snorted and huffed. "I doubt that very much." Then she walked out of the room, pausing at the door. "If that girl makes a fool of herself this evening," she stabbed a finger in Ethelwynne's direction, "I will be placing the blame on you," she stared hard at Abby whose eyes widened as she bobbed her head up and down. Satisfied that her point had been received, Marsha left the two women in relative peace.

"Well you better not screw up," Abby sternly informed Ethelwynne once the door was shut and the sound of Marsha's footsteps had died away. "I've got some plans for tomorrow, and I intend to keep them." Her eyes shifted towards the door as she spoke, before returning to fix on Ethelwynne, and Ethelwynne assumed that those plans had a lot to do with Stewart.

"Who was that?" asked Ethelwynne.

"She's the palace's housekeeper," whispered Abby. "We all try to stay on her good side, and you should probably do the same. So that was good what you did—simply just agreeing with her and doing what she asked."

Abby walked into the bedroom and putdown a small bundle on the vanity. "Well then, let's get that bruise covered up." Ethelwynne walked over and sat down as Abby pulled out the jars. "How'd you manage to bruise your nose? Walk into a door?"

Ethelwynne shrugged and shook her head. "I have no idea anymore, could have been a tree branch, a rock, or a zonkenwae tentacle."

Abby looked at her pointedly before beginning to apply the makeup. "Those things don't exist."

Ethelwynne winced as the brush touched her nose.

Shaking her head, Abby continued, "If you didn't want to tell me, you could have just said so." After a moment, she leaned back to survey her work. "Alright then, let's practice your curtsy."

Abby moved back into the sitting room and demonstrated the proper way to curtsy before a king. "This is probably the most important one for you to know."

Ethelwynne practiced it a couple of times, until it satisfied Abby. As Ethelwynne kept bobbing up and down, Abby began drilling her about how to greet the different nobles.

"I'm never going to remember all of this," Ethelwynne said as she copied another curtsy.

"Sure you will," said Abby as she rattled off the ways that Ethelwynne's curtsy looked different from the one she herself had just done. "Let's try that again."

Trumpets sounded in the courtyard and a team of evlayar spiraled down passed Ethelwynne's window. King Orrin had arrived.

Ethelwynne's heart felt like a stone, and she was thankful for the makeup that was hiding how pale she assumed her face must be. *Will he believe me?* She sank into one of the sitting room's chairs and took a few deep breaths to try and calm herself down. Dots swam across her vision.

"You can do this miss," Abby said soothingly. Her voice sounded very distant.

Ethelwynne felt very cold and leaned forward careful to rest her forehead on her hands.

Abby rubbed her back.

Ethelwynne continued to breathe. In and out. In and out. She could do this. She had been through so much since she first left home. She'd raced through a thunderstorm, escaped slavers, battled mythical creatures, avoided capture, saved Cephas, broke into a palace, and spoke to her own king without an invitation. Slowly her vision cleared. She shivered

320

and rubbed her arms. "Did I smudge my makeup?" she murmured.

Abby cupped Ethelwynne's face in her hands and shook her head. "You alright? Maybe you should lay down for a spell."

Ethelwynne breathed deeply a few more times. "No," she smiled weakly. "I'm sure the king will want to see me soon."

Abby frowned and gave her a quick hug. A sharp rap sounded on the door and she stepped back to open it. Stewart stepped into the room followed by Captain Henryk. The captain's assessment was swift as he strode across the room and knelt down in front of her. "How do you feel?" he asked.

"I'm fine," Ethelwynne whispered. She made to stand up.

Henryk put his hand on her shoulder to stop her. "I'd rather you didn't faint. Go slowly." He offered her his arm to help support her.

Ethelwynne murmured her thanks as she put her arm around his and with more of his help than she would have needed under normal circumstances, she shakily stood up. Once she was standing, the captain waited a few more moments before guiding her towards the bedroom door.

"I thought you were here to bring me before King Orrin." The room spun slightly.

"You did well this morning, but you won't survive a questioning by the elven king like this. Rest. We will distract him for an hour."

Ethelwynne sat on the edge of her bed and bit her lower lip. "Have you heard anything about Cephas or Jocasta yet?"

He shook his head, "It's still too soon for the scouts to have returned. While you provided us with a good description of the area, much of your trek was after dark and the first part was along a well-traveled path. It will be tricky for the scouts to retrace your steps without you there. But worry not, I'm sure he's fine."

"I could have gone with the scouts. I could still go. It only took me half a night to walk from there to here, so it shouldn't take me any more time to go back the other way."

Captain Henryk shook his head. "No, not if what you claim about the elvish prince is true." He laid his hands on her shoulders. "You are too valuable to let you wander off on your own."

"But—"

"No. There is no way that can happen." He turned to speak with Stewart who was returning to resume his post trapping her inside the room.

She lay back against the pillow. Ethelwynne had noticed the absence of Jocasta from his response. *I really don't want to hear that someone else had died because of me.* She closed her eyes. *Life would be much simpler if I knew nothing of Prince Damien's plot.* She sighed. *A plot, which, in all honesty, he will deny.*

"I accused the elf prince of treason," she said softly as the realization dawned on her. She looked over at Abby. "What if he does deny it? What happens to me then?" She asked without expecting an answer, then rolled over and rested her face on her arms. "Here I was thinking that this whole mess was going to be over now."

Abby patted her back soothingly.

"I just want to go home."

"I know miss," said Abby as she continued to rub her back.

Silence lingered in the room.

Ethelwynne turned her head to look at Abby again. She didn't want to think about her upcoming encounter with the king. Worrying would only make her sick. "What are you doing tomorrow?"

"You really want to know?" Abby smiled and looked at the door. "Okay. If you're not going to nap, perhaps you'd like some tea. I always find tea helps me calm down."

When Ethelwynne nodded and sat up, Abby spun out of the room and returned with a steaming pot of tea and a couple of tea cups. "Do you like sugar in your tea? I never actually asked yesterday."

Ethelwynne shook her head.

"Well, you are a strange person. Maybe you should pretend to take sugar if the king invites you to tea. Missus Marsha might not think it proper to have it with just milk."

Ethelwynne laughed and winced as the movement aggravated the bruises and bumps across her chest and sides. "I will try. So about those plans."

Abby's already rosy cheeks deepened and she hugged Ethelwynne's teacup close. "Me and your very charming guard are going to The Bear for some drinks. Who knows what might happen after." She winked and handed Ethelwynne the cup. "But you can't tell anyone, especially not Missus Marsha, she doesn't like us distracting them."

The door to her sitting room slammed open. "Please, sir, at least let me announce you and make sure she's decent." Stewart's voice was higher pitched than normal and sounded more rushed with each word that came out.

CHRISTINA VAN STARKENBURG

— CHAPTER TWENTY-TWO —

The Temperament of Elves

The door to her bedchamber flew open and clattered against the table beside it rattling the teapot.

Ethelwynne pushed her hair behind her ears so the strands were out of her face as she turned to face the regal-looking elf who just barged into her room followed by a scandalized-looking Stewart.

Stewart licked his lips. "His majesty King Orrin," Stewart squeaked before stepping back into a corner out of the way.

"She looks decent." The king glared at Ethelwynne.

Ethelwynne looked at him incredulously before she remembered who he was. As she rose and dipped into a curtsy without spilling the tea in her cup, Ethelwynne felt grateful for the amount of effort Abby put into teaching her how to do it properly. "Your Majesty."

He stepped forward and grabbed her by the shoulders shoving her into the wall behind her. Hot tea sloshed out of the cup and onto her clothes. His fingernails dug into her arms through the fabric. "What lies have you been telling about my brother?"

Ethelwynne's stomach clenched into a knot. She opened

her mouth to answer, but it wasn't fast enough to satisfy the elven king and he slammed her into the wall again knocking the air from her lungs. Her cup clattered to the ground spilling the rest of the liquid on her and the floor.

Abby yelped.

"Please sir," Stewart interjected.

"Silence! I will have my question answered." He stared at Ethelwynne. A vein bulged in his forehead as his brows furrowed deeper.

She wheezed and gasped as she tried to regain her breath.

"Your majesty, please unhand the girl." Captain Henryk's calm voice commanded moments before he slipped his body in between the two of them forcing the king to back up. "She will answer your questions, but she is also our guest and will be treated as such until such a time as we can determine the truth of her statements one way or the other."

Ethelwynne shivered. She watched the king with wide eyes. For a moment she thought he was going to deck the captain and try to toss him out of the way, but then he stepped back and harrumphed as he shook out his collar.

"Have it your way then." King Orrin spun on his heel and stalked out of the room.

Ethelwynne sank to the floor.

Abby collapsed into the chair behind her. Her ashen face a perfect reflection of the way Ethelwynne felt.

"I would compose yourself quickly if I were you," Captain Henryk said as he strode from the room ushering Stewart out ahead of him. "I will not be able to keep him at bay for long." The door thudded shut behind him.

From her spot on the floor, Ethelwynne could see the shadows of Henryk's boots underneath the door. "Captain Marino was right; he is as bad as his brother." Ethelwynne shuddered. This was not going to be pleasant. She leaned forward and pushed herself to her knees. "Abby, can you help me with that necklace?" She pointed to the amulet and chain on the vanity. Abby nodded mutely and tried to fasten it, but her hands were shaking too much.

"Here, let me," Ethelwynne said as she took it from Abby. She winced as she raised her arms to fasten it around her neck. Centering the cool green stone on the base of her throat, Ethelwynne ran over the simple meditation Idra had taught her the first time she wore it.

"Is there anything else for me to wear?"

Abby wobbled over to the wardrobe and pulled out a deep green gown. After carrying it safely over the puddle, she helped Ethelwynne into it. She gasped when she saw the bruises over Ethelwynne's body.

As Abby did up the final buttons on the back of the gown, Ethelwynne looked at her reflection in the mirror. Over her shoulder she saw Abby's expression. The young maid looked like she was about to cry. Ethelwynne turned and smiled. "He's not going to bother you, and I will be fine."

Abby sniffed and nodded.

With a final glance at her reflection over her shoulder, Ethelwynne decided that no one would know she'd been running for her life two days ago. "I'm ready."

"Good luck miss," Abby whispered. She curtsied as she opened the door.

Captain Henryk moved aside as Ethelwynne stepped out into her overly crowded sitting room. King Orrin, Stewart, and the captain, had been joined by King Kellan, Lady Tamara, Lord Dariel, and a few of Orrin's advisors.

The conversations stopped as Ethelwynne entered the room. All of the elves scowled at her. As she curtsied, she started to lift her hand to the necklace for reassurance, but she reminded herself how important it was for her to appear calm. Rising, she smoothed out her skirt and turned to face King Orrin. "I'm sorry the news I bring distresses you, sire,"

Ethelwynne began in elvish. Several of the advisors' eyebrows shot up, and Stewart's mouth dropped open. "I truly wish I bore better news, but that doesn't make it less true." She gestured towards King Kellan. "I trust that His Royal Majesty King Kellan has shown you the wayward key. I am not from the capital, nor is my home along the early spring trade routes so news travels slowly to me. How would I have known that it was missing or even where to look for it had I not heard something from your brother?" She lowered her hands and steepled her fingers as she rested them on the folds of her skirt in front of her.

"There are lots of ways an urchin such as yourself might have come across that information," one of King Orrin's advisors shot back at her. A bit of spittle sprayed from his mouth with each syllable.

Ethelwynne stared at him calmly. She bit the insides of her cheeks to prevent herself from smiling as Stewart tried to surreptitiously wipe some of the spit off his face.

"You could be lying about where you're from," he continued, "you could have been the one to steal it from Prince Damien in the first place, and came back here to, to... or you could have been trying to steal something from the palace and overheard the chatter and decided that this was an easier way to make money." He gave a sharp nod as he finished.

"I agree," said the other elf from where she stood in front of the window. Her lips curled, "She is almost certainly a thief and a liar. Besides, if I recall correctly, Prince Damien was angry enough about the loss of the key that he was refusing to speak to anyone. If that's the case, how on earth would this peasant merit a conversation with him?"

"I did not steal anything from your brother, nor did I ask for money in exchange for the key your Excellency." She rested her gaze briefly on the two advisors who had spoken, then turned to face King Orrin. "I overheard your brother's plot to trap you here when I went to Heatherfield Manor to enquire about the gates. My family is trapped on the other side, but the messages trickling to us from merchants were unclear." She paused. "Sire, surely the best way to determine the truth is not to question me but to speak with your brother. I cannot tell you anything I have not already told my king."

King Orrin frowned at her and folded his arms across his chest.

King Kellan put his hand on the elf king's shoulder. "You know she speaks sense. Let us summon your brother so we may put these accusations to the test, or simply return to your realm and let the gates be open once more."

King Orrin turned his head towards King Kellan. He glared at him for a moment before nodding. "Let us summon my brother then." He pointed towards Ethelwynne, "For your sake, I hope you are telling the truth. I would hate to be the one to ruin my family's livelihood by having them forever banished from their trade route." He started for the door.

King Kellan followed him out along with the rest of their entourages. But Captain Henryk and Stewart both stayed behind.

"I know you said you could speak elvish," remarked the captain, "but you sound so natural doing it. I don't think the elves were expecting that." He turned to Stewart and motioned for him to leave the room. "We will not be hosting the feuding royals here," said Henryk. "The king already has preparations underway to take us to Prince Damien's camp. You will remain here until we leave. Both Stewart and I will remain outside the door so no one comes in and threatens you in the meantime. Should you need anything, send Abby out to request it." With that, he shut the door behind him and left the two women alone to wait.

Abby peeked out from the bedroom. "They're gone?"

Ethelwynne nodded.

Abby played with her skirt and glanced at the door. "Is

329

Stewart okay?"

"Yes," Ethelwynne smiled, "but he's outside with the captain, so you'll probably have to wait until later to ask him about it."

Abby wilted a little. "Oh." She ambled around the suite picking up the cup that had been knocked over, righting a chair, and pushing the sitting room table back to its original spot.

"Miss Tregown," Stewart called out as he rapped on the door.

Ethelwynne looked up.

Abby froze.

Stewart knocked again.

"We should answer that."

Abby jumped and darted to the door. "Right miss. Of course, the door." She dusted off her skirt and smoothed out her hair before she opened the door. Cephas was leaning against the opposite wall. His leg was tightly bandaged and his hands rested on a cane in front of him.

"Cephas!" Ethelwynne jumped up from her chair and ran to embrace him. "You're okay. You're alive."

He grunted and winced as she hugged him. "I'm fine." He wrapped one of his arms around her.

Ethelwynne stepped back and frowned. "You should sit down." Cephas didn't argue as she waved him into her sitting room. "Are you sure you're fine?"

"Ye—"

"How did you get down the mountain? Your leg was broken."

"Well—"

"How did you avoid the prince's elves?"

"Ethelwynne." Cephas grabbed her arms. "If you don't stop talking, I can't answer anything."

Ethelwynne blushed. "I'm sorry. I'm just so happy that you're okay," she waved towards his leg, "relatively speaking."

He laughed and sat down in one of the chairs. "I'm fine. Nothing that a little bit of rest won't cure."

"Do you want something to drink? We probably still have tea here." Ethelwynne spun in a circle looking for the teapot. She was sure it was still here.

"I'm fine," Cephas repeated again, at the same time as Abby said "I have the pot here miss," and began to pour them both a cup. She handed Cephas his first. He took a slow sip, while he waited for Ethelwynne to sit down.

She pulled her chair closer. "Okay. I'm ready. How did you get down the mountain? Did King Kellan's men find you?"

Before he could answer her question, Captain Henryk knocked on the open door. "It's time to head down to the docks, Ethelwynne."

Cephas put the cup on the table and pulled himself up. "I'm coming too." Ethelwynne glanced at the cane in his hand and started to tell him she didn't think it was a good idea, but the look on his face changed her mind. She would not be convincing him to stay.

She turned to see what Captain Henryk would say and prayed the man would tell Cephas to get the rest he had just admitted he needed.

Henryk nodded. "A horse has already been prepared for you to ride to the skyship."

Ethelwynne looked at Henryk incredulously and pointed to Cephas's leg.

"You'll likely want a cloak," said the captain as he handed her one.

As she draped it over her shoulders, she followed Henryk out the door. While they walked down the hall, she did up the buckle to keep it secure.

Right before they turned the corner, she glanced back at the room that had been her cage. She wistfully hoped that if she wasn't able to convince King Orrin of his brother's treachery her next cage would be as nice. She'd even settle for half as nice. She was going to miss that bed.

They made it down to the courtyard where there were a couple of carriages and horses ready to transport the guests to the skyships. Captain Henryk helped Ethelwynne onto one horse. "Having you ride with me is easier than figuring out which carriage would be appropriate for you to ride in," he said as he climbed up behind her, "and it still assures everyone that you're not going to try and run for it."

Ethelwynne sighed.

As they made their way to the docks, Ethelwynne watched the city roll by. Shopkeepers stood on their steps and hollered their wares and prices at passersby to see if they'd be interested in stopping and buying anything. She mostly ignored them, although it did make her appreciative of the lack of competition in her own town, she would feel rather foolish hanging out her door and yelling at Mrs. Cohen to come and buy some fabric as she walked down the street to buy vegetables at the market.

The sky ports rose up before them. The men and women in the carriages stepped out and onto the wooden lifts. Once the bar was secured in place, the men on the ground turned a heavy wheel that wound the rope and pulled the lift up to the platform. As the last individual moved safely to the dock, a worker from the top called down, and the men lowered the lift once more.

Captain Henryk rested his hand on her shoulder as he guided her onto the lift once it touched the ground again. "I suggest you hold on to the railing." He nodded to the workers to start pulling the rope and lifting them into the air. The wooden tray slowly climbed up the wall. It swayed in the wind and rocked and lurched with each tug of the rope.

Ethelwynne clenched onto the railing until her fingers turned white. Once she was on the ship she was going to head inside and stay there until they landed at Prince Damien's camp.

The lift clattered into the dock. Ethelwynne unsteadily stepped off and saw the ship that they would be traveling on was *The Passerine*. "Oh no." Ethelwynne moaned.

"You alright girl?" asked Captain Henryk. "If the lift bothers you this much, I suppose we will need to find you a bucket for the ride."

"I'm fine," she whispered.

Henryk's grin faded as she studied her. "Are you going to faint on me again?"

Cephas limped off the lift and burst out laughing. "It's the ship I used to work on," he explained. "The last time Ethelwynne rode this one she fell off."

She felt her cheeks warming up.

"Perhaps we should keep her inside," King Kellan said as he strode past them on the deck. "A mountain, a window, and a skyship." He shook his head and climbed the steps to the top deck where Captain Marino was standing with King Orrin.

Cephas continued to chuckle as he was helped on the ship. One of the crew members whose name she couldn't remember grabbed him a chair to sit on and a second one to prop his bandaged leg on.

Ethelwynne groaned. She just had to keep reminding herself that her hair was a different color and she was in a dress. It's possible that no one on the ship would recognize her. She did not need the captain to accuse her of thievery right now. The nobles had all heard that tale already, she didn't need them reminded of it once more.

With the repairs completed she couldn't tell that it had been attacked by pirates and burned a short while ago. Captain Marino and her first mate Emily were greeting King Kellan as well the lords and ladies who were accompanying him. Bart watched as the ramp was lifted and the rails were shut behind it, securing the deck for take-off. As he called the "all clear," Captain Marino showed the kings where they could stand and watch the launch.

Ethelwynne looked back at the dock. She pulled her hood over her head and held it with a hand to block out some of the wind and hide her face enough to avoid recognition. She leaned against the wall beside Cephas to watch the launch.

Captain Henryk kept glancing her direction as they sailed away from White Shield.

"Does he think I'm going to jump?" she asked the third time she noticed him looking at her.

Cephas laughed. "Well, you've done it before."

Ethelwynne swatted him.

He just laughed more.

Once the initial lurching ended, the elves went inside the captain's cabin to wait. Ethelwynne had no intention of following them. She took a deep breath and thumbed the amulet. She could do this.

The wind whipped her hood off her head. Ethelwynne gasped and pulled it back up as she glanced around the edges to see if any of the crew had noticed. No one appeared to be staring at her suspiciously. She gave a small sigh of relief. So far, so good. She just had to survive the rest of the trip unnoticed.

Ethelwynne closed her eyes to block out the sight of the ground far below. She leaned further into the cabin wall behind her. This was the exact spot Bart had made her stand when they entered the pass. She grabbed onto the stair railing with the hand that wasn't holding her hood. Her knuckles turned white.

"Are you alright Ethelwynne?"

She opened her eyes and looked at Cephas who was looking up at her. "Yes," she squeaked.

Cephas frowned at her but didn't press it. Instead, he

quietly told her about how he made it down the mountain. "There's a village at the base of the mountain. We fell close enough to it that some of the villagers heard us scream. They arrived shortly after you left."

Ethelwynne nodded and clenched her eyes tight. "What about your leg? How are you walking?"

"It wasn't broken—the knee shifted out of place."

Ethelwynne peeked over at him.

Cephas shuddered as he spoke. "After they wrenched it back into place, they brought me to the village and bandaged it."

The wind jostled the skyship, and Ethelwynne took a sharp breath in.

"You're in the middle of the ship. There are no pirates. You are not going to fall off," Cephas whispered and leaned over to rest his hand on her white-knuckled one. "I promise."

Ethelwynne gave him a small smile and tried to think of anything other than what it felt like to be falling. She licked her dry, chapped lips. "Did the guards find you there?" she whispered.

Cephas nodded.

Whistles chirped from some of the ship's officers. Ethelwynne looked up and noticed the trees growing closer before they opened up into an open plain. The river drifted by to the ship's left.

Cephas squeezed her hand. "Take these in case you need them," he whispered as he handed her three knives when Henryk wasn't looking.

She slipped them under her cloak and into her pocket as Captain Henryk walked over to stand beside them. "We are here."

Ethelwynne let go of her hood. The ship was low enough that the wind was no longer threatening to rip it right off her head.

"You will have to wait here," Henryk said to Cephas as

he pointed to where the rope ladder was being fastened to the gate.

"Keep her safe," Cephas said almost too quietly for Ethelwynne to catch.

Captain Henryk nodded.

Cephas squeezed her hand once more. Ethelwynne gave him a weak smile before she walked to the ladder. Captain Henryk went first then she swung over the edge onto the first rung with help from Bartholomew. As she did her hood fell off, Bartholomew's eyes widened in recognition. Ethelwynne blushed and quickly climbed down a few steps before he could decide what to do.

"So much better than falling off," she muttered to herself when she was about halfway down. Still, she was much happier when her feet were back on the ground.

Ethelwynne looked up at the ship. Two evlayar landed on it to carry the kings to the ground. She followed the animals with her eyes as they circled lower and touched down on the grass beside River Ems. Prince Damien strode up to greet his brother flanked by two other elf guards. Their cloaks billowed out behind them as the wind picked up again. Even from where she stood Ethelwynne could tell their greeting was strained.

It started to rain as they walked back to the prince's camp. Ethelwynne was grateful when they entered a tent before the dampness settled into her skin.

Prince Damien walked to the far side of the tent and rested his hands on the table separating him and his brother. His gaze fell on Ethelwynne. "Why have you brought that thieving wretch to my camp?" The vein in his forehead bulged so much Ethelwynne was sure it was going to burst.

She instinctively took a step back.

King Orrin sneered in her direction and Ethelwynne barely suppressed a shudder. "This wretch claims she overheard you bragging about your plan to overthrow me."

Prince Damien scoffed. "Have you sunk so low that we must be enslaved by the pathetic fallacies of a peasant?"

"You dare insult me?" King Orrin bellowed.

King Kellan put his hand on the other ruler's shoulder.

Orrin shook it off. "Do not touch me." He leveled his gaze at Kellan who returned it unflinchingly.

"Surely we will accomplish more if you both control yourselves and don't digress into brotherly disagreements."

Orrin's nostrils flared as he steamed at King Kellan.

Ethelwynne felt rooted to the spot. Her heart raced as she waited for Orrin to make his move. Out of the corner of her eye, she watched Captain Henryk half draw his sword.

Orrin huffed and turned back to his brother. "Very well. This time I will relent."

Ethelwynne's skin crawled as the two brothers glowered at each other.

"Tell us your lies girl," Orrin demanded without taking his attention from Damien.

A pit formed in Ethelwynne's stomach. She swallowed in a pitiful attempt to return moisture to her mouth. "I went to Heatherfield Manor to learn why the gates remained closed. None of the merchants traveling through my town had believable information, but my parents are trapped in your realm, so I needed to know." As she spoke the confidence she was faking began to take hold of her. Her stomach loosened and her breathing eased.

"When I got there, I heard some elves speaking to each other in the garden. It turned out to be Prince Damien and him," she pointed to Akimos. "They mentioned that the key had been lost in the River Ems."

"This isn't treason," roared King Orrin.

Ethelwynne shook her head, addressing Orrin. "No, but taking the key from the Gatekeeper is. As is trying to use the key to trap you in our realm so he can rule yours. Both of which he has done and is still trying to do."

"Lies," hollered Damien. "You can't believe this nonsense. Look at her. Pathetic."

"It doesn't matter if you believe me Your Majesty. You have the key to return to your lands now. You can go home. But watch him. Because if you don't and I am speaking the truth about his treachery, you may not have another chance."

King Orrin glared at her.

Every part of her wanted to step back and hide behind Captain Henryk, but she refused to move. She refused to drop the king's gaze. She refused to bow to the fear that gripped her.

Orrin sneered. "Very well, I will leave you to the justice system of your own people. Your parents may return to your lands when the gates open, but should anyone from your family be foolish enough to cross into my lands, they will answer for your crimes." He spun to face Kellan. "Here you may not care if the peasantry insults nobility, but we take that nonsense very seriously."

Ethelwynne let a small sigh of relief escape her lips as Orrin began to stalk out of the tent. "Bring my brother," he snapped at two of the guards who came with him.

Ethelwynne started; she didn't think he would listen to her advice.

"What?" The table shook as Damien slammed his hands onto it. "You believe that thing?"

Orrin laughed. "As much as I believe you, Damien."

"Then you are a fool." Damien's lips curled in disgust as he nodded to the guards who had entered the tent with them.

One shoved Ethelwynne to the ground as he grabbed Henryk. Others killed the elf king's guards and one grabbed King Kellan.

Damien drew his sword and smiled. "The girl was right Orrin, but you brought her right to me. And you came to my camp, filled with my soldiers. All of who are loyal to me and think your reign is a mockery of all that we stand for. Your ineptitude will bring ruin to our glorious country."

He swung at Orrin.

King Orrin shifted his weight, throwing Damien's soldier into the path of the sword.

The elf yelped and released the king as Damien's blade cut him down.

Roaring the prince swung again.

Faster than Ethelwynne thought possible Orrin had his sword in hand and sliced through his remaining captor's throat. The same fluid motion brought his sword in front of him. The blade rang out against his brother's weapon as the king and prince fought.

Forgotten, Ethelwynne slipped backward and stood up. The tent's entrance was so close, she could just run. But, would she be able to run fast enough to find someone who could save the king, or would she just run into more of Damien's guards.

With a final glance at the entrance, she drew two of her knives and stabbed the elf holding Henryk. His weight slumped onto the Captain of the Guards. Henryk shook the elf off and ran him through with his spear. Then he turned to stab the elf holding King Kellan.

That elf realized what was happening and turned to use Kellan as a shield.

He needs an opening. Ethelwynne darted around the edge of the tent. The guard focusing on Henryk apparently hadn't seen her role in the captain's escape. She dragged her dagger along the back of his arms.

He screamed and as Kellan shook off his wounded arm, Henryk's spear dove into his opposite shoulder.

Ethelwynne jumped back to avoid being cut as the point came through the elf's back.

Henryk freed his blade and pulled King Kellan out of the tent.

Orrin stepped back cutting off Ethelwynne's escape as

Damien lunged at him again.

Ethelwynne scrambled out of the way and tried to run around the table to get out of the tent.

Damien howled as the king knocked his sword aside and slashed Damien down his left side.

Prince Damien staggered. He clutched his side as he turned around to face his brother again. Snarling he swung his sword at his brother's head. The king moved to block, but Prince Damien adjusted his swing and slashed the king's hand.

King Orrin cried out in pain as his weapon clattered to the ground. Prince Damien slashed him across his chest. The king stumbled backward. Blood darkened his shirt as he fell to the ground.

Damien turned to face Ethelwynne. He smirked. "Well girl, how's it feel to know it was all for nothing? The elf king is dead. And yours is as good as captured." He laughed and took a step towards her, but he stumbled. Damien put his hand on his side. Blood dripped from the cut his brother gave him.

Ethelwynne darted backward. Her back brushed the tent wall.

"Don't worry." He steadied himself on the table leaving a red print on the wood and started moving towards her again. "After you've died, and all of the elves are through the gate, I'll release your king. It won't matter if he knows that I killed my brother once the gates are shut. I'll tell the elves that a human assassin killed him, and then the kingdom will be mine and they won't care if the gateways are never opened again."

He propelled himself off the wobbly table and dashed towards her.

Ethelwynne stepped forward and threw one of her daggers at him.

He gasped as the blade sunk into his chest, just below his

right shoulder.

She darted around the table and raced for the entrance. If she could get outside, maybe she could make it to the ship.

Prince Damien pushed up on the bottom of the tabletop. As the wooden slab slid off of the small stump that had been supporting it, he pulled the blade out and dropped it on the ground.

The tabletop thudded to the ground in front of her, cracking across the middle and forcing her back.

She spun to face him as she drew her final knife. Any moment an elf could come in, and then she would be done for. It wouldn't matter if they were one of Orrin's or Damien's elves, all they would see was a dead king and her fighting the prince.

He swung his sword at her. There was no grace or coordination in his movements, blood oozed out of his wounds.

Ethelwynne deflected the shaky blow with her knives. She wished Cephas was here.

Damien coughed and staggered a few steps back.

Ethelwynne stepped onto the fallen table.

Snarling, Damien charged towards her. "You're never getting out of here. And once I've killed you, I will make sure your family dies working in a mine." He swung his sword at her.

Ethelwynne dodged and blocked the backswing. She sliced the prince's throat with her free hand. Tears and blood mingled on her cheeks as she staggered backward. She tripped over the king as she fled the tent.

Orrin groaned.

CHRISTINA VAN STARKENBURG

— CHAPTER TWENTY-THREE —

Goodbyes and a Long Ways Home

Ethelwynne ran until she reached where *The Passerine* was docked.

Captain Henryk and a few other soldiers were helping the injured guards onto the ship's lifts. His eye's widened when he saw her.

"The king," Ethelwynne gasped.

"He's already on board," Henryk responded. "Come, there's room for you on this one."

Ethelwynne shook her head. "I meant the elf king. I tripped over him when I fled the prince and he moaned."

Henryk called one of the guards over and sent him to pass along the news. As the man nodded and went to find one of the lords who were loyal to Orrin, Henryk guided Ethelwynne onto the lift.

The board swayed as it climbed to the ship. Ethelwynne clung to the rope. The adrenaline was already beginning to fade, but the blood on her hands was not disappearing. She felt weak and nauseous from the motion and the memories.

The lift thudded against *The Passerine's* side. Bartholomew pulled Ethelwynne onto the deck. She stumbled out of the way as a soldier was lowered to the wood. She looked away from the bloodied man and saw Cephas still in his chair. She went to him and wrapped her arms around his neck and sobbed as he gently rubbed her back.

Ethelwynne hiccoughed. "I'm sorry I only brought back two of your knives."

Cephas chuckled gently. "That's alright. I'm just thankful you were able to come back." He cupped her chin and looked into her eyes. "I'm sorry I wasn't able to be there for you."

Wiping her eyes, she leaned back and turned towards the prince's camp. "Me too." She shuddered. "But I would be dead if you hadn't taught me to fight."

"You've told me many times that you can take care of yourself; I'm glad it was finally true."

Ethelwynne looked at him, but he was watching the elves carrying their fallen king off the lift. "They're closing the gate. That must be the last of the wounded."

The ship lurched. Ethelwynne grabbed onto the stair railing to stop from falling over. As she did so, she noticed King Kellan and Captain Henryk climbing down them.

The king and captain stopped before them. From what she could see, with the exception of a bruise under his left eye, Kellan looked unharmed, though quite tired. His gaze flicked across the different patches of blood on her skin and clothes. "I'll have one of the surgeons come and make sure your injuries aren't severe when they have a moment."

"I'm fine. The blood…" Her voice drifted off and she wrapped her arms around her middle.

"Very well," said King Kellan. "The elven lords and ladies wish to express their gratitude for uncovering the plot against their king, and for alerting them to his situation." Kellan glanced towards the captain's cabin where the elves were watching their king. "Perhaps someday they will even thank you for killing the prince."

"Will he make it?" Cephas asked as he gestured towards King Orrin.

King Kellan nodded. "They believe so. The evlayar are racing to the capital ahead of us to prepare for their departure. The time is right for the gateways to open, so they will let their healers work their magic in their own realm."

Ethelwynne's gaze snapped back to the king from the cabin. "They're going to open the gates. She looked at the mountains surrounding them. "My parents!" The tension flowed out of her body.

"Yes," continued the king. "Your parents and all of the others who were trapped will be able to return home." With that, he left them to check on the wounded.

Ethelwynne sank to the floor beside Cephas's chair and rested her head on his lap as the ship's gentle rocking lulled her to sleep.

*   *   *

Cephas woke her when the ship landed in the capital.

The procession back to the palace was slow and somber. Ethelwynne was grateful when the castle walls came into sight. She retreated to her rooms to clean up. Cephas limped beside her, but she didn't have the energy to tell him she was going to bathe and sleep.

He opened the door for her. Abby bounced towards them. "You're alive! And not going to be thrown in prison!" She spun in a circle, stopping when she saw the teapot. "Let me get you some tea." She bounded over to the pot and attempted to pour some tea into a cup. She gasped when she realized it was empty. "Let me go get a fresh pot," she called behind her as she ran from the room.

Ethelwynne wandered into her bedchamber as Cephas sank into one of the sitting room chairs. She removed the necklace and spun the amulet around her fingers. She glanced from it to Cephas. "Here." She walked over to Cephas and handed it to him. "I suspect the Reverend Mother will want this back. Can you give it to your mother to return it to her?"

"Keep it," he said. Standing up, he refastened the chain around her neck. "If the Reverend Mother does want it back, I can always come get it later."

His fingers brushed her neck and sent tingles down her spine. She looked over her shoulder at him. "Thank you."

Abby sauntered back into the room. "There. I got you a fresh pot of tea." She turned to address Cephas. "Would you like milk and sugar in it?"

Cephas stepped back. "No, I'll let Ethelwynne get cleaned up." He left the room with a slight bow.

Ethelwynne watched him leave then turned her attention to Abby, who was now looking at her. "Yes please," Ethelwynne answered. She walked over to retrieve her cup from the woman. Ethelwynne sank into a chair and sipped the tea while Abby drew her a bath.

"It's ready," Abby called from the other room.

Ethelwynne put down the unfinished teacup, and wandered into the other chamber where Abby helped her disrobe and slip into the water. Her muscles ached as she scrubbed the blood, sweat, and grime from her body. "I'm never leaving home again," she muttered to herself. She was also not going to lounge in a pool of water any time soon. She shuddered as the memory of tentacles slithered through her brain and stepped out of the rusty brown water.

*   *   *

"When are you planning on heading home?" she asked Cephas when he joined her in her sitting room for a private breakfast the next morning. "There might still be time for you to join the guard."

He arched an eyebrow in her direction. "Trying to get rid

of me again?"

She opened her mouth to respond, but before she could he smiled. "After I see you home safely. Once you're home, then I will apply again." He bit into the flaky pastry in front of him and savored the taste. "Sooner or later, someone is going to quit or retire. I'm sure I'll get in then."

"Oh," Ethelwynne licked her lips and took a slow sip of tea. "I'm sorry you missed out because of me."

Cephas shrugged. "I've come to terms with it. It was important for you to make it here alive." He pulled another piece off of the pastry and ran it through the egg yolk on his plate. "What about you?" he said without looking up. "How long are you intending to stay here before you head home to see your family?"

"As soon as they let me leave. My brother is going to kill me for running away like that."

Cephas chuckled, but it didn't seem to reach his eyes. "What about what's-his-name? The one you actually stole from. When will you see him?"

"Michael," she shuddered. "I still have to pay him back. I have no idea what I'll say."

"Thanks for lending me some clothes when my life was in danger. Here's the money I owe you for them?"

Ethelwynne nodded half-heartedly. "I'm not entirely sure that would work with Michael or his parents."

There was a knock on the door.

"Come in," Ethelwynne called.

Captain Henryk stepped into the sitting room. He was followed by a servant who placed a bag into Ethelwynne's bedchamber. "I suppose you may have your items back now that you are no longer accused of thievery."

"I was enjoying wearing dresses again," Ethelwynne said frowning at the bag. "And I don't think anything in that bag actually belongs to me. The weapons are yours, and the clothes are Michaels."

Cephas laughed. "You can keep the knives. You may have noticed, they're not all that difficult to come by."

"I'm sure the king will not mind if you continue to wear the gowns in your closet," said Henryk. "Especially since your presence is requested at the farewell luncheon for the elves this afternoon. Though not all of the elves are willing to admit it, King Kellan wishes to formally thank you for finding the key and for saving him and King Orrin."

Missus Marsha strode through the open door. A servant girl with the green silk dress draped over her arm came in a few steps behind her.

"You," Missus Marsha pointed at Cephas, "You should not be in here. It's improper."

Henryk walked out as Cephas grabbed his cane to follow.

"Wait," Ethelwynne darted to the doorway.

"This is not the time for this," Marsha scolded.

Ethelwynne could sense Abby's horror without even looking behind her, but she ignored both women for the moment and walked to where Henryk had stopped. "Do you know if anyone has heard anything about Jocasta?"

Cephas followed her out of the room and rested his hand on Ethelwynne's back while he too waited for Henryk's answer.

She bit her lip as Henryk examined her silently. Her heart pounded as she studied him in return and wondered if his silence was because he didn't know the answer, or because he didn't think she could handle the answer.

"There was a lot going on yesterday," Henryk said after a moment. "Perhaps we will learn more about her whereabouts before the luncheon." He turned and continued to walk down the hall. "Come along Cephas," he called out behind him.

Cephas squeezed her shoulder as he limped after the captain.

Ethelwynne watched them go mutely. Jocasta had saved their lives many times. She pulled them out of the lake. She got Cephas to breathe again. She had to be somewhere. She couldn't be dead.

Ethelwynne blinked in confusion when the resounding thud of the men's departing footsteps was replaced by a quick patter from behind her.

Abby touched her shoulder and spoke softly, "Come on miss. Let's get you back to your rooms."

Ethelwynne looked at her blankly for a moment before nodding and following the other woman back to her chambers.

Marsha stood in the middle of the room with her arms folded across her chest. She tutted indignantly about the reckless manners of uncivilized people and told Ethelwynne to stand in front of her. "This is for the luncheon," she said pointing to the gown. "Do not spill any food or drink on it, or roll around in the grass in it, or whatever else your foolish mind might come up with. Do you hear me?" She waited until Ethelwynne nodded before she bit into Abby. "I expect you to teach her how to act proper. Do not let that boy in here again."

Abby nodded weakly as the housekeeper left the room.

"Ugh," Ethelwynne groaned. "I just want to go home. Think anyone would notice if I just slipped out of the castle and left?"

Abby's eyes widened and she clapped her hands to her chest.

"That's what I thought." Exhausted, Ethelwynne pulled a chair towards the window and looked out over the mountains. "She has to be alright," Ethelwynne said softly before succumbing to silence.

"It's time to get ready," said Abby.

With a sigh, Ethelwynne stood up and let the curtain fall across the window. With Abby's help, she slipped into the gown Missus Marsha left for her.

Once the final button was done up, Ethelwynne sat down on a chair so Abby could pin up her hair into some semblance of style. Then Ethelwynne absentmindedly played with the amulet while she waited for Captain Henryk to come and guide her to the garden.

At first, Abby kept up a constant stream of chatter, but when Ethelwynne neither responded nor stood up after Abby finished her hair, the young woman settled into silence as well. The quietness was only broken by the arrival of the captain and Cephas.

As they left, Ethelwynne asked again about Jocasta. "After," the captain simply said, and her heart sank.

The garden Captain Henryk led her to turned out not to be the small one she had first seen when she entered the castle; Henryk informed her that was the queen's private garden. Only a select few people were ever granted admittance to it.

Instead, he led her and Cephas to the backdoor which led into the main gardens. "I will not be coming out with you, I have some other duties to attend to first," Henryk said as the servants held the doors open for them.

Nodding, Ethelwynne continued onto the back deck and gazed out at the gardens. Perfectly manicured shrubs lined the walks and separated the rose garden from the orchids. Grapes and sweet peas draped down from trellises. Statues of mermaids and men seemed to dance in the mists the fountains created. Apple, pear, and cherry trees provided shade at the far end.

Ethelwynne gasped when she saw it. "My whole town could fit in here," Ethelwynne murmured as they climbed down the stairs.

King Kellan and Queen Colette were standing in front of the rose garden with some nobles and elves. They beckoned for Ethelwynne and Cephas to join them.

"Your adventure has brought the two of you far from the safety and security of your homes," King Kellan began. "As a result, you have lost family, friends, and very nearly your own lives. Because of that you have protected our neighbors from Prince Damien's treachery, found the key to restore the passageway between our countries, saved King Orrin's life, and helped free me from capture. For that, we thank you."

Ethelwynne smiled as Kellan handed Cephas a new sword to replace the one that had been battered over their journey. Cephas took the blade reverently and slowly stepped back to admire it.

Kellan beckoned her forward. "For everything you have done," he said as his wife handed him an ornately carved box. He opened it and showed her the exquisite jewellery inside.

Ethelwynne gasped softly. "Thank you."

"These will complement the gowns you're going home with," he said as he handed her the box. "I hope you enjoy them." He looked up and addressed the crowd as a whole. "And now, I believe the food is ready for us to eat." With that, he and his wife led the way to the banquet table that had been set up in the garden.

Once everyone had eaten their fill of the feast, the guests split off to enjoy the gardens. As Cephas and Ethelwynne walked along the greens, Lord Yole and Lady Layla approached them and demanded to hear their stories. After the first time they relayed their tale, Ethelwynne demurred since they had already heard her version of events and let Cephas tell their story. She watched the fish swimming under the bridge and tried to let the gentle splashing water drown out the tale. It was all too recent; she didn't want to relive it. But from the gasps and laughs coming from the growing circle of nobles around Cephas, she got the idea that they didn't mind hearing his version of the events.

She left him to the nobles and walked away as his story

ventured into the Maudinmere. She didn't need to hear about how the zonkenwae had nearly taken him captive; she already saw that and felt the creature's cool tentacles run across her body in her dreams.

As she wove through the hedges, she met up with King Kellan and Queen Colette walking with their guards. She turned to give them some privacy, but Kellan called her over. Barely containing a sigh, she walked towards them and curtsied as she prayed the queen would not ask to hear what happened.

"Where's Cephas?" asked King Kellan. "After everything the two of you have been through, I would have thought you wouldn't want to let him out of your sight."

Ethelwynne shrugged and pointed in the direction she left Cephas. "Lady Layla, Lord Yole, and some others wished to hear what happened."

The queen smiled. "And you weren't interested in telling it. Yes, escaping and hiding in the hedges is the best way to avoid that situation. Though, there are prettier spots in our gardens. Come." Colette glided past her and led the way to the garden with the fruit trees. The hedges changed as they got closer, and Ethelwynne realized that they were actually well-kept berry bushes in this part of the garden.

The sweet smell of flowers and berries wafted through the air. Some servants laid out a blanket and Kellan helped Colette sit on it. He motioned for Ethelwynne to join his wife, but before he sat, Captain Henryk entered the fruit garden and the king went to meet him. When Cephas hobbled out after him, Ethelwynne excused herself and went to join the conversation.

"I spoke to the elf who killed Jocasta," Henryk said once Ethelwynne reached them. "I'm sorry, your friend is no more."

Ethelwynne felt her heart breaking. Jocasta had given her life for them, and she never fully believed that the prince's treachery was true. She had fully expected to face severe consequences for her actions, and still she gave her life so that they could reach the kings. The greenery blurred. Ethelwynne closed her eyes and breathed deep. When she opened her eyes again, the plants were clear once more. "Thank you for telling me." She turned to face the king and curtsied, "If you would excuse me sire, I would like to go home now."

"The day is nearly over." Henryk shook his head. "You two would only just make it out of the city before you'd need to make camp for the night."

"Yes," said Ethelwynne still focusing on the king, "but then we'd be that much closer to home."

The king nodded. "You may go." He motioned to one of the servants watering the plants nearby, "See to it that there are horses prepared for them. While we cannot spare any evlayar, you need not walk all the way to your homes."

Ethelwynne curtsied again as Cephas bowed. Then they followed Henryk back to Ethelwynne's rooms. Evidently the king had foreseen that Ethelwynne and Cephas would not wish to remain longer than necessary, for when they got there Abby had already packed everything but a riding gown into two bags.

Abby sobbed as she helped Ethelwynne change clothes.

"Take care Abby," whispered Ethelwynne so as not to be overheard by the men waiting in the hall. "I'm sorry you didn't get to tell me about your night at The Bear."

Abby flushed and packed the final gown and chest of jewels into one of the bags. "What with the king being attacked and the key being found and all, it didn't happen. We're going to try again later. Maybe next week."

"Good luck," Ethelwynne said as she left the room.

Cephas had gone ahead to the guards' quarters where he had bunked to change into something more suitable for riding, so Ethelwynne followed Henryk down to the stables.

"Captain," Ethelwynne asked as they climbed down the stairs, "why didn't you say anything when I ran into the king's study? I didn't see you enter, so you had to have been there the whole time."

"Through here," he said opening a door. "I didn't stop you because you looked scared and startled when the maids came in, which led me to believe you weren't hoping to harm someone. More importantly, I also saw the key when you shut the door. It didn't look like a palace key, but given how ornate it was I suspected it might be the missing key. And since I could see you through the shelves as you hid, I decided to wait."

Henryk pushed open another door and the two of them stepped outside and walked across the courtyard to the stables. The servant who was carrying Ethelwynne's belongings handed the bags to the stable hands who tied them to the saddle before double-checking the saddle straps.

Cephas came out while Henryk was helping Ethelwynne into the saddle. The captain then held Cephas's cane as he mounted his horse.

"Leave the horses with Lady Kiran when you return to Stormont," he instructed Cephas. "We can collect them from her later."

Cephas nodded and then the two of them were off.

As the walls of White Shield rose up behind them Ethelwynne felt as though she was leaving a weight with them. She was finally going home.

*   *   *

The third night on the road Ethelwynne lay down on her sleeping mat and looked up at the stars that were just beginning to become visible in the darkening sky. She thumbed the necklace and rolled over and faced Cephas. "Do you really think Michael would have survived the bandit attack?"

Cephas sighed. "You survived and I survived. It's not unrealistic to think others survived too. Besides, not that I was looking, but I didn't see him among the dead."

Ethelwynne smiled briefly at Cephas's caveat. "Why don't you like him? You don't know anything about him."

"Besides the fact that you panic or flinch when you think about him?"

Ethelwynne sat up and hugged her knees through her blanket. "That's not fair. I stole from the man I thought I was going to marry. It's not unsurprising that I would be nervous about the way he responds." She rested her cheek on her knees and studied the trees and whispered, "I still want him to like me."

Cephas scoffed. "You're better off without him. He doesn't really care about you. He just wants your elven trading license."

Ethelwynne snapped upright and glared at Cephas. "And you know that how?"

Cephas pinched the bridge of his nose. "When I was looking for a caravan in Aspen Grove I ran into Michael. The girl on his arm was gushing about how brave he was for traveling the forest below, but once he learned how to sail her father's ships and took over her family's business, he would never have to deal with the woods again."

"He didn't even care that I could have been dead." Her heart fell, and she wondered if the reason he left her in Bewdley so abruptly was because he figured her trading license was as good as useless. "I wonder if he even went back the next day to help me see the elves." She looked over at Cephas. "Why? Why even say he'll bring me to Bewdley? Why not just say no?"

Cephas shrugged. "To keep up his appearances with the rest of Sweet Briar?"

Her gaze dropped to her wrists. The bruises he left were

long faded and replaced by marks from mountains and monsters. She let her hands drop to her sides. A rock bit into her right palm, and she picked it up and threw it at a tree. It bounced off the trunk with a satisfying thunk. She heard Cephas move as she watched the stone skitter across the ground.

He draped his arm around her shoulder and hugged her tightly. "I'm sorry," he whispered into her hair.

"Thank you," she said leaning into him. "Besides the elves, his family is our biggest trading partner."

"I don't understand why guys like him have to play with your emotions. Why can't he just get his own license?"

Ethelwynne shifted so she could look up at him. Cephas looked angry and frustrated all at the same time. "An elvish trading license isn't as easy to come by as one for a merchant train or even a skyship one. Captain Marino could have purchased her license to use *The Passerine* to trade—it's expensive, but possible. A license to trade with the elves has to be earned."

"How did your family earn it?"

"Honestly, I don't know. We've held it for generations." Ethelwynne groaned. "We *had it* for generations."

Cephas looked over at her sympathetically, "He never actually said you would lose your ability to trade with the elves."

Ethelwynne winced. "Let's hope he remembers that. I told my parents nothing would happen to their shop while they were away. If I've lost the license forever, they will never trust me again." She sighed and tried not to think about what would happen if Michael's family also chose not to trade with them when they found out she took clothes from them.

She lifted her hands and hugged Cephas's arm. Let Michael marry whoever he chose, she could still act professionally around him. But, if Michael wanted to break all ties between their families when everything came out, she would be fine. She didn't need him.

*   *   *

After a few weeks on the road, Ethelwynne had to admit flying was certainly faster, but she was grateful for the ground beneath her horse's hooves as they rode past Riderless Ridge.

A wagon was stuck in the ditch just beyond the junction. Cephas reined his horse and got down to help. Ethelwynne followed.

The driver stepped around the side of the wagon. Ethelwynne almost fell off of her horse as she rushed to get down. "Father!"

William wrapped her in a hug and kissed her hair. "Ethelwynne." Tears ran down his cheeks.

Ethelwynne relaxed in his arms. "I've missed you so much."

"I've missed you too," he whispered into her hair.

Ethelwynne gulped back her sobs and pulled back from William to look around. "Where's mother?"

"Your mother went for help while I tried to get us out." He gestured towards the wagon. "But I think we were too hard on the horses in our excitement to get back. They're exhausted, so we could be here a while."

"Why don't we hitch our horses to the wagon?" Cephas suggested.

William started and looked at Cephas as though he had completely forgotten the two of them were not alone. "Who is this?" he asked.

Ethelwynne watched his facial expression change and she assumed he just realized she shouldn't be there.

A thought that was confirmed a moment later when he asked, "What were you doing here? Why aren't you watching the store?"

Ethelwynne's cheeks prickled, and she opted to answer his first question first. "This is Cephas Merrilin. He um..." she ran her fingers through her hair as she decided what to say. "He helped me open the gates."

William looked at her and blinked a few times. "The gates? As in the ones between the realms?"

"Yes," said Ethelwynne haltingly. "Cephas can tell you the story." She looked at him and tried to convey that she wanted him to relay the story without going into too much detail about the danger she had been in. The grin he gave her made her doubt he would listen to that message, even though she was sure he understood it. "Actually," she restarted, "I'll tell you, but maybe we should wait until we catch up to mother. She might want to know too."

Cephas laughed and walked over to begin taking the saddles and saddlebags off of their horses. As Ethelwynne carefully added their bundles to the wagon, Cephas and William traded the horses and tethered the exhausted pair to the back of the wagon.

Cephas walked alongside the wagon, while Ethelwynne peppered her father with questions about what life had been like on the opposite side of the gate.

Soon they saw Victor Mayer and one of his stable hands leading horses to the gate, while Bethany looked to be supporting Meredith's weight. Even from the distance Ethelwynne could see and hear the sobs escaping her mother.

Victor shouted and waved as he rode over to make sure they didn't need any more help. His jaw dropped when he was close enough to realize that it was Ethelwynne sitting beside her father. "We were just telling your wife that Ethelwynne went missing," he said to William as he stared at Ethelwynne.

Victor turned his horse around and followed them back to the edge of his property, but Ethelwynne noticed that he kept looking at her and shaking his head.

"Oh look, Meredith," said Bethany as they approached, "someone came along and helped William. Let's get you back on the wagon and then I'll grab some food for your supper."

Meredith buried her face in her hands and sobbed as she walked towards the wagon. "Oh William, it's awful…" Her voice broke and she stopped speaking. William and Ethelwynne hopped off the wagon.

"It's alright, love," whispered William.

Bethany returned with a pot of soup. "Here you go Meredith, I'll just place this on your wagon."

"I can take it," said Ethelwynne.

The pot slipped from Bethany's hands as she stared agape at Ethelwynne.

Meredith's head shot up from where it was buried in her husband's collarbone. "Ethie?" She stumbled around her husband. "They said…" Her gaze wandered all over her daughter, and Ethelwynne imagined her taking in her hair, her clothes, her presence.

"It's me," said Ethelwynne embracing her. "I'm home too."

Meredith pulled back and traced her hands over Ethelwynne's cheek. "Bethany said you were dead. That you went to Bewdley and never came back."

"I know." Ethelwynne looked over her mother's shoulder at her father, Bethany and Victor, Annie, and the stable hands who had left their chores to see what was happening. "I'm sorry I worried you all. My short trip to Heatherfield Manor didn't go the way I planned."

William coughed. "Apparently our Ethie is partially responsible for us being able to come home."

Ethelwynne watched the question form on her mother's face. "It's a long story, and I promise I will tell you what happened. But for now, can we go home. Danny should know we're back." When Ethelwynne moved towards the wagon, her mother moved with her, as though unwilling to let more than a foot come between her and the child she had just been told had died.

Cephas helped the two women onto the wagon, then mounted one of the horses the Mayers' offered to quicken their journey to the store. William hopped onto the other horse, while Ethelwynne took the reins.

As the drove towards Sweet Briar, Ethelwynne introduced her mother to Cephas, who in turn began to regale her parents with some of the lighter moments of their journey together. He somehow managed to make their meeting and falling off the skyship sound like a delightful misadventure instead of a horrible misunderstanding and near-death experience. By the time they approached the final bend, both Meredith and William were laughing at his stories.

When they rounded the final bend Ethelwynne saw her brother. Danny's back was towards them and his shoulders were slumped as he swept off the steps in front of their shop. Their wagon rattled to a stop behind him.

"The store's closed," he said without turning around. "Come back tomorrow," he sighed heavily, "it'll be open for a bit then."

"That's no way to run a store," said William. "I suppose that's why you're a farmer."

Danny dropped the broom as he turned around. His mouth dropped open and he stared at them while they hopped off the wagon and wrapped him up in a hug.

"I'm so sorry I left you here on your own," Ethelwynne said.

"You should be." He pushed her back and tried to look stern, but the tears rushing down his chin mocked the attempt. "Do you have any idea what I went through?"

Ethelwynne looked at Cephas who was still sitting on his horse and thought about what he said about Xiamara. "I think

I have some idea. I should have told you what I was thinking."

Word traveled through town about their return and soon after the horses were taken care of and the supplies piled in the shop the first family arrived with a hot meal. After the third family knocked on their door the Tregowns abandoned the idea of a quiet evening and headed to the village green for an impromptu picnic.

Ethelwynne hugged Meghan as the two friends sat in front of the bonfire. "It's good to be home."

*   *   *

Danny and Annie were married the next day. After waiting for so long, the two lovers had decided not to wait even a moment longer lest someone else disappear.

When the ceremony was over, Ethelwynne and Cephas lounged on a picnic blanket watching the other villagers dance. Ethelwynne nibbled the apple pie Annie's mother had prepared, but she barely tasted the pastry as she studied Cephas beside her. "I guess you'll be heading out soon."

Cephas rubbed the back of his neck and nodded. "Xia will be pretty worried."

William looked over at the two of them. "You're leaving?"

Cephas nodded again.

"How can I thank you for keeping my daughter safe?"

"I would like to point out that I saved his life several times too," said Ethelwynne.

Cephas patted her shoulder and smiled. "There's no need sir, it was the right thing to do."

Ethelwynne crossed her arms and frowned at Cephas. "I did."

Cephas grinned and took another bite of his pie.

"At least let us give you some supplies for the journey,"

said Meredith after William told her what was being said.

"Thank you, Mrs. Tregown."

Ethelwynne watched as her parents walked away to speak with other guests. "They don't believe me." She turned to face Cephas. "And now, thanks to you, they never will."

As he ate the final bite of his pie, Cephas shook his head. "I've already shared tales of your heroism with your parents." He turned towards her parents who were now hugging Danny and Annie. "I don't think they're ready to believe any of it happened yet. To admit that you saved the king, or that you found the key to the gates, means they have to admit that you were in a lot of danger." He rested his hand on hers. "Give them time. Once other merchants start rolling in and sharing tales of your adventures, they'll have to admit you're not a child anymore."

*   *   *

Two days later, as Cephas was getting ready to go, Michael's wagon rolled in.

"Ethelwynne!" Michael hopped down from the wagon. "You're back. I died when I found out you hadn't returned." He pulled her into a tight hug.

"I'm fine," she said as she tried to push him away.

"I'm never letting you do anything so stupid again. What were you thinking?" He let her go and ran his fingers through his hair. "You don't know anything about being out there on your own."

"I'm fine," she reiterated. Ethelwynne bit her lip and reached into her pocket for the change. "This is for you."

Her cheeks prickled as he arched an eyebrow in confusion.

"After I visited Heatherfield Manor I ended up in Helmsville in desperate need of a change of clothes, but I didn't want to pull you into the mess." She brushed some dust off her skirt. "This should cover it."

He took the money and counted it before putting it in his pocket. "You stole from me?"

Ethelwynne braced herself under his darkening gaze. "Yes. As you may have heard, I was being chased by the elves and I needed a way to hide. Since your family has always been close with ours, I trusted that you would be willing to help me when I needed it most." She clasped her hands in front of her as she continued to meet his gaze. "But now that the issue that prevented me from asking for your help has been resolved, I would like to pay you for the clothes I took. If that change doesn't cover the cost of the pants and shirt, let me know."

His fists balled.

Ethelwynne instinctively stepped back and felt Cephas's hand come to rest on the small of her back.

Michael's eyes flicked over her shoulder to Cephas. He sneered. "The caravan guards? Was that a set-up too? Now that I think about it, it seems awfully convenient that you were the one to sound the alarm."

Cephas pulled Ethelwynne back as Michael swung his fist in their direction. The blow missed.

"Your pathetic attempt at being a guard cost me an entire shipment!" Michael swung again.

Cephas blocked it and returned a jab of his own.

Michael wheezed as it connected. He stepped back and yanked his shirt to straighten it. His eyes burned as he pulled the coins out of his pocket and threw them on the ground at their feet. "This doesn't begin to cover what I lost." Michael spat on the ground. "And believe me, I will get back every penny from you."

He stormed back to his wagon and rolled into town.

Cephas turned to face Ethelwynne. "See that wasn't so bad."

Ethelwynne gave him a small smile. "I think he hates

me."

"Better off without him."

"Except he's one of the main people we trade with."

"Well if he's petty enough to cut all ties with you because you were trying to protect his family from losing their license, then I'm sure there are better people out there to trade with. I mean you already trade with elves, could you not swing your caravan the other way and trade with people in Helmsville too?"

"And when he tells them I'm a thief?" she laughed ruefully. "His family lives in Helmsville."

Cephas shrugged, "Remind them you're a hero who knows the king personally."

Ethelwynne flushed and turned to the horses behind him. "I suppose we should get you ready to go."

Cephas cupped her chin. "Do you want me to stay until he leaves?"

She leaned forward and rested her head on his chest. "No," she lied. Stepping back, Ethelwynne looked him in the eyes, "He can't do anything here. It would damage his trade with the area." She hugged him. "Thank you for asking."

He took her hand and kissed it. "I'll see you again Ethelwynne." Without another word he hopped onto his horse and spurred both beasts into motion.

Ethelwynne waved as she watched him ride down the road and around the corner. When he was no longer in sight, she dropped her hand to the amulet around her throat and watched him ride away through the trees and turns as the amulet's magic and her own memories of the road showed her where he was.

Christina Van Starkenburg lives on the Canadian West Coast with her husband, two sons, daughter, and cat.

Visit her at www.christinavanstarkenburg.com. Or leave her a message on Instagram @christinavanstarkenburg and Facebook @christinavanstarkenburg.